P9-DHJ-275

DATE DUE

PENGUIN BOOKS

# WRITERS AT WORK

NINTH SERIES

WILLIAM STYRON is the author of a number of critically acclaimed novels, including *Lie Down in Darkness, The Long March, Set This House on Fire, The Confessions of Nat Turner*, for which he won the Pulitzer Prize, and *Sophie's Choice*, which won him the American Book award. His nonfiction includes *This Quiet Dust and Other Writings* and *Darkness Visible*. Among his honors is the *legion d'honneur*. An appropriate choice to introduce this volume of *Writers at Work*, Styron wrote the preamble for the first number of the *Paris Review* (1953), in which he set forth its aims.

The *Paris Review* was founded in 1953 by a group of young Americans including Peter Matthiessen, Harold L. Humes, George Plimpton, Thomas Guinzburg, and Donald Hall. While the emphasis of its editors was on publishing creative work rather than nonfiction (among writers who published their first short stories were Philip Roth, Terry Southern, Evan S. Connell, Mary Lee Settle, Norman Rush, T. C. Boyle, Alan Gurganus, Jay McInerney, and Samuel Beckett), part of the magazine's success can be attributed to its continuing series of interviews on the craft of writing.

*Previously Published*

WRITERS AT WORK
The *Paris Review* Interviews

FIRST SERIES

Edited by GEORGE PLIMPTON and introduced by MALCOLM COWLEY

| | |
|---|---|
| E. M. Forster | Frank O'Connor |
| François Mauriac | Robert Penn Warren |
| Joyce Cary | Alberto Moravia |
| Dorothy Parker | Nelson Algren |
| James Thurber | Angus Wilson |
| Thornton Wilder | William Styron |
| William Faulkner | Truman Capote |
| Georges Simenon | Françoise Sagan |

SECOND SERIES

Edited by GEORGE PLIMPTON and introduced by VAN WYCK BROOKS

| | |
|---|---|
| Robert Frost | Aldous Huxley |
| Ezra Pound | Ernest Hemingway |
| Marianne Moore | S. J. Perelman |
| T. S. Eliot | Lawrence Durrell |
| Boris Pasternak | Mary McCarthy |
| Katherine Anne Porter | Ralph Ellison |
| Henry Miller | Robert Lowell |

THIRD SERIES

Edited by GEORGE PLIMPTON and introduced by ALFRED KAZIN

| | |
|---|---|
| William Carlos Williams | Saul Bellow |
| Blaise Cendrars | Arthur Miller |
| Jean Cocteau | James Jones |
| Louis-Ferdinand Céline | Norman Mailer |
| Evelyn Waugh | Allen Ginsberg |
| Lillian Hellman | Edward Albee |
| William Burroughs | Harold Pinter |

FOURTH SERIES

Edited by GEORGE PLIMPTON and introduced by WILFRID SHEED

| | |
|---|---|
| Isak Dinesen | John Dos Passos |
| Conrad Aiken | Vladimir Nabokov |
| Robert Graves | Jorge Luis Borges |
| George Seferis | John Berryman |
| John Steinbeck | Anthony Burgess |
| Christopher Isherwood | Jack Kerouac |
| W. H. Auden | Anne Sexton |
| Eudora Welty | John Updike |

FIFTH SERIES

Edited by GEORGE PLIMPTON and introduced by
FRANCINE DU PLESSIX GRAY

| | |
|---|---|
| P. G. Wodehouse | Joyce Carol Oates |
| Pablo Neruda | Archibald MacLeish |
| Henry Green | Isaac Bashevis Singer |
| Irwin Shaw | John Cheever |
| James Dickey | Kingsley Amis |
| William Gass | Joseph Heller |
| Jerzy Kosinski | Gore Vidal |

Joan Didion

SIXTH SERIES

Edited by GEORGE PLIMPTON and introduced by FRANK KERMODE

Rebecca West — Kurt Vonnegut, Jr.
Stephen Spender — Nadine Gordimer
Tennessee Williams — James Merrill
Elizabeth Bishop — Gabriel García Márquez
Bernard Malamud — Carlos Fuentes
William Goyen — John Gardner

SEVENTH SERIES

Edited by GEORGE PLIMPTON and introduced by JOHN UPDIKE

Malcolm Cowley — Arthur Koestler
William Maxwell — May Sarton
Philip Larkin — Eugene Ionesco
Elizabeth Hardwick — John Ashbery
Milan Kundera — John Barth
Edna O'Brien — Philip Roth
Raymond Carver

EIGHTH SERIES

Edited by GEORGE PLIMPTON and introduced by JOYCE CAROL OATES

E. B. White — Elie Wiesel
Leon Edel — Derek Walcott
Robert Fitzgerald — E. L. Doctorow
John Hersey — Anita Brookner
James Laughlin — Robert Stone
Cynthia Ozick — Joseph Brodsky
John Irving

# Writers at Work

## The *Paris Review* Interviews

NINTH SERIES

*Edited by George Plimpton*
*Introduction by William Styron*

PENGUIN BOOKS

X808.3
P23w
ser.9
(1)

PENGUIN BOOKS
Published by the Penguin Group
Viking Penguin, a division of Penguin Books USA Inc.,
375 Hudson Street, New York, New York 10014, U.S.A.
Penguin Books Ltd, 27 Wrights Lane,
London W8 5TZ, England
Penguin Books Australia Ltd, Ringwood,
Victoria, Australia
Penguin Books Canada Ltd, 10 Alcorn Avenue, Suite 300,
Toronto, Ontario, Canada M4V 3B2
Penguin Books (N.Z.) Ltd, 182–190 Wairau Road,
Auckland 10, New Zealand

Penguin Books Ltd, Registered Offices:
Harmondsworth, Middlesex, England

First published in
simultaneous hardcover and paperback editions
by Viking Penguin, a division of
Penguin Books USA Inc. 1992

1 3 5 7 9 10 8 6 4 2

Copyright © The Paris Review, Inc., 1992
All rights reserved

Interview with Doris Lessing,
© Doris Lessing, 1988.
By permission of Jonathan Clowes Ltd., London,
on behalf of Doris Lessing.

ISBN 0 14 01.6684 X
ISSN 0510-9671

Printed in the United States of America

Set in Electra

Except in the United States of America, this
book is sold subject to the condition that it
shall not, by way of trade or otherwise, be lent,
re-sold, hired out, or otherwise circulated
without the publisher's prior consent in any form
of binding or cover other than that in which it
is published and without a similar condition
including this condition being imposed on the
subsequent purchaser.

# Acknowledgments

In addition to the interviewers, the editor would like to acknowledge the help of the following in the preparation of this volume: Tanuja Desai, Dan Kunitz, Rowan Gaither, and Claudia Grazioso.

# Contents

# Introduction

Since I was one of the first writers to be interviewed for the *Paris Review* series, I think I can beg the reader's indulgence and set down a brief reminiscence about that episode of—astonishing to realize!—almost four decades ago. I assume that anyone interested enough in the art of fiction (and, in the case of this volume, theater, poetry, and criticism) to want to read these interviews might be curious as to how the whole idea began; it's an appropriate moment, too, to reflect on the evolution of this series from its somewhat crude and callow beginnings to the rich, free-flowing dialogues that have made the *Paris Review* interviews a kind of minor art form and, at their best, the standard by which such literary colloquies are measured. I think it's not entirely clear why the *Paris Review* interviews have been so successful. Needless to say, the editors of the magazine didn't stumble on a new concept, and since the beginning of the series in 1953 numerous other literary journals have carried interviews with writers. It may be that the *Paris Review* interviews have simply established a continuity through which readers interested in writers and the writing process have discovered a seriousness of purpose and consistent intelligence of discourse they will rarely find anywhere else.

Speaking of interviews in general, writers themselves are often responsible for the superficiality of most of the product. Always excepting J. D. Salinger or Thomas Pynchon, virtually every contemporary writer will, over the course of his or her career, give countless interviews—in many cases more than is prudent, since writers are usually eager communicators and frequently forget the advantages of taciturnity. Sometimes the interviews, which are commonly in newspapers, turn out to be reasonable replicas of what was actually said. But just as often the writer's garrulous good nature will lead him to stray into a hostile area where, he will later understand to his dismay, his chat with the affable interviewer was in reality an adversarial procedure, a face-off in which much of what he uttered ended up being willfully misinterpreted and the rest so garbled as to make him appear an egregious jackass.

In the long history of the *Paris Review* interviews, the interviewees have reflected fragments of their central or peripheral selves in myriad ways: they have been witty, haughty, rancorous, jocular, fretful, abrasive, opinionated, evasive, prickly, windy, self-effacing, pompous; but never, it is safe to say, has any one of them appeared to be an egregious jackass. The writers asked to be interviewed for the series would not, one can faithfully attest, fall into such a category anyway; but the possibilities of being misquoted, misrendered, or otherwise wronged have been minimized to the vanishing point through the civilized procedure developed by *PR* over the years. As Joyce Carol Oates put it in her introduction to the previous volume of interviews, the reader will find here "no verbatim transcripts, no fumbling, no groping, 'spontaneous' utterances, no trailings off into baffled silence . . . no misstatements the subject clearly wished afterward to delete, but was prevented from doing so by journalistic exigency or malice." In short, the writers have been pretty much in full command of the dialogue, subject only to the natural arbitrariness of the interviewer's questions. What small loss accruing from the possible absence of spontaneity has been more than adequately made up for by the writer's capacity to review the transcript, make alterations and emendations, and shape the whole according to his own sense of fitness. And this is as it should be in these serious (though thankfully not too often solemn) autobiographical disclosures. In such a way the reader knows for once that he's getting it straight from the horse's mouth—with no lapses or excuses possible—while the writer has avoided the dread sensation, so commonly felt in the aftermath of more casual interviews, of a stiletto being inserted into the spine.

Credit must be given to technology when owed. Certainly it is the tape recorder—despite the prejudice against it held by a few subjects—that has made the greatest difference in the technique of the *PR* interview over the years. If nothing else, the tiny machine has allowed a copious, leisurely, and unimpeded flow of dialogue to be captured for transcription, and this emphasizes the serious disadvantages of the earlier method of getting it all down back in the 1950s, when interviews were conducted by persons scratching away with pen or pencil while the subject aired his views slowly and haltingly out of consideration for the interlocutor. This traditional procedure produced some good interviews at the beginning, but there can be no doubt—if one compares the examples of the first decade with the interviews conducted more recently—that the tape recorder, together with a generally more polished and sophisticated approach on the part of the interviewers, has been an important factor in making these encounters livelier and more comprehensive, more densely textured and satisfying. The earliest *Paris Review* interviews with such literary figures as E. M. Forster, François Mauriac, Alberto Moravia, and Irwin Shaw are illuminating and in their own way fascinating; however, they have a certain stiffness and formality that appears to come partly from the old-fashioned interviewing technique but, even more significantly, from the fact that the young editors and their cohorts, most of them fresh out of college, may have had an overly reverential attitude toward these literary moguls.

I was anything but a literary mogul when I arrived in Paris for the first time in the spring of 1952, but I had recently published a first novel called *Lie Down in Darkness* and I was flattered when George Plimpton and Peter Matthiessen, the co-founders of the *Paris Review*, deemed me of sufficient stature to be a participant in the series of interviews they were planning to make a regular feature of their still embryonic magazine. Several subjects had already been corralled—I recall being stunned to learn through a noninterview comment from Plimpton, who had encountered Forster at Cambridge University, that the revered novelist had a lover who was a large, hirsute police official—but I was the first targeted writer who could be termed a contemporary. I was living in a hotel of *troisième classe* called the Libéria on the rue de la Grande-Chaumière, a small atelier-lined street just around the corner from the busy intersection of the boulevards Raspail and Montparnasse. It was the dawn of the Cold War: all empty walls were plastered with the legend U.S. GO HOME. My bidet-equipped but toiletless room (facilities down the hall) at the Libéria cost me eight dollars a week; this was but one small reflection of the supremacy of the post–World War II dollar. An item in my notebook of the period mentions lunch for one at a nearby bistro: steak, *pommes frites*, *haricots verts, tarte aux pommes, carafe de vin rouge, café filtre*—total cost, $1.85. I was hard at work but lonely in my room; a measure of my isolation is my forlorn memory of Reed Hall, the residence of Smith College students abroad, which was opposite my window, and my voyeuristic attempts to catch glimpses of the girls as they sashayed down the hallway from the shower—always, however, chastely robed.

Plimpton and Matthiessen rescued me from my cell and we became friends and drinking companions. I was toiling away at a short novel, *The Long March*, and their friendship made it possible for me to look forward to cheery social evenings whose usual venue was a smoky but clean nightclub called La Chaplain. There we drank cognac and soda since scotch, later relatively cheap and plentiful in France, cost a fortune. Midmorning coffee was usually taken at Le Dôme, which was not then a swank seafood establishment but still retained the run-down, even squalid character of previous times, when Hemingway hung out there. A post-Hemingway touch was an all-pervading odor of cannabis—you could almost suffocate from pot in the downstairs *lavabos*—but the spirit of Papa was still evident in the extraordinary number of young men sitting at tables who were dead ringers for Hemingway, wearing the cropped mustache, flashing bright teeth, and scribbling away at some fifties update of *The Sun Also Rises*. My *PR* interview, which by all rights should have been conducted at Le Dôme, was for some reason transferred across the boulevard to the terrace of a café called Patrick's. More pot. I recall that we all had ferocious hangovers. The transparency of my recollection is enhanced by the fact that I was limping and in pain; two nights before, Matthiessen, gunning his car in a rearward lunge over the curb in front of Le Chaplain, had run me down, leaving me miraculously upright but with a deep dent from the bumper imprinted so solidly in my calf that it remained there for weeks. Plimpton and Matthiessen shot their questions at me across a tiny round table where we sat for perhaps an hour and a half. The interrogation and the answers were, as I've said, set down in longhand and a full year passed before I saw the results, transferred to a typescript that reached me where I was living in Ravello, Italy. I recall that I made very few changes or emendations on the final transcript. At twenty-six I was nothing if not self-assured and my staccato, cocky, know-it-all tone, which pains me a little upon rereading, must have pleased me immensely. At any rate, I plainly didn't do what the editors of the *Paris Review* have so generously encouraged the writers to do in the years thereafter, and that is to revise, expand, emend, and otherwise enrich the text, to the extent that some of these interviews have, as Joyce Carol Oates said, "acquired reputations, with the passage of time, as masterpieces of their genre."

Posterity will judge whether this volume, the ninth in the series, contains masterpieces, but certainly the offerings displayed here have an extraordinary variety and range. Quite aside from the intellectual territory covered by these writers in their conversations, there is bound to be an arresting diversity when the writers themselves had their beginnings in such far-flung places as Peru; Richmond, Virginia; the Bronx; Czechoslovakia; Arkansas; and Persia. And for many of these writers those beginnings are entwined with a sense of place: Where One Comes From is not a negligible factor in the total reckoning. Southerners like Walker Percy and Maya Angelou are unable to avoid the South even when, as in Angelou's case, they want to; Dixie is ineluctably a component of their work. Angelou relates how, after forty years of deliberate absence from the South, which has been a constant presence in her autobiographical narratives, she was finally drawn back to the region of her birth and now makes her home there. Percy, a dyed-in-the-wool Southerner if there ever was one, but a man who maintained a healthy and droll skepticism about that sometimes schizophrenic world, speaks engagingly of those mysterious qualities that make the South forever "different." "All I know," he says, "is that there is still something about living in the South which turns one inward, makes one secretive, shy, and scheming, makes one capable of a degree of malice, humor, and outrageousness." For Wallace Stegner, a Westerner, the consciousness of place—of Westernness—allows him to contemplate both the advantages and drawbacks of being a writer situated at the edge of the Pacific Basin. Regretting the lack of a "usable past" which has been the birthright of so many Southern writers, he notes nonetheless the benefits of the West, where writers "see aspects of the future, and we hear the sounds of alien ideas that are less apparent farther east. And we hear the interior of the continent more plainly." The work of the novelist William Kennedy, the bard of Albany, is so indissolubly bound up with the capital city of the state of New York that he has, like the creator of Yoknapatawpha County, virtually become its proprietor. He speaks with eloquent intensity of his passion to render his hometown with the verisimilitude of Faulkner's *The Sound and the Fury*, his desire to give the similar effect of "an entire cosmos." Place for Kennedy is as crucially important to writing as the words themselves.

What about influences? Of all the questions leveled at writers, the one most commonly asked (unless it be "What did you think of the movie Fox made of your novel *Godolphin the Magnificent*?") is probably the one that concerns the literary movers and shakers that sparked one's electric excitement in youth or that shaped one's thinking in the struggle and growth toward mature creative achievement. There is a splendid diversity of genius in the rosters of literary antecedents and modern mentors that have affected the work of the present writers, who acknowledge their gurus and gods with varying shades of grace. Tom Wolfe expresses his early (and continuing) enthusiasm for his namesake, Thomas Wolfe. That both Harold Bloom and Maya Angelou refer to the Bible as having had an abiding influence on the way in which they apprehend the world tells much about the power and the eclectic reach of the Judeo-Christian tradition. Like so many Latin-American writers, Mario Vargas Llosa confesses his great indebtedness to Faulkner. For the playwright Tom Stoppard there was less influence, oddly, from his fellow dramatists—Beckett, Pinter, John Osborne—than in the prose work of Hemingway and Evelyn Waugh. As a young woman in Australia, P. L. Travers was smitten with the work of the poet AE, and after much hesitancy, formed a friendship with the great man. Walker Percy points to the "breathtaking" stories of Chekhov, which he reread, as comprising fresh inspiration. And so it goes. The roll call of predecessors is fascinating and, in many instances, occasion for the reader's genuine surprise.

In 1953 the editors of the *Paris Review* asked me to write an introduction to the first issue of their journal, and in that prolegomenon I set down, in fairly top-lofty tones, some of the aims of the brave venture. The New Criticism was then in full blossom; like its latter-day descendant, the ominously named Deconstructionism, it tended, despite solemn disclaimers from its practitioners, to exalt itself and, at its most pushy, to make writers and poets feel pale and shrunken in the shadow of critical theory, which was really being peddled as a greater good in itself than anything purely creative. It was certainly in reaction to this dogma that I insisted, on behalf of the editors, that criticism within the pages of the journal would be zealously avoided. This was a considerable departure for a literary magazine. And the standard, if such it may be called, has been adhered to until this day: no writing of a strictly critical nature has ever invaded any one of the 122 issues that have appeared to date. It is a somewhat dramatic development, then, that this volume contains the initial interview in a series called "The Art of Criticism," and that its exemplar is the eminent critic Harold Bloom. Bloom's interview is powerful, wide-ranging, acidulous, judgmental, enormously erudite, and wickedly provocative. Our critic is anything but politically correct and his animadversions on contemporary pieties—academic cultism, loony feminism, the canonization of the mediocre, "that whole semiotic cackle"—are expressed with a consummate hauteur that will delight some and make the faint-hearted miserable. It seems likely that as a model his interview will be the one to which future critics will have to aspire.

And so in this volume will be found no ultimate answers concerning the creative process but much talk that is suggestive, some that is annoying, and very little that is not consistently interesting. The interviews may be read on fluctuating levels of seriousness and levity, and parts of them at least can be appreciated as the most entertaining kind of literary gossip, which is fine, since only those readers who are reverential owls would deny the appeal of gossip at its best, especially when embedded in texts that are generally so thoughtful and illuminating about the high purpose of literature. Thus Maya Angelou's lively description of her return to Stamps, Arkansas, is a bright counterpoint to her meditation on the musical language of the Scriptures. In a lecture hall at a German university Doris Lessing confronts, in the form of four professors, Teutonic blockheadedness at its most impenetrable; the effect is hilarious and contrasts nicely with her shrewd reflections on her art. What really happened in Mexico City during the alleged fistfight between Mario Vargas Llosa and Gabriel García Márquez? Vargas Llosa's reticence prevents us from knowing, but he does give us a sweet glimpse of the great Borges, blind and peeing, making the priceless comment, "The Catholics, do you think they are serious? Probably not." As in most of these interviews, such mordant vignettes add spice to the earnest task of self-examination.

As for my task, it has been pleasant to introduce this rich new collection, and to recommend its challenges and pleasures, nearly forty years after my own encounter on the boulevard Montparnasse, where I spoke my thoughts and the smells of marijuana and hydrocarbons mingled as harbingers of this second half-century.

—WILLIAM STYRON

# 1. Samuel Beckett

In the brief span of three months, Samuel Beckett wrote the play that was to become the cornerstone of modern drama, *Waiting for Godot*, the tale of two tramps who do just as the title says: wait for Godot, the maybe-savior who never arrives. Beckett himself was born on Good Friday, April 13, 1906, the birthdate of those who, according to superstition, are clairvoyant. He completed his schooling at Trinity College, where he studied French and Italian; after receiving his master's degree he lectured on English in Paris, where he befriended James Joyce. "Whoroscope," his first poem, appeared in 1930 and in 1931 his essay on Marcel Proust. In 1937, he moved—for good—to Paris.

During the war Beckett and his wife both took an active part in the French Resistance and had to live in hiding to escape the Gestapo. During that period Beckett wrote *Watt*, the last novel he wrote in English. Afterward he wrote his novels in French. He was his own translator for all of his work.

In 1947, Beckett finished his first play, *Eleutheria*. This was the start of his most creative period, his middle years, during which he wrote his trilogy of novels, *Molloy*, *Malone Dies*, and *The Unnamable*, and *Waiting for Godot*, which opened in 1953 to a bewildered audience and skyrocketed Beckett to fame.

In 1969 Beckett received the Nobel Prize for a body of work that "has transformed the destitution of man into his exaltation." He died in Paris of respiratory problems at the age of eighty-three.

Beckett hated the interview form, but he had no objection to Lawrence Shainberg writing an account of their various meetings, which explains the narrative form that follows.

*A manuscript page from Samuel Beckett's one-act play* Krapp's Last Tape, *in which an aging man plays back the monologues that he taped when young and listens with a cynical ear to the hopes and dreams he had once had and which amounted to nothing.*

© Jerry Bauer

# *Exorcising Beckett*

I met Beckett in 1981, when I sent him, with no introduction, a book I'd written, and to my astonishment, he read the book and replied almost at once. Six weeks later, his note having emboldened me to seek a meeting, our paths crossed in London, and he invited me to sit in on the rehearsals of *Endgame* which he was then conducting with a group of American actors for a Dublin opening in May.

It was a happy time for him. Away from his desk, where his work, he said (I've never heard him say otherwise), was not going well at all, he was exploring a work which, though he'd written it thirty years before, remained among his favorites. The American group, called the San Quentin Theatre Workshop because they had discovered his work—through a visiting production of *Waiting for Godot*—while inmates at San Quentin, was particularly close to his heart, and working in London he was accessible to the close-knit family that collects so often where he or his work appears. Among those who came to watch were Billie Whitelaw, Irene Worth, Nicol Williamson, Alan Schneider, Israel Horovitz, Siobhan O'Casey (Sean's daughter), three writers with Beckett books in progress, two editors who'd published him and one who wanted to, and an impressive collection of madmen and Beckett freaks who had learned of his presence via the grapevine. One lady, in her early twenties, came to ask if Beckett minded that she'd named her dog after him (Beckett: "Don't worry about me. What about the dog?"), and a wild-eyed madman from Scotland brought flowers and gifts for Beckett and everyone in the cast and a four-page letter entitled "Beckett's Cancer, Part Three," which begged him to accept the gifts as "a sincere token of my deep and long-suffering love for you," while remembering that "I also hold a profound and comprehensive loathing for you, in response to all the terrible corruption and suffering which you have seen fit to inflict upon my entirely innocent personality."

The intimacy and enthusiasm with which Beckett greeted his friends as well as newcomers like myself—acting for all the world as if I'd done him an enormous favor to come—was a great surprise for me, one of many ways in which our meetings would force me to reconsider the conception of him which I had formed during the twenty years I'd been reading and, let's be honest about it, worshiping him. Who would expect the great master of grief and disenchantment to be so expansive, so relaxed in company? Well, as it turned out, almost everyone who knew him. My surprise was founded not in his uncharacteristic behavior but in the erroneous, often bizarre misunderstandings that had gathered about him in my mind. Certainly, if there's one particular legacy that I take from our meetings it is the way in which those misunderstandings were first revealed and then corrected. In effect, Beckett's presence destroyed the Beckett myth for me, replacing it with something at once larger and more ordinary. Even today I haven't entirely understood what this correction meant to me, but it's safe to say that the paradoxical effects of Beckett incarnate—inspiring and disheartening, terrifying, reassuring, and humbling in the extreme—are nowhere at odds with the work that drew me to him in the first place.

The first surprise was the book to which he responded. Because it was journalism—an investigation of the world of neurosurgery—I had been almost embarrassed to send it, believing that he of all people would not be interested in the sort of information I'd collected. No, what I imagined he'd really appreciate was the novel that had led me to neurosurgery, a book to which I had now returned, which dealt with brain damage and presented it with an ambiguity and dark humor that, as I saw it, clearly signaled both his influence and my ambition to go beyond it. As it turned out, I had things exactly backward. For the novel, the first two chapters of which he read in London, he had little enthusiasm, but the nonfiction book continued to interest him. Whenever I saw him, he questioned me about neurosurgery, asking, for example, exactly how close I had stood to the brain while observing surgery, or how much pain a craniotomy entailed, or, one day during lunch at rehearsals: "How is the skull removed?" and "Where do they put the skull bone while they're working inside?" Though I'd often heard it said of him that he read nothing written after 1950, he remembered the names of the patients I'd mentioned and inquired as to their condition, and more than once he expressed his admiration for the surgeons. Later he did confess to me that he read very little, finding what he called "the intake" more and more "excruciating," but I doubt that he ever lost his interest in certain kinds of information, especially those which concerned the human brain. "I have long believed," he'd written me in his first response to my book, "that here in the end is the writer's best chance, gazing into the synaptic chasm."

Seventy-four years old, he was very frail in those days, even more gaunt and wizened than his photos had led me to expect, but neither age nor frailty interfered with his sense of humor. When I asked him how he was doing one morning at the theater, he replied with a great display of exhaustion and what I took to be a sly sort of gleam in his eye, "No improvement." Another day, with an almost theatrical sigh, "A little wobbly." How can we be surprised that on the subject of his age he was not only unintimidated but challenged, even inspired? Not five minutes into our first conversation he brought us round to the matter: "I always thought old age would be a writer's best chance. Whenever I read the late work of Goethe or W. B. Yeats I had the impertinence to identify with it. Now, my memory's gone, all the old fluency's disappeared. I don't write a single sentence without saying to myself, 'It's a lie!' So I know I was right. It's the best chance I've ever had." Two years later—and older—he explored the same thoughts again in Paris. "It's a paradox, but with old age, the more the possibilities diminish, the better chance you have. With diminished concentration, loss of memory, obscured intelligence—what you, for example, might call 'brain damage'—the more chance there is for saying something closest to what one really is. Even though everything seems inexpressible, there remains the need to express. A child needs to make a sand castle even though it makes no sense. In old age, with only a few grains of sand, one has the greatest possibility." Of course, he knew that this was not a new project for him, only a more extreme version of the one he'd always set himself, what he'd laid out so clearly in his famous line from *The Unnamable*: ". . . it will be the silence, where I am, I don't know, I'll never know, in the silence you don't know, you must go on, I can't go on, I'll go on." It was always here, in "the clash," as he put it to me once, "between can't and must" that he took his stand. "How is it that a man who is completely blind, completely deaf, must see and hear? It's this impossible paradox which interests me. The unseeable, the unbearable, the inexpressible." Such thoughts of course were as familiar to me as they would be to any attentive reader of Beckett, but it was always amazing to hear how passionately—and innocently—he articulated them. Given the pain in his voice, the furrowed, struggling concentration on his face, it was impossible to believe that he wasn't unearthing these thoughts for the first time. Absurd as it sounds, they seemed less familiar to him than to me. And it was no small shock to realize this. To encounter, I mean, the author of some of the greatest work in our language, and find him, at seventy-four, discovering his vision in your presence. His excitement alone was riveting, but for me the greatest shock was to see how intensely he continued to work on the issues that had preoccupied him all his life. So much so that it didn't matter where he was or who he was with, whether he was literally "at work" or in a situation that begged for small talk. I don't think I ever had a conversation with him in which I wasn't, at some point, struck by an almost naive realization of his sincerity, as if reminding myself that he was not playing the role one expected him to play, but simply pursuing the questions most important to him. Is it possible that no one surprises us more than someone who is (especially when our expectations have been hyperbolic) exactly what we expect? It was as if a voice in me said, "My God, he's serious!" or, "So he's meant it all along!" And this is where my misunderstandings became somewhat embarrassing. Why on earth should he have surprised me? What did it say of my own sense of writing and reading or the culture from which I'd come that integrity in a writer—for this was after all the simple fact that he was demonstrating—should have struck me as so extraordinary?

Something else he said that first night in London was familiar to me from one of his published interviews, but he said this too as if he'd just come upon it, and hearing it now, I felt that I understood, for the first time, that aspect of his work which interested me the most. I'm speaking of its intimacy and immediacy, the uncanny sense that he's writing not only in a literary but an existential present tense, or more precisely, as John Pilling calls it in his book *Samuel Beckett*, an imperfect tense. The present tense of course is no rare phenomenon in modern, or for that matter, classical fiction, but unlike most writers who write *in* the present, Beckett writes *from* the present and remains constantly vulnerable to it. It is a difference of which he is acutely aware, one which distinguishes him even from a writer he admires as much as he does Kafka. As he said in a 1961 interview, "Kafka's form is classic, it goes on like a steamroller, almost serene. It seems to be threatened all the time, but the consternation is in the form. In my work there is consternation behind the form, not in the form." It is for this reason that Beckett himself is present in his work to a degree that, as I see it, no other writer managed before him. In most of his published conversations, especially when he was younger and not (as later) embarrassed to speak didactically, he takes the position that such exposure is central to the work that he considers interesting. "If anything new and exciting is going on today, it is the attempt to let Being into art." As he began to evolve a means by which to accommodate such belief, he made us realize not only the degree to which Being had been kept out of art but *why* it had been kept out, how such exclusion is, even now, the *raison d'être* of most art, and how the game changes, the stakes rising exponentially, once we let it in. Invaded by real time, narrative time acquires an energy and a fragility and, not incidentally, a truth which undermines whatever complacency or passivity the reader—not to mention the writer—has brought to the work, the assumption that enduring forms are to be offered, that certain propositions will rise above the flux, that "pain-killers," which Hamm seeks in vain throughout *Endgame,* will be provided. In effect, the narrative illusion is no longer safe from the narrator's reality. "Being," as he said once, "is constantly putting form in danger," and the essence of his work is its willingness to risk such danger. Listen to the danger he risks in this sentence from *Molloy:* "A and C I never saw again. But perhaps I shall see them again. But shall I be able to recognize them? And am I sure I never saw them again?"

The untrustworthy narrator, of course, had preceded Beckett by at least a couple of centuries, but his "imperfect" tense deprives Molloy of the great conceit that most authors have traditionally granted their narrators—a consistent, dependable memory. In effect, a brain that is neither damaged, in that it doesn't suffer from amnesia, nor normal, in that it is consistent, confident of the information it contains, and immune to the assaults that time and environment mount on its continuities. But Beckett's books are not *about* uncertainty any more than they're *about* consternation. Like their author, like the Being which has invaded them, they are themselves uncertain, not only in their conclusions but their point of view. Form is offered, because as he has so often remarked, that is an obligation before which one is helpless, but any pretense that it will endure is constantly shown to be just that, pretense and nothing more. A game the author can no longer play and doesn't dare relinquish. "I know of no form," he said, "that does not violate the nature of Being in the most unbearable manner." Simply stated, what he brought to narrative fiction and drama was a level of reality that dwarfed all others that had preceded it. And because the act of writing—i.e., his own level of reality, at the moment of composition—is never outside his frame of reference, he exposes himself to the reader as no writer has before him. When Molloy changes his mind it's because Beckett has changed his mind as well, when the narrative is inconsistent it's not an esthetic trick but an accurate reflection of the mind from which that narrative springs. Finally, what Molloy doesn't know Beckett doesn't know either. And this is why, though they speak of Joyce or Proust or other masters in terms of genius, so many writers will speak of Beckett in terms of courage. One almost has to be a writer to know what courage it takes to stand so naked before one's reader or, more important, before oneself, to relinquish the protection offered by separation from the narrative, the security and order which, in all likelihood, were what drew one to writing in the first place.

That evening, speaking of *Molloy* and the work that followed it, he told me that, returning to Dublin after the war, he'd found that his mother had contracted Parkinson's Disease. "Her face was a mask, completely unrecognizable. Looking at her, I had a sudden realization that all the work I'd done before was on the wrong track. I guess you'd have to call it a revelation. Strong word, I know, but so it was. I simply understood that there was no sense adding to the store of information, gathering knowledge. The whole attempt at knowledge, it seemed to me, had come to nothing. It was all haywire. What I had to do was investigate not-knowing, not-perceiving, the whole world of incompleteness." In the wake of this insight, writing in French ("Perhaps because French was not my mother tongue, because I had no facility in it, no spontaneity") while still in his mother's house, he had begun *Molloy* (the first line of which is "I am in my mother's room"), thus commencing what was to be the most prolific period of his life. Within the first three paragraphs of his chronicle, Molloy says "I don't know" six times, "perhaps" and "I've forgotten" twice, and "I don't understand" once. He doesn't know how he came to be in his mother's room, and he doesn't know how to write anymore, and he doesn't know why he writes when he manages to do so, and he doesn't know whether his mother was dead when he came to her room or died later, and he doesn't know whether or not he has a son. In other words, he is not an awful lot different from any other writer in the anxiety of composition, considering the alternative roads offered up by his imagination, trying to discern a theme among the chaos of messages offered by his brain, testing his language to see what sort of relief it can offer. Thus, Molloy and his creator are joined from the first, and the latter—unlike most of his colleagues, who have been taught, even if they're writing about their own ignorance and uncertainty, that the strength of their work consists in their ability to say the opposite—is saying "I don't know" with every word he utters. The whole of the narrative is therefore time-dependent, neurologically and psychologically suspect and contingent on the movement of the narrator's mind. And since knowledge, by definition, requires a subject and an object, a knower and a known, two points separated on the temporal continuum, Beckett's "I don't know" has short-circuited the fundamental dualism upon which all narrative, and for that matter, all language, has before him been constructed. If the two points cannot be separated on the continuum, what is left? No time, only the present tense. And if you must speak at this instant, using words which are by definition object-dependent, how do you do so? Finally, what is left to know if knowledge itself has been, at its very root, discredited? Without an object, what will words describe or subjugate? If subject and object are joined, how can there be hope or memory or order? What is hoped for, what is remembered, what is ordered? What is Self if knower and known are not separated by self-consciousness?

Those are the questions that Beckett has dealt with throughout his life. And before we call them esoteric or obtuse, esthetic, philosophical or literary, we'd do well to remember that they're not much different from the questions many of us consider, consciously or not, in the course of an ordinary unhysterical day, the questions which, before Molloy and his successors, had been excluded, at least on the surface, from most of the books we read. As Beckett wrote once to Alan Schneider, "The confusion is not my invention. . . . It is all around us and our only chance is to let it in. The only chancc of renovation is to open our eyes and see the mess. . . . There will be new form, and . . . this form will be of such a type that it admits the chaos and does not try to say that it is really something else."

At the time of his visit with his mother, Beckett was thirty-nine years old, which is to say the same age as Krapp, who deals with a similar revelation in his tape-recorded journals and ends (this knowledge, after all, being no more durable than any other) by rejecting it: "What a fool I was to take that for a vision!" That evening, however, as we sat in his hotel room, there was no rejection in Beckett's mind. In the next three years, he told me, he wrote *Molloy*, *Malone Dies*, *The Unnamable*, *Stories and Texts for Nothing*, and—in three months, with almost no revision of the first draft—*Waiting for Godot*. The last, he added, was "pure recreation." The novels, especially *The Unnamable*, had taken him to a point where there were no limits, and *Godot* was a conscious attempt to reestablish them. "I wanted walls I could touch, rules I had to follow." I asked if his revelation—the understanding, as he'd put it, that all his previous work had been a lie—had depressed him. "No, I was very excited! There was no effort in the writing. I worked all day and went out to the cafés at night."

He was visibly excited by the memory, but it wasn't long before his mood shifted, and his excitement gave way to sadness and nostalgia. The contrast between the days he had remembered and the difficulty he was having now—"racking my brains," as he put it, "to see if I can go a little farther"—was all too evident. Sighing loudly, he put his long fingers over his eyes, then shook his head. "If only it could be like that again."

So this is the other side of his equation, one which I, like many of his admirers, have a tendency to forget. The enthusiasm he had but moments before expressed for his diminishments did not protect him from the suffering those diminishments had caused. Let us remember that this is a man who once called writing "disimproving the silence." Why should he miss such futile work when it deserts him? So easy, it is, to become infatuated with the way he embraces his ignorance and absurdity, so hard to remember that when he does so he isn't posturing or for that matter "writing," that what keeps his comedy alive is the pain and despair from which it is won. The sincerity of writers who work with pain and impotence is always threatened by the vitality the work itself engenders, but Beckett has never succumbed to either side of this paradox. He has never, that is to say, put his work ahead of his experience. Unlike so many of us, who found in the Beckett vision—"Nothing is funnier than unhappiness," says Nell in *Endgame*—a comic esthetic which had us, a whole generation of writers, I think, collecting images of absurdity as if mining precious ore, he has gazed with no pleasure whatsoever at the endless parade of light and dark. For all the bleakness of *Endgame*, it remains his belief, as one of the actors who did the play in Germany recalls, that "Hamm says no to nothingness." Exploit absurdity though he does, there is no sign, in his work or his conversation, that he finds life less absurd for having done so. Though he has often said that his real work began when he "gave up hope for meaning," he hates hopelessness and longs for meaning as much as anyone who has never read *Molloy* or seen *Endgame*.

One of our less happy exchanges occurred because of my tendency to forget this. In other words, my tendency to underestimate his integrity. This was three years later, on a cold, rainy morning in Paris, when he was talking, yet again, about the difficulties he was having in his work. "The fact is, I don't know what I'm doing. I can't even bring myself to open the exercise book. My hand goes out to it, then draws back as if on its own." As I say, he often spoke like this, sounding less like a man who'd been writing for sixty years than one who'd just begun, but he was unusually depressed that morning, and the more he talked, the more depressed I became myself. No question about it, one had to have a powerful equanimity that his grief might leave it intact. When he was inside his suffering, the force of it spreading out from him could feel like a tidal wave. The more I listened to him that morning, the more it occurred to me that he sounded exactly like Molloy. Who else but Molloy could speak with such authority about paralysis and bewilderment, in other words, a condition absolutely antithetical to authority itself? At first I kept such thoughts to myself, but finally, unable to resist, I passed them along to him, adding excitedly that, if I were forced to choose my favorite of all Beckett lines, it would be Molloy's: "If there's one question I dread, to which I've never been able to invent a satisfactory reply, it's the question, 'What am I doing?' " So complete was my excitement that for a moment I expected him to share it. Why not? It seemed to me that I'd come upon the perfect antidote to his despair in words of his own invention. It took but a single glance from him—the only anger I ever saw in his eyes—to show me how naive I'd been, how silly to think that Molloy's point of view would offer him the giddy freedom it had so often offered me. "Yes," he murmured, "that's my line, isn't it?" Not for Beckett the pleasures of Beckett. As Henry James once said in a somewhat different context: "My job is to write those little things, not read them."

One of the people who hung around rehearsals was a puppeteer who cast his puppets in Beckett plays. At a cast party one night he gave a performance of *Act Without Words* which demonstrated, with particular force, the consistency of Beckett's paradox and the relentlessness with which he maintains it. For those who aren't familiar with it, *Act Without Words* is a silent, almost Keatonesque litany about the futility of hope. A man sits beside a barren tree in what seems to be a desert, a blistering sun overhead. Suddenly, offstage, a whistle is heard and a glass of water descends, but when the man reaches for it, it rises until it's just out of reach. He strains for it, but it rises to elude him once again. Finally he gives up and resumes his position beneath the tree. Almost at once the whistle sounds again, and a stool descends to rekindle his hope. In a flurry of excitement, he mounts, stretches, grasps, and watches the water rise beyond his reach again. A succession of whistles and offerings follows, each arousing his hope and dashing it until at last he ceases to respond. The whistle continues to sound but he gives no sign of hearing it. Like so much Beckett, it's the bleakest possible vision rendered in comedy nearly slapstick, and that evening, with the author and number of children in the audience and an ingenious three-foot-tall puppet in the lead, it had us all, children included, laughing as if Keaton himself were performing it. When the performance ended, Beckett congratulated the puppeteer and his wife, who had assisted him, offering—with his usual diffidence and politeness—but a single criticism. "The whistle isn't shrill enough."

As it happened, the puppeteer's wife was a Buddhist, a follower of the path to which Beckett himself paid homage in his early book on Proust, when he wrote, "the wisdom of all the sages, from Brahma to Leopardi . . . consists not in the satisfaction but the ablation of desire." As a devotee and a Beckett admirer, this woman was understandably anxious to confirm what she, like many people, took to be his sympathies with her religion. In fact, not a few critical opinions had been mustered, over the years, concerning his debt to Buddhism, Taoism, Zen, the Noh theater, all of it received—as it was now received from the puppeteer's wife—with curiosity and appreciation and absolute denial by the man it presumed to explain. "I know nothing about Buddhism," he said. "If it's present in the play, it is unbeknownst to me." Once this had been asserted, however, there remained the possibility of unconscious predilection, innate Buddhism, so to speak, so the woman had another question, which had stirred in her mind, she said, since the first time she'd seen the play. "When all is said and done, isn't this man, having given up hope, finally liberated?" Beckett looked at her with a pained expression. He'd had his share of drink that night, but not enough to make him forget his vision or push him beyond his profound distaste for hurting anyone's feelings. "Oh, no," he said quietly. "He's *finished*."

I don't want to dwell on it, but I had a personal stake in this exchange. For years I'd been studying Zen and its particular form of sitting meditation, and I'd always been struck by the parallels between the practice and Beckett's work. In fact, to me, as to the woman who questioned him that evening, it seemed quite impossible that he didn't have some explicit knowledge, perhaps even direct experience, of Zen, and I had asked him about it that very first night at his hotel. He answered me as he answered her: he knew nothing of Zen at all. Of course, he said, he'd heard Zen stories and loved them for their "concreteness," but other than that he was ignorant on the subject. Ignorant, but not uninterested. "What do you do in such places?" he asked. I told him that mostly we looked at the wall. "Oh," he said, "you don't have to know anything about Zen to do that. I've been doing it for fifty years." (When Hamm asks Clov what he does in his kitchen, Clov replies: "I look at the wall." "The wall!" snaps Hamm. "And what do you see on your wall? . . . naked bodies?" Replies Clov, "I see my light dying.") For all his experience with wall-gazing, however, Beckett found it extraordinary that people would seek it out of their own free will. Why, he asked, did people do it? Were they seeking tranquility? Solutions? And finally, as with neurosurgery: "Does it hurt?" I answered with growing discomfort. Even though I remained convinced that the concerns of his work were identical with those of Zen, there was something embarrassing about discussing it with him, bringing self-consciousness to bear, I mean, where its absence was the point. This is not the place for a discussion of Zen, but since it deals, as Beckett does, with the separation of subject and object ("No direct contact is possible between subject and object," he wrote in his book on Proust, "because they are automatically separated by the subject's consciousness of perception. . . ."), the problems of Self, of Being and Non-being, of consciousness and perception, all the means by which one is distanced or removed from the present tense, it finds in Beckett's work a mirror as perfect as any in its own literature or scripture.

This in itself is no great revelation. It's not terribly difficult to find Zen in almost any great work of art. The particular problem, however, what made my questions seem—to me at least—especially absurd, is that such points—like many where Beckett is concerned—lose more than they gain in the course of articulation. To point out the Zen in Beckett is to make him seem didactic or, even worse, therapeutic, and nothing could betray his vision more. For that matter, the converse is also true. Remarking on the Beckett in Zen betrays Zen to the same extent and for the same reasons. It is there that their true commonality lies, their mutual devotion to the immediate and the concrete, the Truth which becomes less True if made an object of description, *the Being which form excludes*. As Beckett put it once, responding to one of the endless interpretations his work has inspired, "My work is a matter of fundamental sounds. Hamm as stated, Clov as stated. . . . That's all I can manage, more than I could. If people get headaches among the overtones, they'll have to furnish their own aspirin."

So I did finally give up the questions, and though he always asked me about Zen when we met—"Are you still looking at the wall?"—I don't think he held it against me. His last word on the matter came by mail, and maybe it was the best. In a fit of despair I had written him once about what seemed to me an absolute, insoluble conflict between meditation and writing. "What is it about looking at the wall that makes the writing seem obsolete?" Two weeks later, when I'd almost forgotten my question, I received this reply, which I quote in its entirety:

Dear Larry, When I start looking at walls, I begin to see the writing. From which even my own is a relief.

As ever,

Sam

Rehearsals lasted three weeks and took place in a cavernous building, once used by the BBC, called the Riverside Studios. Since it was located in a section of London with which I was not familiar, Beckett invited me that first morning to meet him at his hotel and ride out in the taxi he shared with his cast. Only three of his actors were present that day—Rick Cluchey, Bud Thorpe, and Alan Mandell (Hamm and Clov and Nagg, respectively)—the fourth, Nell, being Cluchey's wife, Teresita, who was home with their son, Louis Beckett Cluchey, and would come to the theater in the afternoon. The group had an interesting history, and it owed Beckett a lot more than this production, for which he was taking no pay or royalties. Its origins dated to 1957 when Cluchey, serving a life sentence for kidnapping and robbery at San Quentin, had seen a visiting production of *Waiting for Godot* and found in it an inspiration that had completely transformed his life. Though he'd never been in a theater—"not even," he said, "to rob one"—he saw to the heart of a play which at the time was baffling more sophisticated audiences. "Who knew more about waiting than people like us?" Within a month of this performance, Cluchey and several other inmates had organized a drama group which developed a Beckett cycle—*Endgame, Waiting for Godot*, and *Krapp's Last Tape*—that they continued, in Europe and the United States, after their parole. Though Cluchey was the only survivor of that original workshop, the present production traced its roots to those days at San

Quentin and the support which Beckett had offered the group when word of their work had reached him. Another irony was that Mandell, who was playing Nagg in this production, had appeared with the San Francisco Actors' Workshop in the original production at San Quentin. By now Beckett seemed to regard Rick and Teri and their son, his namesake, as part of his family, and the current production was as much a gift to them as a matter of personal or professional necessity. Not that this was uncharacteristic. In those days much of his work was being done as a gift to specific people. He'd written *A Piece of Monologue* for David Warrilow, and in the next few years he'd write *Rockaby* for Billie Whitelaw and *Ohio Impromptu* for S. E. Gontarski, a professor at Georgia Tech, who was editor of the *Journal of Beckett Studies.* When I met him later in Paris he was struggling to write a promised piece for Cluchey at a time when he had, he said, no interest in work at all. In my opinion, this was not merely because he took no promise lightly or because at this point in his life he valued especially this sort of impetus, though both of course were true, but because the old demarcations, between the work and the life, writing and speaking, solitude and social discourse, were no longer available to him. If his ordinary social exchanges were less intense or single-minded than his work it was certainly not apparent to me. I never received a note from him that didn't fit on a 3 × 5 index card, but (as the previously mentioned note on Zen illustrates) there wasn't one, however lighthearted, that wasn't clearly Beckett writing. Obviously, this was not because of any particular intimacy between us, but because, private though he was, and fiercely self-protective, he seemed to approach every chance as if it might be his last. You only had to watch his face when he talked—or wait out one of those two- or three-minute silences while he pondered a question you'd asked—to know that language was much too costly and precarious for him to use mindlessly or as a means of filling gaps.

Wearing a maroon polo sweater, gray flannel pants, a navy blue jacket, no socks, and brown suede sneaker-like shoes, he was dressed, as Cluchey told me later, much the same as he'd been every time they'd met for the past fifteen years. As the taxi edged through London's morning rush hour, he lit up one of the cheroots he smoked and observed to no one in particular that he was still unhappy with the wheelchair they'd found for Hamm to use in this production. Amazing how often his speech echoed his work. "We need a proper wheelchair!" Hamm cries. "With big wheels. Bicycle wheels!" One evening, when I asked him if he was tired, his answer—theatrically delivered—was a quote from Clov: " 'Yes, tired of all our goings on.' " And a few days later, when a transit strike brought London to a standstill, and one of the actors suggested that rehearsals might not go on, he lifted a finger in the air and announced with obvious self-mockery, "Ah, but we must go on!" I'm not sure what type of wheelchair he wanted but several were tried in the next few days until one was found that he accepted. He was also unhappy with the percussion theme he was trying to establish, two pairs of knocks or scrapes which recur throughout the play—when Nagg, for example, knocks Nell's ashcan to rouse her, when Hamm taps the wall to assure himself of its solidity, or when Clov climbs the two steps of his ladder with four specific scrapes of his slippers. For Beckett, these sounds were a primary musical motif, a fundamental continuity. It was crucial that they echo each other. "Alan," he said, "first thing this morning, I want you to rehearse your knock." Most discussions I was to hear about the play were like this, dealing in sound or props or other tangibles, with little or no mention of motivation, and none at all of meaning. Very seldom did anyone question him on intellectual or psychological ground, and when they did, he usually brought the conversation back to the concrete, the specific. When I asked him once about the significance of the ashcans which Nagg and Nell inhabit, he said, "It was the easiest way to get them on and off stage." And when Mandell inquired, that morning in the taxi, about the meaning of the four names in the play—four names which have been subject to all sorts of critical speculation—Beckett explained that Nagg and Clov were from "noggle" and "clou," the German and French for nail, Nell from the English "nail" and Hamm from the English "hammer." Thus, the percussion motif again: a hammer and three nails. Cluchey remembered that when Beckett directed him in Germany in *Krapp's Last Tape* a similar music had been developed around the words "Ah well," which recur four times in the play, and with the sound of Krapp's slippers scraping across the stage. "Sam was obsessed with the sound of the slippers. First we tried sandpapering the soles, then layering them with pieces of metal, then brand new solid leather soles. Finally, still not satisfied, he appeared one day with his own slippers. 'I've been wearing these for twenty years,' he said. 'If they don't do it nothing will.' " More and more, as rehearsals went on, it would become apparent that music—"The highest art form," he said to me once. "It's never condemned to explicitness"—was his principal referent. His directions to actors were frequently couched in musical terms. "More emphasis there . . . it's a crescendo," or, "The more speed we get here, the more value we'll find in the pause." When Hamm directs Clov to check on Nagg in his garbage can—"Go and see did he hear me. Both times"—Beckett said, "Don't play that line realistically. There's music there, you know." As Billie Whitelaw has noted, his hands rose and fell and swept from side to side, forming arcs like a conductor's as he watched his actors and shaped the rhythm of their lines. You could see his lips move, his jaw expanding and contracting, as he mouthed the words they spoke. Finally, his direction, like his texts, seemed a process of reduction, stripping away, reaching for "fundamental sound," transcending meaning, escaping the literary and the conceptual in order to establish a concrete immediate reality, beyond the known, beyond the idea, which the audience would be forced to experience directly, without mediation of intellect.

What Beckett said once of Joyce—"his work is not about something. It is something"—was certainly true of this production. The problem, of course, what Beckett's work can neither escape nor forget, is that words are never pure in their concreteness, never free of their referents. To quote Marcel Duchamp, himself a great friend and chess partner of Beckett's, "Everything that man has handled has a tendency to secrete meaning." And such secretion, because he is too honest to deny it, is the other side of Beckett's equation, the counterweight to his music that keeps his work not only meaningful, but (maniacally) inconclusive and symmetrical, its grief and rage always balanced with its comedy, its yearning for expression constantly humbled by its conviction that the Truth can only be betrayed by language. Rest assured that no Beckett character stands on a rug that cannot be pulled out from under him. When Didi seeks solace after Godot has disappointed them again—"We are not saints, but at least we have our appointment. How many people can say as much?"—Vladimir wastes no time in restoring him to his futility: "Billions."

But more than anyone else it is Hamm who gets to the heart of the matter, when he cries out to Clov in a fit of dismay, "Clov! We're not beginning to . . . to . . . mean something?"

"Mean something!" Clov cries. "You and I, mean something. Ah that's a good one!"

"I wonder. If a rational being came back to earth, wouldn't he be liable to get ideas into his head if he observed us long enough? 'Ah good, now I see what it is, yes, now I understand what they're at!' And without going so far as that, we ourselves . . . we ourselves . . . at certain moments . . . to think perhaps it won't all have been for nothing!"

As promised, Nagg's knock was the first order of business after we reached the theater. This is the point in the play where Nagg has made his second appearance, head rising above the rim of the ashcan with a biscuit in his mouth, while Hamm and Clov—indulging in one of their habitual fencing matches—are discussing their garden. ("Did your seeds come up?" "No." "Did you scratch the ground to see if they have sprouted?" "They haven't sprouted." "Perhaps it's too early." "If they were going to sprout they would have sprouted. They'll never sprout!") A moment later, Clov having made an exit, and Hamm drifted off into a reverie, Nagg leans over to rouse Nell, tapping four times—two pairs—on the lid of her bin. Beckett demonstrated the sound he wanted, using his bony knuckle on the lid, and after Mandell had tried it six or seven times—not "Tap, tap, tap, tap," or "Tap . . . tap . . . tap . . . tap," but "tap, tap . . . tap, tap"—appeared to be satisfied. "Let's work from here," he said. Since Teri had not arrived, he climbed into thc can himself and took Nell's part, curling his bony fingers over the edge of the can, edging his head above the rim, and asking, in a shaky falsetto that captured Nell better than anyone I'd ever heard in the part: "What is it, my pet? Time for love?"

As they worked through the scene, I got my first hint of the way in which this *Endgame* would differ from others I'd seen. So much so that, despite the fact that I'd seen six or seven different productions of the play, I would soon be convinced that I'd never seen it before. Certainly, though I'd always thought *Endgame* my favorite play, I realized that I had never really understood it or appreciated the maniacal logic with which it pursues its ambiguities. Here, as elsewhere, Beckett pressed for speed and close to flat enunciation. His principal goal, which he never realized, was to compress the play so that it ran in less than ninety minutes. After the above line, the next three were bracketed for speed, then a carefully measured pause established before the next section—three more lines—began. "Kiss me," Nagg begs. "We can't," says Nell. "Try," says Nagg. And then, in another pause, they crane their necks in vain to reach each other from their respective garbage cans. The next section was but a single line in length (Nell: "Why this farce, day after day?"), the next four, the next seven, and so on. Each was a measure, clearly defined, like a jazz riff, subordinate to the rhythm of the whole. Gesture was treated like sound, another form of punctuation. Beckett was absolutely specific about its shape—the manner in which, for example, Nagg and Nell's fingers curled above the rim of their cans—and where it occurred in the text. "Keep these gestures small," he said to Cluchey, when they reached a later monologue. "Save the big one for 'All that loveliness!' " He wanted the dialogue crisp and precise but not too realistic. It seemed to me he yearned to stylize the play as much as possible, underline its theatricality, so that the actors, as in most of his plays, would be seen as clearly acting, clearly playing the roles they're doomed to play forever. The text, of course, supports such artifice, the actors often addressing each other in language which reminds us that they're on stage. "That's an aside, fool," says Hamm to Clov. "Have you never heard an aside before?" Or Clov, after his last soliloquy, pausing at the edge of the stage: "This is what they call . . . making an exit." Despite this, Beckett wanted theatrical flourish kept to a minimum. It seemed to me that he stiffened the movement, carving it like a sculptor, stripping it of anything superfluous or superficial. "Less color please," he said to Alan while they were doing Nagg and Nell together, "if we keep it flat, they'll get it better." And later, to Thorpe: "Bud, you don't have to move so much. Only the upper torso. Don't worry. They'll get it. Remember: you don't even want to be out here. You'd rather be alone, in your kitchen."

Though the play was thirty years old for him, and he believed that his memory had deteriorated, his memory of the script was flawless and his alertness to its detail unwavering. "That's not 'upon.' It's 'on.' " He corrected "one week" with "a week," "crawlin' " with "crawling." When Cluchey said to Thorpe, "Cover me with a sheet," Beckett snapped: "*The* sheet, Rick, *the* sheet." And when Clov delivered the line, "There are no more navigators," he corrected, "There's a pause before navigators." He made changes as they went along—"On 'Good God' let's leave out the 'good' "—sometimes cutting whole sections, but had no interest in publishing a revised version of the play. For all the fact that he was "wobbly," he seemed stronger than anyone else on the set, rarely sitting while he worked and never losing his concentration. As so many actors and actresses have noted, he delivered his own lines better than anyone else, and this was his principal mode of direction. When dealing with certain particular lines, he often turned away from the cast and stood at the edge of the stage, facing the wall, working out gestures in pantomime. For those of us who were watching rehearsals, it was no small thing to see him go off like this and then hear him, when he'd got what he wanted, deliver his own lines in his mellifluous Irish pronunciation, his voice, for all its softness, projecting with force to the seats at the back of the theater:

> " 'They said to me, That's love, yes, yes, not a doubt, now you see how easy it is. They said to me, That's friendship, yes, yes, no question, you've found it. They said to me, Here's the place, stop, raise your head and look at all that beauty. That order! They said to me, Come now, you're not a brute beast, think upon these things and you'll see how all becomes clear. And simple! They said to me, What skilled attention they get, all these dying of their wounds.' "

To say the least, such moments produced an uncanny resonance. Unself-conscious, perfectly in character, one felt that he was not only reading the lines but writing them, discovering them now as he'd discovered them thirty years before. That we, as audience, had somehow become his first witness, present at the birth of his articulations. If his own present tense—the act of writing—had always been his subject, what could be more natural or inevitable than showing us this, the thoughts and meaning "secreted" and rejected, the words giving form, the form dissolving in the silence that ensued. For that was the message one finally took from such recitations, the elusiveness of the meanings he had established, the sense of the play as aging with him, unable to arrest the flow of time and absolutely resolved against pretending otherwise. Why should Hamm and Clov be spared the awareness of Molloy: "It is in the tranquility of decomposition that I remember the long confused emotion which was my life."

Perhaps it was for this reason, that he was never far removed from what he'd written, that if an actor inquired about a line, his answers could seem almost naive. When Cluchey asked him why Hamm, after begging Clov to give him his stuffed dog, throws it to the ground, Beckett explained, "He doesn't like the feel of it." And when he was asked for help in delivering the line "I'll tell you the combination of the larder if you promise to finish me," he advised, "Just think, you'll tell him the combination if he'll promise to kill you." Despite—or because of—such responses, all four members of the cast would later describe the experience of his direction in language that was often explicitly spiritual. "What he offered me," said Cluchey, "was a standard of absolute authority. He gave my life a spiritual quotient." And Thorpe: "When we rehearsed, the concentration was so deep that I lost all sense of myself. I felt completely empty, like a skeleton, the words coming through me without thought of the script. I'm not a religious person, but it seemed a religious experience to me. Why? Maybe because it was order carried to its ultimate possibility. If you lost your concentration, veered off the track for any reason, it was as if you'd sinned." Extreme though such descriptions are, I doubt that anyone who watched these rehearsals would find in them the least trace of exaggeration. More than intense, the atmosphere was almost unbearably internalized, self-contained to the point of circularity. In part, obviously, this was because we were watching an author work on his own text. In addition to this, however, the text itself—because *Endgame* is finally nothing but theater, repetition, a series of ritualized games that the actors are doomed to play forever—was precisely about the work that we were watching. When Clov asks Hamm, "What keeps me here?" Hamm replies, "The dialogue." Or earlier, when Hamm is asking him about his father, "You've asked me these questions millions of times." Says Hamm, "I love the old questions . . . ah, the old questions, the old answers, there's nothing like them!" If the play is finally about nothing but itself, the opportunity to see it repeated, again and again for two weeks, offered a chance to see Beckett's intention realized on a scale at once profound and literal, charged with energy but at the same time boring, deadening, infuriating. (A fact of which Beckett was hardly unaware. While we were working on the line "This is not much fun," he advised Cluchey, "I think it would be dangerous to have any pause after that line. We don't want to give people time to agree with you.") To use his own percussion metaphor, watching these rehearsals was to offer one's head up for *Endgame*'s cadence to be hammered into it. Finally, after two weeks of rehearsal, the play became musical to a hypnotic extent, less a theatrical than a meditative experience in that one could not ascribe to it any meaning or intention beyond its own concrete and immediate reality. In effect, the more one saw of it, the less it contained. To this day the lines appear in my mind without reason, like dreams or memory-traces, but the play itself, when I saw it in Dublin, seemed an anticlimax, the goal itself insignificant beside the process that had produced it. If *Waiting for Godot* is, as Vivian Mercier has written, "a play in which nothing happens, twice," it might be said of *Endgame* that it is an endless rehearsal for an opening night that never comes. And therefore that its true realization was the rehearsals we saw rather than its formal production later in Dublin. Could this be why, one reason at least, Beckett did not accompany his cast to Ireland or, for that matter, why he has never attended his own plays in the theater?

He left London the day after rehearsals ended, and I did not see him again until the following spring in Paris. At our first meeting, he seemed a totally different person, distant and inaccessible, physically depleted, extremely thin, his eyes more deeply set and his face more heavily lined than ever. He spoke from such distance and with such difficulty that I was reminded again of Molloy, who describes conversation as "unspeakably painful," explaining that he hears words "a first time, then a second, and often even a third, as pure sounds, free of all meaning." We met in the coffee shop of a new hotel, one of those massive gray skyscrapers that in recent years have so disfigured the Paris skyline. Not far from his apartment, it was his favorite meeting place because it offered anonymity. He wasn't recognized during this or any subsequent meeting I had with him there. Early on in our conversation, I got a taste of his ferocious self-protection, which was much more pronounced here, of course, where he lived, than it had been in London. "How long will you be here?" he said. "Three weeks," I said. "Good," he said. "I want to see you *once* more." Given his politeness, it was easy to forget how impossible his life would have been had he not been disciplined about his schedule, how many people must have sought him out as I had sought him out myself. What was always amazing to me was how skillful he was in letting one know where one ranked in his priorities. Couching his decision in courtesy and gentleness, he seemed totally vulnerable, almost passive, but his softness masked a relentless will and determination. He left one so disarmed that it was difficult to ask anything of him, much less seek more time than he had offered. Though he promptly answered every letter I wrote him, it was three years before he gave me his home address, so that I would not have to write him in care of his publisher, and he has never given me a phone number, always arranging that he will call me when I come to town. Why not? Rick Cluchey told me that whenever Beckett went to Germany a documentary film crew followed him around without his permission, using a telephoto lens to film him from a distance.

As it turned out, however, there was another reason for his distance now. In London, the only unpleasant moment between us had occurred when, caught up in the excitement of the rehearsals, I'd asked if I could write about him. Though his refusal, again, had been polite ("Unless of course you want to write about the work . . .") and I had expressed considerable regret about asking him, it would soon become clear that he had not forgotten. Even if he had, the speed with which I was firing questions at him now, nervously pressing all the issues I had accumulated since I'd seen him last, would have put him on his guard. Beckett is legendary, of course, for his hatred of interviews, his careful avoidance of media and its invasions (the *Paris Review* has tried for years, with no success, to interview him for its "Writers at Work" series), and the next time we met, he made it clear that before we continued he must know what I was after. "Listen, I've got to get this off my chest. You're not interviewing me, are you?"

We had just sat down at a restaurant to which he had invited me. The only restaurant he ever frequented, it was a classic bistro on the edge of Montparnasse where he kept his own wine in the cellar and the waiters knew his habits so well that they always took him to the same table and brought him, without his having to order, the dish he ate—filet of sole and french fries—whenever he went there. Though I had my notebook in my pocket and upon leaving him would, as always, rush to take down everything I could remember about our conversation, I assured him that I certainly was not interviewing him and had no intention of writing about him. At this point in time, there was nothing but truth in my disclaimer. (And I might add that he obviously trusted me on this score, since he gave me permission to publish this article, and so far as I can see, has never held it against me.) Since I was not yet even dimly conscious of the ambiguous, somewhat belligerent forces that led to this memoir, the notes I took were for myself alone, as I saw it, a result of the emotion I felt when I left him and the impulse, common if not entirely handsome in a writer, to preserve what had transpired between us. Taking me at my word, Beckett relaxed, poured the wine, and watched with pleasure as I ate while he picked at his food like a child who hated the dinner table. "You're not hungry?" I said. "No," he said. "I guess I'm not too interested in food anymore." And later, when I asked him if he'd ever eaten in any of the Japanese restaurants that were just beginning to open in Paris: "No. But I hear they make good rice."

Considering how thin he was, I wasn't surprised to hear that the desire for food—like almost all other desires, I believe, except those which involved his work—was a matter of indifference to him. What did surprise me, as the wine allowed us to speak of things more commonplace, was the view of his domestic situation—evenings at home with his wife, and such—which emerged during the course of the evening. He told me that he'd been married for forty years, that he and his wife had had just two addresses during all their time in Paris, that it had sometimes been difficult for them—"many near-ruptures, as a matter of fact"—but that the marriage had grown easier as they'd got older. "Of course," he added, "I do have my own door." Since I'd always thought of him as the ultimate solitary, isolated as Krapp and as cynical about sex as Molloy, I confessed that I couldn't imagine him in a situation so connubial. "Why should you find it difficult?" he said with some surprise. In fact, he seemed rather pleased with his marriage, extremely grateful that it had lasted. It was one more correction for me, and more important, I think, one more illustration of the symmetry and tension, the dialectic he maintains between his various dichotomies. Just as "can't" and "must" persist with equal force in his mind, the limitations of language no more deniable than the urgent need to articulate, the extreme loneliness which he's explored throughout his life—the utter skepticism and despair about relationships in general and sexuality in particular—has had as its counterpoint a marriage which has lasted forty years. But lest one suspect that the continuity and comfort of marriage had tilted the scales so far that the dream of succession had taken root in his mind, "No," he replied, when I asked if he'd ever wanted children, "that's one thing I'm proud of."

For all my conviction that I did not intend to write about him, I always felt a certain amount of shame when I took up my notebook after I left him. For that matter, I am not entirely without shame about what I'm writing now. One does not transcribe a man like Beckett without its feeling like a betrayal. What makes me persist? More than anything, I believe, it is something I began to realize after our meetings in Paris—that the shame I felt in relation to him had not begun with my furtive attempts to preserve him in my notebook, but rather had been a constant in our relationship long before I'd met him. To put it simply, it began to strike me that Beckett had been, since the moment I discovered *Molloy*, as much a source of inhibition as inspiration. For all the pleasure it had given me, my first reading of the trilogy had almost paralyzed me (as indeed it had paralyzed any number of other writers I knew), leaving me traumatized with shame and embarrassment about my own work. It wasn't merely that, in contrast to his, my language seemed inauthentic and ephemeral, but that he made the usual narrative games—the insulated past tense, the omniscient narrator, form which excluded reference to itself, biographical information—seem, as he put it in *Watt*, "solution clapped on problem like a snuffer on a candle." More than any other writer I knew, Beckett's work seemed to point to that which lay beyond it. It was as if, though its means were Relative, its goals were Absolute, its characters beyond time precisely because (again and again) they seemed to age before our eyes. And such accomplishment was not, it seemed to me, simply a matter of talent or genius but of a totally different approach to writing, a connection between his life and his work which I could covet but never achieve. It was this union—the joining, if you like, of "being" and "form"—that I envied in him and that caused me finally to feel that the very thought of Beckett, not to mention the presence of one of his sentences in my mind, made writing impossible. And once again: it was not merely a matter of talent. I could read Joyce or Proust or Faulkner without such problems, and I had no lack of appreciation for them. It was just that they were clearly *writers*, while Beckett was something else, a sort of meta-writer who, even as he wrote, transcended the act of writing.

Oddly enough, if there was anyone else I knew who stood in such relation to his work, it was Muhammad Ali, who seemed to laugh at boxing even as he took it to higher levels of perfection, who not only defeated but humiliated his opponents, establishing such possession of their minds that he won many fights before the first round began, because he stood outside the game in which his adversary was enclosed. One cannot play a game unless one believes in it, but Ali managed such belief without the attachment to which it usually leads. Say that he found the cusp that separates belief from attachment, concentration from fixation, and on the other hand, play from frivolity, spontaneity from formlessness. And it seems to me that Beckett has done the same. No writer has lived who took language more seriously, but none has been more eloquent about its limitations and absurdities. Like Ali, he shows us where we are imprisoned. The danger is that, in doing so, he will imprison us in his example. If some fighters tried, playing the clown, to imitate Ali, and ended by making fools of themselves in addition to being defeated, writers with Beckett too much in mind can sound worse than the weakest student in a freshman writing class. After reading Joyce or Proust, one can feel embarrassed about one's lack of music or intelligence, but in the wake of one of Beckett's convoluted, self-mocking sentences, one can freeze with horror at the thought of any form that suggests "Once upon a time," anything in fact which departs from the absolute present. But if you take that too far you lose your work in the ultimate swamp, the belief that you can capture both your subject and your object in the instant of composition: "Here I am, sitting at my desk, writing 'Here I am, sitting at my desk.' "

None of this of course is historically unprecedented. Every generation of artists has to do battle with its predecessors, and each such battle has its own unique configurations. What made it so vivid for me was that now, twenty years after that first reading, his presence affected me much as his work had. Happy though I felt to see him, however amazing I found our time together, I always left him with an acute sense that I'd come up short, failed him somehow, as if the moment had passed before I had awakened to it. As if my conversational and psychological habits had stood between us. Or more to the point, as if the *form* of my social habit had violated the nature of his *Being* in much the same way that literary form, as he'd concluded years before, violated the being it excluded. Sitting across from me in the café, his eyes fierce in their concentration, his silence so completely unapologetic, he seemed to occupy, according to my reverential opinion, a present tense—*this* space, *this* moment in time—which I could merely observe from afar. Despite—no, because of—his humility, his uncertainty, the "impotence" which, as he'd once put it, his work had set out to "exploit,"* he manifested for me, as for years he had for Rick Cluchey, a kind of ultimate authority, a sense of knowledge very near to Absolute. Neither egoism nor self-confidence—the opposite, in fact, of both—such knowledge seemed a by-product of suffering, the pain that was so evident on his face, an earned if not entirely welcome result of having explored and survived an emptiness that people of less courage, if they acknowledged it at all, considered by means of intellect alone.

Exaggerated and romantic though all this seems, I'm sure it's not entirely unjustified. Beckett is indeed an extraordinary being, a man who has traveled in realms that most people don't want to hear about, much less explore. A true writer, an artist who pursues his vision so courageously and with such disregard for easy gratification that his work becomes, in the purest sense, a spiritual practice. What my responses showed, however, my idealization of him and the self-criticism it evoked, was that such authority was nothing if not a hazardous experience. Like all great wisdom, it could bring out the best or the worst in you, challenge or intimidate you, toughen you or make you self-effacing. Finally, if you were a writer, it could inspire you to listen to your own voice or trap you into years of imitating his. Like Joyce or Proust, or for that matter, any other great artist one adopts as a teacher, Beckett is an almost impossible act to follow, but more so than most, I think, because his work is so subjective, so seductive in the permissions it grants, because his apparent freedom from plot and character and his first person present tense can draw you into a swamp in which art and self-indulgence begin to seem identical. It is so easy to think that he opens the gates for anything you're feeling or thinking at the moment you sit down at your desk. How many writers could I count who had

* "The kind of work I do," he explained to Israel Schenker in a *New York Times* interview in 1966, before he'd closed the door to the media, "is one in which I'm not master of my material. The more Joyce knew the more he could. He's tending toward omniscience and omnipotence as an artist. I'm working with impotence, ignorance. I don't think impotence has been exploited in the past."

books like mine, the one I'd shown him, the one he'd criticized because the voice was "not believable," which would not be written until the Beckett had been removed from them? The great irony is that, for all his rejection of authority and knowledge—precisely because of such rejection, in fact—Beckett is almost too much an authority, he knows too much that one must discover on one's own. If you aren't to go on imitating him, you either face the fact that there is nothing you really need to say and find yourself another vocation, or you dig for something truer in yourself, something you don't know, at the bottom of all you do. In other words, you start where he started, after meeting his mother in Dublin. The trouble is that, since most of such digging, if you're an ordinary mortal, is surely doomed to fail, it can seem as if he's taken you out of the game you're capable of playing and signed you up in one for which you've neither the courage, the talent, nor the appetite. Finally, his greatest danger—and his greatest gift—may be his simple reminder that writing is not about reiteration.

But of course there is also the other side to it, one which has explicitly to do with the nature of his vision, the "being" he allows into the work, the void he's faced, the negation he's endured, the grief he's not only experienced but transformed with his imagination. "Yes, the confusion of my ideas on the subject of death," says Molloy, "was such that I sometimes wondered, believe me or not, if it wasn't a state of being even worse than life. So I found it natural not to rush into it and, when I forgot myself to the point of trying, to stop in time." Once we'd got over our laughter and exhilaration, how were we to deal with such a statement? For Beckett, such negation had fueled the work, but for many who presumed to be his successors, it had often become an easy, a facile nihilism, less a game you lost than one you refused to play. Indeed, for some of us, true disciples, it could become one you were ashamed to play. As if, having finally been enlightened as to the absurdity of life, you were too wise to persist at its illusions, too wise to allow enthusiasm, occupy space, to feed the body you knew to be disintegrating. In effect, if you misread him well enough, Beckett could turn you into a sort of literary anorexic, make you too cool or hip, too scared, too detached and disenchanted, to take, by writing, the only food that nourished you. But the irony is that he himself, as he'd shown me in London, in our very first conversation, is anything but anorexic. That's obvious, isn't it? This man who writes, in *Molloy*, "you would do better, at least no worse, to obliterate texts than to blacken margins, to fill in the holes of words till all is blank and flat and the whole ghastly business looks like what it is, senseless, speechless, issueless misery," has published six novels and fourteen plays during his lifetime, not to mention a great body of short prose, poetry, criticism, a number of television and radio plays, and a filmscript. Just fifteen pages later in *Molloy* he writes, "Not to want to say, not to know what you want to say, and never to stop saying, or hardly ever, that is the thing to keep in mind, even in the heat of composition." Much as he can recognize the tyranny of hope or meaning, he cannot deny that there is hope and meaning within such recognition, and he cannot pretend that this hope and meaning is any less exciting or more enduring than the others. It's all part of the equation, however absurd, of being alive, and he's never rejected that condition for its alternative. After all, when Nell says "Nothing's funnier than unhappiness," we laugh at that statement, and—if only for an instant—are less unhappy as we do so. In a sense Beckett is the great poet of negation, but what is poetry for him can easily become, if we use him incorrectly, if we make him too much an authority or if we underestimate the integrity of his paradox, a negation so extreme and absolute that it threatens the very source of one's energy and strength.

Of course, it's not easy to speak of these things. It's always possible that his greatest gift, not only to those of us he's challenged, but the readers we might have enlisted, is the silence toward which he's pressed us. If you can't accept his example, and allow Being into your work, why add your lies to the ocean of print which is drowning the world already? In my opinion, most writers deal with his challenge in one of two ways. Either they ignore his example, go on—as I had, for example, in writing journalism—making forms that exclude Being, accepting the role of explainer, describer, or they try—as I was trying with my novel—to play his game despite the astonomical odds against any possibility of success. For those who take the latter path, the entry of Being into the form often means the entry of self-consciousness, writing about writing about writing. Too late we discover that Beckett, Molloy, Malone, *et al*, though they may be mad, haven't a trace of neurosis or narcissism about them, that their present tense is shaped and objectified by an inherently classical, concrete mind, a sense of self which differs radically from our own. In effect, that the present tense which becomes, inevitably, an imperfect tense for them, remains a merely present—a merely reductive, a totally self-absorbed—tense for us. If you can't take the leap from present to imperfect, you remain rooted in the present. An honorable intention, of course, but if you're honest about it, you have to admit that writing and being in the present are not necessarily compatible, that in fact you're always flirting with contradiction and dishonesty. Tantalized by what amounts to a desire to write and not-write simultaneously, you may be equally loyal to form and being, but you may also be a mother who would keep her child forever in her womb. It's the sort of game in which defeat can lead to farce that's not only hypocritical but blasphemous toward the master one has pretended to revere.

These are just a few of the reasons, I think, I took notes when I left him, and despite my disclaimer, am writing about him now. Why? Perhaps because Beckett himself, as I said earlier, freed me from the Beckett myth. Not entirely for sure, but enough at least to help me resume a voice that differed from the one he once inspired in me. Not for nothing did he show me that he enjoyed my journalism. "Look here, Larry," he said to me once in London, "your line is witnessing." By which I understand him to have meant: take your object and be done with it. Be content to write what you know without acknowledging every moment that you don't. So here I am, witnessing him. Maybe this is all just rationalization, but getting him down like this may be the best homage and the best revenge, the only weapon I have against the attack he mounted on my mind. I can't forget him, and I can't think of anything else to do with his example but reject it. Just as Buddhists say about their own ultimate authority, "If you meet the Buddha on the road, kill him," I say of Beckett that a writer can only proceed from him by recognizing that he is now, having taken his work to all of its ultimate conclusions, utterly emptied of possibility. As Hamm says, "All is absolute. The bigger a man is, the fuller he is . . . and the emptier."

The next time we saw each other, a year later in Paris, our conversation continued, where it had begun and where it had been left, with the difficulties of writing. Because my work (the same novel) was going as badly as his, there wasn't a whole lot of joy in the air. For a moment, in fact, it became a sort of sparring match between us, agony versus agony, but then, remembering whom I was in the ring with and how much he outweighed me, I backed off. "It's not a good time at all," he said with a sigh. "I walk the streets trying to see what's in my mind. It's all confusion. Life is all confusion. A blizzard. It must be like this for the newborn. Not much difference I think between this blizzard and that. Between the two, what do you have? Wind machines or some such. I can't write anything, but I must." He paused a moment, then suddenly brightened, once again repeating a famous Beckett line as if he'd just come upon it, "Yes, that's it! Can't and must! That's my situation!"

He spoke of a sentence that haunted him. "It won't go away, and it won't go farther: 'One night, as he sat, with his head on his hands, he saw himself rise, and go.' " Except for this, however, there was nothing. "It's like the situation I spoke of in my book on Proust. 'Not just hope is gone, but desire.' " When I reminded him—quoting the line I mentioned earlier ("The wisdom of all the sages . . . consists not in the satisfaction but the ablation of desire.")—that according to the book he'd remembered, the loss of desire was not an entirely unwelcome development, he replied, "Well, yes, but the writing was the only thing that made life bearable." Sighing as if in tremendous pain, he seemed to drift off for a moment. "Funny to complain about silence when one has aspired to it for so long. Words are the only thing for me and there's not enough of them. Now, it's as if I'm just living in a void, waiting. Even my country house is lonely when I'm not writing."

Occasionally, when he talked like this, there was an odd sense, absurd as it seems, that he was asking for help, even perhaps advice, but this time was different. Now seventy-eight years old, he appeared to have reached a sort of bottom-line exhaustion. He seemed smaller to me, the lines in his forehead more deeply etched, like a grid. Every gesture seemed difficult, every word a struggle. His blue eyes were shy, gentle, youthful as ever, but incredibly pained and sorrowful. I told him that sometimes I found it amazing that he went on. "Yes," he replied, "often I think it's time I put an end to it. That's all through the new work. But then again . . . there are also times when I think, maybe it's time to begin." He said there had always been so much more in the work than he'd suspected was there, and then added, in what seemed an almost unconscious afterthought, a phrase I've never forgotten, which may have summed up his work as well or better than any other: "Ambiguities infirmed as they're put down. . . ."

"Which is more painful," I asked him, "writing or not writing?"

"They're both painful, but the pain is different."

He spoke a little about the different sorts of pain—the pain of being unable to write, the pain of writing itself, and—as bad as any—the pain of finishing what he'd begun. I said, "If the work is so painful when one does it and so painful when it's done, why on earth does anyone do it?"

This was one of those questions that caused him, as I've mentioned already, to disappear behind his hand, covering his eyes and bending his head toward the table for what must have been two full minutes. Then, just when I'd begun to suspect that he'd fallen asleep, he raised his head and with an air of relief, as if he'd finally resolved a lifelong dilemma, whispered, "The fashioning, that's what it is for me, I think. The pleasure in making a satisfactory object." He explained that the main excitement in writing had always been technical for him, a combination of "metaphysics and technique." "A problem is there and I have to solve it. *Godot*, for example, began with an image—of a tree and an empty stage—and proceeded from there. That's why, when people ask me who Godot is, I can't tell them. It's all gone."

"Why metaphysics?" I said.

"Because," he said, "you've got your own experience. You've got to draw on that."

He tried to describe the work he wanted to do now. "It has to do with a fugitive 'I' [or perhaps he meant 'eye']. It's an embarrassment of pronouns. I'm searching for the non-pronounial."

" 'Non-pronounial'?"

"Yes. It seems a betrayal to say 'he' or 'she.' "

The problem of pronouns, first person versus third, which had been so much explored and illuminated throughout his work, was also the one he addressed in mine. That morning, as always, he was extremely solicitous, asking me question after question about the progress of my novel. Though the book continued to defy me, so much so that I'd begun to wonder if brain damage, as I wanted to approach it, might not be beyond the limits of art, he seemed to know exactly what I wanted to do. It wasn't surprising, of course, that the man who'd once described tears as "liquefied brain" should be familiar with the subject of brain damage, but his questions were so explicit that it was difficult to believe that he hadn't considered, and rejected, the very book I wanted to write. The chapters I'd shown him in London had been written in the first person, which he had considered a mistake. "I know it's impertinent to say this, please forgive me . . . but this book, in my opinion, will never work in the first person." When I told him, here at the café, that I had now moved it to the third person, he nodded, but he knew that problems of point of view were never resolved with pronouns alone. "Still," he said, returning to the point he'd made when we met in London, "you need a witness, right?"

He excused himself from the table—"pardon my bladder"—but when he returned it was clear that he'd taken my book with him. "Well, do you see the end of it?"

"No," I said, "not at all."

He sighed. "It's really very difficult, isn't it?"

He sipped his coffee, then homed in on the principal issue in my book as in so much contemporary fiction—the need for objectivity and knowledge in conjunction with the need for the intimacy and immediacy of a naked subjectivity. "You need a witness and you need the first person, that's the problem, isn't it? One thing that might help . . . you might have a look at an early book of mine, perhaps you know it, *Mercier and Camier*. I had a similar problem there. It begins, 'I know what happened with Mercier and Camier because I was there with them all the time.' "

After I returned from Paris, I looked at *Mercier and Camier* again but found no place for his solution in the problems I had set myself. Still, I wrote an entire version of my novel in the third person, and I can say without a doubt that there were very few days I didn't feel him looking over my shoulder, whispering, "It's really very difficult, isn't it?" or when things were going worse, commenting on me as Nagg comments on Hamm, "What does that mean? That means nothing!" Halfway through, I knew it wasn't working, suspecting strongly that my only hope, despite what Beckett had said, was in the first person, but I pushed on. Certainly, it wasn't merely his recommendation that kept me going in that direction, but how can I pretend it didn't matter? When finally—a year and a half and an entire manuscript later—I turned it around and started over, in the first person, I could not, though I wrote him more than one letter about the book, bring myself to mention it to him. To my mind, the book worked, not only because it was in the first person, but because I had finally succeeded in weaning myself from him. Given all this, I felt no small trepidation when I sent him the manuscript but, as before, he read the book at once and replied with generosity and enthusiasm. There was no sign of his original disappointment and none of his position *vis-à-vis* my point of view. His note, as always, was confined to a 3 × 5 index card, and his scrawl, which had grown progressively worse in the years that I'd corresponded with him, was not completely legible. To my chagrin, in fact, its most important sentence was only half-accessible to me. After offering his compliments and appreciation, he concluded with a sentence that drifted off into a hopeless hieroglyphics after beginning with "And on with you now from . . ."

After "from" was a word which looked like "this," but might have been "thus" or "phis," a word which looked like "new" but might have been "man" or "ran," a word which looked like "thought" or "bought" or "sought," and finally a word which looked like "anew." "And on with you now from this new thought anew"? It didn't sound like Beckett at all. I asked several friends to have a look but none could read his writing any better than I. What absurd apocryphy that a note from Beckett should conclude, "And on with you now from [illegible] [illegible] [illegible]." Finally, unable to stand it any longer, I wrote to ask if, by some chance (after all, more than three weeks had passed since he'd written the note) he could remember what he'd written. Again he answered promptly, ending our dialogue, as I will end this memoir, with a note that was characteristic, not only in its economy and content, but in what it says about his (failing?) memory and the attitude with which he approached his correspondence:

Dear Larry,

I believe I wrote, "And on with you now from this new nought anew."

As ever,

Sam.

LAWRENCE SHAINBERG
1981

[illegible]

thought ends, more or less, and [illegible] the [illegible]
[illegible] to [illegible] any man, [illegible]
I was the first person [illegible]
[illegible]
[illegible] but [illegible] back [illegible]
with [illegible] and [illegible]. There was [illegible]
[illegible] his position [illegible]
[illegible]
[illegible] in the [illegible]
[illegible] was not completely [illegible]
[illegible] sentence was only [illegible]
[illegible] his [illegible] and [illegible]
[illegible]
'And on with you any more.'

[illegible] looked like [illegible]
[illegible] looked like [illegible]
[illegible] looked like [illegible]
[illegible]
[illegible]
[illegible] I [illegible] to have a [illegible]
[illegible] any better than [illegible]
[illegible]
[illegible]
[illegible]
[illegible]
[illegible]
[illegible]
[illegible]
[illegible]

[illegible]

[illegible] with you [illegible]

# 2. P. L. Travers

"We have no idea where childhood ends and maturity begins," says Pamela Lyndon Travers. "It is one unending thread, not a life chopped up into sections out of touch with one another." In touch with a childlike wisdom, joy, and simplicity, this Australian-born woman, while convalescing in a Sussex cottage, wrote *Mary Poppins* in order to amuse herself. Submitted on the advice of a friend, it was published in 1934 and later turned into a film by Walt Disney. Travers followed the instant success of the book with *Mary Poppins Comes Back* (1935), *Mary Poppins Opens the Door* (1944), *Mary Poppins in the Park* (1952), *Mary Poppins in Cherry Tree Lane* (1982), and, in 1989, *Mary Poppins and the House Next Door.* Her other works include *I Go by Sea, I Go by Land* (1944), *The Fox at the Manger* (1962), *Friend Monkey* (1971), *About the Sleeping Beauty* (1975), and three books based on preceding Mary Poppins stories, *Mary Poppins from* A *to* Z (1962), A *Mary Poppins Story for Colouring* (1969), and *Mary Poppins in the Kitchen* (1975). She has published several articles on mythology, children's literature, and her own work, the most important of the latter being "Only Connect" (1967), which was an address to the Library of Congress. She collected her essays and lectures on these topics into *What the Bee Knows: Reflections on Myth, Symbol and Story,* published in 1989. Travers has been writer-in-residence at various American universities, and she has received honorary degrees from universities in the United States and Britain. She makes her home in London.

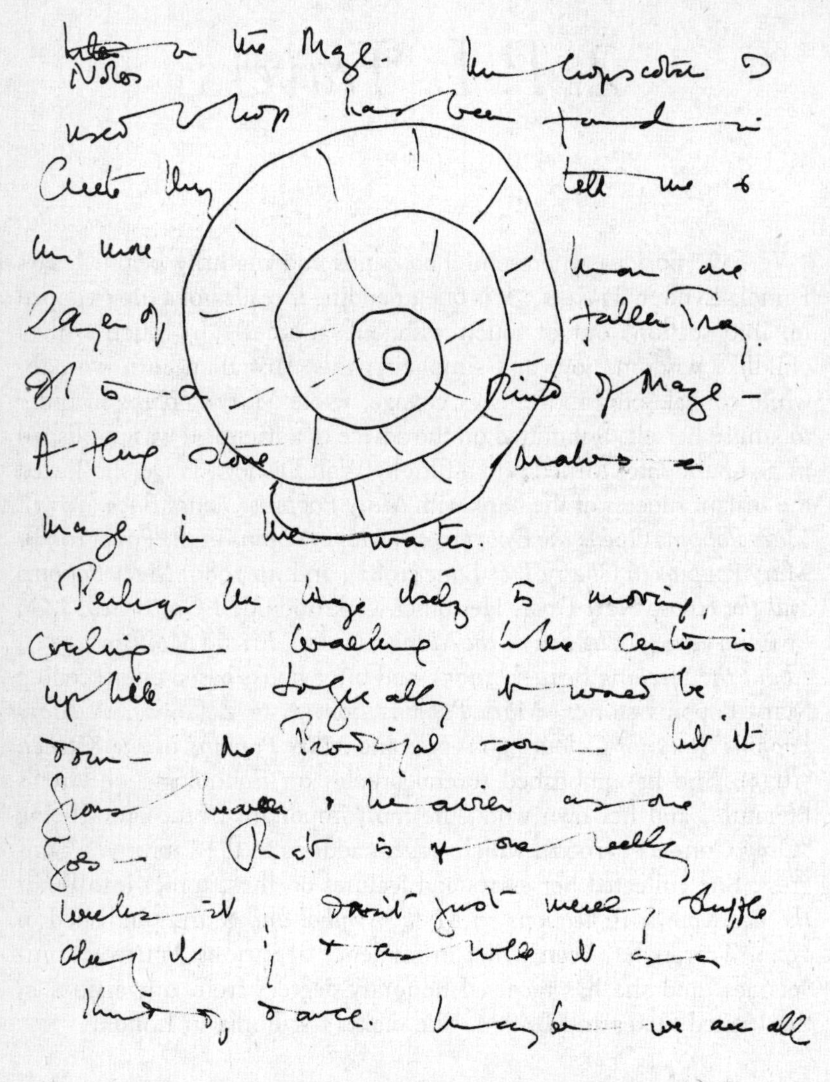

*A manuscript page from P. L. Travers's article "Walking the Maze at Chartres," which was published in* Parabola.

# P. L. Travers

*P. L. Travers's terraced house in Chelsea has a pink door, the color of the cover of* Mary Poppins in Cherry Tree Lane. *In the hall is an antique rocking horse. Her study is at the top of the house: a white-walled room, crowded with books and papers, its austerity relieved by a modern rocking chair. Pamela Travers, tall and handsome, with short whitish hair, is a strong woman of great humor and charm. Once a dancer, she moves smoothly and gracefully; once an actress, she speaks with the deep clear tones of another era. Before answering a question she sometimes closes her eyes as if in meditation. There is something both mythic and modern about her. She was wearing a blue and white flowing dress and white pumps and silver ethnic jewelry. As she spoke, her tongue sometimes darted from the corner of her mouth, reminding one perhaps of the hamadryad in* Mary Poppins*—the wise snake that lectures to the transfixed Banks children. She is a master of pith and anecdote, as shown in the story she tells about Yeats. A young woman* *then, traveling by train in Ireland, it occurred to her to stop and bring a gift to the poet. She persuaded a boatman to take her to the Isle of Innisfree, where she collected great branches of rowan for her gift. A storm came up as she struggled with her branches into the train car. Finally, at Yeats's door in Dublin, a startled maid took her in and dried her clothes by the fire. By this time, Travers, quite embarrassed, was planning an opportune escape, but as she made for the door the servant told her that Yeats was ready to see her. She ascended the stairs to meet a grandfatherly Yeats who proudly showed her an egg his canary had just laid. As they talked, Travers noticed on his desk a vase with a small slip from the colossus of branches she had brought. "That's when I learned," Travers concludes, "that you can say more with less."*

INTERVIEWERS: That recalls your meeting with AE (George Russell). You must have had great courage as a young woman to call on these venerable Irishmen.

P. L. TRAVERS: I read AE's poems when I was a child in Australia. Later I came to England to see my relatives. But before I did that, I sent a poem to AE who was then editing *The Irish Statesman*, and with all the arrogance of youth I didn't put any letter with it explaining myself or saying that I was Irish or anything. I just sent it with a stamped addressed envelope.

And sure enough, the stamped envelope came back. But in it was a check for two guineas and a letter that said: "I'm accepting your poem, which is a very good one, and I think it could not have been written by anyone who wasn't Irish. If you're ever coming to Ireland, be sure to come and see me." Since I was going to Ireland, I did go to see him and was greatly welcomed and more poems were taken. I felt immediate mutuality with him, this great elderly man bothering about me. But he bothered about all young poets. They were always welcome.

After our visit he said to me, "On your way back through Dublin you come and see me again." I said, "Of course, I will." But when the time arrived and I was back in Dublin, an awful timidity came upon me. I thought he was a great man and I shouldn't take up his time; he was doing this for *politesse*. And so I refrained from going to see him and went back to England. Some time later when I opened the door, there was AE. He said to me, "You're a faithless girl. You promised to see me on your way back through Dublin and you didn't." And he added, "I meant to give you my books then and, as you weren't there, I brought them." And there were all his books.

INTERVIEWERS: He sought you out, then?

TRAVERS: Oh, he didn't come to London specially to see me. He had come to see his old friend George Moore. But he took me in during that time, and had time for me. I often went out to Dublin after that and saw a good deal of AE and Yeats and James Stephens. Among the young people like myself was Frank O'Connor who used to be called Michael O'Donovan. He was one of AE's protégés. There were many of them.

INTERVIEWERS: AE's reaction to *Mary Poppins* is very interesting. You report his saying, "Had [Mary Poppins] lived in another age, in the old times to which she certainly belongs, she would undoubtedly have had long golden tresses, a wreath of flowers in one hand, and perhaps a spear in the other. Her eyes would have been like the sea, her nose comely, and on her feet winged sandals. But, this age being the Kali Yuga, as the Hindus call it, she comes in habiliments suited to it." It seems that AE was suggesting that your English nanny was some twentieth-century version of the Mother Goddess Kali.

TRAVERS: Indeed, he was throwing me a clue, but I didn't seize upon that for a long time. I've always been interested in the Mother Goddess. Not long ago, a young person, whom I don't know very well, sent a message to a mutual friend that said: "I'm an addict of *Mary Poppins*, and I want you to ask P. L. Travers if Mary Poppins is not really the Mother Goddess." So, I sent back a message: "Well, I've only recently come to see that. She is either Mother Goddess or one of her creatures—that is, if we're going to look for mythological or fairy tale origins of *Mary Poppins*."

I've spent years thinking about it because the questions I've been asked, very perceptive questions by readers, have led me to examine what I wrote. The book was entirely spontaneous and not invented, not thought out. I never said, "Well, I'll write a story about Mother Goddess and call it *Mary Poppins*." It didn't happen like that. I cannot summon up inspiration; I myself am summoned.

Once when I was in the United States I went to see a psychologist. It was during the war when I was feeling very cut off. I thought, well, these people in psychology always want to see the kinds of things you've done, so I took as many of my books as were then written. I went and met the man, and he gave me another appointment. And at the next appointment the books were handed back to me with the words: "You know, you don't really need me. All you need to do is read your own books."

That was so interesting to me. I began to see, thinking about it, that people who write spontaneously as I do, not with invention, never really read their own books to learn from them. And I set myself to reading them. Every now and then I found myself saying, "But this is true. How did she know?" And then I realized that she is me. Now I can say much more about *Mary Poppins* because what was known to me in my blood and instincts has now come up to the surface in my head.

INTERVIEWERS: Has Mary Poppins changed for you over the years?

TRAVERS: Not at all, not at all.

INTERVIEWERS: Has she changed for other people, do you think? Has their attitude to her altered at all?

TRAVERS: I don't think that she *must* change for other people very much; I think that they would be bitterly disappointed. The other day two little boys accosted me in the street and said to me, "You are the lady who wrote *Mary Poppins*, aren't you?" And I admitted it, and said, "How do you know?" And they said, "Because we sing in the choir, and the vicar told us." So, clearly, they had thrown off their surplices and rushed after me to catch me. So I said, "Well, do you like her?" And they both nodded vigorously. I then said, "What is it you like about her?" And one of them said, "Well, she's so *ordinary* and then . . ." and having said "and then" he looked around for the proper word, and couldn't find it. And I said, "You don't have to say any more. That 'and then' says everything." And the other little boy said, "Yes, and I'm going to marry her when I grow up." And I saw the first one clench his fists and look very belligerent. I felt there might be trouble and so I said, "Well, we'll just have to see what *she* thinks about it, won't we? And in the meantime, my house is just there—come in and have a lemonade." So they did. With regard to your question about her altering, I do not think that people who read her would want her to be altered. And what I liked so much about that—I felt it was the highest praise—was that the boy should say, "Well, she's so *ordinary*." But that's what she is. And it is only through the ordinary that the extraordinary can make itself perceived.

INTERVIEWERS: Speaking about children's reactions, when a little girl was asked why she liked Mary Poppins, she said, "Because she is so *mad*."

TRAVERS: She *is* mad. Only the mad can be so sane. A young man in my house—he's now grown up and has his own children—but when he was sixteen he said to me, "Make me a promise." And I thought, well, an open-ended promise is very difficult and dangerous . . . but he said, "Don't worry, you can easily afford it." (Of course he might have been about to ask me for a Rolls Royce, and what would I have done then?) But I said, "Yes, very well." So he said, "Promise me never to be clever." "Oh," I said, "I can easily do that, because you know I'm a perfect fool and I'm not in the least bit clever. But why do you ask that?" He said, "I've just been reading *Mary Poppins* again, and it could only have been written by a lunatic." That goes with your girl, you see. And I knew perfectly well, because we understand each other's language very well, that he meant "lunatic" as high praise.

INTERVIEWERS: Virginia Woolf when going through a "mad" period thought she heard the birds singing in Greek. This reminds one of the babies in *Mary Poppins* and *Mary Poppins Comes Back* who understand what the Starling says. Maybe it's the same kind of "madness"?

TRAVERS: Possibly. My Starlings in *Mary Poppins* talk Cockney, as far as I remember.

INTERVIEWERS: Mary Poppins is always teaching, isn't she?

TRAVERS: Well, yes, but I think she teaches by the way; I don't think she sets herself up as a governess. You remember there was a governess called Miss Andrew. She's very different from that.

INTERVIEWERS: Miss Andrew's a horror. But is Mary Poppins perhaps instructing the children in the "difficult truths" you mention in "Only Connect" as being contained in fairy tale, myth, and nursery rhyme?

TRAVERS: Exactly. Well, you see, I think if she comes from anywhere that has a name, it is out of myth. And myth has been my study and joy ever since—oh, the age, I would think . . . of three. I've studied it all my life. No culture can satisfactorily move along its forward course without its myths, which are its teachings, its fundamental dealing with truth of things, and the one reality that underlies everything. Yes, in that way you could say that it was teaching, but in no way deliberately doing so.

INTERVIEWERS: Jane and Michael, then, learn about tears and suffering from Mary Poppins when she leaves them?

TRAVERS: She doesn't hold back anything from them. When they beg her not to depart, she reminds them that nothing lasts forever. She's as truthful as the nursery rhymes. Remember that all the King's horses and all the King's men couldn't put Humpty Dumpty together again. There's such a tremendous truth in that. It goes into children in some part of them that they don't know, and indeed perhaps *we* don't know. But eventually they realize—and that's the great truth.

INTERVIEWERS: Does Mary Poppins's teaching—if one can call it that —resemble that of Christ in his parables?

TRAVERS: My Zen master, because I've studied Zen for a long time, told me that every one (and all the stories weren't written then) of the Mary Poppins stories is in essence a Zen story. And someone else, who is a bit of a Don Juan, told me that every one of the stories is a moment of tremendous sexual passion, because it begins with such tension and then it is reconciled and resolved in a way that is gloriously sensual.

INTERVIEWERS: So people can read anything and everything into the stories?

TRAVERS: Indeed. A great friend of mine at the beginning of our friendship (he was himself a poet) said to me very defiantly, "I have to tell you that I *loathe* children's books." And I said to him, "Well, won't you just read this just for my sake?" And he said grumpily, "Oh, very well, send it to me." I did, and I got a letter back saying: "Why didn't you *tell* me? Mary Poppins with her cool green core of sex has me enthralled forever."

INTERVIEWERS: And what about love? Are you implying in the Mary Poppins books that a child needs more than the love of family and friends?

TRAVERS: I have always thought that if the child doesn't need it, it benefits by having that extra, that plus. Every child needs to have for itself not only its loving parents and siblings and friends of its own age, but a grown-up friend. It is the fashion now to make a gap between child and grown-up, but this, I believe, has been made by the media. I was older than Jane and Michael, but I had a grown-up friend when I was about eleven. How wonderful it was to be able to have somebody other than your parents that you could talk to, who treated you as though you were a human being, with your proper place in the world. Your parents did so too (my parents were most loving, I had a most loving childhood), but the extra friend was a tremendous plus.

INTERVIEWERS: That is the kind of love that both Mary Poppins and Friend Monkey give?

TRAVERS: Yes, there is a great deal in common between Mary Poppins and Friend Monkey. *Friend Monkey* is really my favorite of all my books because the Hindu myth on which it is based is my favorite—the myth of the Monkey Lord who loved so much that he created chaos wherever he went.

INTERVIEWERS: Almost a Christ figure?

TRAVERS: Indeed, I hadn't dared to think of that, but yes, indeed, when you read the *Ramayana* you'll come across the story of Hanuman on which I built my version of that very old myth.

I love *Friend Monkey*. I love the story of Hanuman. For many years, it remained in my very blood because he's someone who loves too much and can't help it. I don't know where I first heard of him, but the story remained with me and I knew it would come out of me somehow or other. But I didn't know what shape it would take.

The book hasn't been very well received. It wasn't given very good notices. Everybody said, "Oh, *Friend Monkey*. She's writing about a monkey now. Why not more of Mary Poppins?" I wanted to do something new and, strangely enough, it wasn't something so very new after all.

INTERVIEWERS: Let's talk about another reaction to *Mary Poppins*. As you know, the book was recently removed from the children's shelves of the San Francisco libraries. The charge has been made that the book is racist and presents an unflattering view of minorities.

TRAVERS: The Irish have an expression: "Ah, my grief!" It means "the pity of things." The objections had been made to the chapter "Bad Tuesday" where Mary Poppins goes to the four points of the compass. She meets a mandarin in the East, an Indian in the West, an Eskimo in the North, and blacks in the South who speak in a picaninny language. What I find strange is that, while my critics claim to have children's best interests in mind, children themselves have never objected to the book. In fact, they love it. That was certainly the case when I was asked to speak to an affectionate crowd of children at a library in Port-of-Spain in Trinidad. On another occasion, when a white teacher friend of mine explained how she felt uncomfortable reading the picaninny dialect to her young students, I asked her, "And are the black children affronted?" "Not at all," she replied, "it appeared they loved it." "Minorities" is not a word in my vocabulary. And I wonder, sometimes, how much disservice is done children by some individuals who occasionally offer, with good intentions, to serve as their spokesmen. Nonetheless, I have rewritten the offending chapter, and in the revised edition I have substituted a Panda, Dolphin, Polar Bear, and Macaw. I have done so not as an apology for anything I have written. The reason is much more simple: I do not wish to see Mary Poppins tucked away in the closet. Aside from this issue, there is something else you should remember. I never wrote my books especially for children.

INTERVIEWERS: You have said that before. What do you mean?

TRAVERS: When I sat down to write *Mary Poppins* or any of the other books, I did not know children would read them. I'm sure there must be a field of "children's literature"—I hear about it so often—but sometimes I wonder if it isn't a label created by publishers and booksellers who also have the impossible presumption to put on books such notes as "from five to seven" or "from nine to twelve." How can they know when a book will appeal to such and such an age?

If you look at other so-called children's authors, you'll see they never wrote directly for children. Though Lewis Carroll dedicated his book to Alice, I feel it was an afterthought once the whole was already committed to paper. Beatrix Potter declared, "I write to please myself!" And I think the same can be said of Milne or Tolkien or Laura Ingalls Wilder.

I certainly had no specific child in mind when I wrote *Mary Poppins*. How could I? If I were writing for the Japanese child who reads it in a land without staircases, how could I have written of a nanny that slides up the bannister? If I were writing for the African child who reads the book in Swahili, how could I have written of umbrellas for a child who has never seen or used one?

But I suppose if there is something in my books that appeals to children, it is the result of my not having to go *back* to my childhood; I can, as it were, turn *aside* and consult it (James Joyce once wrote, "My childhood bends beside me"). If we're completely honest, not sentimental or nostalgic, we have no idea where childhood ends and maturity begins. It is one unending thread, not a life chopped up into sections out of touch with one another.

Once, when Maurice Sendak was being interviewed on television a little after the success of *Where the Wild Things Are,* he was asked the usual questions: Do you have children? Do you like children? After a pause, he said with simple dignity: "I was a child." That says it all.

But don't let me leave you with the impression that I am ungrateful to children. They have stolen much of the world's treasure and magic in the literature they have appropriated for themselves. Think, for example, of the myths or Grimm's fairy tales—none of which were written especially for them—this ancestral literature handed down by the folk. And so despite publishers' labels and my own protestations about not writing especially for them, I am grateful that children have included my books in their treasure trove.

INTERVIEWERS: Don't you have a new Mary Poppins book coming out?

TRAVERS: You know, for the longest time I thought I was done with Mary Poppins. Then I found out she was not done with me. My English publisher, William Collins, will release *Mary Poppins in Cherry Tree Lane.* It will be out in the U.S. in the fall of 1982 with Delacorte/Dell. After all those years, Mary Poppins showed me new dimensions of herself and other characters. I will be interested to learn how you and other readers find it. Then in the fall, my English publisher will reissue *Friend Monkey.*

INTERVIEWERS: Could you write a *Mary Poppins* book to order?

TRAVERS: No, never. As I have said, I am summoned. I do not wait around though; I write on other things. For example, I am a regular contributor to the periodical *Parabola: Myth and the Quest for Meaning,* my latest piece being "Leda's Lament." Anyway, everything comes out of living with an idea. If I knew how to summon up inspiration, would I give my secret away?

INTERVIEWERS: Even if you might be termed an "inspired" or mystical writer, do you have to set yourself a daily schedule of writing?

TRAVERS: In a way I'm never not doing it. When I'm going to buy, let us say, a tube of toothpaste, I have it in me. The story or lecture or article is moving. And I make a point of writing, if only a little, every day, as a kind of discipline so that it is not a whim but a piece of work.

INTERVIEWERS: Do you read much before or during writing?

TRAVERS: No. I read myth and fairy tale and books about them a great deal now, but I very seldom read novels. I find modern novels bore me. I can read Tolstoy and the Russians but mostly I read comparative mythology and comparative religion. I need matter to carry with me.
INTERVIEWERS: Do you compose in longhand or at the typewriter?
TRAVERS: I do a little bit of both. It's very strange. My handwriting, when I'm writing on paper before I put it onto the typewriter, is quite different—it's somebody else's handwriting. I'm always surprised to see it. Perhaps I'm not writing at all; perhaps there is somebody else doing it. I so often wonder: do these ideas come into the mind or are they just instinctive or are they . . . ?
INTERVIEWERS: "Throngs of living souls," as AE suggests.
TRAVERS: I just don't know. I don't think I'm a very mental person. When I write it's more a process of listening. I don't pretend that there is some spirit standing beside me that tells me things. More and more I've become convinced that the great treasure to possess is the Unknown. I'm going to write, I hope, a lot about that. It's with my unknowing that I come to the myths. If I came to them knowing, I would have nothing to learn. But I bring my unknowing which is a tangible thing, a clear space, something that's been made room for out of the muddle of ordinary psychic stuff, an empty space.
INTERVIEWERS: In one of your essays you recall the Zen statement "Summoned not created" when speaking about this.
TRAVERS: Yes, that really describes it. You know C. S. Lewis, whom I greatly admire, said: "There's no such thing as creative writing." I've always agreed with that and always refuse to teach it when given the opportunity. He said: "There is, in fact, only one Creator and we mix." That's our function, to mix the elements He has given us. See how wonderfully anonymous that leaves us? You can't say, "I did this; this gross matrix of flesh and blood and sinews and nerves did this." What nonsense! I'm given these things to make a pattern out of. Something gave it to me.

I've always loved the idea of the craftsman, the anonymous man. For instance, I've always wanted my books to be called the work of Anon, because Anon is my favorite literary character. If you look through an anthology of poems that go from the far past into the present time, you'll see that all the poems signed "Anon" have a very specific flavor that is one flavor all the way through the centuries. I think, perhaps arrogantly, of myself as "Anon." I would like to think that *Mary Poppins* and the other books could be called back to make that change. But I suppose it's too late for that.

INTERVIEWERS: What do you think of the books of Carlos Castaneda?

TRAVERS: I like them very much. They take me into a world where I fear I will not belong. It's a bit more occult than my world, but I like Don Juan's idea about what a warrior is and how a warrior should live. In a way, we all have to live like warriors; that's the same as being the hero of one's own story. I feel that Castaneda has been taken into other dimensions of thinking and experiencing. I don't pretend to understand them, and I think I understand why Castaneda is so slow to give interviews and tries to separate himself from all of that. He doesn't want to explain. These things can't be explained in ordinary terms.

You know, in America, everybody thinks there's an answer to every question. They're always saying, "But why and how?" They always think there is a solution. There is a great fortitude in that and a great sense of optimism. In Europe, we are so old that we know there are certain things to which there is not an answer. And you will remember, in this regard, that Mary Poppins's chief characteristic, apart from her tremendous vanity, is that she never explains. I often wonder why people write and ask me to explain this and that. I'll write back and say that Mary Poppins didn't explain, so neither can I or neither will I. So many people ask me, "Where does she go?" Well, I say, if the book hasn't said that, then it's up to you to find out. I'm not going to write footnotes to *Mary Poppins*. That would be absolutely presumptuous, and at the same time it would be assuming that I know. It's the fact that she's unknown that's so intriguing to readers.

INTERVIEWERS: There's that same quality about Castaneda.

TRAVERS: There is. His is a more deliberate unknown. It's as though he were hiding, I often think. And I don't know why, psychologically, he is doing that but I respect that hiding nonetheless. He has some idea in it.

You see, you've got a great wealth of myth in America and he has tapped it. And some of the writers on American Indian affairs have tapped it. But in a way it's foreign to us. You see how often Castaneda, as a modern man and non-Indian, becomes sick, physically sick, with the experiences. It almost seems to be that they're not for us. The Mexican Indians are, after all, a very old race.

I lived with the Indians, or I lived on the reservations, for two summers during the war. John Collier, who was then the Administrator for Indian Affairs, was a great friend of mine and he saw that I was very homesick for England but couldn't go back over those mineswept waters. And he said, "I'll tell you what I'll do for you. I'll send you to live with the Indians." "That's mockery," I replied. "What good will that do me?" He said, "You'll see."

I'd never been out West and I went to stay on the Navaho reservation at Administration House which is at Window Rock beyond Gallup. Collier had sent a letter to the members of the committee at Administration House and asked them to take me about so that I could see the land and meet the Indians. They very kindly did. Fortunately, I was able to ride and I was equipped with jeans and boots and a western saddle. Then I saw that the Indian women wore big, wide, flounced Spanish skirts with little velvet jackets. And I, who don't like trousers very much, said I must have one of those. So they made me a flounced skirt and a velvet jacket, and I rode with the Indians. It was wonderful the way they turned towards me when, instead of being an Eastern dude, I put on their skirt.

One day the head of Administration House asked me if I would give a talk to the Indians. And I said, "How could I talk to them, these ancient people? It is they who could tell me things." He said, "Try." So they came into what I suppose was a clubhouse, a big place with a stage, and I stood on the stage and the place was full of Indians. I told them about England, because she was at war then, and all that was happening. I said that for me England was the place "Where the Sun Rises" because, you see, England is east of where I was. I said, "Over large water." And I told them about the children who were being evacuated from the cities and some of the experiences of the children. I put it as mythologically as I could, just very simple sayings.

At the end there was dead silence. I turned to the man who had introduced me and said, "I'm sorry. I failed, I haven't got across." And he said, "You wait. You don't know them as well as I do." And every Indian in that big hall came up and took me silently by the hand, one after another. That was their way of expressing feeling with me.

I never knew such depths of silence, internally and externally, as I experienced in the Navaho desert. One night I was taken at full moon away into the desert where they were having a meeting before they had their dancing. There were crowds of Indians there, about two thousand under the moon. And before the proceedings began there was no sound in the desert amongst those people except the occasional cry of a baby or the rattle of a horse's harness or the crackling of fire under a pot—those natural sounds that really don't take anything from the silence.

They waited it seemed to me hours before the first man got up to speak. Naturally, I didn't understand what they were saying. But I listened to the speeches and I enjoyed the silences all night long. And when the night was far spent, they began to dance. Not in the usual dances of the corn dance; they had their ordinary clothes on and were dancing two-and-two, going around and around a fire, a man and a woman. And I was told that if you're asked to dance by a man and you don't want to dance, you give him a silver coin. So one Indian did come up but I went with him. I couldn't do the dance, even though it wasn't a very intricate dance; it was more a little short step round and round, just these two people together. So we two strangers danced around the fire. It was very moving to me. And we came back to the House in the early morning.

And, of course, I saw lots of the regular dances with Navahos and the Hopis, and later with the Pueblos. The Indians in the Pueblo tribe gave me an Indian name and they said I must never reveal it. Every Indian has a secret name as well as his public name. This moved me very much because I have a strong feeling about names, that names are a part of a person, a very private thing to each one. I'm always amazed at the way Christian names are seized upon in America as if by right instead of as something to be given. One of the fairy tales, "Rumplestiltskin," deals with the extraordinary privacy and inward nature of the name. It's always been a big taboo in the fairy tales and in myth that you do not name a person. Many primitive people do not like you to speak and praise a child to its face, for instance, and they will make a cross or sign against evil when you do that, even in Ireland sometimes.

INTERVIEWERS: What do you think of the contemporary interest in religion and myth, particularly among young people? Do you sense that in the last few years a large number of people have grown interested in spiritual disciplines—yoga, Zen, meditation, and the like?

TRAVERS: Yes, definitely. It shows the deep, disturbed undercurrents that there are in man, that he is really looking for something that is more than a thing. This is a civilization devoted to things. What they're looking for is something that they cannot possess but serve, something higher than themselves.

I'm all with them in their search because it is my search, too. But I've searched for it all my life. And when I'm asked to speak about myth, I nearly always find it's not known. There's no preparation. There's nothing for the words to fall on. People haven't read the fairy tales.

INTERVIEWERS: What reading would you recommend for children and adults?

TRAVERS: I should send people right back to the fairy tales. The Bible, of course. Even the nursery rhymes. You can find things there. As I was saying, when you think of "Humpty Dumpty"—". . . All the King's horses and all the King's men couldn't put Humpty together again"—that's a wonderful story, a fable that some things are impossible. And when children learn that, they accept that there are certain things that can't be, and it's a most delicate and indirect way to have it go into them.

I feel that the indirect teaching is what is needed. All school teaching is a direct giving of information. But everything I do is by hint and suggestion. That's what I think gets into the inner ear.

INTERVIEWERS: Nowadays, then, you see behind the headlines a renewed interest in the Divine Mother.

TRAVERS: I've said several times that I think women's liberation is, in a way, an aspect of realizing the Divine Mother. Not that I think women's libbers are Divine Mothers. Far from it. But I think the feminine principle, which we could say the Divine Mother embodies, is rising. All I want is that they don't use the feminine principle in order to turn themselves into men. We have all that we need as women. We just don't recognize it, some of us.

I am happily a woman. Nothing in me resents it. All of me accepts it and always has. Mind you, I haven't suffered. I haven't been in a profession where women are paid less than men. Nothing has been hard for me as a woman. But I sympathize with women who want to live themselves to the full. But I don't think you can do that by being a Madison Avenue executive or president of a women's bank. All those things I've never wanted.

Women belong in myth. We have to think of the ideas of yin and yang. So I feel we're really sitting, if we only knew, exactly where we ought to be, where the Divine Mother sits. If we don't know this is so, then it isn't so.

INTERVIEWERS: If Mary Poppins invented you, not vice versa, as you say, can you imagine what would have happened to you if she hadn't come along?

TRAVERS: Oh, I've never thought about it. It has never occurred to me to think that way, because, you see, we aren't given the opportunity of leading parallel lives. What would I have done if I hadn't done this? I have no means of knowing, because one life is all we get. It would have had something to do with the stage, dancing. But then, actresses grow old, dancers grow wobbly, whereas a writer still has a typewriter. And I think I've been learning and growing in writing all these years. If there's a life after death, I want to work.

INTERVIEWERS: Is there going to be another Mary Poppins book?

TRAVERS: Well, I have a sense of another lurking, "lurking" is the word, like a burglar, round and round the house. That's all I can say at the moment.

EDWINA BURNESS
JERRY GRISWOLD
1976, 1981

# 3. Wallace Stegner

Wallace Stegner has written thirteen novels, three short-story collections, sixteen nonfiction titles, and edited eighteen works in the fifty-three years he has been publishing. His first novella, *Remembering Laughter*, won a Little, Brown Prize in 1937; as early as 1944, when Stegner was only thirty-five, Sinclair Lewis hailed him as "one of the most important novelists in America."

There are those who know him as a prizewinning historian, or as the biographer of John Wesley Powell (*Beyond the Hundredth Meridian*, 1954) and Bernard DeVoto (*The Uneasy Chair*, 1974). Others know him as the author of *Angle of Repose* (1971), a transcontinental novel which earned Stegner a Pulitzer Prize. And, too, there are those who know him as a "damned environmentalist."

During the Kennedy administration, Stegner became a special assistant to then Interior Secretary Stewart Udall. Later he served on—and then chaired—the Advisory Board for National Parks, Historical Sites, Buildings and Monuments.

From 1945 to 1971 Stegner taught at Stanford University, where he is remembered through the fellowships, established in September 1946, which bear his name. A partial list of those who have received fellowships attests to his influence and stature, including, among others, Edward Abbey, Max Apple, Peter Beagle, Wendell Berry, Raymond Carver, Jim Houston, Tom McGuane, Larry McMurtry, Tillie Olson, and Robert Stone. In 1990 Random House published Stegner's collected stories.

"What makes you think the camels marked Geebie?" I asked, to keep the revelations flowing. "Has he got a cleft palate, or a hump, or what?"

"He's got their evil disposition," Charity said. "Their evil disposition and their inch-long eyelashes." Her laugh was as unclouded as everything else about her. "Did you notice me trying not to look at Professor Rousselot the other day? Because I'm pregnant again, and I had this feeling that if I looked, this new one might look like *him*."

"Oh, you too?" Sally said. "When? When is it due?"

"Early March. And are *you*? When's yours?"

"Almost the same time!"

They fell on each other. You never saw two ~~happier~~ more delighted people. If they had been twins separated in childhood, and now revealed to one another by some birthmark or other perepetia, they couldn't have been more ~~delighted~~ exhilarated.

"It'll be a *race*," Charity said. "Let's keep notes, and compare. Who's your obstetrician?"

"I haven't got one yet. Is yours a good one?"

A big clear uninhibited laugh, as if parturition, which left both Sally and me clammy with nervous apprehension, were the most fun since Run Sheep Run. "I guess so," Charity said. "I don't really know him very well. He's only interested in my *uterus*."

"Well," Sally said, a little daunted. "I hope he'll like mine."

I made to rise. "Excuse me," I said. "I believe the ~~proper~~ dignified thing to do is blush a deep crimson and leave the room."

Hoo hoo, ha ha. We filled the basement with our laughter and our discovered common concern. Charity wrote the name of her doctor on a three by five card (she carried a deck of them in her purse) and then, turning her watch to the open door, cried that she must go. But first, when could we come to dinner? How was Friday?

Friday was day after tomorrow. It seemed precipitate. It crossed my mind--and if it crossed mine it had already passed through Sally's--that we had a humiliatingly blank calendar. In a quick look we determined that we

*A manuscript page from Wallace Stegner's novel* Crossing to Safety. *Stegner apologized that his markings are not more revealing: "My methods are prelapsarian and prewordprocessarian. It takes me many rewritings to get a first draft, and all the chapters that went into it have been thrown away successively until I get something that will read consecutively. I go through that with an editing pencil and retype it to make a relatively clear second draft."*

© Stanford Publications Service

# Wallace Stegner

*In person, what first impresses many people is Stegner's appearance. Even at the age of eighty-one he looks exceptionally youthful and handsome. He wears his clothes well, whether an old bathrobe or a workshirt and jeans. He rises early—sometimes too early for a houseguest from Idaho—breakfasts, then retreats before first light to the manual typewriter inside the study adjoining the Stegner home. Both the house and the study overlook the woods and meadows of the Los Altos Hills. On cool mornings Stegner lights a low fire in the stove and then writes until lunch.*

*Although far from uncluttered, his study nevertheless seems orderly and neat. On its entrance wall and to the left of it, bookshelves run from floor to ceiling; opposite the entrance, honorary degrees, awards, certificates and memorabilia take the place of bookshelves. To the right sits Stegner's broad wooden desk, on top of it more books, a few cigars, an ashtray, and manuscript pages. Behind the desk are photos of friends like Bernard DeVoto and Robert Frost; below these, more bookshelves tightly packed with contemporary classics.*

INTERVIEWER: When did you decide that you had to be a writer?

WALLACE STEGNER: I'm a writer by the sheerest accident. Nobody in my family had ever gone to college. I did, and there they said, "You've got to major in something." So I said, "Fine. Economics," and I took one course in economics and that cured that. Then, my freshman English teacher thought I had some kind of gift. So he put me in an advanced class, which gave me the notion that I could put words together in some fashion. I wrote some short stories as an undergraduate, won a little prize at one of the local newspapers. But I was selling rugs and linoleum, and, as far as I knew, I would go on selling rugs and linoleum for a living. I wrote this piece of stupidity into the novel *Recapitulation* because it seemed to me nobody above the stage of a cretin could have been so completely unaware, so totally naive, so unsophisticated, wide-eyed, going any way he was pushed. I was silly putty.

When I finished college, a couple of my professors pushed me off to graduate school. When I had finished that, I went back to Salt Lake to teach, and after two years of recovering from the Ph.D., I sat down one afternoon and wrote a story just because I wanted to write a story. I wrote it in about two hours and sent it off to the *Virginia Quarterly*, I think, and they published it. Then you know you're hooked. By that time I was twenty-six or twenty-seven. I hadn't been grinding away at a literary apprenticeship, and I had given writing up as a possible career. It never occurred to me that there was a possibility of making a living at it. So it was all pure, brute accident, with some people who encouraged me along the way. That's probably the way it is. You do get encouraged when you're young and malleable by people who think they know better than you what you're good for. And they may be right. Certainly, I'd have made a terrible economist.

INTERVIEWER: Do you consciously go in search of book projects? How did your novel, *Crossing to Safety*, begin?

STEGNER: No. I don't go in search of projects. Sometimes they appear before my eyes, and sometimes they grow over a long period of time as I brood. Sometimes I know there's a book there, and I have to hunt through an awful lot of research material, as I did with *Angle of Repose*. I have started books without knowing where they were going to end. That's more dangerous. But in the case of *Crossing to Safety* the book just grew, more or less, through personal experience in Vermont,

Wisconsin, and to a small extent, in Italy. In those places what was gradually developing in my mind could find a home. That's how the book came about. It took a long time. I had to do it by trial and error, and I was years in getting it finally sorted out. It's not a conscious process.

INTERVIEWER: Was there any point where you definitely knew this project was a novel?

STEGNER: I knew from the beginning it was going to be a book. You have that feeling. It's like having a fish on the line. You know when it's an old boot and when it's a fish. But I didn't know *what* the book was. I've got piles of manuscripts over there, eight and ten inches high, of stuff written and tossed aside in the process of finding out. At several points the novel was going in entirely different directions. It had different characters from those that now appear, more characters, episodes that never got into the finished book at all. The novel started in a different place. It proceeded toward a different end.

INTERVIEWER: In writing the new novel did you confront any technical challenges you had never faced before?

STEGNER: There were problems in this book, partly because it's a very quiet book. Not much happens in it. It contains none of the things that seem to be essential for contemporary novels. Much goes on in the mind, in memory. I was doing something that I would have advised almost any student of mine not to do: I let nearly the whole book happen in one head, during the course of one day. There's a little bit of front-stage action during the day, but most of the book curls back and picks up the past. It's difficult to do this without being slow and tedious. I don't know if I succeeded or not. I had to work on that problem constantly to keep the story line from appearing to sag and go nowhere. It had to have some forward motion. It had to have some draft. That's a technical problem: by the pure force of the writing to create a sense of involvement in real events. Also, the problem of how to get the essence of the lives of the four main characters into the space of one day is not small. I had done something like that before but never in such a concentrated way. In making fiction, one of the things a writer must do is to make absolutely certain that he knows the mind he's dealing *through*. In *Recapitulation*, I was dealing in third-person narration, but through a particular memory and a particular mind. In *Crossing to Safety*, I'm dealing in first-person; I have to try to become that person as far as possible. If I succeed, I get the tone of voice and the quality of mind that will persuade a reader to see and hear a real and credible human being, not a mouthpiece or a construct. As Henry James said, if fiction is going to be successful, it depends helplessly upon that sense of reality.

INTERVIEWER: You have to convince the reader that the world that he or she is entering is the real world and not the world of dream or memory only. Is that it?

STEGNER: I believe the real world exists. I haven't any philosophical doubts about that. Moreover, before you can convince the reader, you have to convince yourself that, in effect, you have invaded and become the person you're speaking through. Every morning you have to read over what you did yesterday, and if it doesn't persuade you, it has to be redone. Sometimes it takes me three hours in the morning to get over the feeling that I've been wasting my time for the past week and that everything I've written up to that point is drivel. Until I can convince myself that I am speaking in the plausible, believable voice of the person I have invented, I can't go on. So the first job is to convince yourself, the second is to convince the reader. If you do the first, the second more or less follows.

INTERVIEWER: Can we properly speak of traditional forms in fiction in the same sense that we can speak of traditional forms in poetry?

STEGNER: Sonnets and rondels? No. But it seems to me that every story has its own form, which can't be imposed upon the material but must be discovered within it. I don't believe, for instance, in such a thing as an all-inclusive form at all. I don't think there is such a thing in philosophy, either. I don't believe in method-makers, system-makers; it doesn't seem to me that life conforms to systems. Only systems conform to systems. The people who feel compelled to make systems, whether out of philosophy or out of human life, or out of words, are deluding themselves. I would rather follow the flow of life as it happens than of life as I can imagine it to be. I don't think strait-jackets are the way to get at fiction. I would rather define the novel as Stendhal did, as a mirror in the roadway. Whatever happens in the road is going to happen in the mirror, too. You can't systematize that.

INTERVIEWER: What is originality in fiction?

STEGNER: It's often thought to be technical innovation, experimentation of one kind or another, which never intrigued me. Whatever originality is, you can tell when it *isn't* there. If everything in a story can be anticipated from the start, if the writer begins with a situation and the story develops and concludes in absolutely anticipated ways, then I would say it is unoriginal. The writer is following a pattern practically imprinted on the material. Some element of the unexpected is necessary, or some element, at least, of the—what would you call it?—profound. For a writer to be original, he or she would have to see deeply enough into characters to say something that makes a reader really pause, something the reader might never have thought of at that point in the fiction. And ultimately, the writer would have to make the reader go the writer's way, too.

INTERVIEWER: Both John Fowles's *The French Lieutenant's Woman* and your *Angle of Repose* employ similar narrative techniques, some we had not seen in the novel for perhaps as long as a century.

STEGNER: They are both traditional, which doesn't bother me one bit. I don't really aspire to write a novel that can be read backward as well as forward, that turns chronology on its head, has no continuity, no narrative, that, in effect, tries to create a novel by throwing all the pieces in a bag and shaking it. If a writer has to do *that* to be original, then I don't care about being original. In fact, I don't think the word "originality," as it's usually defined, is particularly useful. It usually seizes upon some innovation that often turns out to be frivolous or essentially unimportant. An awful lot of mutations, which is what these things are, turn out to be monsters that can't live. I'm content with the species, with turning out two-legged animals with one head.

INTERVIEWER: Judging by the whole body of your fiction, you seem to me a highly self-conscious novelist. I mean that as a compliment.

STEGNER: That depends on what you mean by "self-conscious." I'm not careless, and I don't like to write things that fail to cast any shadow at all. On the other hand, I do, as I said, like to follow the flow of what I perceive to be the reality of observed life. I don't like to risk messing with that. If I'm lucky, things will come together.

INTERVIEWER: How much of your fiction is autobiographical? You are often taken for your fictional narrators, Joe Allston and Lyman Ward in particular.

STEGNER: What does Wallace Stegner have to do with it? The very fact that some of my experience goes into the book is all but inescapable, and true for almost any writer I can name. Which is real and which is invented is (a) nobody's business and (b) a rather silly preoccupation and (c) impossible to answer. By the time I'm through converting my life to fiction, it's half fiction at least and maybe more. People still come to me and say, "Oh, it's too bad about your son who drowned in that surfing accident." Because some of *All the Little Live Things* reflects my immediate circumstances, they assume all of it does. People ought to learn to read better than that. The kind of *roman à clef* reading determining biographical facts in fiction is not a good way to read. Read the fiction. The life, like all kinds of other things, is just raw material for the fiction. Insofar as the life is usable, it's used; insofar as it's unusable, something else is used. When I get through a book that involves some aspects of my own experience, as this new one does, I often don't know myself what I invented and what I didn't.

INTERVIEWER: Is that because you have made the experience real?

STEGNER: It's because I have thought my way into it in fictional terms. I never want the end product to be taken as autobiography or biography. Because it isn't. No, the moment I begin to say, "This fictional person is so-and-so," I am lying through my teeth. My fictional people are no more real people than Larry Morgan is me. They are constructs with some relations and roots in real life, but they are certainly not people. If I said they *were* people, real people would begin to say, "Well, you did me wrong." And they would have every reason to say so. But as long as my characters are constructs and understood to be such, I have only borrowed, shall we say, some characteristics and experience for fictional purposes—and I hope transformed them.

INTERVIEWER: My own limited experience in creating fiction tells me I have no choice but to draw upon my own experience as well as that of my friends, parents, children, if I am going to shape characters. I sometimes feel as if I am stealing.

STEGNER: You can't steal anything that's already yours—in a literary sense. If you can surround it, understand it, comprehend it, it's yours unless you steal word for word—which is another matter. If the material is yours and it fits your concepts and the growing pattern in a novel, then it's already yours.

INTERVIEWER: How important are literary friendships? How important are friends to a writer?

STEGNER: I would hate to think that friends were simply purpose-servers, utilitarian. There's no question at all that literary conversation with people who know what they're talking about and whose books you have read, with whom you have some kind of friendly occupational relationship, is important. When you read a book you're bound to get a closer glimpse of people than a lot of the glimpses you get in real life. And so literary conversation, the companionship of people of like minds, is very pleasurable. I wouldn't want to think of it strictly as a useful business, although once in a while it happens that way. Malcolm Cowley helped me a time or two just with his wisdom.

INTERVIEWER: Did you consider him a friend?

STEGNER: Oh, yes. One of the best. I was writing *Wolf Willow*, and I couldn't make it come together. It was an anthology in the first place. Malcolm said, "Let me look at it," which was very friendly of him, and he looked and he said, "You know, I think if you just move this 'Dump Ground' chapter from the beginning to the end"—or vice versa, I've fogotten which—"the book will come together better." And it did, like a puzzle when you find the key piece. I had a blind spot he did not have. So there is often a great usefulness in literary friends, but that isn't what you have them for. You don't have any friend *for* anything. You just have him. Or her.

INTERVIEWER: What others do you think of as literary friends?

STEGNER: I don't have many because I haven't lived a literary life. Most writers either live in New York or in their own pieces of the hinterlands. Frank O'Connor was a good and close friend. So was Storm Jameson. But most of my literary friends are friendly acquaintances or ex-students—a separate category.

INTERVIEWER: Do the women in your fiction seem to you stronger than the men? Doesn't your fiction address this question frequently? By "stronger" I mean physiologically as well as psychologically. I'm thinking, too, of one of your critics—a man—who claims your novels *use* women but are ultimately *about* men.

STEGNER: I wouldn't think such a generalization would be easy. There are some women in my fiction, like the discombobulated woman in *A Shooting Star*, who are not strong characters. I've known a lot of women, particularly in the more distant past, back a way: attractive, well-educated, with nothing to do. Simply brought up and well-educated to a dead-end. Society wives. That kind often ends up alcoholic or something else self-destructive. They can't be called strong characters.

I think Elsa in *Big Rock Candy Mountain*, who has a good many qualities in common with my mother, is a strong character, stronger than her husband who is a lot more active and in some ways more imaginative. In *Angle of Repose* I would guess that it's a stand-off. Susan is more talented in many ways than Oliver. She shows off better. But while I wrote that book, thinking that I was writing about her as a heroine, I came to the end of it thinking maybe *he* is the hero because there is a flaw in her, a flaw of snobbery. She doesn't adequately appreciate the kind of person he is, or the kind of work he does. That's a story not about either men or women, but about a relationship, a novel about a marriage.

I have been lucky, in some ways, writing about women. My mother was a very strong woman, and I got an example of the kind of patience and endurance that even an unlucky woman can display. And I was lucky in writing *Angle of Repose* because the record was so complete. I couldn't have been a Victorian gentlewoman without taking a lot of material out of the letters of Mary Hallock Foote, who was, in her way, a quite remarkable character. Women sometimes ask me, "How do you know so much about women?" I don't know anything about women. I'm writing about people. It's not as if only women can write about women or men about men. After all, neither *Madame Bovary* nor *Anna Karenina* was written by a woman. I know novels about men written by women that are perfectly strong and true. I don't want to dismiss the sexes or dismantle them. I just don't want to choose between them.

INTERVIEWER: Is there a point where a writer's consciousness ought to take over his intuitive responses, when the character begins to cast a longer shadow on the page and assume symbolic values? I'm thinking of the evolutionary process: first by accident, then by design.

STEGNER: Oh, I suppose. Again, I would insist that those patterns are discovered and not imposed. When a writer finds them he helps them along. You would be foolish not to play any scene that is given to you to play. Benny DeVoto said, in effect, "You run out your hits as far as you can. You don't stop on second." But the author's consciousness certainly ought never to be obvious. It's imposed, of course it's imposed. But the author's view of his own characters may be arrived at through a long period of inductive thinking about them. You don't put placards up for the reader saying, "This is my meaning."

The whole business of writing is an attempt to arrive at truth, insofar as you can see it, as far as your capacity to unearth it permits. Truth is to be handled gingerly. That's an egg with a very thin shell. I'm not writing fables—where the moral is literally part of the form. I'm writing something from which the reader is supposed to deduce or induce any mortal that's there. The moral value ought to be hiding in the material.

INTERVIEWER: The last time we spoke I pointed out to you a few of the interpretive possibilities for the first name of your narrator, Lyman, in *Angle of Repose*; "Lie-Man," I exclaimed. "What a wonderful name for a storyteller." You denied making any conscious association.

STEGNER: I never thought of that pun on Lyman's name until you suggested it to me, so if it was unconscious on my part, it was *totally* unconscious. Such things seem to me a form of gamesmanship and pedantry I really don't want to play. *Lang*, for instance, in the new novel is just a name. I don't know where that came from. I wanted a Scottish name. It came, I suppose, because I happened to run across Andrew Lang, a translator of certain Greek classics. "Lang" is just a Scotch name. It might as well have been McDermit.

INTERVIEWER: But it wasn't McDermit! It was *Lang*. What about the name *Ward*, the family name in *Angle of Repose*? Lyman, the narrator, and his whole family are literally orphans. Lyman considers himself both a cultural guardian and watchman, as well as a dependent. He, at least, is aware of himself as a *ward*.

STEGNER: Well, I suppose I'm entitled to anything you can find in me. I'll accept that. But I'm certainly not doing anything like that on purpose. If I were Vladimir Nabokov, that's the kind of game I might play. I'm a very different kind of writer.

INTERVIEWER: Will you comment on the way you choose the names of your fictional characters?

STEGNER: Sure. Which ones?

INTERVIEWER: Well, how about Lyman Ward?

STEGNER: While I hate to lose credit for ingenuity, I have to say that most of my characters' names are pure accident. I probably named him Lyman because the president of Stanford at the time was named Dick Lyman, and I borrowed his name. Ward? I don't know where I picked up Ward except for Julia Ward Howe and other people related to my historical models. I wanted an old, eastern, established name. Even though Ward came a little close to some of the ancestors of the people I used as models, I still felt it was legitimate. It wasn't the name of either family. It was on a collateral edge of one of the families. I guess that's where that name comes from, but I also wanted to use the fellow in Leadville, the wizard of Wall Street, the man who broke Ulysses Grant and more or less disgraced him.

INTERVIEWER: Who was that?

STEGNER: W. S. Ward. He appears in the book just briefly as a foil for the relatively square, unimaginative integrity of his cousin.

INTERVIEWER: It must be outright unnerving to write a book like *Angle of Repose* and then watch the *New York Times* ignore it, even when the Pulitzer committee nods benevolently. What do you do then?

STEGNER: I was made aware of the situation by all kinds of friends of mine, including many in the East, who kept writing to the *Times* and saying, "When are you going to review this book, because it's a book we admire very much?" Eventually, months later, the *Times* ran a retrospective review, which was a little condescending, and kind of snobby. I don't know. The reasons they ignored it could have been personal. Wright Morris and I talk about which one of us is the more neglected. We compete for the role. Neither of us wants it.

INTERVIEWER: But then, after *Angle of Repose*, you published *The Spectator Bird* and won a National Book Award. Did the *Times* review it?

STEGNER: No. They didn't. But that's all water under the bridge. Let's not bring on anything with a rain dance. The *Los Angeles Times* didn't review *The Spectator Bird*, either. That, I found out later, was because Robert Kirsch, the book editor, was abroad and terminally ill, and somebody in his place just overlooked it. I wouldn't make a case for the *Los Angeles Times* being unfriendly, because they have been friendly. They've given me a prize. These things seldom happen through calculated neglect.

INTERVIEWER: You once claimed in an essay published in *The Sound of Mountain Water* that a publisher's map of the United States would look like a barbell: New York at one end, California at the other, and United Airlines in between. Does that comparison still hold?

STEGNER: The publishing world used to be a narrow world, pinched between about Thirty-third and Sixty-fifth Streets and between Third Avenue and the Avenue of the Americas. That world has widened in recent years as regional and university presses have enlarged their activities. Though the New York skyline still obscures the view to some extent, publishers certainly do know that the West Coast exists, and some have even discovered the interior West. The concentration of publishing, the reviews, and the advertising industry in New York makes New York indisputably the center, but it's less necessary than it used to be to live in New York, or to make frequent visits, if you want to be a writer. It is possible—not optimal but possible—to live a long way from the center and not get lost.

Twenty years ago I could not have said that, probably. I taught at Harvard for a half-dozen years in the 1940s, and because of the proximity to New York I felt more a part of the literary world than I have ever felt since moving back west. Personal contacts, acquaintances, visibility, all have practical usefulness. But they are not now as absolutely essential as they were then. The principal danger is that, like a character in a radio play who says nothing for a minute or two, you may disappear.

INTERVIEWER: When you say it is useful for a writer to be visible, what do you mean?

STEGNER: For practical purposes, to be visible to editors, publishers, critics, agents, and for the possibilities of personal growth and stimulation, to other writers. Not being in New York means not knowing, or at least not seeing regularly, some of the best and brightest people in the world, people who might take can-openers to your mind, the kind of people who give off sparks when struck.

INTERVIEWER: Are you speaking about fruitful cultural differences?

STEGNER: Of course. I am probably going to look provincial to a born-and-bred New Yorker. He is probably going to look parochial to me. We need each other as correctives. For just one thing: cliques tend to form, coteries, fads, mind-sets, coagulations of ideas. Inevitably, we in the West are farther from Europe; the examples and stimulations that come from there are pretty attentuated after crossing the Atlantic and the North American continent. Just as surely, New York is farther from Asia than we are. Sitting on the edge of the Pacific Basin, we see aspects of the future, and we hear the sounds of alien ideas that are less apparent farther East. And we hear the interior of the continent more plainly. But the main problem is that the prestigious review journals come out of New York, and they tend to ignore what they can't hear, or to review it less seriously.

INTERVIEWER: Can we talk about the question of age and writing well? Conrad started at forty. Hardy, of course, wrote his best poetry—

STEGNER: After *Jude the Obscure*. I don't know anybody in this country who's writing fiction at a really advanced age and still writing well. Robert Penn Warren was very productive in poetry. Malcolm Cowley went on producing books, too, but his health and energy finally ran down. There are a few. Sophocles wrote *Oedipus at Colonus* when he was ninety. Goethe finished *Faust* when he was very old. But those were people with remarkable vigor and stamina, and most were not writing fiction. Not just anybody can do it. Some people are senile at sixty, some at twenty.

INTERVIEWER: What about you?

STEGNER: When I was in my prime, so to speak, I would generally get anywhere from three to five or six pages a day, stuff that might have to be rewritten tomorrow, but that would essentially stay. That doesn't happen now. It takes more combing to do it now.

INTERVIEWER: Perhaps you're only being a more cantankerous and harsher critic, more difficult to please. You once told me that the critic inside the writer ought to come to the work at a "different hour" than the creator and scribe.

STEGNER: Well, I still think that's true. It's important to get *on* with the writing, particularly when you're young and you can hardly wait to get down to work because you're boiling with something. But I'm not boiling that hard anymore. The critic is taking charge, and I'm just driving the cab. That's why it takes me so much longer now.

INTERVIEWER: Are there no advantages to age for a writer?

STEGNER: Oh, of course there are. There are even advantages to being fifty years in the business of writing books, because one hand has a tendency to wash the other. People know one book and get reminded of another. A reputation is, to some extent, a cumulative affair. I suppose that's the best kind of reputation, one you've earned over a long period of time. That's the kind I would covet, if I were coveting.

INTERVIEWER: Are there no other advantages of age? Even if you only end up keeping one page a day you can easily have a book every year or every other year.

STEGNER: Yes, one page would be pretty good. There are advantages. You should know more. You should be able to estimate people better. You should have, if not a more mellow, at least a less distorted view of the world. But a lot of the business of writing books is, as Hemingway said, selling energy. The disadvantage of age is that your energy level goes down. You have less to sell. And eventually the level goes down so far you haven't any to sell, and you quit writing books.

INTERVIEWER: I've heard this before. The last time we spoke you told me, "I don't know if I'm going to have another novel."

STEGNER: Well, all right. I'll go on like a fool until I'm ninety—and then wish I hadn't written the last three. There are other things that happen when you get to be my age. Literary fashions change, leaving you stranded. Still, at my age you care less. You just plain care less. You get tired of people's problems, and you take less interest in them. You think, "Oh, to hell with them. I'll go out and tend to the garden." The kinds of problems you can care about in your old age are different from the kinds of problems you care about when you're thirty. And they are probably different from the kinds of problems most of your readers care about. So you tend to move away from all the heat and calamity of living and get into a kind of serenity that is not very creative.

INTERVIEWER: That's one option. If you could literally go back and change anything, would you do it?

STEGNER: Oh, I don't know. It's a kind of fruitless speculation, isn't it?

INTERVIEWER: Maybe. Not necessarily for a novelist, I would think.

STEGNER: If I could go back? There are many, many things I would do differently if I could go back. Of course. I would go back and study different things. If we're in the self-improvement business, which we seem to be on the basis of this last book, there are many ways I could improve myself.

INTERVIEWER: You would study biology and anthropology.

STEGNER: I would study both of those. I would waste far less time.

INTERVIEWER: You've produced fifty or more books in as many years. Where did you waste a second of time and when?

STEGNER: I'm thinking up to the time I was about twenty—twenty-two, maybe—no, twenty. You waste your youth. I wasted mine working too much. I fiddled. I played a lot of cards, for one thing . . . like Solo. I spent a lot of time reaching for "spread misères." It's a laydown hand in Solo. " 'I guess I'll make it a spread misère,' said Dangerous Dan McGrew." I suppose I didn't waste a lot of time, but I was a frivolous youth. I really was.

INTERVIEWER: Isn't that what youth is for?

STEGNER: It doesn't seem so. I had plenty of reasons to be serious. If I could go back, I would waste less. And I would waste less of it at frivolous and unproductive work. I worked my way through college being a clerk in a rug and linoleum store forty hours a week. There was nothing in that work that taught me anything. I did it for a long time—and was glad to do it because it was the only way to go to school. If I were going back I'd find some other way. There were so many books I wanted to know and would know now if I hadn't worked those forty-hour weeks, four years of my life.

INTERVIEWER: Do you recall these words? "Nobody has quite made a western Yoknapatawpha County or discovered a historical continuity comparable to that which Faulkner traced from Ikkemotubbe the Chickasaw to Montgomery Ward Snopes. Maybe it isn't possible, but I wish someone would try. I might even try myself." Haven't you been trying?

STEGNER: Not systematically, no. When I wrote that statement, sometime in the fifties maybe, I was wishing that somebody could do it; I suppose I was aware that in many people's eyes, and perhaps in my own, I was becoming a western writer; I was curious to know what that meant, curious to know if it was some kind of fence I was stuck inside of. If I was going to be stuck inside the fence, what was I going to do with the territory in there? I pretty well decided, then or later, that the territory was a little too vast and various, that you couldn't make a Yoknapatawpha County out of it. There was not enough homogeneity in the material.

I don't know how systematic Faulkner was in writing the Yoknapatawpha County books; I suspect he wasn't a systematic kind of man. But he was dealing with material that was homogeneous, that related one book to another through three generations of a family of characters. In the West, there is not that kind of continuity to deal with, even if I wanted to. If I had been tempted to try to make some kind of saga like that, I couldn't possibly have done it without confining myself to a particular part of the West, Salt Lake City, say or Saskatchewan, Montana, parts of the West I knew. Here again we run into the lack of a usable past. There wasn't enough in those places to produce that kind of saga—I thought. So, I'm scattered. Even when I'm writing about the things I know, I'm inevitably scattered. The only related things I was able to do were a trailer to *The Big Rock Candy Mountain* in *Recapitulation*, two Joe Allston books, and another little Joe Allston novella about this part of contemporary California. Those are not sagas. They are only minimal crystallizations and coagulations. All of Faulkner's people tend to revolve around the courthouse square, the Confederate monument. It's a different, much more concentrated country in the South. It's a rural tradition with a relatively homogeneous population, homogeneous problems—the problem of slavery and its consequences; it's a rural society and notably traditional.

INTERVIEWER: One of your critics writes, "Stegner reminds me of Faulkner, a mythologizer notoriously unreliable in his comments about his own work. . . . Stegner treats myth and tradition as does Faulkner, who uses them in terms which absolutely surround them and encompass them and melt them down and make them into something else . . . [who] transcends and transforms his tradition."

STEGNER: It would be nice to think I have all those powers. I don't understand, really, what the critic is talking about. I am, so far as I know, unaware of myth in my work—notoriously unreliable as I am. Again, if these things are found in my fiction, I'm happy. I have been, as you suggest, trying to make a historical continuity between past and present, but I don't understand that as myth. I don't believe the myth matches either past or present. The mythic western is pure hokum. It applies to very small numbers of people over very short periods of time and not at all to nine-tenths of the people who lived here—as a personification of Individualism and Self-Reliance. I guess I like things that are closer to the actual facts of experience.

INTERVIEWER: Have you been conscious of attempting to debunk the myths, statements like "Rain follows the plow" or "Gold is anywhere you stick your shovel"?

STEGNER: I'd call those delusions, not myths; but sure, I grew up doubting the Big-Bonanza-Just-Over-the-Next-Rise notion because for years I watched my family chase it. I got pretty jaundiced on that subject. A little realism would have helped my family a good deal. Instead of expecting to make a big strike somewhere, which is a very American notion, encouraged by free land, by opportunity, by freedom of action or nearly complete freedom of action, I would have liked to see a little more just plain stick-to-itiveness at times. The longest journey begins with a single step—I believe that more than I believe in the fortune over the next rise. My father always refused to make the first step. He always wanted the step to be a one-hundred-yard broad-jump. Broad-jumping is not the way you travel. It leads to a succession of falls.

INTERVIEWER: Is it possible for a writer to open up "new" territory for fiction?

STEGNER: "No new ways to be new," as Frost said. I think that's a reasonably good statement. "There's nothing new under the sun," sayeth the Preacher. "All the rivers run into the sea, yet the sea is not full." I think more circularly than linearly. I don't think there are beginnings and destinations so much as circles which end by closing and starting over again. I can't think of any fiction that introduces new elements of what used to be called "Human Nature," nothing that isn't present, say, in *The Iliad* and *The Odyssey*. The qualities of character, the machinery of suspense and climax, of mounting action and falling action: I don't think we've seen anything new in that way. There are new clothes, because civilization can change, and we get out of armor and into doublet and hose, and then Brooks Brothers pants, but we're still the same people, and doing the same things essentially. I think it's a mistake to think originality amounts to that much.

I know people, for instance, including former students of mine, who got into the sexual revolution and thought they had opened up really new material for fiction. They felt like renaissance men and women discovering a new world with fifty-seven positions. But it's there in *One Thousand and One Nights*, it's there in the *Satyricon* of Petronius. There's nothing new about it. I doubt there's much Cain didn't know as soon as he got acquainted east of Eden. I don't think that's a way of getting anywhere to pretend that there's anything new to be said. What's important is a larger understanding of what has always been. I believe some things have been added in that respect.

INTERVIEWER: Like what?

STEGNER: Many would say depth psychology has given us both new soil and new tools. I'm not sure. I've never seen an Id—and I will run in another direction if I ever do! Freud's theory of the personality doesn't always strike me as plausible. I'm half-inclined to agree with Nabokov on the subject of Freud: a great witch-doctor. I would say that I doubt psychoanalysis has produced many cures, though it has produced a good many novels.

I don't mean to say the species is absolutely incapable of change.

But often what we change to may have already been there, but neglected. Aldo Leopold's American land ethic is, in some ways, for example, prefigured in Stoic philosophy. Marcus Aurelius: "What's bad for the beehive can't be good for the bee." It's certainly there in Saint Francis, in Zen, in American Indian religions: that attitude toward the earth that is respectful and reverent, that goes *with* the flow of the earth instead of against it. If we all adopted Leopold's land ethic tomorrow we would not be doing anything new. We might be going in a different direction from the one we're headed toward, but it wouldn't be a new direction, only a change of direction, one already inscribed in the books.

INTERVIEWER: Is it possible for a writer to protect the places he or she loves by writing about them?

STEGNER: It doesn't help to write about them in celebratory ways because all you do is stimulate the tourist industry. I have sometimes carefully avoided writing in celebratory ways about places I love on the earth. On the other hand, you can write, as Leopold did, about attitudes toward the earth and do some educating. The problem is not wickedness or evil. Lynn White calls it a development of the Judeo-Christian tradition which makes man the center of the earth and all creatures subservient to him. The problem, as stated in Genesis, is a piece of early Jewish arrogance. But many peoples have felt it. The Navaho call themselves Diné, The People. Many, many people have called themselves *the* people, as if no other people existed, and have thought of themselves as the center of the universe. We have to get over that. I am profoundly of the opinion that *that* attitude has to go or we destroy our own habitat. So without innovating anything, I would just rather get a little more American Indian than Judeo-Christian in my attitudes toward the earth, and a little more Zen and Saint Francis-like in my attitude toward other animals.

INTERVIEWER: You've observed that the "new man" Crèvecoeur defined had become something else by the time Henry James got around to writing *The American*. Is there anything you can tell us that might help the species survive?

STEGNER: Crèvecoeur's notion is touched by the Rousseauian idea of the naturally good human being given new opportunity. And new opportunity—Crèvecoeur never got around to saying this—is often abused. People take advantage of it to extend beyond their normal appetites. Wendell Berry was right when he said we've gone about as far as we *can* go with that American notion, the new man in a new country. It's time to change direction and quit thinking of the American as simply an animated economic opportunity. That's Ronald Reagan's way of looking at America. I'm profoundly opposed to enterprise when enterprise is uncontrolled by any notion of the public good, of the *polis,* the way in which people relate one to another. Instead, we find Individualism gone berserk. I don't know if you're familiar with a book by Robert N. Bellah called *Habits of the Heart,* the title of which comes from Tocqueville. It's an examination of American attitudes, of Individualism without what Wendell Berry calls "membership," without association, without a notion of a *polis.* According to Bellah, individualism often results in a lifestyle that changes as often as the coat or tie, the absolute repudiation of commitment or obligation to anything. You're not obligated by religion, you're not obligated by a social conscience, you're not obligated by family: you change your family, you get a divorce and start over. You're not even obligated to stay with one sex. You're absolutely free. And absolutely, it seems to me, in a vacuum. I would agree with Bellah: that kind of Individualism gone berserk, gone rampant, leads down to some cold ninth circle of hell. That's no way for any people to continue to live. We had better get over precisely the kind of thing Ronald Reagan urges us to get back to.

INTERVIEWER: You also wave a hand of dismissal to the whole idea that T. H. Watkins raises in a recent article: that you've been one of "the central figures in the modern conservation movement." You worked for Stewart Udall in the Kennedy administraton; before that as an active freelancer in Bernard DeVoto's camp; and you've been on the Advisory Board for National Parks, Historical Sites, Buildings and Monuments as well as on the Governing Council of the Wilderness Society.

STEGNER: I told Tom Watkins, "I am not a good soldier in the environmental armies because I don't seem to work well in bodies with other people." Here's an irony. I'm against Individualism gone rampant, but I don't actually seem to be a very good team player. I become recalcitrant. Even when I agree wholeheartedly with the people who are urging me along, I don't like to be pushed. So some of the work of conservation, which is by necessity touched with zealotry, I resist. I'm not fooling when I tell Tom I'm not really a good team player. I have the complete conviction and conversion, but I seem to have to do it on my own. That means I write when I feel it and not when the tactics of the moment call for it.

I have been unable to bring much of my thought about conservation into fiction because I suspect myself when I begin to be doctrinaire. I consider the integrity of the material to be of greater value than any message I might want to get across. If the material itself dictates that message, it would be in there, but I don't seem to be able to put it in by force or will: that seems to me a dilution of the essential.

INTERVIEWER: But it does surface. Plenty of public servants turn up: John Wesley Powell, for instance, and there are plenty of examples in your DeVoto biography. Bruce Mason is a public servant. Oliver Ward has a kind of civic-mindedness.

STEGNER: Oliver's notion of how to be a public servant in the West was mistaken, but he did have the notion of public service. His notion was to build a dam that he hoped would do a lot of good. Well, I happen to be an anti-dam man, so I have to go against my own character in a way. Oliver is not a Bo Mason, but neither is he a Powell. Even Powell I would have to disagree with on certain things because he didn't live long enough to see what the development of the dry country would do to it.

INTERVIEWER: What's the most difficult thing to teach about writing? And what's the most difficult thing for students to learn?

STEGNER: Assuming that the student is at a stage where he is still teachable—there *is* a time when you shouldn't try to teach him, when he is technically proficient and subtle and has his own ways for going about what he wants to say—one of the hardest things to teach him is *Revise! Revise! Revise!* And they *won't* revise, often. Many of them would rather write a new book than revise the old one. Revision is what separates the men from the boys. Sooner or later, you've got to learn to revise. On the other hand, there's occasionally somebody like Bob Stone, who won the National Book Award for *Dog Soldiers*. Quite wacky, really. Quite mad. He got the notion in the middle of the year that he had a brain tumor. He came in and sat across from my desk and big drops of sweat formed on his forehead. "I'm going blind!" he said, scared to death. He had just used up his fellowship. So I quickly reinstated his fellowship so that he could get free medical care. He swore later they bored a hole into his head and blew him out with a pressure hose, but they didn't find any brain tumor. He came bald-headed to a party when Bill Styron was there talking. But Stone was someone you couldn't teach *not* to revise. He was so finicky that it would take him a term to produce a chapter. He would be working on it all the time, but he wouldn't really let anybody see it until it satisfied him completely. He's an exception, though, and a very good writer.

INTERVIEWER: If you were to outline a course of study for a writer at the outset of his undergraduate career, what would it include? Or is the question too broad?

STEGNER: That's pretty broad. It might be different for every individual. I would ask some questions. I suppose I would ask, "Are you a reader?" If you aren't a reader, you might as well forget trying to be a writer. I don't think it's necessary to take a lot of courses in English literature. I sound prejudiced against the English Departments, but in a sense, if you had some kind of guidance, if you had a tutor who could suggest books for you to read, it would be better, I think, than taking regular English Department courses. To know something substantive, to have some kind of skill, some body of knowledge, is terribly useful. I don't care what it is. It will be useful in writing sooner or later. If you only play tennis well, if you're a doctor—whatever you do. I know what I would do if I were doing it again. I would take courses in biology and anthropology, though that's my particular bias. Whatever your choice, there's no substitute for knowing something. As Benny DeVoto once said in a dour martini-lit moment, "Literary people always tend to overbid their knowledge." At the same time, while you're learning something, I suspect that you should keep writing. Use it or lose it. Creation is a knack which is empowered by practice, and like almost any skill, it is lost if you don't practice it.

INTERVIEWER: Is the proliferation of creative writing programs on the nation's campuses in any way dangerous?

STEGNER: Yes. It's dangerous because, if you'll pardon the expression, a lot of people in English Departments should never be trusted to run a program. Their training is all in the other direction, all analytical, all critical. It's all a reader's training, not a writer's training, so they have no notion of how to approach the opportunity.

INTERVIEWER: During some of the years you taught at Stanford, you shared the corridors with Yvor Winters, a formidable critic. Former students like Ed Loomis say they were "very much aware of dominions and borders that were taken very seriously in these little intellectual baronies. There was a certain amount of distrust—or perhaps dislike would be a more accurate characterization."

STEGNER: Yvor Winters was, as you say, a formidable critic, positive and often unyielding in his opinions, and intolerant of ideas that conflicted with his. He was not a man you could debate with, because he never debated, he asserted. On the other hand, he was learned, utterly serious, and a devoted teacher to those with whom he could work, and who could work with him. We had our differences, which were never mortal, and we generally operated, as Ed Loomis suggests, by a division of territory. Yvor kept his poets close, away from contamination, with the result, which I never liked, that poets and fiction writers had too little contact. That situation has not applied since Yvor's retirement and death, and so far as I am able to observe, poets and fiction writers mix and blend and influence one another in the present-day program.

INTERVIEWER: As a nation, are we pursuing the best course by subsidizing fiction writers and poets and the publication of their work through the auspices of the National Endowment?

STEGNER: I suppose it could be said that arts that require public support don't justify themselves, and should be allowed to wither. But the arts have always needed support, because they are a product of a highly evolved society with plenty of leisure, and few of them can count on a mass audience big enough to keep them solvent and flourishing. I have no difficulty with the spectacle of the federal government playing modest Maecenas. After all, when I was breaking in, there was outright support for the arts through WPA, essentially a welfare program. The only problem is that a leaky tap will always attract lapping tongues. Any fellowship program, even such university programs as Stanford's, must keep a careful eye out for plausible fellowship lushes. Fellowships are best applied to young writers with big ambitions, to help them over the first hump. I don't know the hazards of other arts—I suspect composers have it worst—but any beginning artist needs time to develop, and fellowships, federal or otherwise, buy him time.

INTERVIEWER: What do you do when you simply want to relax—apart from reading and writing, teaching and lecturing, stumping for conservation?

STEGNER: Walking, reading, gardening. I am past tennis because of a shoulder separation, past skiing because I hate the cold, and past being a beach bum for obvious reasons.

INTERVIEWER: What role has your wife, Mary Stuart Page, played in your life and career?

STEGNER: She has had no role in my life except to keep me sane, fed, housed, amused, and protected from unwanted telephone calls, also to restrain me fairly frequently from making a horse's ass of myself in public, to force me to attend to books and ideas from which she knows I will learn something; also to mend my wounds when I am misused by the world, to implant ideas in my head and stir the soil around them, to keep me from falling into a comfortable torpor, to agitate my waking hours with problems that I would not otherwise attend to; also to remind me constantly—not by precept but by example—how fortunate I have been to live for fifty-six years with a woman that bright, alert, charming, and supportive.

INTERVIEWER: Another great American writer once wrote, "Death is the mother of beauty, mystical/ Within whose burning bosom we devise/ Our earthly mothers waiting, sleeplessly." Is one life ever enough?

STEGNER: I would like to think that one life is enough, and that when I see it coming to an end I can meet the darkness with resignation and perhaps acceptance. I have been lucky. I came from nowhere, and had no reason to expect as much from this one life as I have got. I owe God a death, and the earth a pound or so of chemicals. Now let's see if I can remember that when the time comes.

INTERVIEWER: In your only formal statement on your personal beliefs, you write, "I am terribly glad to be alive; and when I have wit enough to think about it, terribly proud to be a man and an American, with all the rights and privileges that those words connote; and most of all I am humble before the responsibilities that are also mine. For no right comes without a responsibility, and being born luckier than most of the world's millions, I am also born more obligated." What new obligations and responsibilities do you feel confronting you now? Or are there any?

STEGNER: No new ones—haven't we agreed with Frost that there are no new ways to be new?—but only reiterated and intensified versions of the old ones: the obligation to use oneself to the bone, to be as good as one's endowments and circumstances let one be, to project one's actions over and beyond the personal. The only things I owe to myself, I owe to my notions of justice. But I owe a great deal, in the way not only of obligation but of tenderness, to my family and my friends.

Chekhov said he worked all his life to get the slave out of himself. I guess I feel my obligation is to get the selfishness and greed, which often translates as the Americanism, out of myself. I want to be a citizen of the culture, of the best the culture stands for, not of a nation or a party or an economic system.

JAMES R. HEPWORTH
Spring 1990

# 4. Octavio Paz

Octavio Paz was born in 1914 in Mexico City. He began to write at an early age; in 1937 he traveled to Valencia, Spain, to participate in the Second International Congress of Anti-Fascist Writers. In 1943 he traveled on a Guggenheim Fellowship to the United States, where he became immersed in Anglo-American Modernist poetry; two years later, he entered the Mexican diplomatic service and was sent to France, where he wrote his fundamental study of Mexican identity, *The Labyrinth of Solitude*, and actively participated with André Breton in various surrealist activities and publications. In 1962 Paz was appointed Mexican ambassador to India, an important moment in both the poet's life and work, as witnessed in various books written during his stay there, especially *The Grammarian Monkey* and *East Slope*. In 1968, however, he resigned from the diplomatic service in protest against the government's bloodstained suppression of the student demonstrations in Tlatelolco during the Olympic Games in Mexico. Since then, Paz has continued his work as an editor and publisher, having founded two important magazines dedicated to the arts and politics: *Plural* (1971–1976) and *Vuelta*, which he has been publishing since 1976. In 1980 he was named honorary doctor at Harvard. Recent prizes include the Cervantes Award in 1981—the most important award in the Spanish-speaking world—and the Nobel Prize in 1990.

Paz's poetry has been collected in *Poemas 1935–1975* (1981) and *Collected Poems, 1957–1987* (1987). A remarkable prose stylist, Paz has written a prolific body of essays—including several book-length studies—in poetics and literary and art criticism, as well as on Mexican history, politics, and culture.

(135)

Todas las artes, especialmente la pintura y la escul-
tura, ~~son formas y cosas~~ materiales, al ser formas materiales
son cosas: pueden guardarse o venderse y transformarse
en objetos de especulación monetaria. La poesía también
es cosa pero es muy poca cosa: está hecha de palabras-
ecos, horadada de aire que no ocupa lugar en el espacio.
A la inversa del cuadro, el poema no muestra imágenes
ni figuras: es un conjunto verbal que provoca en el
lector (o en el oyente) un sentido de imágenes insólitas.
La poesía se oye en los oídos pero se ve en el entendi-
miento.

La discordia entre poesía y modernidad no es

accidental sino consustancial. La oposición entre
ambos aparece desde el comienzo de nuestra época
con los primeros románticos. La paradoja es que la
~~quizá~~ incompatibilidad es uno de los atributos,
quizá el central, de la poesía moderna. Sólo los mo-
dernos pueden ser tan total y desgarradoramente an-
ti-modernos como lo han sido todos nuestros grandes
poetas. La modernidad, fundada en la crítica,
secreta de un modo natural la crítica de sí-
misma. La poesía ha sido una de las manifestaciones
más enérgicas y vivaces de esa crítica. Pero su crítica
no ha sido ni racional ni filosófica sino pasional y en
nombre de realidades negadas o humilladas por la Edad
Moderna. La poesía ha sido la réplica y el antídoto de
la modernidad. Así, al negarla, la ha criticado

*Two manuscript pages from* The Other Voice, *an essay on poetry by Octavio Paz.*

© Nina Subin, New Directions

# Octavio Paz

*Though small in stature and well into his seventies, Octavio Paz, with his piercing eyes, gives the impression of being a much younger man. In his poetry and his prose works, which are both erudite and intensely political, he recurrently takes up such themes as the experience of Mexican history, especially as seen through its Indian past, and the overcoming of profound human loneliness through erotic love. Paz has long been considered, along with César Vallejo and Pablo Neruda, to be one of the great South American poets of the twentieth century; three days after this interview, which was conducted on Columbus Day 1990, he joined Neruda among the ranks of Nobel laureates in literature.*

*During this interview, which took place in front of an overflow audience at the 92nd Street Young Men's and Young Women's Hebrew Association in New York, under the auspices of the Poetry Center, Paz displayed the energy and power typical of him and of his poetry, which draws upon an eclectic sexual mysticism to bridge the gap between the individual and society. Appropriately, Paz seemed to welcome this opportunity to communicate with his audience.*

INTERVIEWER: Octavio, you were born in 1914, as you probably remember . . .

OCTAVIO PAZ: Not very well!

INTERVIEWER: . . . virtually in the middle of the Mexican Revolution and right on the eve of World War I. The century you've lived through has been one of almost perpetual war. Do you have anything good to say about the twentieth century?

PAZ: Well, I have survived, and I think that's enough. History, you know, is one thing and our lives are something else. Our century has been terrible—one of the saddest in universal history—but our lives have always been more or less the same. Private lives are not historical. During the French or American revolutions, or during the wars between the Persians and the Greeks—during any great, universal event—history changes continually. But people live, work, fall in love, die, get sick, have friends, moments of illumination or sadness, and that has nothing to do with history. Or very little to do with it.

INTERVIEWER: So we are both in and out of history?

PAZ: Yes, history is our landscape or setting and we live through it. But the real drama, the real comedy also, is within us, and I think we can say the same for someone of the fifth century or for someone of a future century. Life is not historical, but something more like nature.

INTERVIEWER: In *The Privileges of Sight*, a book about your relationship with the visual arts, you say: "Neither I nor any of my friends had ever seen a Titian, a Velázquez, or a Cézanne. . . . Nevertheless, we were surrounded by many works of art." You talk there about Mixoac, where you lived as a boy, and the art of early twentieth-century Mexico.

PAZ: Mixoac is now a rather ugly suburb of Mexico City, but when I was a child it was a small village. A very old village, from pre-Columbian times. The name Mixoac comes from the god Mixcoatl, the Nahuatl name for the Milky Way. It also meant "Cloud Serpent," as if the Milky Way were a serpent of clouds. We had a small pyramid, a diminutive pyramid, but a pyramid nevertheless. We also had a seventeenth-century convent. My neighborhood was called San Juan, and the parish church dated from the sixteenth century, one of the oldest in the area. There were also many eighteenth- and nineteenth-century houses, some with extensive gardens, because at the end of the nineteenth century Mixoac was a summer resort for the Mexican bourgeoisie. My family in fact had a summer house there. So when the revolution came, we were obliged, happily I think, to have to move there. We were surrounded by small memories of two pasts that remained very much alive, the pre-Columbian and the colonial.

INTERVIEWER: You talk in *The Privileges of Sight* about Mixoac's fireworks.

PAZ: I am very fond of fireworks. They were a part of my childhood. There was a part of the town where the artisans were all masters of the great art of fireworks. They were famous all over Mexico. To celebrate the feast of the Virgin of Guadalupe, other religious festivals, and at New Year's, they made the fireworks for the town. I remember how they made the church façade look like a fiery waterfall. It was marvelous. Mixoac was alive with a kind of life that doesn't exist anymore in big cities.

INTERVIEWER: You seem nostalgic for Mixoac, yet you are one of the few Mexican writers who live right in the center of Mexico City. Soon it will be the largest city in the world, a dynamic city, but, in terms of pollution, congestion, and poverty, a nightmare. Is living there an inspiration or a hindrance?

PAZ: Living in the heart of Mexico City is neither an inspiration nor an obstacle. It's a challenge. And the only way to deal with challenges is to face up to them. I've lived in other towns and cities in Mexico, but no matter how agreeable they are, they seem somehow unreal. At a certain point, my wife and I decided to move into the apartment where we live now. If you live in Mexico, you've got to live in Mexico City.

INTERVIEWER: Could you tell us something about the Paz family?

PAZ: My father was Mexican, my mother Spanish. An aunt lived with us—rather eccentric as aunts are supposed to be and poetic in her own absurd way. My grandfather was a lawyer and a writer, a popular novelist. As a matter of fact, during one period we lived off the sales of one of his books, a best-seller. The Mixoac house was his.

INTERVIEWER: What about books? I suppose I'm thinking about how Borges claimed he never actually left his father's library.

PAZ: It's a curious parallel. My grandfather had a beautiful library, which was the great thing about the Mixoac house. It had about six or seven thousand books, and I had a great deal of freedom to read. I was a voracious reader when I was a child and even read "forbidden" books because no one paid attention to what I was reading. When I was very young, I read Voltaire. Perhaps that led me to lose my religious faith. I also read novels that were more or less libertine, not really pornographic, just racy.

INTERVIEWER: Did you read any children's books?

PAZ: Of course. I read a lot of books by Salgari, an Italian author very popular in Mexico. And Jules Verne. One of my great heroes was an American, Buffalo Bill. My friends and I would pass from Alexandre Dumas's *Three Musketeers* to the cowboys without the slightest remorse or sense that we were warping history.

INTERVIEWER: You said once that the first time you saw a surrealist painting—a picture where vines were twisting through the walls of a house—you took it for realism.

PAZ: That's true. The Mixoac house gradually crumbled around us. We had to abandon one room after another because the roofs and walls kept falling down.

INTERVIEWER: When you were about sixteen in 1930, you entered the National Preparatory School. What did you study, and what was the school like?

PAZ: The school was beautiful. It was built at the end of the seventeenth century, the high point of the baroque in Mexican architecture. The school was big, and there was nobility in the stones, the columns, the corridors. And there was another aesthetic attaction. During the twenties, the government had murals painted in it by Orozco and Rivera—the first mural Rivera painted was in my school.

INTERVIEWER: So you felt attracted to the work of the muralists then?

PAZ: Yes, all of us felt a rapport with the muralists' expressionist style. But there was a contradiction between the architecture and the painting. Later on I came to think that it was a pity the murals were painted in buildings that didn't belong to our century.

INTERVIEWER: What about the curriculum?

PAZ: It was a mélange of the French tradition mixed with American educational theories. John Dewey, the American philosopher, was a big influence. Also the "progressive school" of education.

INTERVIEWER: So the foreign language you studied was French?

PAZ: And English. My father was a political exile during the revolution. He had to leave Mexico and take refuge in the United States. He went ahead and then we joined him in California, in Los Angeles, where we stayed for almost two years. On the first day of school, I had a fight with my American schoolmates. I couldn't speak a word of English, and they laughed because I couldn't say "spoon" during lunch hour. But when I came back to Mexico on my first day of school I had another fight. This time with my Mexican classmates and for the same reason—because I was a foreigner! I discovered I could be a foreigner in both countries.

INTERVIEWER: Were you influenced by any of your teachers in the National Preparatory School?

PAZ: Certainly. I had the chance to study with the Mexican poet Carlos Pellicer. Through him I met other poets of his generation. They opened my eyes to modern poetry. I should point out that my grandfather's library ended at the beginning of the twentieth century, so it wasn't until I was in the National Preparatory School that I learned books were published after 1910. Proust was a revelation for me. I thought no more novels had been written after Zola.

INTERVIEWER: What about poetry in Spanish?

PAZ: I found out about the Spanish poets of the Generation of 1927: García Lorca, Rafael Alberti and Jorge Guillén. I also read Antonio Machado and Juan Ramón Jiménez, who was a patriarch of poetry then. I also read Borges at that time, but remember Borges was not yet a short story writer. During the early thirties he was a poet and an essayist. Naturally, the greatest revelation during that first period of my literary life was the poetry of Pablo Neruda.

INTERVIEWER: You went on to university, but in 1937 you made a momentous decision.

PAZ: Well, I made several. First I went to Yucatán. I finished my university work, but I left before graduating. I refused to become a lawyer. My family, like all Mexican middle-class families at that time, wanted their son to be a doctor or a lawyer. I only wanted to be a poet and also in some way a revolutionary. An opportunity came for me to go to Yucatán to work with some friends in a school for the children of workers and peasants. It was a great experience—it made me realize I was a city boy and that my experience of Mexico was that of central Mexico, the uplands.

INTERVIEWER: So you discovered geography?

PAZ: People who live in cities like New York or Paris are usually provincials with regard to the rest of the country. I discovered Yucatán, a very peculiar province of southern Mexico. It's Mexico, but it's also something very different thanks to the influence of the Mayas. I found out that Mexico has another tradition besides that of central Mexico, another set of roots—the Maya tradition. Yucatán was strangely cosmopolitan. It had links with Cuba and New Orleans. As a matter of fact, during the nineteenth century, people from the Yucatán traveled more often to the United States or Europe than they did to Mexico City. I began to see just how complex Mexico is.

INTERVIEWER: So then you returned to Mexico City and decided to go to the Spanish Civil War?

PAZ: I was invited to a congress, and since I was a great partisan of the Spanish Republic I immediately accepted. I left the Yucatán school and went to Spain, where I stayed for some months. I wanted to enroll in the Spanish Loyalist Army—I was twenty-three—but I couldn't because as a volunteer I would have needed the recommendation of a political party. I wasn't a member of the Communist party or any other party, so there was no one to recommend me. I was rejected, but they told me that was not so important because I was a young writer—I was the youngest at the congress—and that I should go back to Mexico and write for the Spanish Republic. And that is what I did.

INTERVIEWER: What did that trip to Spain mean to you, above and beyond politics and the defense of the Spanish Republic?

PAZ: I discovered another part of my heritage. I was familiar, of course, with the Spanish literary tradition. I have always viewed Spanish literature as my own, but it's one thing to know books and another thing to see the people, the monuments, and the landscape with your own eyes.

INTERVIEWER: So it was a geographical discovery again?

PAZ: Yes, but there was also the political or, to be more precise, the moral aspect. My political and intellectual beliefs were kindled by the idea of fraternity. We all talked a lot about it. For instance, the novels of André Malraux, which we all read, depicted the search for fraternity through revolutionary action. My Spanish experience did not strengthen my political beliefs, but it did give an unexpected twist to my idea of fraternity. One day—Stephen Spender was with me and might remember this episode—we went to the front in Madrid, which was in the university city. It was a battlefield. Sometimes in the same building the loyalists would only be separated from the fascists by a single wall. We could hear the soldiers on the other side talking. It was a strange feeling: those people facing me—I couldn't see them but only hear their voices—were my enemies. But they had human voices, like my own. They were like me.

INTERVIEWER: Did this affect your ability to hate your enemy?

PAZ: Yes. I began to think that perhaps all this fighting was an absurdity, but of course I couldn't say that to anyone. They would have thought I was a traitor, which I wasn't. I understood then, or later, when I could think seriously about that disquieting experience, I understood that real fraternity implies that you must accept the fact that your enemy is also human. I don't mean that you must be a friend to your enemy. No, differences will subsist, but your enemy is also human, and the moment you understand that you can no longer accept violence. For me it was a terrible experience. It shattered many of my deepest convictions.

INTERVIEWER: Do you think that part of the horror of the situation resulted from the fact that the fascist soldiers were speaking your language?

PAZ: Yes. The soldiers on the other side of the wall were laughing and saying, "Give me a cigarette," and things like that. I said to myself, "Well, they are the same as we on this side of the wall."

INTERVIEWER: You didn't go straight back to Mexico, however.

PAZ: Of course not. It was my first trip to Europe. I had to go to Paris. Paris was a museum, it was history, it was the present. Walter Benjamin said Paris was the capital of the nineteenth century, and he was right, but I think Paris was also the capital of the twentieth century, the first part at least. Not that it was the political or economic or philosophic capital, but the artistic capital. For painting and the plastic arts in general but also for literature. Not because the best artists and writers lived in Paris but because of the great movements, right down to surrealism.

INTERVIEWER: What did you see that moved you?

PAZ: I went to the Universal Exposition and saw *Guernica*, which Picasso had just painted. I was twenty-three and had this tremendous opportunity to see the Picassos and Mirós in the Spanish pavilion. I didn't know many people in Paris, and by pure chance I went to an exhibition where I saw a painting by Max Ernst, *Europe after the Rain*, which made a deep impression on me.

INTERVIEWER: What about people?

PAZ: I met a Cuban writer who became very famous later, Alejo Carpentier. He invited me to a party at the house of the surrealist poet Robert Desnos. There was a huge crowd, many of them quite well known—but I didn't know a soul and felt lost. I was very young. Looking around the house, I found some strange objects. I asked the pretty lady of the house what they were. She smiled and told me they were Japanese erotic objects, "godemiches," and everyone laughed at my innocence. I realized just how provincial I was.

INTERVIEWER: You were back in Mexico in 1938. So were André Breton and Trotsky: did their presence mean anything to you?

PAZ: Of course. Politically, I was against Breton and Trotsky. I thought our great enemy was fascism, that Stalin was right, that we had to be united against fascism. Even though Breton and Trotsky were not agents of the Nazis, I was against them. On the other hand, I was fascinated by Trotsky. I secretly read his books, so inside myself I was a heterodox. And I admired Breton. I had read *L'Amour Fou*, a book that really impressed me.

INTERVIEWER: So in addition to Spanish and Spanish-American poetry you plunged into European modernism.

PAZ: Yes, I would say there were three texts that made a mark on me during this period: the first was Eliot's "Waste Land," which I read in Mexico in 1931. I was seventeen or so, and the poem baffled me. I couldn't understand a word. Since then I've read it countless times and still think it one of the great poems of the century. The second text was Saint-John Perse's *Anabase*, and the third was Breton's small book, which exalted free love, poetry and rebellion.

INTERVIEWER: But despite your admiration you wouldn't approach Breton?

PAZ: Once a mutual friend invited me to see him, telling me I was wrong about Breton's politics. I refused. Many years later, I met him and we became good friends. It was then—in spite of being criticized by many of my friends—I read with enthusiasm the *Manifesto for a Revolutionary Independent Art* written by Breton and Trotsky and signed by Diego Rivera. In it Trotsky renounces political control of literature. The only policy the revolutionary state can have with regard to artists and writers is to give them total freedom.

INTERVIEWER: It would seem as though your internal paradox was turning into a crisis.

PAZ: I was against Socialist Realism, and that was the beginning of my conflicts with the Communists. I was not a member of the Communist party, but I was friendly with them. Where we fought first was about the problem of art.

INTERVIEWER: So the exposition of surrealism in Mexico City in 1940 would have been a problem for you.

PAZ: I was the editor of a magazine, *Taller*. In it one of my friends published an article saying the surrealists had opened new vistas, but that they had become the academy of their own revolution. It was a mistake, especially during those years. But we published the article.

INTERVIEWER: Publish or perish.

PAZ: We must accept our mistakes. If we don't, we're lost, don't you think? This interview is in some ways an exercise in public confession—of which I am very much afraid.

INTERVIEWER: Octavio, despite the fact that you are a poet and an essayist, it seems that you have had novelistic temptations. I'm thinking of that "Diary of a Dreamer" you published in 1938 in your magazine *Taller* and *The Monkey Grammarian* of 1970.

PAZ: I wouldn't call that diary novelistic. It was a kind of notebook made up of meditations. I was probably under the spell of Rilke and his *Notebooks of Malte Laurids Brigge*. The truth is that the novel has always been a temptation for me. But perhaps I am not suited to it. The art of the novel unites two different things. It is like epic poetry, a world peopled by characters whose actions are the essence of the work. But, unlike the epic, the novel is analytical. It tells the deeds of the characters and, at the same time, criticizes them. Tom Jones, Odette de Crécy, Ivan Karamazov, or Don Quixote are characters devoured by criticism. You don't find that in Homer or Virgil. Not even in Dante. The epic exalts or condemns; the novel analyzes and criticizes. The epic heroes are one-piece, solid characters; novelistic characters are ambiguous. These two poles, criticism and epic, combine in the novel.

INTERVIEWER: What about *The Monkey Grammarian*?

PAZ: I wouldn't call that a novel. It's on the frontier of the novel. If it's anything, that book is an anti-novel. Whenever I'm tempted to write a novel, I say to myself, "Poets are not novelists." Some poets, like Goethe, have written novels—rather boring ones. I think the poetic genius is synthetic. A poet creates syntheses while the novelist analyzes.

INTERVIEWER: If we could return to Mexico during the war years, I would like to ask you about your relationship with Pablo Neruda, who was sent to Mexico as Consul General of Chile in 1940.

PAZ: As I said earlier, Neruda's poetry was a revelation for me when I started to read modern poetry in the thirties. When I published my first book, I sent a copy to Neruda. He never answered me, but it was he who invited me to the congress in Spain. When I reached Paris in 1937, I knew no one. But just as I was getting off the train, a tall man ran up to me shouting, "Octavio Paz! Octavio Paz!" It was Neruda. Then he said, "Oh you are so young!" and we embraced. He found me a hotel, and we became great friends. He was one of the first to take notice of my poetry and to read it sympathetically.

INTERVIEWER: So what went wrong?

PAZ: When he came to Mexico, I saw him very often, but there were difficulties. First, there was a personal problem. Neruda was very generous, but also very domineering. Perhaps I was too rebellious and jealous of my own independence. He loved to be surrounded by a kind of court made up of people who loved him—sometimes these would be intelligent people but often they were mediocre. The second problem was politics. He became more and more Stalinist, while I became less and less enchanted with Stalin. Finally we fought—almost physically—and stopped speaking to each other. He wrote some not terribly nice things about me, including one nasty poem. I wrote some awful things about him. And that was that.

INTERVIEWER: Was there a reconciliation?

PAZ: For twenty years we didn't speak. We'd sometimes be at the same place at the same time, and I knew he would tell our mutual friends to stop seeing me because I was a "traitor." But then the Khrushchev report about the Stalinist terrors was made public and shattered his beliefs. We happened to be in London at the same poetry festival. I had just remarried, as had Pablo. I was with Marie-José, my wife, when we met Matilde Urrutia, his wife. She said, "If I'm not mistaken, you are Octavio Paz." To which I answered, "Yes, and you are Matilde." Then she said, "Do you want to see Pablo? I think he would love to see you again." We went to Pablo's room, where he was being interviewed by a journalist. As soon as the journalist left, Pablo said, "My son," and embraced me. The expression is very Chilean—"*mijito*"—and he said it with emotion. I was very moved, almost crying. We talked briefly, because he was on his way back to Chile. He sent me a book, I sent him one. And then a few years later, he died. It was sad, but it was one of the best things that has ever happened to me—the possibility to be friends again with a man I liked and admired so very much.

INTERVIEWER: The early forties were clearly difficult times for you, and yet they seem to have forced you to define your own intellectual position.

PAZ: That's true. I was having tremendous political problems, breaking with former friends—Neruda among them. I did make some new friends, like Victor Serge, a Franco-Russian writer, an old revolutionary. But I reached the conclusion that I had to leave my country, exile myself. I was fortunate because I received a Guggenheim Fellowship to go to the United States. On this second visit, I went first to Berkeley and then to New York. I didn't know anyone, had no money, and was actually destitute. But I was really happy. It was one of the best periods of my life.

INTERVIEWER: Why?

PAZ: Well, I discovered the American people, and I was thrilled. It was like breathing deeply and freely while facing a vast space—a feeling of elation, lightness, and confidence. I feel the same way every time I come to your country, but not with the same intensity. It was vivifying just to be in the States in those days, and, at the same time, I could step back from politics and plunge into poetry. I discovered American poetry in Conrad Aiken's *Anthology of Modern American Poetry*. I had already read Eliot, but I knew nothing about William Carlos Williams or Pound or Marianne Moore. I was slightly acquainted with Hart Crane's poetry—he lived his last years in Mexico, but he was more a legend than a body of poetry. While I was in Berkeley, I met Muriel Rukeyser who very generously translated some of my poems. That was a great moment for me. A few years later, she sent them to *Horizon*, which Spender and Cyril Connolly were editing in London, where they were published. For me it was a kind of . . .

INTERVIEWER: Small apotheosis?

PAZ: A very small apotheosis. After New York, where I became a great reader of *Partisan Review*, I went on to Paris and caught up with some friends I'd met in Mexico. Benjamin Péret, for example. Through him, I finally met Breton. We became friends. Surrealism was in decline,

but surrealism for French literary life was something healthy, something vital and rebellious.
INTERVIEWER: What do you mean?
PAZ: The surrealists embodied something the French had forgotten: the other side of reason, love, freedom, poetry. The French have a tendency to be too rationalistic, to reduce everything to ideas and then to fight over them. When I reached Paris, Jean-Paul Sartre was the dominant figure.
INTERVIEWER: But for you existentialism would have been old hat.
PAZ: That's right. In Madrid, the Spanish philosopher Ortega y Gasset—and later his disciples in Mexico City and Buenos Aires—had published all the main texts of phenomenology and existentialism, from Husserl to Heidegger, so Sartre represented more a clever variation than an innovation. Also, I was against Sartre's politics. The one person connected to French existentialism with whom I was friendly and who was very generous to me was Albert Camus. But I must say I was nearer to the surrealist poets.
INTERVIEWER: By the end of the forties you had published two major books, the poems collected in *Freedom on Parole (Libertad bajo palabra)* and *The Labyrinth of Solitude.* I've always been curious about the title of *Freedom on Parole.* Does it have anything to do with the futurist poet Marinetti's "words on leave" *(parole in libertà)?*
PAZ: I'm afraid not. Marinetti wanted to free words from the chains of syntax and grammar, a kind of aesthetic nihilism. *Freedom on Parole* has more to do with morals than aesthetics. I simply wanted to say that human freedom is conditional. In English, when you are let out of jail you're "on parole," and "parole" means speech, word, word of honor. But the condition under which you are free is language, human awareness.
INTERVIEWER: So for you freedom of speech is more than the right to speak your mind?
PAZ: Absolutely. Ever since I was an adolescent I've been intrigued by the mystery of freedom. Because it is a mystery. Freedom depends on the very thing that limits or denies it, fate, God, biological or social determinism, whatever. To carry out its mission, fate counts on the complicity of our freedom, and to be free, we must overcome fate. The dialectics of freedom and fate is the theme of Greek tragedy and Shakespeare, although in Shakespeare fate appears as passion (love,

jealousy, ambition, envy) and as chance. In Spanish theater—especially in Calderón and Tirso de Molina—the mystery of freedom expresses itself in the language of Christian theology: divine providence and free will. The idea of conditional freedom implies the notion of personal responsibility. Each of us, literally, either creates or destroys his own freedom. A freedom that is always precarious. And that brings up the title's poetic or aesthetic meaning: the poem—freedom—stands above an order—language.

INTERVIEWER: You wrote *Freedom on Parole* between 1935 and 1957, more than twenty years. . . .

PAZ: I wrote and rewrote the book many times.

INTERVIEWER: Is it an autobiography?

PAZ: Yes and no. It expresses my aesthetic and personal experiences, from my earliest youth until the beginning of my maturity. I wrote the first poems when I was twenty-one, and I finished the last when I turned forty-three. But the real protagonist of those poems is not Octavio Paz but a half-real, half-mythical figure: the poet. Although that poet was my age, spoke my language, and his vital statistics were identical with my own, he was someone else. A figure, an image derived from tradition. Every poet is the momentary incarnation of that figure.

INTERVIEWER: Doesn't *The Labyrinth of Solitude* also have an autobiographical dimension?

PAZ: Again, yes and no. I wrote *The Labyrinth of Solitude* in Paris. The idea came to me in the United States when I tried to analyze the situation of the Mexicans living in Los Angeles, the *pachucos* or Chicanos as they're called now. I suppose they were a kind of mirror for me—the autobiographical dimension you like to see. That on one side. But there is also the relationship between Mexico and the United States. If there are two countries in the world that are different, they are the United States and Mexico. But we are condemned to live together forever. So we should try to understand each other and also to know ourselves. That was how *The Labyrinth of Solitude* began.

INTERVIEWER: That book deals with ideas such as difference, resentment, the hermetic nature of Mexican man, but it doesn't touch on the life of the poet.

PAZ: True. I tried to deal with that subject in a short essay called "Poetry of Solitude and Poetry of Communion." That article in some ways is the poetic equivalent to *The Labyrinth of Solitude* because it presents my vision of man, which is very simple. There are two situations for every human being. The first is the solitude we feel when we are born. Our first situation is that of orphanhood, and it is only later that we discover the opposite, filial attachment. The second is that because we are thrown, as Heidegger says, into this world, we feel we must find what the Buddhists call "the other share." This is the thirst for community. I think philosophy and religion derive from this original situation or predicament. Every country and every individual tries to resolve it in different ways. Poetry is a bridge between solitude and communion. Communion, even for a mystic like Saint John of the Cross, can never be absolute.

INTERVIEWER: Is this why the language of mysticism is so erotic?

PAZ: Yes, because lovers, which is what the mystics are, constitute the greatest image of communion. But even between lovers solitude is never completely abolished. Conversely, solitude is never absolute. We are always with someone, even if it is only our shadow. We are never one—we are always "we." These extremes are the poles of human life.

INTERVIEWER: All in all, you spent some eight years abroad, first in the United States, then in Paris, and then in the Mexican diplomatic service. How do you view those years in the context of your career as a poet?

PAZ: Actually, I spent nine years abroad. If you count each of those years as a month, you'll find that those nine years were nine months which I lived in the womb of time. The years I lived in San Francisco, New York, and Paris were a period of gestation. I was reborn, and the man who came back to Mexico at the end of 1952 was a different poet, a different writer. If I had stayed in Mexico, I probably would have drowned in journalism, bureaucracy, or alcohol. I ran away from that world and also, perhaps, from myself.

INTERVIEWER: But you were hardly greeted as the prodigal son when you reappeared. . . .

PAZ: I wasn't accepted at all, except by a few young people. I had broken with the predominant aesthetic, moral, and political ideas and was instantly attacked by many people who were all too sure of their dogmas and prejudices. It was the beginning of a disagreement which has still not come to an end. It isn't simply an ideological difference of opinion. Certainly those polemics have been bitter and hard-fought, but even that does not explain the malevolence of some people, the pettiness of others, and the reticence of the majority. I've experienced despair and rage, but I've just had to shrug my shoulders and move forward. Now I see those quarrels as a blessing: if a writer is accepted, he'll soon be rejected or forgotten. I didn't set out to be a troublesome writer, but if that's what I've been, I am totally unrepentant.

INTERVIEWER: You left Mexico again in 1959.

PAZ: And I didn't come back until 1971. An absence of twelve years —another symbolic number. I returned because Mexico has always been a magnet I can't resist, a real passion, alternately happy and wretched like all passions.

INTERVIEWER: Tell me about those twelve years. First you went back to Paris, then to India as the Mexican ambassador, and later to England and the United States.

PAZ: When I'd finished the definitive version of *Freedom on Parole*, I felt I could start over. I explored new poetic worlds, knew other countries, lived other sentiments, had other ideas. The first and greatest of my new experiences was India. Another geography, another humanity, other gods—a different kind of civilization. I lived there for just over six years. I traveled around the subcontinent quite a bit and lived for periods in Ceylon and Afghanistan—two more geographical and cultural extremes. If I had to express my vision of India in a single image, I would say that I see an immense plain: in the distance, white, ruinous architecture, a powerful river, a huge tree and in its shade a shape (a beggar, a Buddha, a pile of stones?). Out from among the knots and forks of the tree, a woman arises. . . . I fell in love and got married in India.

INTERVIEWER: When did you become seriously interested in Asian thought?

PAZ: Starting with my first trip to the East in 1952—I spent almost a year in India and Japan—I made small incursions into the philosophic and artistic traditions of those countries. I visited many places and read some of the classics of Indian thought. Most important to me were the poets and philosophers of China and Japan. During my second stay in India, between 1962 and 1968, I read many of the great philosophic and religious texts. Buddhism impressed me profoundly.

INTERVIEWER: Did you think of converting?

PAZ: No, but studying Buddhism was a mental and spiritual exercise that helped me begin to doubt the ego and its mirages. Ego worship is the greatest idolatry of modern man. Buddhism for me is a criticism of the ego and of reality. A radical criticism that does not end in negation but in acceptance. All the great Buddhist sanctuaries in India (the Hindu sanctuaries as well, but those, perhaps because they're later, are more baroque and elaborate) contain highly sensual sculptures and reliefs. A powerful but peaceful sexuality. I was shocked to find that exaltation of the body and of natural powers in a religious and philosophic tradition that disparages the world and preaches negation and emptiness. That became the central theme of a short book I wrote during those years, *Conjunctions and Disjunctions*.

INTERVIEWER: Was it hard to balance being Mexican ambassador to India with your explorations of India?

PAZ: My ambassadorial work was not arduous. I had time, I could travel and write. And not only about India. The student movements of 1968 fascinated me. In a certain way I felt the hopes and aspirations of my own youth were being reborn. I never thought it would lead to a revolutionary transformation of society, but I did realize that I was witnessing the appearance of a new sensibility that in some fashion *rhymed* with what I had felt and thought before.

INTERVIEWER: You felt that history was repeating itself?

PAZ: In a way. The similarity between some of the attitudes of the 1968 students and the surrealist poets, for example, was clear to see. I thought William Blake would have been sympathetic to both the words and the actions of those young people. The student movement in Mexico was more ideological than in France or the United States, but it too had legitimate aspirations. The Mexican political system, born out of the Revolution, had survived but was suffering a kind of historical arteriosclerosis. On October 2, 1968, the Mexican government decided to use violence to suppress the student movement. It was a brutal action. I felt I could not go on serving the government, so I left the diplomatic corps.

INTERVIEWER: You went to Paris and then to the United States before spending that year at Cambridge.

PAZ: Yes, and during those months I reflected on the recent history of Mexico. The Revolution began in 1910 with great democratic ambitions. More than half a century later, the nation was controlled by a paternalistic, authoritarian party. So in 1969 I wrote a postscript to *The*

*Labyrinth of Solitude*, a "critique of the pyramid," which I took to be the symbolic form of Mexican authoritarianism. I stated that the only way of getting beyond the political and historical crisis we were living through—the paralysis of the institutions created by the Revolution—was to begin democratic reform.

INTERVIEWER: But that was not necessarily what the student movement was seeking.

PAZ: No. The student leaders and the left-wing political groups favored violent social revolution. They were under the influence of the Cuban Revolution—and there are still some who defend Fidel Castro even today. My point of view put me in opposition, simultaneously, to the government and the left. The "progressive" intellectuals, almost all of whom wanted to establish a totalitarian socialist regime, attacked me vehemently. I fought back. Rather, *we* fought back: A small group of younger writers agreed with some of my opinions. We all believed in a peaceful, gradual move toward democracy. We founded *Plural*, a magazine that would combine literature, art, and political criticism. There was a crisis, so we founded another, *Vuelta* ("Return"), which is still going strong and has a faithful, demanding readership. Mexico has changed, and now most of our old enemies say they are democratic. We are living through a transition to democracy, one that will have its setbacks and will seem too slow for some.

INTERVIEWER: Do you see yourself as part of a long line of Latin American statesmen-writers, one that could include Argentina's Sarmiento in the nineteenth and Neruda in the twentieth century?

PAZ: I don't think of myself as a "statesman-poet," and I'm not really comparable to Sarmiento or Neruda. Sarmiento was a real statesman and a great political figure in addition to being a great writer. Neruda was a poet, a great poet. He joined the Communist party, but for generous, semi-religious reasons. It was a real conversion. So his political militance was not that of an intellectual but of a believer. Within the Party, he seems to have been a political pragmatist, but, again, he was more like one of the faithful than a critical intellectual. As for me, well, I've never been a member of any political party, and I've never run for public office. I have been a political and social critic, but always from the marginal position of an independent writer. I'm not a joiner, although of course I've had and have my personal preferences. I'm different from Mario Vargas Llosa, who did decide to intervene directly in his country's politics. Vargas Llosa is like Havel in Czechoslovakia or Malraux in France after World War II.

INTERVIEWER: But it is almost impossible to separate politics from literature or any aspect of culture.

PAZ: Since the Enlightenment, there has been a constant confluence of literature, philosophy, and politics. In the English-speaking world you have Milton as an antecedent as well as the great Romantics in the nineteenth century. In the twentieth century, there are many examples. Eliot, for instance, was never an active participant in politics, but his writing is an impassioned defense of traditional values, values that have a political dimension. I mention Eliot, whose beliefs are totally different from my own, simply because he too was an independent writer who joined no party. I consider myself a private person, although I reserve the right to have opinions and to write about matters that affect my country and my contemporaries. When I was young, I fought against Nazi totalitarianism and later on against the Soviet dictatorship. I don't regret either struggle in the slightest.

INTERVIEWER: Thinking about your time in India now and its effect on your poetry, what would you say about the influence of India?

PAZ: If I hadn't lived in India, I could not have written *Blanco* or most of the poems in *Eastern Slope*. The time I spent in Asia was a huge pause, as if time had slowed down and space had become larger. In a few rare moments, I experienced those states of being in which we are at one with the world around us, when the doors of time seem to open, if only slightly. We all live those instants in our childhood, but modern life rarely allows us to reexperience them when we're adults. As regards my poetry, that period begins with *Salamander*, culminates in *Eastern Slope*, and ends with *The Monkey Grammarian*.

INTERVIEWER: But didn't you write *The Monkey Grammarian* in 1970, the year you spent at Cambridge University?

PAZ: I did. It was my farewell to India. That year in England also changed me. Especially because of what we must necessarily refer to as English "civility," which includes the cultivation of eccentricity. That taught me not only to respect my fellow man but trees, plants, and birds as well. I also read certain poets. Thanks to Charles Tomlinson, I discovered Wordsworth. *The Prelude* became one of my favorite books. There may be echoes of it in A *Draft of Shadows*.

INTERVIEWER: Do you have a schedule for writing?

PAZ: I've never been able to maintain a fixed schedule. For years, I wrote in my few free hours. I was quite poor and from an early age had to hold down several jobs to eke out a living. I was a minor employee in the National Archive; I worked in a bank; I was a journalist; I finally found a comfortable but busy post in the diplomatic service, but none of those jobs had any real effect on my work as a poet.

INTERVIEWER: Do you have to be in any specific place in order to write?

PAZ: A novelist needs his typewriter, but you can write poetry any time, anywhere. Sometimes I mentally compose a poem on a bus or walking down the street. The rhythm of walking helps me fix the verses. Then when I get home, I write it all down. For a long time when I was younger, I wrote at night. It's quieter, more tranquil. But writing at night also magnifies the writer's solitude. Nowadays I write during the late morning and into the afternoon. It's a pleasure to finish a page when night falls.

INTERVIEWER: Your work never distracted you from your writing?

PAZ: No, but let me give you an example. Once I had a totally infernal job in the National Banking Commission (how I got it, I can't guess) which consisted in counting packets of old banknotes already sealed and ready to be burned. I had to make sure each packet contained the requisite three thousand pesos. I almost always had one banknote too many or too few—they were always fives—so I decided to give up counting them and to use those long hours to compose a series of sonnets in my head. Rhyme helped me retain the verses in my memory, but not having paper and pencil made my task much more difficult. I've always admired Milton for dictating long passages from *Paradise Lost* to his daughters. Unrhymed passages at that!

INTERVIEWER: Is it the same when you write prose?

PAZ: Prose is another matter. You have to write it in a quiet, isolated place, even if that happens to be the bathroom. But above all to write it's essential to have one or two dictionaries at hand. The telephone is the writer's devil, the dictionary his guardian angel. I used to type, but now I write everything in longhand. If it's prose, I write it out one, two, or three times and then dictate it into a tape recorder. My secretary types it out, and I correct it. Poetry I write and rewrite constantly.

INTERVIEWER: What is the inspiration or starting-point for a poem? Can you give an example of how the process works?

PAZ: Each poem is different. Often the first line is a gift, I don't know if from the gods or from that mysterious faculty called inspiration. Let me use *Sun Stone* as an example: I wrote the first thirty verses as if someone were silently dictating them to me. I was surprised at the fluidity with which those hendecasyllabic lines appeared one after another. They came from far off and from nearby, from within my own chest. Suddenly the current stopped flowing. I read what I'd written: I didn't have to change a thing. But it was only a beginning, and I had no idea where those lines were going. A few days later, I tried to get started again, not in a passive way but trying to orient and direct the flow of verses. I wrote another thirty or forty lines. I stopped. I went back to it a few days later and, little by little, I began to discover the theme of the poem and where it was all heading.

INTERVIEWER: A figure began to appear in the carpet?

PAZ: It was a kind of review of my life, a resurrection of my experiences, my concerns, my failures, my obsessions. I realized I was living the end of my youth and that the poem was simultaneously an end and a new beginning. When I reached a certain point, the verbal current stopped, and all I could do was repeat the first verses. That is the source of the poem's circular form. There was nothing arbitrary about it. *Sun Stone* is the last poem in the book that gathers together the first period of my poetry: *Freedom on Parole* (1935–1957). Even though I didn't know what I would write after that, I was sure that one period of my life and my poetry had ended, and another was beginning.

INTERVIEWER: But the title seems to allude to the cyclical Aztec concept of time.

PAZ: While I was writing the poem, I was reading an archeological essay about the Aztec calendar, and it occurred to me to call the poem *Sun Stone*. I added or cut—I don't remember which—three or four lines so that the poem would coincide with the 584 days of the conjunction of Venus with the Sun. But the time of my poem is not the ritual time of Aztec cosmogony but human, biographical time, which is linear.

INTERVIEWER: But you thought seriously enough about the numerical symbolism of 584 to limit the number of verses in the poem to that number.

PAZ: I confess that I have been and am still fond of numerological combinations. Other poems of mine are also built around certain numerical proportions. It isn't an eccentricity, but a part of the Western tradition. Dante is the best example. *Blanco*, however, was completely different from *Sun Stone*. First I had the *idea* for the poem. I made notes and even drew some diagrams which were inspired, more or less, by Tibetan mandalas. I conceived it as a spatial poem which would correspond to the four points on the compass, the four primary colors, etc. It was difficult because poetry is a temporal art. As if to prove it, the words themselves wouldn't come. I had to call them and, even though it may seem I'm exaggerating, *invoke* them. One day, I wrote the first lines. As was to be expected they were about words, how they appear and disappear. After those first ten lines, the poem began to flow with relative ease. Of course, there were, as usual, anguishing periods of sterility followed by others of fluidity. The architecture of *Blanco* is more sharply defined than that of *Sun Stone*, more complex, richer.

INTERVIEWER: So you defy Edgar Allan Poe's injunction against the long poem?

PAZ: With great relish. I've written other long poems, like *A Draft of Shadows* and *Carta de creencia*, which means "letter of faith." The first is the monologue of memory and its inventions—memory changes and recreates the past as it revives it. In that way, it transforms the past into the present, into presence. *Carta de creencia* is a cantata where different voices converge. But, like *Sun Stone*, it's still a linear composition.

INTERVIEWER: When you write a long poem, do you see yourself as part of an ancient tradition?

PAZ: The long poem in modern times is very different from what it was in antiquity. Ancient poems, epics or allegories, contain a good deal of stuffing. The genre allowed and even demanded it. But the modern long poem tolerates neither stuffing nor transitions, for several reasons. First, with inevitable exceptions like Pound's *Cantos*, because our long poems are simply not as long as those of the ancients. Second, because our long poems contain two antithetical qualities: the *development* of the long poem and the *intensity* of the short poem. It's very difficult to manage. Actually, it's a new genre. And that's why I admire Eliot: his long poems have the same intensity and concentration as short poems.

INTERVIEWER: Is the process of writing enjoyable or frustrating?

PAZ: Writing is a painful process that requires huge effort and sleepless nights. In addition to the threat of writer's block, there is always the sensation that failure is inevitable. Nothing we write is what we wish we could write. Writing is a curse. The worst part of it is the anguish that precedes the act of writing—the hours, days, or months when we search in vain for the phrase that turns the spigot that makes the water flow. Once that first phrase is written, everything changes: the process is enthralling, vital, and enriching, no matter what the final result is. Writing is a blessing!

INTERVIEWER: How and why does an idea seize you? How do you decide if it is prose or poetry?

PAZ: I don't have any hard-and-fast rules for this. For prose, it would seem that the idea comes first, followed by a desire to develop the idea. Often, of course, the original idea changes, but even so the essential fact remains the same: prose is a means, an instrument. But in the case of poetry, the poet becomes the instrument. Whose? It's hard to say. Perhaps language. I don't mean automatic writing. For me, the poem is a *premeditated* act. But poetry flows from a psychic well related to language, that is, related to the culture and memory of a people. An ancient, impersonal spring intimately linked to verbal rhythm.

INTERVIEWER: But doesn't prose have a rhythm as well?

PAZ: Prose does have a rhythm, but that rhythm is not its constitutive element as it is in poetry. Let's not confuse metrics with rhythm: meter may be a manifestation of rhythm, but it is different because it has become mechanical. Which is why, as Eliot suggests, from time to time meter has to return to spoken, everyday language, which is to say, to the original rhythms every language has.

INTERVIEWER: Verse and prose are, therefore, separate entities?

PAZ: Rhythm links verse to prose: one enriches the other. The reason why Whitman was so seductive was precisely because of his surprising fusion of prose and poetry. A fusion produced by rhythm. The prose poem is another example, although its powers are more limited. Of course, being prosaic in poetry can be disastrous, as we see in so many inept poems in "free verse" every day. As to the influence of poetry on prose—just think about Chateaubriand, Nerval, or Proust. In Joyce, the boundary between prose and poetry sometimes completely disappears.

INTERVIEWER: Can you always keep that boundary sharp?

PAZ: I try to keep them separate, but it doesn't always work. A prose piece, without my having to think about it, can become a poem. But I've never had a poem turn into an essay or a story. In some books—*Eagle or Sun?* and *The Monkey Grammarian*—I've tried to bring the prose right up to the border with poetry, I don't know with how much success.

INTERVIEWER: We've talked about premeditation and revision: how does inspiration relate to them?

PAZ: Inspiration and premeditation are two phases in the same process. Premeditation needs inspiration and vice-versa. It's like a river: the water can only flow between the two banks that contain it. Without premeditation, inspiration just scatters. But the role of premeditation—even in a reflexive genre like the essay—is limited. As you write, the text becomes autonomous, changes, and somehow forces you to follow it. The text always separates itself from the author.

INTERVIEWER: Then why revise?

PAZ: Insecurity. No doubt about it. Also a senseless desire for perfection. I said that all texts have their own life, independent of the author. The poem doesn't express the poet. It expresses poetry. That's why it is legitimate to revise and correct a poem. Yes, and at the same time respect the poet who wrote it. I mean the poet, not the man we were then. I was that poet, but I was also someone else—that figure we talked about earlier. The poet is at the service of his poems.

INTERVIEWER: But just how much revising do you do? Do you ever feel a work is complete, or is it abandoned?

PAZ: I revise incessantly. Some critics say too much, and they may be right. But if there's a danger in revising, there is much more danger in not revising. I believe in inspiration, but I also believe that we've got to help inspiration, restrain it and even contradict it.

INTERVIEWER: Thinking again on the relationship between inspiration and revision, did you ever attempt the kind of automatic writing the surrealists recommended in the first surrealist manifesto?

PAZ: I did experiment with "automatic writing." It's very hard to do. Actually, it's *impossible*. No one can write with his mind blank, not thinking about what he's writing. Only God could write a real automatic poem because only for God are speaking, thinking, and acting the same thing. If God says, "A horse!" a horse immediately appears. But a poet has to *reinvent* his horse, that is, his poem. He has to think it, and he has to make it. All the automatic poems I wrote during the time of my friendship with the surrealists were thought and written with a certain deliberation. I wrote those poems with my eyes open.

INTERVIEWER: Do you think Breton was serious when he advocated automatic writing?

PAZ: Perhaps he was. I was extremely fond of André Breton, really admired him. It's no exaggeration to say he was a solar figure because his friendship emitted light and heat. Shortly after I met him, he asked me for a poem for a surrealist magazine. I gave him a prose poem, "*Mariposa de obsidiana*"—it alludes to a pre-Columbian goddess. He read it over several times, liked it, and decided to publish it. But he pointed out one line that seemed weak. I reread the poem, discovered he was right, and removed the phrase. He was charmed, but I was confused. So I asked him, "What about automatic writing?" He raised his leonine head and answered without changing expression: "That line was a journalistic intromission. . . ."

INTERVIEWER: It's curious, Octavio, how often a tension allows you to find your own special place—the United States and Mexico, the *pachuco* and Anglo-American society, solitude and communion, poetry and prose. Do you yourself see a tension between your essays and your poetry?

PAZ: If I start to write, the thing I love to write most, the thing I love most to create, is poetry. I would much rather be remembered for two or three short poems in some anthology than as an essayist. However, since I am a modern and live in a century that believes in reason and explanation, I find I am in a tradition of poets who in one way or another have written defenses of poetry. Just think of the Renaissance and then again of the Romantics—Shelley, Wordsworth in the preface to *Lyrical Ballads*. Well, now that I'm at the end of my career, I want to do two things: to keep on writing poetry and to write another defense of poetry.

INTERVIEWER: What will it say?

PAZ: I've just written a book, *The Other Voice*, about the situation of poetry in the twentieth century. When I was young, my great idols were poets and not novelists—even though I admired novelists like Proust or Lawrence. Eliot was one of my idols, but so were Valéry and Apollinaire. But poetry today is like a secret cult whose rites are celebrated in the catacombs, on the fringes of society. Consumer society and commercial publishers pay little attention to poetry. I think this is one of society's diseases. I don't think we can have a good society if we don't also have good poetry. I'm sure of it.

INTERVIEWER: Television is being criticized as the ruination of twentieth-century life, but you have the unique opinion that television will be good for poetry as a return to the oral tradition.

PAZ: Poetry existed before writing. Essentially, it is a verbal art, that enters us not only through our eyes and understanding but through our ears as well. Poetry is something spoken and heard. It's also something we see and write. In that we see the importance in the Oriental and Asian traditions of calligraphy. In the West, in modern times, typography has also been important—the maximum example in this would be Mallarmé. In television, the aural aspect of poetry can join with the visual and with the idea of movement—something books don't have. Let me explain: this is a barely explored possibility. So I'm not saying television *will* mean poetry's return to an oral tradition but that it *could* be the beginning of a tradition in which writing, sound, and images will unite. Poetry always uses all the means of communication the age offers it: musical instruments, printing, radio, records. Why shouldn't it try television? We've got to take a chance.

INTERVIEWER: Will the poet always be the permanent dissident?

PAZ: Yes. We have all won a great battle in the defeat of the Communist bureaucracies by themselves—and that's the important thing: they were defeated by themselves and not by the West. But that's not enough. We need more social justice. Free-market societies produce unjust and very stupid societies. I don't believe that the production and consumption of things can be the meaning of human life. All great religions and philosophies say that human beings are more than producers and consumers. We cannot reduce our lives to economics. If a society without social justice is not a good society, a society without poetry is a society without dreams, without words, and, most importantly, without that bridge between one person and another that poetry is. We are different from the other animals because we can talk, and the supreme form of language is poetry. If society abolishes poetry it commits spiritual suicide.

INTERVIEWER: Is your extensive critical study of the seventeenth-century Mexican nun Sor Juana Inés de la Cruz a kind of projection of the present onto the past?

PAZ: In part, but I also wanted to recover a figure I consider essential not only for Mexicans but for all of the Americas. At first, Sor Juana was buried and forgotten; then she was disinterred and mummified. I wanted to bring her back into the light of day, free her from the wax museum. She's alive and has a great deal to tell us. She was a great poet, the first in a long line of great Latin American women poets—let's not forget that Gabriela Mistral from Chile was the first Latin American writer to win the Nobel Prize. Sor Juana was also an intellectual of the first rank (which we can't say for Emily Dickinson) and a defender of women's rights. She was put on a pedestal and praised, then persecuted and humiliated. I just had to write about her.

INTERVIEWER: Finally, whither Octavio Paz? Where do you go from here?

PAZ: Where? I asked myself that question when I was twenty, again when I was thirty, again when I was forty, fifty . . . I could never answer it. Now I know something: I have to persist. That means live, write and face, like everyone else, the other side of every life—the unknown.

ALFRED MACADAM
October 1990

# 5. Walker Percy

As one of America's foremost novelists, Percy likened his role to that of "the canary the coal miners used to take down into the shaft with them to test the air." His books—*The Moviegoer* (1961, winner of the National Book Award), *The Last Gentleman* (1966, nominated for the National Book Award), *Love in the Ruins* (1971, National Catholic Book Award for fiction), *Lancelot* (1977), *The Second Coming* (1980, winner of the *Los Angeles Times* Book Prize for fiction), and *The Thanatos Syndrome* (1987), as well as a book of nonfiction, *Lost in the Cosmos* (1983) and a collection of essays, *The Message in the Bottle* (1975)—reflect that sense of prophetic mission.

Born in Alabama in 1916 and raised by his adoptive father, the poet and memoirist William Alexander Percy, Percy grew up more interested in science than in writing. He originally intended to become a doctor, but after his studies at Columbia Medical School were halted by his contracting tuberculosis, he turned elsewhere. He never abandoned his interest in the sciences, particularly psychiatry, but during his long convalescence he began a study of philosophy, coming to realize, he said, that the individual "will be left out of even the most rigorous scientific formulation."

Percy was a member of the National Institute of Arts and Letters and a fellow of the American Academy of Arts and Sciences. He received the University of Notre Dame's 1989 Laetare Medal and was the only American ever to receive the T. S. Eliot Award. Percy died on May 10, 1990, in Louisiana. *Signposts in a Strange Land*, a collection of his previously uncollected essays on a variety of topics, from language and literature to religion and philosophy, was published by Farrar, Straus & Giroux in July 1991.

I Thanatos—

For some time now I have noticed that something strange is occurring in our region. I have noticed it both in the patients I have treated and in ordinary encounters with people. At first there were only suspicions. But yesterday my suspicions were confirmed. I was called to the hospital for a consultation and there was an opportunity to make an examination.

It began with little things, certain small clinical changes which I

*A manuscript page from Walker Percy's novel* The Thanatos Syndrome. *In Greek mythology, Thanatos was Death represented as a person and was the twin brother of Hypnos (Sleep).*

# Walker Percy

*This interview was conducted by mail, from May to October 1986, at an enormous geographical distance; but the interviewer does cherish the memory of a personal meeting. It was on May 4, 1973, a warm Louisiana evening, at Percy's home in Covington, a small town at the northern end of the causeway running above Lake Pontchartrain (New Orleans is at the southern end). The house is in a wooded area by the bayou, along the Bogue Falaya River. Percy was a tall, slender, handsome man, with a distinguished and thoughtful mien. His manner that day was unassuming, gracious, and gentle. Even later, judging from our correspondence, he was still the same warm, helpful, generous, and patient person, as the very existence of this interview, carried out under such difficult circumstances, will testify.*

INTERVIEWER: How did you spend your seventieth birthday?
WALKER PERCY: An ordinary day. I went with my wife and some friends to a neighborhood restaurant in New Orleans. I think I had crawfish. What distinguishes Louisianians is that they suck the heads.

INTERVIEWER: You and your wife recently celebrated your fortieth anniversary. Is it easy, do you imagine, to be married to a writer?

PERCY: Mine has been a happy marriage—thanks mainly to my wife. Who would want to live with a novelist? A man underfoot in the house all day? A man, moreover, subject to solitary funks and strange elations. If I were a woman, I'd prefer a traveling salesman. There is no secret, or rather the secrets are buried in platitudes. That is to say, it has something to do with love, commitment, and family. As to the institution, it is something like Churchill's description of democracy: vicissitudinous yes, but look at the alternatives.

INTERVIEWER: What are the decisive moments, turning points that you regard as the milestones of those seven decades?

PERCY: What comes to mind is something like this: one, losing both parents in my early teens and being adopted by my uncle, a poet, and being exposed to the full force of a remarkable literary imagination; two, contracting a non-fatal case of tuberculosis while serving as an intern in Bellevue Hospital in New York, an event which did not so much change my life as give me leave to change it; three, getting married; four, becoming a Catholic.

INTERVIEWER: If you had the chance, would you decide to be reborn or to flee back into William Blake's "the vales of Har"?

PERCY: No vales of Har, thank you. No rebirth either, but I wouldn't mind a visit in the year 2050—a short visit, not more than half an hour—say, to a park bench at the southeast corner of Central Park in New York, with a portable radio. Just to have a look around, just to see whether we made it and if so, in what style. One could tell in half an hour. By "we" of course, I do not mean just Americans, but the species. *Homo sapiens sapiens*.

INTERVIEWER: Once you said that if you were starting over, you might like to make films. Would there be other decisions that would be different?

PERCY: I might study linguistics—not in the current academic meanings of the word, but with a fresh eye, like Newton watching the falling apple: How come? What's going on here?

INTERVIEWER: Apropos of your fascination with film, most of it finds its way into your novels on the thematic level, especially in *The Moviegoer* and *Lancelot*. Does it happen that film or television influences you in less noticeable ways as well, such as cinematic structuring of material and so on?

PERCY: I can only answer in the most general way: that what television and movies give the writer is a new community and a new set of referents. Since nearly everyone watches television a certain number of hours a day (whether they admit it or not), certain turns of plot are ready-made for satirical use, namely the Western shoot-out, one man calling another out, a mythical dance of honor. In my last novel I described one character as looking something like Blake Carrington. Now you may not know who Blake Carrington is—though sooner or later most Hungarians will. A hundred million Americans do know.*

INTERVIEWER: Could you tell me how you feel about your inspiring beliefs, how faithful you have remained to them?

PERCY: If you mean, am I still a Catholic, the answer is yes. The main difference after thirty-five years is that my belief is less self-conscious, less ideological, less polemical. My ideal is Thomas More, an English Catholic—a peculiar breed nowadays—who wore his faith with grace, merriment, and a certain wryness. Incidentally, I reincarnated him again in my new novel and I'm sorry to say he has fallen upon hard times; he is a far cry from the saint, drinks too much, and watches reruns of *M*A*S*H* on TV.

INTERVIEWER: As for philosophy and religion, do you still regard yourself as a philosophical Catholic existentialist?

PERCY: Philosophical? Existentialist? Religion? Pretty heavy. These are perfectly good words—except perhaps "existentialist"—but over the years they have acquired barnacle-like connotative excrescences. Uttering them induces a certain dreariness and heaviness in the neck muscles. As for "existentialist," I'm not sure it presently has a sufficiently clear referent to be of use. Even "existentialists" forswear the term. It fell into disuse some years ago when certain novelists began saying things like: I beat up my wife in an existential moment—meaning a sudden, irrational impulse.

INTERVIEWER: Is it possible to define your Catholic existentialism in a few sentences?

PERCY: I suppose I would prefer to describe it as a certain view of man, an anthropology, if you like; of man as wayfarer, in a rather conscious contrast to prevailing views of man as organism, as encultured creature, as consumer, Marxist, as subject to such and such a scientific or psy-

* He is John Forsythe's character in the television series *Dynasty*.

chological understanding—all of which he is, but not entirely. It is the "not entirely" I'm interested in—like the man Kierkegaard described who read Hegel, understood himself and the universe perfectly by noon, but then had the problem of living out the rest of the day. It, my "anthropology," has been expressed better in an earlier, more traditional language—e.g., scriptural: man born to trouble as the sparks fly up; Gabriel Marcel's *Homo viator*.

INTERVIEWER: You converted to Catholicism in the 1940s. What was the motive behind that decision?

PERCY: There are several ways to answer the question. One is theological. The technical theological term is grace, the gratuitous unmerited gift from God. Another answer is less theological: what else is there? Did you expect me to become a Methodist? A Buddhist? A Marxist? A comfortable avuncular humanist like Walter Cronkite? An exhibitionist like Allen Ginsberg? A proper literary-philosophical-existentialist answer is that the occasion was the reading of Kierkegaard's extraordinary essay: "On the Difference Between a Genius and an Apostle." Like the readings that mean most to you, what it did was to confirm something I suspected but that it took Sören Kierkegaard to put into words: that what the greatest geniuses in science, literature, art, philosophy utter are sentences which convey truths *sub specie aeternitatis*, that is to say, sentences which can be confirmed by appropriate methods and by anyone, anywhere, any time. But only the apostle can utter sentences which can be accepted on the authority of the apostle, that is, his credentials, sobriety, trustworthiness as a newsbearer. These sentences convey not knowledge *sub specie aeternitatis* but news.

INTERVIEWER: I noticed that you rarely refer to other converted novelists like Graham Greene and Evelyn Waugh when discussing your ideas. Or if you do, it is rarely, if ever, in this context.

PERCY: Maybe it's because novelists don't talk much about each other. Maybe this is because novelists secrete a certain B.O. which only other novelists detect, like certain buzzards who emit a repellent pheromone detectable only by other buzzards, which is to say that only a novelist can know how neurotic, devious, underhanded a novelist can be. Actually I have the greatest admiration for both writers, not necessarily for their religion, but for their consummate craft.

INTERVIEWER: Can we discuss the "losangelized" and re-Christianized New South? Is there anything new in the way the South is developing in the 1980s or in the way you read the South or your own relation to it?

PERCY: The odd thing I've noticed is that while of course the South is more and more indistinguishable from the rest of the country (Atlanta, for example, which has become one of the three or four megalopolises of the U.S., is in fact, I'm told by blacks, their favorite American city), the fact is that as Faulkner said fifty years ago, as soon as you cross the Mason-Dixon Line, you still know it. This, after fifty years of listening to the same radio and watching millions of hours of *Barnaby Jones*. I don't know whether it's the heat or a certain lingering civility but people will slow down on interstates to let you get in traffic. Strangers speak in post offices, hold doors for each other without being thought queer or running a con game or making a sexual advance. I could have killed the last cab driver I had in New York. Ask Eudora Welty, she was in the same cab.

INTERVIEWER: Have your views concerning being a writer in the South undergone a change during the past decades? Is being a writer in the South in 1987 the same as it was when you started to write?

PERCY: Southern writers—that's the question everybody asks. I still don't know the answer. All I know is that there is still something about living in the South which turns one inward, makes one secretive, sly, and scheming, makes one capable of a degree of malice, humor, and outrageousness. At any rate, despite the losangelization of the South there are right here, in the New Orleans area, perhaps half a dozen very promising young writers—which is more than can be said of Los Angeles. It comes, not from the famous storytelling gregariousness one hears about, but from the shy, sly young woman, say, who watches, listens, gets a fill of it, and slips off to do a number on it. And it comes, not from having arrived at last in the Great American Mainstream along with the likes of Emerson and Sandburg, but from being close enough to have a good look at one's fellow Americans, fellow Southerners, yet keep a certain wary distance, enough to nourish a secret, subversive conviction: I can do a number on those guys—and on me—and it will be good for all of us.

INTERVIEWER: Apropos of Southern writing, does regionalism still apply?

PERCY: Sure, in the better sense of the word, in the sense that Chekhov and Flaubert and Mark Twain are regionalists—not in the sense that Joel Chandler Harris and Bret Harte were regionalists.

INTERVIEWER: You studied science at Chapel Hill and became a medical doctor at Columbia. In your recently published essay "The Diagnostic Novel" you suggest that serious art is "just as cognitive" as science is and "the serious novelist is quite as much concerned with discovering reality as a serious physicist." Art explores reality in a way which "cannot be done any other way." What are some of the ways that are specific to artistic as opposed to scientific exploration of reality?

PERCY: The most commonplace example of the cognitive dimension in fiction is the reader's recognition —sometimes the shock of recognition—the "verification" of a sector of reality which he had known but not known that he had known. I think of letters I get from readers which may refer to a certain scene and say, in effect, yes! that's the way it is! For example, Binx in *The Moviegoer* describes one moviegoing experience, going to see *Panic in the Streets*, a film shot in New Orleans, going to a movie theater in the very neighborhood where the same scenes in the movie were filmed. Binx tells his girlfriend Kate about his reasons for enjoying the film—that it, the film, "certifies" the reality of the neighborhood in a peculiar sense in which the direct experience of the neighborhood, living in the neighborhood, does not. I have heard from many readers about this and other such scenes—as have other novelists, I'm sure—saying they *know* exactly what Binx is talking about. I think it is reasonable to call such a transaction cognitive, sciencing. This sort of sciencing is closely related to the cognitive dimension of psychoanalysis. The patient, let's say, relates a dream. Such and such happened. The analyst suggests that perhaps the dream "means" such and such. It sometimes happens that the patient—perhaps after a pause, a frown, a shaking of head—will suddenly "see" it. Yes, by God! Which is to say: in sciencing, there are forms of verification other than pointer-readings.

INTERVIEWER: As for your view that it is a mistake to draw a moral and be edifying in art—is Lancelot's naive-fascistoid idea of the Third Revolution illustrative of this?

PERCY: I was speaking of the everyday use of the words "moral" and "edifying"—which is to say, preachy—in the sense that, say, Ayn Rand's novels are preachy, have a message, but may in the deepest sense of the word be immoral. So is Lancelot's "Third Revolution" in the deepest sense immoral and, I hope, is so taken by the reader. To tell the truth, I don't see how any serious fiction-writer or poet can fail to be moral and edifying in the technical non-connotative sense of these words, since he or she cannot fail to be informed by his own deep sense of the way things should be or should not be, by a sense of pathology and hence a sense of health. If a writer writes from a sense of outrage—and most serious writers do—isn't he by definition a moral writer?

INTERVIEWER: The influence of Dostoyevsky, Camus, Sartre, and other novelists upon you has often been discussed. Is there any literary influence that joined the rest recently?

PERCY: Chekhov reread—in a little reading group we have here in Covington. His stories "In the Ravine" and "Ward Six" are simply breathtaking. Also recently, the German novelist Peter Handke whose latest, *The Weight of the World*, is somehow exhilarating in the spontaneity of its free-form diary entries. The accurate depiction of despair can be exhilarating, a cognitive emotion.

INTERVIEWER: What is your attitude towards the reader?

PERCY: I hold out for some sort of contractual relationship between novelist and reader, however flawed, misapprehended, or fragmentary. Perhaps the contract is ultimately narratological, perhaps not. But something keeps—or fails to keep—the reader reading the next sentence. Even the "antinovel" presupposes some sort of contractual venture at the very moment the "antinovelist" is attacking narrativity. Such a venture implies that the writer is up to something, going abroad like Don Quixote—if only to attack windmills—and that the reader is with him. Otherwise why would the latter bother? The antinovelist is like a Protestant. His protests might be valid, but where would he be without the Catholic Church? I have no objection to "anti-story" novels. What I object to is any excursion by the author which violates the novelistic contract between writer and reader which I take to be an intersubjective transaction entailing the transmission of a set of symbols, a text. The writer violates the contract when he trashes the reader by pornography or scatological political assaults, e.g., depicting President Nixon in a novel buggering Ethel Rosenberg in Times Square, or LBJ plotting the assassination of JFK. Take pornography, a difficult, slippery case. It is not necessary to get into a discussion of First Amendment rights—for all I know it has them. And for all I know, pornography has its uses. All I suggest is that pornography and literature stimulate different organs. If we can agree that a literary text is a set of signals transmitted from sender to receiver in a certain code, pornography is a different set of signals and a different code.

INTERVIEWER: Can it be said that in your case the primary business of literature and art is cognitive whereas with John Gardner it is "to be morally judgmental"? It is clear that you and Gardner are not talking about the same thing.

PERCY: I expect there is an overlap between Gardner's "moral fiction" and my "diagnostic novel." But Gardner makes me nervous with his moralizing. When he talks about literature "establishing models of human action," he seems to be using literature to influence what people do. I think he is confusing two different orders of reality. Aquinas and the Schoolmen were probably right: art is making, morality is doing. Art is a virtue of the practical intellect, which is to say making something. This is not to say that art, fiction, is not moral in the most radical sense—if it is made right. But if you write a novel with the goal of trying to make somebody do right, you're writing a tract—which may be an admirable enterprise but it is not literature. Dostoyevsky's *Notes from Underground* is in my opinion a work of art, but it would probably not pass Gardner's moral test. Come to think of it, I think my reflexes are medical rather than normal. This comes, I guess, from having been a pathologist. Now I am perfectly willing to believe Flannery O'Connor when she said, and she wasn't kidding, that the modern world is a territory largely occupied by the devil. No one doubts the malevolence abroad in the world. But the world is also deranged. What interests me as a novelist is not the malevolence of man—so what else is new?—but his looniness. The looniness, that is to say, of the "normal" denizen of the Western world who, I think it fair to say, doesn't know who he is, what he believes, or what he is doing. This unprecedented state of affairs is, I suggest, the domain of the "diagnostic" novelist.

INTERVIEWER: Are there any trends or authors in contemporary American innovative fiction that you regard with sympathy?

PERCY: Yes, there are quite a few younger writers whom I will not name but whom I would characterize as innovative "minimalist" writers who have been influenced by Donald Barthelme without succumbing to him, which is easy to do, or as young Southern writers who have been influenced by Faulkner and Welty without succumbing to them, which is also easy to do.

INTERVIEWER: If I were asked whose work I feel to be closest to yours—the whole terrain of contemporary American fiction considered—I would choose Saul Bellow.

PERCY: Why?

INTERVIEWER: Because of the philosophical bent, because both of you are satirical moralists, because Bellow's is also a quest informed by an awareness that man *can* do something about alienation, and because philosophical abstraction and concrete social commentary are equally balanced.

PERCY: I take that kindly. I admire Barth, Pynchon, Heller, Vonnegut—you could also throw in Updike, Cheever, and Malamud—but perhaps Bellow most of all. He bears the same relationship to the streets of Chicago and upper Broadway—has inserted himself into them—the way I have in the Gentilly district of New Orleans or a country town in West Feliciana Parish in Louisiana.

INTERVIEWER: What exactly moves you to write? An idea? An image? A character? A landscape? A memory? Something that happened to you or to someone else? You have said about *The Moviegoer* that you "liked the idea of putting a young man down in a faceless suburb."

PERCY: The spark might have come from Sartre's Roquentin in *Nausea* sitting in that library watching the Self-Taught Man or sitting in that café watching the waiter. Why not have a younger, less perverse Roquentin, a Southerner of a certain sort, and put him down in a movie house in Gentilly, a middle-class district of New Orleans, not unlike Sartre's Bouville.

INTERVIEWER: If every writer writes from his own predicament, could you give a few hints as to how *The Moviegoer* illustrates this point?

PERCY: After the war, not doing medicine, writing and publishing articles in psychiatric, philosophical, and political journals, I was living in New Orleans and going to the movies. You can't make a living writing articles for *The Journal of Philosophy and Phenomenological Research*. The thought crossed my mind: why not do what French philosophers often do and Americans almost never—novelize philosophy, incarnate ideas in a person and a place, which latter is after all a noble Southern tradition in fiction.

INTERVIEWER: Did you model any character on your brothers, wife, children, grandchildren?

PERCY: Not in any way anyone would recognize.

INTERVIEWER: In connection with *Message in the Bottle,* a collection of essays that had been published over two-and-a-half decades, what attracted you to linguistics and semiotics, to the theories of language, meaning, signs, and symbols?

PERCY: That's the big question, too big to answer in more than a couple of sentences. It has to do with the first piece of writing I ever got published. I was sitting around Saranac Lake getting over a light case of tuberculosis. There was nothing to do but read. I got hold of Susanne Langer's *Philosophy in a New Key* in which she focuses on man's unique symbol-mongering behavior. This was an eye-opener to me, a good physician-scientist brought up in the respectable behaviorist tradition of U.N.C. and Columbia. I was so excited, I wrote a review and sent it to *Thought* quarterly. It was accepted! I was paid by twenty-five reprints. That was enough. What was important was seeing my scribble in *print*!

INTERVIEWER: Can you recollect what was involved in your getting started with *The Last Gentleman*?

PERCY: I wanted to create someone not quite as flat as Binx in *The Moviegoer*, more disturbed, more passionate, more in love, and, above all, *on the move*. He is in pilgrimage without quite knowing it—doing a Kierkegaardian repetition, that is, going back to his past to find himself, then from home and self to the *West* following the summons of a queer sort of apostle, mad Doctor Sutter. "Going West" is U.S. colloquial for dying.

INTERVIEWER: *Love in the Ruins*?

PERCY: *Love in the Ruins* was a picnic, with everything in it but the kitchen sink. It was written during the Time of Troubles in the sixties, with all manner of polarization in the country, black vs. white, North vs. South, hippie vs. square, liberal vs. conservative, McCarthyism vs. commies, etc.—the whole seasoned with a Southern flavor and featuring sci-fi, futurism and Dr. More, a whimsical descendant of the saint. After the solemnities of *The Moviegoer* and *The Last Gentleman*, why not enjoy myself? I did. Now I have seen fit to resurrect Dr. More in the novel I just finished, *The Thanatos Syndrome*. He is in trouble as usual and I am enjoying it.

INTERVIEWER: *Lancelot*?

PERCY: *Lancelot* might have come from an upside-down theological notion, not about God but about sin, more specifically the falling into disrepute of the word "sin." So it seemed entirely fitting that Lancelot, a proper Southern gent raised in a long tradition of knightly virtues, chiefly by way of Walter Scott, the most widely read novelist in the South for a hundred years, should have undertaken his own sort of quest for his own perculiar Grail, i.e., sin, which quest is after all a sort of search for God. Lancelot wouldn't be caught dead looking for God but he is endlessly intrigued by the search for evil. Is there such a thing—malevolence over and beyond psychological and sociological categories? The miscarriage of his search issues, quite logically I think, in his own peculiar brand of fascism, which is far more attractive and seductive, I think, than Huey Long's.

INTERVIEWER: Let me ask about *The Second Coming*, too, since although it developed into a sequel to *The Last Gentleman*, originally it was not conceived as a sequel.

PERCY: *The Second Coming* was a sure-enough love story—a genre I would ordinarily steer clear of. What made it possible was the, to me, appealing notion of the encounter of Allie and Will, like the crossing of two lines on a graph, one going up, and other down: the man who has "succeeded" in life, made it, has the best of worlds, and yet falls down in sand traps on the golf course, gazes at clouds and is haunted by memory, is in fact in despair; the girl, a total "failure," a schizophrenic who has flunked life, as she puts it, yet who despite all sees the world afresh and full of hope. It was the paradox of it that interested me. What happens when he meets her? What is the effect on his ghostlike consciousness of her strange, yet prescient, schizophrenic speech?

INTERVIEWER: Nonfiction. *Lost in the Cosmos*?

PERCY: *Lost in the Cosmos* was a sly, perhaps even devious, attempt to approach a semiotic of the self. Circumspection was necessary here, because semioticists have no use for the self, and votaries of the self—poets, humanists, novel-readers, etc.—have no use for semiotics. It was a quite ambitious attempt actually, not necessarily successful, to derive the self, a very nebulous entity indeed, through semiotics, specifically the emergence of self as a consequence of the child's entry into the symbol-mongering world of men—and even more specifically, through the acquisition of language. What was underhanded about the book was the insertion of a forty-page "primer of semiotics" in the middle of the book with a note of reassurance to the reader that he could skip it if he wanted to. Of course I was hoping he, or more likely she, would be sufficiently intrigued to take the dare and read it, since it is of course the keystone of the book. Having derived the self semiotically, then the fun came from deriving the various options of the self semiotically—the various "re-entries" of the self from the orbits most people find themselves in. Such options are ordinarily regarded as the territory of the novelist, the queer things his characters do. The fun was like the fun of Mendeleyev who devised his periodic table of elements and then looked to see if all the elements were there. Technically speaking, it was a modest attempt to give the "existentialia" of Heidegger some semiotic grounding—this, of course, in the ancient tradition of Anglo-Saxon empiricism administering therapy to the European tendency to neurotic introspection. It was also fun to administer a dose of semiotics to Phil Donahue and Carl Sagan, splendid fellows both, but who's perfect?

INTERVIEWER: Which of your novels do you expect to weather time best and why?

PERCY: I've no idea.

INTERVIEWER: Would you rewrite any of your works from any aspect at any point if you could?

PERCY: No, I hardly think about them. Sometimes in the middle of the night, however, something will occur to me which I would use in a revision. For example, in the chapter called "Metaphor as Mistake" in *The Message in the Bottle* I wish I had used this example: in Charity Hospital in New Orleans, which serves mainly poor blacks, the surgical condition, fibroids of the uterus, an accurate if somewhat prosaic definition, is known to many patients more creatively as "fireballs of the Eucharist."

INTERVIEWER: Is it correct to say that your *oeuvre* forms an organic whole and that there is a consistent logic that takes you from one work to the next as you explore reality step by step?

PERCY: Yes, I hope so—though the organic quality, if there is any, occurred more by happenstance than by design. The "fruits of the search" are there—to the extent they are allowed in the modest enterprise of the novel. That is to say, the novelist has no business setting up as the Answer Man. Or, as Binx says in the epilogue of *The Moviegoer:*

"As for my search, I have not the inclination to say much on the subject. For one thing, I have not the authority, as the great Danish philosopher declared, to speak of such matters . . ."

But the novelist is entitled to a degree of artifice and cunning, as Joyce said; or the "indirect method," as Kierkegaard said; or the comic-bizarre for shock therapy, as Flannery O'Connor did. For example, a hint of the resolution of Binx's search is given in a single four-word sentence on page 240.* The reader should know by now that Binx, for all his faults, never bullshits, especially not with children. In *Lancelot* the resolution of the conflict between Lancelot and Percival is given by a single word, the last word in the book. Which holds out hope for Lancelot.

INTERVIEWER: Hope in what sense? Isn't he beyond reach for Percival anyway?

PERCY: No, Lancelot is not beyond the reach of Percival and accordingly Lancelot is not beyond hope. The entire novel is Lancelot's spiel to Percival. Percival does not *in the novel* reply in kind. At the end Lancelot asks him if he has anything to say. Percival merely says, "yes." Lancelot, presumably, will listen. It is precisely my perception of the esthetic limitations of the novel-form that this is all Percival can say. But the novelist is allowed to nourish the secret hope that the reader may remember that in the legend it was only Percival and Lancelot, of all the knights, who saw the Grail.

INTERVIEWER: I guess *Lancelot* was meant as your bicentenary novel. But the two radical points of view, Lancelot's "pagan Greco-Roman Nazi and so on tradition" and Percival's orthodox Christianity, are unacceptable for most people, as you once explained. So, another guess, what you could teach America in *Lancelot* was what was wrong, and what you could work out in *The Second Coming* was what you could *recommend* to the nation.

PERCY: If you say so, though I had nothing so grand in mind as "recommending to the nation." I never lose sight of the lowly vocation of the novelist. He is mainly out to give pleasure to a reader—one would hope, esthetic pleasure. He operates in the esthetic sphere, not the

* "He'll be like you."

religious or even the ethical. That is to say, he is in business, like all other artists, of making, not doing, certainly not lecturing to the nation. He hopes to make well and so sell what he makes.

INTERVIEWER: Isn't it safe to say, though, that *Lancelot* and *The Second Coming* are twin novels in the sense that while Lance embarks on a quest to meet the devil, Barrett's quest is to meet God? The latter's physical journey downwards seems to be an ironic counterpart to his yearning, which is upward. Barrett's route leads him—through his fall into the greenhouse—to a different reality: perhaps the correction of direction you recommend to the South and to America. Is this stretching things too far?

PERCY: Yes indeed. Will Barrett falls out of the cave into Allie's arms, i.e., out of his nutty gnostic quest into sacramental reality. I liked the idea of falling out of a cave. I permitted myself a veiled optimism here, that one can in fact fall out of a cave, i.e., despair and depression, when aware of themselves as such, can be closest to life. From cave to greenhouse, courtesy of Sören Kierkegaard and Dr. Jung. Some reservation, however, about "a message to the South." The South is by and large in no mood for messages from Walker Percy, being, for one thing, too busy watching *Dallas*, *Love Boat*, and the NFL on the tube. Or Jimmy Swaggart.

INTERVIEWER: Do the times have anything to do with your reaching this breakthrough to eros, affirmation, and celebration in 1980 and not before? In other words, could *The Second Coming* have been written in the fifties or sixties? Or was your own age and life experience needed to reach this stage?

PERCY: Yes, no, yes. Also artistic development. Also luck—as I said before. You're sitting at your typewriter, nine in the morning, a bad time, or four in the afternoon, a worse time. Sunk as usual. In the cave. What's going to happen to these poor people? They're on their own. I'll be damned if I'm going to impose a solution on them, a chic unhappy existential ending or an upbeat Fannie Hurst ending. What does this poor guy do? He falls out of the cave, what else?

INTERVIEWER: Can we look at much of what goes on in innovative fiction, when it is not self-indulgent and cynical, in light of what you call "defamiliarization" in *Lost in the Cosmos*? That is, the artist tries to "wrench signifier out of context and exhibit it in all its queerness and splendor"?

PERCY: Absolutely, but I would apply the principle even more broadly, indeed to much that is beautiful in poetry. Take Shakespeare's lovely lines: "Daffodils that come before the swallow dares/ And take the winds of March with beauty." Surely the wrenching out of context and hence defamiliarization of such ordinary words as *daffodils, swallow, dare, March*, and even the curious use of *take*, has something to do with the beauty. Obviously Empson's theory of ambiguity in poetry is closely akin.

INTERVIEWER: It is clear that once we are dealing with a "post-religious technological society," transcendence is possible for the self by science or art but not by religion. Where does this leave the heroes of your novels with their metaphysical yearnings—Binx, Barrett, More, Lance?

PERCY: I would have to question your premise, i.e., the death of religion. The word itself, *religion*, is all but moribund, true, smelling of dust and wax—though of course in its denotative sense it is accurate enough. I have referred to the age as "post-Christian" but it does not follow from this that there are not Christians or that they are wrong. Possibly the age is wrong. Catholics—who are the only Christians I can speak for—still believe that God entered history as a man, founded a church, and will come again. This is not the best of times for the Catholic Church, but it has seen and survived worse. I see the religious "transcendence" you speak of as curiously paradoxical. Thus it is only by a movement, "transcendence," toward God that these characters, Binx *et al.*, become themselves, not abstracted like scientists but fully incarnate beings in the world. Kierkegaard put it more succinctly: the self only becomes itself when it becomes itself transparently before God.

INTERVIEWER: The second half of the question still applies: is it possible to describe Binx and the others in terms of your semiotic typology of the self?

PERCY: I would think in terms of the semiotic typology of self described in *The Message in the Bottle*. The semiotic receptor or "self" described here is perceived as being—unlike the "responding organism" of Skinner or Morris or Ogden-and-Richards—attuned to the reception of *sentences*, asserted subject-predicate pairings, namings, etc. There is adumbrated here a classification of sentences—not grammatically but existentially, that is, how the semiotic self construes the sentences in relation to his "world" (*Welt* not *Umwelt*), the latter itself a semiotic construction. Thus:

I. Sentences conveying "island news": there is fresh water in the next cove; the price of eggs is fifty cents a dozen; Nicaragua has invaded El Salvador; my head hurts; etc.

II. Sentences conveying truths *sub specie aeternitatis* (i.e., valid on any island anywhere): 2 plus 2 equals 4; $E = MC^2$ (mathematical sentences); to thine own self be true, etc. (poetic sentences); wolves are carnivorous (scientific sentences, true of all known wolves anywhere).

III. Sentences announcing news from across the seas: The French fleet is on its way to Saint Helena to rescue you (a sentence of possible significance to Napoleon). Or: A certain event occurred in history, in the Middle East some two thousand years ago, which is of utmost importance to every living human. Presumably it was just some such sentence, however indirectly, obscurely, distortedly uttered, which might have been uttered or was about to be uttered to Binx Bolling, Will Barrett, at the end of these novels—by such unlikely souls as Sutter. Notice too that it is only this last sort of sentence, the good news from across the seas, which requires the credential of the newsbearer. Or, as Kierkegaard phrased the sentence: Only I, an apostle (that is, messenger), have the authority to bring you this piece of news. It is true and I make you eternally responsible for whether or not you believe it. Certainly it is not the business of the novelist to utter sentences of Class III, but only a certain sort of Class II sentence. Also, *mutatis mutandis*, it is Dr. Thomas More who, in *The Thanatos Syndrome*, hears the Class III sentence as a non-sentence, devalued, ossified, not so much nonsense as part merely of a religious decor, like the whiff of incense or a plastic Jesus on the dashboard, or a bumper sticker common here in Louisiana: Jesus Saves.

INTERVIEWER: Is it possible that the idea central to your semiotic theory of the self—namely, that the self has no sign of itself—has something to do with Jung's idea in his *Modern Man in Search of a Soul* where he speaks about the difficulty man has expressing the inexpressible in his language?

PERCY: Actually I would suppose that my notions about the "semiotic origins" of the self are more closely related, at least in my own mind, to the existentialist philosophers, Heidegger and Marcel and Jaspers, and to the existentialist school of psychiatrists. Some years ago I published a paper which sought to do precisely that: derive many of the so-called "existentialia"—anxiety, notion of a "world"—from this very structure of man's peculiar triadic relation to his environment: interpreter-symbol-referent.

INTERVIEWER: The Jungian idea in *The Thanatos Syndrome* is mentioned in the book—that anxiety and depression might be trying to tell the patient something he does not understand. Doesn't this contradict the "semiotic-predicament-of-the-self" theory in *Cosmos*, i.e., its unspeakableness in a world of signs?

PERCY: I don't think so. The concept of an unsignificant self stranded in a world of solid signs (trees, apples, Alabama, Ralphs, Zoltáns) is very useful in thinking about the various psychiatric ways patients "fall" into inauthenticity, the way frantic selves grope for any mask at hand to disguise their nakedness. Sartre's various descriptions of bad faith in role-playing are marvelous phenomenological renderings of this quest of the self for some, any, kind of habiliment. This being the case, perhaps the patient's "symptoms"—anxiety, depression, and whatnot—may be read as a sort of warning or summons of the self to itself, of the "authentic" self to the "fallen"or inauthentic self. Heidegger speaks of the "fall" of the self into the "world." I am thinking of the first character you encounter in *The Thanatos Syndrome* through the eyes of Dr. More: the woman who lives at the country club and thinks she has everything and yet is in the middle of a panic attack. She is also the last person you encounter in the book—after being "relieved" of her symptoms by the strange goings-on in the book. So here she is at the end confronting her anxiety. She is about to listen to herself tell herself something. The last sentence in the novel is: *She opens her mouth to speak*. Jung, of course, would have understood this patient as this or that element of the self speaking to itself, perhaps anima-self to animus-self. Perhaps he is right, but I find it more congenial and less occult to speak in terms of observables and semiotic elements. Perhaps it is the Anglo-Saxon empiricist in me.

INTERVIEWER: One way to sum up *The Thanatos Syndrome*—without giving away the plot—is to call it an ecological novel. What made you turn to the ecological theme?

PERCY: I wasn't particularly aware of the ecological theme. It is true that the Louisiana of the novel is an ecological mess—as indeed it is now—but this I took to be significant only insofar as it shows the peculiar indifference of the strange new breed of Louisianians in the novel. After all, chimp-like creatures do not generally form enviromental-protection societies.

INTERVIEWER: Novels like Cheever's *Oh! What a Paradise It Seems,* Gardner's *Mickelsson's Ghosts,* and Don DeLillo's *White Noise* are about the contamination of the environment. Were you influenced by those novels or by any others with similar topics?

PERCY: Not really. If you want to locate a contemporary influence, it would be something like a cross between Bellow and Vonnegut—aiming at Bellow's depth in his central characters and Vonnegut's outrageousness and satirical use of sci-fi.

INTERVIEWER: Did you make up the "pre-frontal cortical deficit," the Tauber test, and other things, the way you invented Hausmann's Syndrome for inappropriate longing in *The Second Coming*?

PERCY: No, they're not made up. There is just enough present-day evidence to make my "syndrome" plausible, or at least credible. One advantage of futuristic novel-writing is that it relieves one of restriction to the current state of the art of brain function. Another way of saying this is that, fortunately, the present knowledge of cortical function is so primitive that it gives the novelist considerable carte blanche.

INTERVIEWER: What about in *The Thanatos Syndrome*—is the pharmacological effect of $Na^{24}$ on the cortex known?

PERCY: Not that I know of, but perhaps some shrink will write me, as one did about Hausmann's Syndrome, and report that, sure enough, administration of $Na^{24}$ to patients in the Veteran's Hospital in Seattle has been shown to reduce anxiety and improve sexual performance both in quantity and quality and variety (for example, presenting rearward).

INTERVIEWER: What led you to the idea of cortex manipulation?

PERCY: Well of course the cortex is the neurological seat of the primate's, and man's, "higher functions." But I was particularly intrigued by the work of neurologists like John Eccles who locate the "self" in the language areas of the cortex—which squares very well with the semiotic origins of the self in the origins of language—as that which gives names, utters sentences. It seems, despite the most intensive training, chimps do neither.

INTERVIEWER: The idea of man regressing to a pre-lingual stage must be a satiric device to get at what you experience in human communicative behavior today?

PERCY: Well, I might have had at the edge of my mind some literary critics, philosophers, and semioticians, who seem hell-bent on denying the very qualities of language and literature which have been held in such high esteem in the past: namely, that it is possible to know something about the world, that the world actually exists, that one person can actually say or write about the world and that other people can understand him. That, in a word, communication is possible. Some poets and critics outdo me in regression. I was content to regress some characters to a rather endearing pongid-primate level. But one poet I read about claimed that the poet's truest self could only be arrived at if he regressed himself clear back to the inorganic level, namely, a stone.

INTERVIEWER: When at the end of the book you hint that earlier poets wrote two-word sentences, uttered howls, or routinely exposed themselves during their readings, I thought you meant the counterculture.

PERCY: I was thinking of Ginsberg and company—and some of his imitators who can be found in our genteel Southern universities. I do not imply that Ginsberg had been intoxicated by $Na^{24}$, but only that such poets might suffer cortical deficits of a more obscure sort. The fact that American writers-in-residence and poets-in-residence often behave worse than football players does not necessarily imply that they are more stoned than the latter. There is more than one way to assault the cortex.

INTERVIEWER: You have said literature can be a living social force, that the segregationists could feel the impact of a satirical line about Valley Forge Academy in *Love in the Ruins*. Do you expect *The Thanatos Syndrome* to be effective in that way?

PERCY: I would hope that it would have some small influence in the great debate on the sanctity of life in the face of technology. For one thing, I would hope to raise the level of the debate above the crude polemics of the current pro-abortion/pro-life wrangle. When people and issues get completely polarized, somebody needs to take a step back, take a deep breath, take a new look.

INTERVIEWER: Aren't there more immediate ways besides writing satirical fiction? Have you ever been engaged in political activity?

PERCY: Only in a small way in the sixties. For a while I had the honor of being labeled a nigger-lover and a bleeding heart. One small bomb threat from the Klan and one interesting night in the attic with my family and a shotgun, feeling both pleased and ridiculous and beset with ambiguities—for I knew some of the Klan people and they are not bad fellows, no worse probably than bleeding-heart liberals.

INTERVIEWER: Is there any concrete issue that engages your attention most in connection with what is going on in America at the moment?

PERCY: Probably the fear of seeing America, with all its great strength and beauty and freedom—"Now in these dread latter days of the old violent beloved U.S.A.," and so on—gradually subside into decay through default and be defeated, not by the Communist movement, demonstrably a bankrupt system, but from within by weariness, boredom, cynicism, greed, and in the end helplessness before its great problems. Probably the greatest is the rise of a black underclass. Maybe Faulkner was right. Slavery was America's Original Sin and the one thing that can defeat us. I trust not.

INTERVIEWER: In connection with what is going on in the world?

PERCY: Ditto: the West losing by spiritual acedia. A Judaic view is not inappropriate here: Communism may be God's punishment for the sins of the West. Dostoyevsky thought so.

INTERVIEWER: You have often spoken about the postpartum depression you are in when you finish a novel. To put the question in Lost-in-the-Cosmos terms: now that you have finished another novel, which re-entry option is open to you?

PERCY: Thanks for taking re-entries seriously. Probably re-entry travel (geographical—I'm going to Maine, where I've never been). Plus re-entry anaesthesia—a slight dose of bourbon.

INTERVIEWER: In 1981 you spoke about a novel you were writing about two amnesiacs traveling on a Greyhound bus. You also said that you had been at that novel for two years. *Thanatos* is obviously not that novel. Did you give up on that one?

PERCY: I can't remember.

INTERVIEWER: Do you have any plans for future works?

PERCY: It is in my mind to write a short work on semiotics showing how the current discipline has been screwed up by followers of Charles Peirce and de Saussure, the founders of modern semiotics. The extraordinary insight of Peirce into the *triadic* nature of meaning for humans and of de Saussure into the nature of the sign—as a union of the signifier and the signified—has been largely perverted by the current European tradition of structuralism and deconstruction and the American version of "dyadic" psychology, that is, various versions of behaviorism, so-called "cognitive" psychology, artificial intelligence, and so on. It would be nice if someone pursued Peirce's and de Saussure's breakthroughs. On the other hand, I may not have the time or the energy.

INTERVIEWER: Are there hopes that you would like the eighth decade of your life to fulfill?

PERCY: I was thinking of getting a word processor.

INTERVIEWER: The minimum a seventy-year-old man deserves is a birthday present. Since the person in question happens to be a writer, and since he has shown in a self-interview that he is the best man to answer the questions, the birthday present is that he can *ask* the last question.

PERCY: Question: Since you are a satirical novelist and since the main source of the satirist's energy is anger about something amiss or wrong about the world, what is the main target of your anger in *The Thanatos Syndrome*?

Answer: It is the widespread and ongoing devaluation of human life in the Western world—under various sentimental disguises: "quality of life," "pointless suffering," "termination of life without meaning," etc. I trace it to a certain mind-set in the biological and social sciences which is extraordinarily influential among educated folk—so much so that it has almost achieved the status of a quasi-religious orthodoxy. If I had to give it a name, it would be something like: The Holy Office of the Secular Inquisition. It is not to be confused with "secular humanism" because, for one thing, it is anti-human. Although it drapes itself in the mantle of the scientific method and free scientific inquiry, it is neither free nor scientific. Indeed it relies on certain hidden dogma where dogma has no place. I can think of two holy commandments which the Secular Inquisition lays down for all scientists and believers. The first: In your investigations and theories, Thou shalt not find anything unique about the human animal even if the evidence points to such uniqueness. Example: Despite heroic attempts to teach sign language to other animals, the evidence is that even the cleverest chimpanzee has never spontaneously named a single object or uttered a single sentence. Yet dogma requires that, despite traditional belief in the soul or the mind, and the work of more recent workers like Peirce and Langer in man's unique symbolizing capacity, *Homo sapiens sapiens* be declared to be not qualitatively different from other animals. Another dogma: Thou shalt not suggest that there is a unique and fatal flaw in *Homo sapiens sapiens* or indeed any perverse trait that cannot be laid to the influence of Western civilization. Examples: (1) An entire generation came under the influence of Margaret Mead's *Coming of Age in Samoa* and its message: that the Samoans were an innocent, happy, and Edenic people until they were corrupted by missionaries and technology. That this turned out not to be true, that indeed the Samoans appear to have been at least as neurotic as New Yorkers, has not changed the myth or the mind-set. (2) The gentle Tasaday people of the Philippines, an isolated Stone Age tribe, were also described as innocents, peace-loving, and benevolent. When asked to describe evil, they replied: "We cannot think of anything that is not good." That the Tasaday story has turned out to be a hoax is like an *erratum* corrected in a footnote and as inconsequential. (3) The ancient Mayans are still perceived as not only the builders of a high culture, practitioners of the arts and sciences, but a gentle folk—this despite the fact that recent deciphering of Mayan hieroglyphs have disclosed the Mayans to have been a cruel, warlike people capable of tortures even more vicious than the Aztecs. Scholars, after ignoring the findings, have admitted that the "new image" of the Mayans is perhaps "less romantic" than we had supposed. Conclusion: It is easy to criticize the absurdities of fundamentalist beliefs like "scientific creationism"—that the world and its creatures were created six thousand years ago. But it is also necessary to criticize other dogmas parading as science and the bad faith of some scientists who have their own dogmatic agendas to promote under the guise of "free scientific inquiry." Scientific inquiry should in fact be free. The warning: If it is not, if it is subject to this or that ideology, then do not be surprised if the history of the Weimar doctors is repeated. Weimar leads to Auschwitz. The nihilism of some scientists in the name of ideology or sentimentality and the consequent devaluation of individual human life leads straight to the gas chamber.

ZOLTAN ABÁDI-NAGY
May–October 1986

# 6. *Doris Lessing*

Born of British parents in Persia in 1919, Doris Lessing went with her family to southern Rhodesia when she was five years old. After growing up there she moved to England in 1949 at the age of thirty with the manuscript of her first novel, *The Grass Is Singing* (1950), and has lived there as a writer ever since. She has published over twenty-five books of fiction, essays, journalism, and poetry. Her most acclaimed novels include A *Proper Marriage* (1954), *Briefing for a Descent into Hell* (1971), *Shikasta* (1979)—the first work in the "Canopus in Argus: Archives" series of futuristic novels in which images of humans interact on six "levels of being"—and *The Good Terrorist* (1986), which received the W. H. Smith Literary Award in 1986 and the Palermo Prize and Premio Internazionale Mondello in 1987. The book for which she is arguably best known, *The Golden Notebook*, was at the time of its publication in 1962 a groundbreaking novel, both for its technical innovation and for its sociological and particularly feminist focus, yet it was the one book about which Lessing refused to answer questions. ("You'll find what you need in the preface; I said everything there.") Among her most significant short-story collections are *The Habit of Loving* (1958), *African Stories* (1965), and *The Stories of Doris Lessing* (1978). "Once upon a time," she has written, "when I was young, I believed things easily, both religious and political; now I believe less and less. But I wonder about more. . . ." In 1988 her book *The Fifth Child* was published.

everything they said. Words in their mouths – now in June's – had a labouring effortful quality – dreadful, because of the fluencies so easily available, but to others.

The children went off at last, June lingering behind. From her look around the room, I could see she did not want to go. She was regretting, not the act, but the consequences of it, which might sever her from her beloved Emily.

"What was that about?" I asked.

Emily's bossiness dropped from her, and she slumped, a worried and tired child, near Hugo. He licked her cheek.

"Well, they fancied some of your things, that's all."

"Yes, but ..." My feeling was, <u>But I'm a friend and they shouldn't have picked on me!</u> Emily caught this, and with her dry little smile she said, "June had been here, she knew the lay-out, so when the kids were wondering what place to do next, she suggested yours."

"Makes sense, I suppose."

"Yes," she insisted, raising serious eyes to me, so that I shouldn't make light of her emphasis. "Yes, it does make sense."

"You mean, I shouldn't think there was anything per-sonal in it?"

Again the smile, pathetic because of its knowing-ness, its precocity – but what an old-fashioned word that was, depending for its force on certain standards.

"Oh, no, it was personal ... a compliment, if you like!"

She put down her face into Hugo's yellow fur and ~~shook with laughter~~ laughed. I knew ~~that at night as well~~ [illegible]

Gal. 58

A *manuscript page from Doris Lessing's novel* Memoirs of a Survivor.

# *Doris Lessing*

*Doris Lessing was interviewed at the home of Robert Gottlieb, in Manhattan's east forties. Her editor for many years at Knopf, Mr. Gottlieb was then the editor of* The New Yorker. *Ms. Lessing was briefly in town to attend some casting sessions for the opera Philip Glass has based on her novel* The Making of the Representative for Planet 8, *for which she had written the libretto. Plans for the opera had been in more or less constant flux, and it was only after a minor flurry of postcards—Ms. Lessing communicates most information on postcards, usually ones from the British Museum—that the appointment was finally arranged.*

*While the tape recorder was being prepared, she said, "This is a noisy place here, when you think we're in a garden behind a row of houses." She points across the way at the townhouse where Katharine Hepburn lives; the talk is about cities for a while. She has lived in London for almost forty years, and still finds that "everything all the time in a city is extraordinary!" More speculatively, as she has remarked elsewhere, "I would not be at all surprised to find out . . . that the dimensions of buildings affect us in ways we don't guess." She spoke about spending six months in England before the age of five, saying, "I think kids ought to travel. I think it's very good to carry kids around. It's good for them. Of course it's tough on the parents."*

*The interview was conducted on the garden patio. Silvery-streaked dark hair parted in the middle and pulled back in a bun, a shortish skirt, stockings, blouse, and jacket, she looked much like her book jacket photos. If she seemed tired, it was hardly surprising considering the extent of her recent travels. She has a strong, melodious voice which can be both amused and acerbic, solicitous and sarcastic.*

INTERVIEWER: You were born in Persia, now Iran. How did your parents come to be there?

DORIS LESSING: My father was in the First World War. He couldn't stick England afterwards. He found it extremely narrow. The soldiers had these vast experiences in the trenches and found they couldn't tolerate it at home. So he asked his bank to send him somewhere else. And they sent him to Persia, where we were given a very big house, large rooms and space, and horses to ride on. Very outdoors, very beautiful. I've just been told this town is now rubble. It's a sign of the times, because it was a very ancient market town with beautiful buildings. No one's noticed. So much is destroyed, we can't be bothered. And then they sent him to Tehran, which is a very ugly city, where my mother was very happy, because she became a part of what was called the "legation set." My mother adored every second of that. There were dinner parties every night. My father hated it. He was back again with convention. Then in 1924, we came back to England where something called the Empire Exhibition (which turns up from time to time in literature) was going on and which must have had an enormous influence. The southern Rhodesian stand had enormous maize-cobs, corn-cobs, slogans saying "Make your fortune in five years" and that sort of nonsense. So my father, typically for his romantic temperament, packed up everything. He had this pension because of his leg, his war wounds—minuscule, about five thousand pounds—and he set off into unknown country to be a farmer. His childhood had been spent near Colchester, which was then a rather small town, and he had actually lived the life of a farmer's child and had a country childhood. And that's how he found himself in the veldt of Rhodesia. His story is not unusual for that time. It took me some time, but it struck me quite forcibly when I was writing *Shikasta* how many wounded ex-servicemen there were out there, both English and German. All of them had been wounded, all of them were extremely lucky not to be dead, as their mates were.

INTERVIEWER: Perhaps a minor version of the same thing would be our Vietnam veterans coming back here and being unable to adjust, completely out of society.

LESSING: I don't see how people can go through that kind of experience and fit in at once. It's asking too much.

INTERVIEWER: You recently published a memoir in the magazine *Granta* which, according to its title, was about your mother. In some ways it really seemed to be more about your father.

LESSING: Well, how can one write about them separately? Her life was, as they used to say, devoted to his life.

INTERVIEWER: It's astonishing to read about his gold-divining, his grand plans, his adventures . . .

LESSING: Well, he was a remarkable bloke, my father. He was a totally impractical man. Partly because of the war, all that. He just drifted off, he couldn't cope. My mother was the organizer, and kept everything together.

INTERVIEWER: I get the feeling that he thought of this gold-divining in a very progressive and scientific way.

LESSING: His idea was—and there's probably something true about it somewhere—that you could divine gold and other metal if you only knew how to do it. So he was always experimenting. I wrote about him actually, in a manner of speaking, in a story I called "Eldorado." We were living in gold country. Gold mines, little ones, were all around.

INTERVIEWER: So it wasn't out of place.

LESSING: No! Farmers would always keep a hammer or a pan in the car, just in case. They'd always be coming back with bits of gold-bearing rock.

INTERVIEWER: Were you around a lot of storytelling as a child?

LESSING: No . . . the Africans told stories, but we weren't allowed to mix with them. It was the worst part about being there. I mean I could have had the most marvelously rich experiences as a child. But it would have been inconceivable for a white child. Now I belong to something called a "Storytellers' College" in England. About three years ago a group of people tried to revive storytelling as an art. It's doing rather well. The hurdles were—I'm just a patron, I've been to some meetings—first that people turn up thinking that storytelling is telling jokes. So they have to be discouraged! Then others think that storytelling is like an encounter group. There's always somebody who wants to tell about their personal experience, you know. But enormous numbers of real storytellers have been attracted. Some from Africa—from all over the place—people who are still traditional hereditary storytellers or people who are trying to revive it. And so, it's going on. It's alive and well. When you have storytelling sessions in London or anywhere, you get a pretty good audience. Which is quite astonishing when you think of what they could be doing instead—watching *Dallas* or something.

INTERVIEWER: What was it like coming back to England? I remember J. G. Ballard, coming there for the first time from Shanghai, felt very constrained; he felt that everything was very small and backward.

LESSING: Oh yes! I felt terribly constricted, very pale and damp; everything was shut in, and too domestic. I still find it so. I find it very pretty, but too organized. I don't imagine that there's an inch of the English landscape that hasn't been dealt with in some way or another. I don't think there is any wild grass anywhere.

INTERVIEWER: Do you have any deep urges or longings to go back to some kind of mythical African landscape?

LESSING: Well, I wouldn't be living in that landscape, would I? It wouldn't be the past. When I went back to Zimbabwe three years ago, which was two years after independence, it was very clear that if I went I would be from the past. My only function in the present would be as a kind of token. Inevitably! Because I'm the "local girl made good." Under the white regime I was very much a baddie. No one had a good word to say for me. You've got no idea how wicked I was supposed to be. But now I'm "okay."

INTERVIEWER: Were you bad because of your attitude to blacks?

LESSING: I was against the white regime. There was a total color bar. This phrase has completely gone now: "color bar." The only contact I had with blacks was what I had with servants. As for the political Africans it is very difficult. It's very hard to have a reasonable relationship with black people who have to be in at nine o'clock because there's a curfew, or who are living in total poverty and you are not.

INTERVIEWER: In the *Granta* memoir there's the image of you as a child, toting guns around, shooting game . . .

LESSING: Well, there was a great deal of game around then. There's very little these days, partly because the whites shot it out.

INTERVIEWER: Did you have a desire to be a writer in those early days? You mention hiding your writings from your mother, who tried to make too much of them.

LESSING: My mother was a woman who was very frustrated. She had a great deal of ability, and all this energy went into me and my brother. She was always wanting us to *be* something. For a long time she wanted me to be a musician, because *she* had been a rather good musician. I didn't have much talent for it. But everybody had to have music lessons then. She was always pushing us. And, of course, in one way it was very good, because children need to be pushed. But she would then take possession of whatever it was. So you had to protect yourself. But I think probably every child has to find out the way to possess their own productions.

INTERVIEWER: I just wondered if you thought of yourself as becoming a writer at an early age.

LESSING: Among other things. I certainly could have been a doctor. I would have made a good farmer, and so on. I became a writer because of frustration, the way I think many writers do.

INTERVIEWER: Because you've written novels in so many different modes, do people feel betrayed when you don't stick in one camp or another? I was thinking of the science fiction fans, quite narrow-minded, who resent people who write "science fiction" who don't stick within their little club.

LESSING: Well, it is narrow-minded, of course it is. Actually, the people who regard themselves as representatives of that community seem now to want to make things less compartmentalized. I've been invited to be Guest of Honor at the World Science Fiction Convention, in Brighton. They've invited two Soviet science fiction writers too. In the past there's always been trouble; now they're hoping that *glasnost* might allow their writers to actually come. Actually, it never crossed my mind with these later books that I was writing science fiction or anything of the kind! It was only when I was criticized for writing science fiction that I realized I was treading on sacred ground. Of course, I don't really write science fiction. I've just read a book by the *Solaris* bloke, Stanislav Lem. Now that's real classic science fiction . . . full of scientific ideas. Half of it, of course, is wasted on me because I don't understand it. But what I do understand is fascinating. I've met quite a lot of young people—some not so young either, if it comes to that—who say "I'm very sorry, but I've got no time for realism" and I say "My God! But look at what you're missing! This is prejudice." But they don't want to know about it. And I'm always meeting usually middle-aged people who say, "I'm very sorry. I can't read your non-realistic writing." I think it's a great pity. This is why I'm pleased about being Guest of Honor at this convention, because it does show a breaking down.

INTERVIEWER: What I most enjoyed about *Shikasta* was that it took all the spiritual themes that are submerged or repressed or coded in science fiction, and brought them up into the foreground.

LESSING: I didn't think of that as science fiction at all when I was doing it, not really. It certainly wasn't a book beginning, I don't know, say, "At three o'clock on a certain afternoon in Tomsk, in 1883 . . ."—which is, as opposed to the cosmic view, probably my second most favorite kind of opening, this kind of beginning!

INTERVIEWER: You've written introductions for many collections of Sufi stories and prose. How did your interest and involvement with Sufism come about?

LESSING: Well, you know, I hate talking about this. Because really, what you say gets so clichéd, and it sounds gimmicky. All I really want to say is that I was looking for some discipline along those lines. Everyone agrees that you need a teacher. I was looking around for one, but I didn't like any of them because they were all "gurus" of one kind or another. Then I heard about this man Shah, who is a Sufi, who really impressed me. So I've been involved since the early sixties. It's pretty hard to summarize it all, because it's all about what you experience. I want to make a point of that because a lot of people walk around saying "I am a Sufi," probably because they've read a book and it sort of sounds attractive. Which is absolutely against anything that real Sufis would say or do. Some of the great Sufis have actually said, "I would never call myself a Sufi—it's too large a name." But I get letters from people, letters like this: "Hi, Doris! I hear you're a Sufi too!" Well, I don't know what to say, really. I tend to ignore them.

INTERVIEWER: I imagine that people try to set you up as some sort of guru, whether political or metaphysical.

LESSING: I think people are always looking for gurus. It's the easiest thing in the world to become a guru. It's quite terrifying. I once saw something fascinating here in New York. It must have been in the early seventies—guru time. A man used to go and sit in Central Park, wearing elaborate golden robes. He never once opened his mouth, he just sat. He'd appear at lunchtime. People appeared from everywhere, because he was obviously a holy man, and this went on for months. They just sat around him in reverent silence. Eventually he got fed up with it and left. Yes. It's as easy as that.

INTERVIEWER: Let me ask you one more question along these lines. Do you think that reincarnation is a plausible view?

LESSING: Well, I think it's an attractive idea. I don't believe in it myself. I think it's more likely that we "dip into" this realm on our way on a long journey.

INTERVIEWER: That this planet is merely one single stop?

LESSING: We're not encouraged—I'm talking about people studying with Shah—to spend a great deal of time brooding about this, because the idea is that there are more pressing things to do. It's attractive to brood about all this, of course, even to write books about it! But as far as I was concerned, in *Shikasta* the reincarnation stuff was an attractive metaphor, really, or a literary idea, though I understand that there are people who take *Shikasta* as some kind of a textbook.

INTERVIEWER: Prophecy, perhaps?

LESSING: It was a way of telling a story—incorporating ideas that are in our great religions. I said in the preface to *Shikasta* that if you read the Old Testament and the New Testament and the Apocrypha and the Koran you find a continuing story. These religions have certain ideas in common, and one idea is, of course, this final war or apocalypse, or whatever. So I was trying to develop this idea. I called it "space fiction" because there was nothing else to call it.

INTERVIEWER: I have the feeling that you are an extremely intuitive kind of fiction writer, and that you probably don't plan or plot out things extensively, but sort of discover them. Is that the case, or not?

LESSING: Well, I have a general plan, yes, but it doesn't mean to say that there's not room for an odd character or two to emerge as I go along. I knew what I was going to do with *The Good Terrorist*. The bombing of Harrod's department store was the start of it. I thought it would be interesting to write a story about a group who drifted into bombing, who were incompetent and amateur. I had the central character, because I know several people like Alice—this mixture of very maternal caring, worrying about whales and seals and the environment, but at the same time saying, "You can't make an omelette without breaking eggs," and who can contemplate killing large numbers of people without a moment's bother. The more I think about that, the more interesting it becomes. So I knew about her; I knew about the boyfriend, and I had a rough idea of the kinds of people I wanted. I wanted people of different kinds and types, so I created this lesbian couple. But then what interested me were the characters who emerged that I hadn't planned for, like Faye. And then Faye turned into this destroyed person, which was surprising to me. The little bloke Phillip turned up like this: right about then I was hearing about an extremely fragile young man, twenty-one or twenty-two, who was out of work, but was always being offered work by the authorities. I mean, loading very heavy rolls of paper onto lorries, in fact! You'd think they were lunatics! So he always got the sack at the end of about three days. I think it's quite a funny book.

INTERVIEWER: Really?

LESSING: Well, it is comic, in a certain way. We always talk about things as if they are happening in the way they're supposed to happen, and everything is very efficient. In actual fact, one's experience about anything at all is that it's a complete balls-up. I mean everything! So why should this be any different? I don't believe in these extremely efficient terrorists, and all that.

INTERVIEWER: Conspiracies, and so on?

LESSING: There's bound to be messes and muddles going on.

INTERVIEWER: Do you work on more than one fictional thing at a time?

LESSING: No, it's fairly straight. I do sometimes tidy up a draft of a previous thing while I'm working on something else. But on the whole I like to do one thing after another.

INTERVIEWER: I'd imagine then that you work from beginning to end, rather than mixing around. . . .

LESSING: Yes, I do. I've never done it any other way. If you write in bits, you lose some kind of very valuable continuity of form. It is an invisible inner continuity. Sometimes you only discover it is there if you are trying to reshape.

INTERVIEWER: Do you have a feeling of yourself as having evolved within each genre that you employ? For instance, I thought the realistic perspective in *The Good Terrorist*, and even sometimes in the Jane Somers books, was more detached than in your earlier realism.

LESSING: It was probably due to my advanced age. We do get detached. I see every book as a problem that you have to solve. That is what dictates the form you use. It's not that you say, "I want to write a science fiction book." You start from the other end, and what you have to say dictates the form of it.

INTERVIEWER: Are you producing fairly continuously? Do you take a break between books?

LESSING: Yes! I haven't written in quite a while. Sometimes there are quite long gaps. There's always something you have to do, an article you have to write, whether you want to or not. I'm writing short stories at the moment. It's interesting, because they're *very* short. My editor, Bob Gottlieb, said, quite by chance, that no one ever sends him very short stories, and he found this interesting. I thought, "My God, I haven't written a very short story for years." So I'm writing them around 1,500 words, and it's good discipline. I'm enjoying that. I've done several, and I think I'm going to call them "London Sketches," because they're all about London.

INTERVIEWER: So they're not parables, or exotic in any way?

LESSING: No, not at all. They're absolutely realistic. I wander about London quite a lot. And any city, of course, is a theater, isn't it?

INTERVIEWER: Do you have regular working habits?

LESSING: It doesn't matter, because it's just habits. When I was bringing up a child I taught myself to write in very short concentrated bursts. If I had a weekend, or a week, I'd do unbelievable amounts of work. Now those habits tend to be ingrained. In fact, I'd do much better if I could go more slowly. But it's a habit. I've noticed that most women write like that, whereas Graham Greene, I understand, writes 200 perfect words every day! So I'm told! Actually, I think I write much better if I'm flowing. You start something off, and at first it's a bit jagged, awkward, but then there's a point where there's a click and you suddenly become quite fluent. That's when I think I'm writing well. I don't write well when I'm sitting there sweating about every single phrase.

INTERVIEWER: What kind of a reader are you these days? Do you read contemporary fiction?

LESSING: I read a great deal. I'm very fast, thank God, because I could never cope with it otherwise. Writers get sent enormous amounts of books from publishers. I get eight or nine or ten books a week which is a burden, because I'm always very conscientious. You do get a pretty good idea of what a book's like in the first chapter or two. And if I like it at all, I'll go on. That's unfair, because you could be in a bad mood, or terribly absorbed in your own work. Then there are the writers I admire, and I'll always read their latest books. And, of course, there's a good deal of what people tell me I should read. So I'm always reading.

INTERVIEWER: Could you tell us more about how you put the "Jane Somers" hoax over on the critical establishment? It strikes me as an incredibly generous thing to do, first of all, to put a pseudonym on two long novels to try to show the way young novelists are treated.

LESSING: Well, it wasn't going to be two to begin with! It was meant to be one. What happened was, I wrote the first book and I told the agent that I wanted to sell it as a first novel . . . written by a woman journalist in London. I wanted an identity that was parallel to mine, not too different. So my agent knew, and he sent it off. My two English publishers turned it down. I saw the readers' reports, which were very patronizing. Really astonishingly patronizing! The third publisher, Michael Joseph (the publisher of my first book), was then run by a very clever woman called Phillipa Harrison, who said to my agent, "This reminds me of the early Doris Lessing." We got into a panic because we didn't want her going around saying that! So we took her to lunch and I said, "This *is* me, can you go along with it?" She was upset to begin with, but then she really enjoyed it all. Bob Gottlieb, who was then my editor at Knopf in the States, guessed, and so that was three people. Then the French publisher rang me up and said, "I've just bought a book by an English writer, but I wonder if you haven't been helping her a bit!" So I told him. So in all, four or five people knew. We all expected that when the book came out, everyone would guess. Well, before publication it was sent to all the experts on my work, and none of them guessed. All writers feel terribly caged by these experts

—writers become their property. So, it was bloody marvelous! It was the best thing that happened! Four publishers in Europe bought it not knowing it was me, and that was nice. Then the book came out, and I got the reviews a first novel gets, small reviews, mostly by women journalists, who thought that I was one of their number. Then "Jane Somers" got a lot of fan letters, mostly non-literary, from people looking after old people and going crazy. And a lot of social workers, either disagreeing or agreeing, but all saying they were pleased I'd written it. So then I thought, "Okay, I shall write another one." By then I was quite fascinated with Jane Somers. When you're writing in the first person, you can't stray too far out of what is appropriate for that person. Jane Somers is middle class, English, from a very limited background. There are very few things more narrow than the English middle class. She didn't go to university. She started working very young, went straight to the office. Her life was in the office. She had a marriage that was no marriage. She didn't have children. She didn't really like going abroad. When she went abroad with her husband, or on trips for her firm and her office, she was pleased to get home. She was just about as narrow in her experience as you can get. So in the writing, I had to cut out all kinds of things that came to my pen, as it were. Out! Out! She's a very ordinary woman. She's very definite in her views about what is right and what is wrong.

INTERVIEWER: What to wear . . .

LESSING: Everything! I have a friend who is desperately concerned with her dress. The agonies she goes through to achieve this perfection I wouldn't wish on anyone! Jane Somers was put together from various people. Another was my mother. I wondered what she would be like if she were young now, in London. A third one was a woman I knew who used to say, "I had a perfectly happy childhood. I adored my parents. I liked my brother. We had plenty of money. I loved going to school. I was married young, I adored my husband"—she goes on like this. But then, her husband dies suddenly. And from becoming a rather charming child-woman, she became a person. So I used all these things to make one person. It's amazing what you find out about yourself when you write in the first person about someone very different from you.

INTERVIEWER: Your original idea with the Jane Somers books was to probe the literary establishment?

LESSING: Yes. I've been close to the literary machine now for a long time. I know what's good about it and what's bad about it. It's not the publishers I've had it in for so much as the reviewers and the critics, whom I find extraordinarily predictable. I knew everything that was going to happen with that book! Just before I came clean I had an interview with Canadian television. They asked, "Well what do you think's going to happen?" and I said, "The English critics are going to say that the book is no good." Exactly! I had these sour nasty little reviews. In the meantime the book did very well in every other country.

INTERVIEWER: In your preface to *Shikasta* you wrote that people really didn't know how extraordinary a time this was in terms of the availability of all kinds of books. Do you feel that in fact we're going to be leaving the culture of the book? How precarious a situation do you see it?

LESSING: Well, don't forget, I remember World War II when there were very few books, very little paper available. For me to walk into a shop or look at a list and see anything that I want, or almost anything, is like a kind of miracle. In hard times, who knows if we're going to have that luxury or not?

INTERVIEWER: Do you feel any sense of responsibility in presenting these prophesies aside from telling a good story?

LESSING: I know people say things like, "I regard you as rather a prophet." But there's nothing I've said that hasn't been, for example, in the *New Scientist* for the last twenty years. Nothing! So why am I called a prophet, and they are not?

INTERVIEWER: You write better.

LESSING: Well, I was going to say, I present it in a more interesting way. I do think that sometimes I hit a kind of wavelength—though I think a lot of writers do this—where I anticipate events. But I don't think it's very much, really. I think a writer's job is to provoke questions. I like to think that if someone's read a book of mine, they've had—I don't know what—the literary equivalent of a shower. Something that would start them thinking in a slightly different way perhaps. That's what I think writers are for. This is what our function is. We spend all our time thinking about how things work, why things happen, which means that we are more sensitive to what's going on.

INTERVIEWER: Did you ever do any of those sixties' experiments with hallucinogens, that sort of thing?

LESSING: I did take mescaline once. I'm glad I did, but I'll never do it again. I did it under very bad auspices. The two people who got me the mescaline were much too responsible! They sat there the whole time, and that meant, for one thing, that I only discovered the "hostess" aspect of my personality, because what I was doing was presenting the damn experience to them the whole time! Partly in order to protect what I was really feeling. What should have happened was for them to let me alone. I suppose they were afraid I was going to jump out of a window. I am not the kind of person who would do such a thing! And then I wept most of the time. Which was of no importance, and they were terribly upset by this, which irritated me. So the whole thing could have been better. I wouldn't do it again. Chiefly because I've known people who had such bad trips. I have a friend who took mescaline once. The whole experience was a nightmare that kept on being a nightmare—people's heads came rolling off their shoulders for months. Awful! I don't want that.

INTERVIEWER: Do you travel a great deal?

LESSING: Too much; I mean to stop.

INTERVIEWER: Mostly for obligations?

LESSING: Just business, promoting, you know. Writers are supposed to sell their books! Astonishing development! I'll tell you where I've been this year, for my publishers: I was in Spain . . . Barcelona and Madrid, which is enjoyable, of course. Then I went to Brazil, where I discovered—I didn't know this—that I sell rather well there. Particularly, of course, space fiction. They're very much into all that. Then I went to San Francisco. They said, "While you're here, you might as well . . ."—that phrase, "you might as well"—"pop up the coast to Portland." You've been there?

INTERVIEWER: No, never.

LESSING: Now there is an experience! In San Francisco, they're hedonistic, cynical, good-natured, amiable, easygoing, and well-dressed—in a casual way. Half an hour in the plane and you're in a rather straight-laced formal city that doesn't go in for casual behavior at all. It's amazing, just up the coast there. This is what America's like. Then I went to Finland for the second time. They've got some of the best bookstores in the world! Marvelous, wonderful! They say it's because of those long, dark nights! Now I'm here. Next I'm going to be in Brighton, for the science fiction convention. Then I won a prize in Italy called the Mondello Prize, which they give in Sicily. I said, "Why

Sicily?" and they said, deadpan, "Well, you see, Sicily's got a bad image because of the Mafia . . ." So I'll go to Sicily, and then I shall work for all the winter.

INTERVIEWER: I hear you've been working on a "space opera" with Philip Glass.

LESSING: What happens to books is so astonishing to me! Who would have thought *The Making of the Representative for Planet 8* would turn into an opera? I mean it's so surprising!

INTERVIEWER: How did that come about?

LESSING: Well, Philip Glass wrote to me, and said he'd like to make an opera, and we met.

INTERVIEWER: Had you known much of his music before?

LESSING: Well, no I hadn't! He sent some of his music. It took quite a bit of time for my ears to come to terms with it. My ear was always expecting something else to happen. You know what I mean? Then we met and we talked about it, and it went very well, which is astonishing because we couldn't be more different. We just get on. We've never had one sentence worth of difficulty over anything, ever. He said the book appealed to him, and I thought he was right, because it's suitable for his music. We met, usually not for enormous sessions, a day here and a day there, and decided what we would do, or not do. I wrote the libretto.

INTERVIEWER: Have you ever done anything like that before?

LESSING: No, never with music.

INTERVIEWER: Did you have music to work from?

LESSING: No, we started with the libretto. We've done six versions of the story so far, because it is a story, unlike most of the things he does. As something was done, he would do the music, saying he'd like six more lines here or three out there. That was a great challenge.

INTERVIEWER: Can you say anything about your next project?

LESSING: Yes, my next book is a little book. It's a short story that grew. The joke is that a short novel in England is very much liked. They're not terribly popular here in the U.S. They like big books here. Getting your money's worth. It's about a very ordinary family that gives birth to a goblin. And this is realism. I got the idea from two sources. One was this fantastic writer called Loren Eiseley. He wrote a piece—I can't remember what it was actually about—where he's walking up the seashore in the dusk, and on a country road he sees a girl that he says is a Neanderthal girl: a country girl in a country district, nothing very much to be asked of her, hardly noticed except as a stumpy girl with a clumsy skull. It's just the most immensely touching, sad piece. It stuck in my mind, and I said, "If Neanderthals, why not Cro-Magnons, why not dwarves, goblins, because all cultures talk about these creatures?" The other source was the saddest piece in a magazine, from a woman who wrote in and said, "I just want to write about this or I shall go crazy." She'd had three children, I think. Her last child, who was now seven or eight, had been born, she said, a devil. She put it in those terms. She said that this child had never done anything but hate everyone around. She's never done anything normal, like laugh or be happy. She destroyed the family, who couldn't stand her. The mother said, "I go in at night and I look at this child asleep. I kiss her while she's asleep because I don't dare kiss her while she's awake." So, anyway, all this went into the story. The main point about this goblin is, he's perfectly viable in himself. He's a normal goblin. But we just cannot cope with him.

INTERVIEWER: Is the space series going to continue?

LESSING: Yes. I haven't forgotten it. If you read the last one, *The Sentimental Agents*—which is really satire, not science fiction—you'll see that I've ended it so that I've pointed it all to the next volume. [The book ends in the middle of a sentence.] In the next book, I send this extremely naive agent off to . . . What's the name of my bad planet?

INTERVIEWER: Shammat?

LESSING: Yes, to Shammat, in order to reform everything. It's going to be difficult to write about Shammat because I don't want to make it much like Earth! That's too easy! I have a plot, but it's the tone I need. You know what I mean?

INTERVIEWER: Do you do many public readings of your own work?

LESSING: Not very many. I do when I'm asked. They didn't ask me to in Finland. I don't remember when was the last. Oh, Germany last year, my God! That was the most disastrous trip. It was some academic institution in Germany. I said to them, "Look, I want to do what I always do. I'll read the story and then I'll take questions." They said, the way academics always do, "Oh you can't expect our students to ask questions." I said, "Look, just let me handle this, because I know how." Anyway, what happened was typical in Germany: we met at four o'clock in order to discuss the meeting that was going to take place at eight. They cannot stand any ambiguity or disorder—no, no! Can't bear it. I said, "Look, just leave it." The auditorium was very large and I read a story in English and it went down very well, perfectly okay. I said, "I will now take questions." Then this bank of four bloody professors started to answer questions from the audience and debate among themselves, these immensely long academic questions of such tedium that finally the audience started to get up and drift out. A young man, a student sprawled on the gangway—as a professor finished something immensely long—called out, "BLAH, BLAH, BLAH, BLAH, BLAH." So with total lack of concern for the professors' feelings I said, "Look, I will take questions in English from the audience." So they all came back and sat down, and it went well . . . perfectly lively questions! The professors were absolutely furious. So that was Germany. German academics are the worst.

INTERVIEWER: Recently, you've turned to writing nonfiction.

LESSING: I've just written a book, a short book, about the situation in Afghanistan. I was there looking at the refugee camps, because what happens is that men usually go for the newspapers, and men can't speak to the women because of the Islamic attitudes. So we concentrated on the women. The book's called *The Wind Blows Away Our Words*, which is a quote from one of their fighters, who said, "We shout to you for help but the wind blows away our words."

INTERVIEWER: Did you ever worry about what sort of authority you could bring to such an enormous story, being an outsider visiting only for a short time?

LESSING: Do journalists worry about the authority they bring, visiting countries for such a short time? As for me, rather more than most journalists, I was well briefed for the trip, having been studying this question for some years knowing Afghans and Pakistanis (as I made clear in the book) and being with people who knew Farsi—this last benefit not being shared by most journalists.

INTERVIEWER: Your methods of reportage in that book have been the target of some criticism by American journalists, who charge that your trip to Afghanistan was sponsored by a particular pro-Afghan organization. How do you respond to that?

LESSING: This is the stereotypical push-button criticism from the left, from people who I do not think can expect to be taken seriously, for

I made it clear in the book that the trip was not organized by a political organization. I went for something called Afghan Relief, set up by some friends, among them myself, which has helped several people to visit Pakistan, but not with money. I paid my own expenses, as did the others I went with. The point about Afghan Relief is that it has close links with Afghans, both in exile and fighting inside Afghanistan, and includes Afghans living in London, as advisors. These Afghans are personal friends of mine, not "political." Afghan Relief has so far not spent one penny on administration; all the fund-raising work, here and in Pakistan, is done voluntarily. To spell it out: no one has made anything out of Afghan Relief except the Afghans.

INTERVIEWER: From the tag that you used for the Jane Somers book: "If the young knew/ If the old could . . ." Do you have any things you would have done differently, or any advice to give?

LESSING: Advice I don't go in for. The thing is, you do not believe I know everything in this field is a cliché, everything's already been said, but you just do not believe that you're going to be old. People don't realize how quickly they're going to be old, either. Time goes very fast.

THOMAS FRICK
Summer 1988

# 7. William Kennedy

January 1983, the month of his fifty-fifth birthday, heralded the beginning of an era of fame and fortune in William Kennedy's life. *Ironweed*, Kennedy's fourth novel, was published to widespread critical acclaim, and that same week the MacArthur Foundation awarded him a six-figure tax-free grant to use as he pleased. Two of his previous novels, *Legs* (1975) and *Billy Phelan's Greatest Game* (1978), were reissued in paperback, and later in 1983 Kennedy began a collaboration with Francis Ford Coppola on *The Cotton Club* screenplay.

Using part of his MacArthur grant, Kennedy established the Writers Institute at the University of Albany, which would bring internationally known writers such as William Styron, Seamus Heaney, John Updike, and Toni Morrison to Kennedy's hometown for lectures and workshops. In December 1983, Kennedy published *O Albany!*, a book of lyric essays celebrating the real life of the city he has recreated as a mythic entity in his novels.

Kennedy was on a literary roll. In 1984 he won the Pulitzer Prize and the National Book Critics' Circle Award for *Ironweed;* his first novel, *The Ink Truck* (1969), was reissued in both hardcover and paperback. Mario Cuomo declared that Albany had "found its Homer," adding the New York Governor's Arts Award to Kennedy's collections of honors. Kennedy sold the film rights to three novels, and signed contracts to write the screenplays (*Ironweed* became a film in 1987). Later in 1984 the New York legislature renamed the Writers Institute the New York State Writers Institute and provided a $100,000 grant for it. Kennedy's novels had put Albany on the map. In 1988 he published his most recent novel, *Quinn's Book*. Currently he is finishing his novel *Very Old Bones*, to be published in 1992 by Viking Penguin, which will also publish a collection of his journalistic pieces later in 1992.

lemon weed - 100

and considered the death he caused in this life, consider the fact that Helen was dying, and that he was perhaps the principal agent of her death, even as his whole being directed to keeping her from freezing to death in a the dust like Sandra, even to the point of accepting cuckoldry at the hand of Finny, and perhaps Mac, and perhaps Little Red, given the threatfulness of the crepuscular mood.

I don't want to die before you do, Helen, is what Francis thought. You'll be lost in the world without me.

Francis thought of his father flying through the air in his fatal arc and he knew the man was in heaven. The good leave us behind to think about the deeds they did. His mother would be in purgatory, with luck for goddamn ever. She wasn't evil enough for hell, nor could he conceive of a bitch such as she shrew of shrews, denier of life, ever ascending to heaven, if they ever got such a place.

The frigid air of November lay on like a blanket of glass. It rendered him motionless, brought peace to his body, and the stillness brought a cessation of anguish to his brain. In a dream he was only just beginning to enter, horns and mountains rose out of the earth. The horns, ethereal trumpets, were in virtuosity the perilousness of the crags and cornices of the mountains paths. Francis recognized the song bodily into the world where had been composed.

1st drfaft to here, 1:10 a.m.
Feb. 1, 1979, at day begun on
Jan. 31, 1979 at 8 a.m., and in
which 17 pp were written, a record, (all-time)

*A manuscript page from William Kennedy's* Ironweed, *the third and final novel in his "Albany Cycle."*

© Thomas Victor

# William Kennedy

*The first interview session took place in July 1984 as Kennedy was finishing a magazine piece about working on the screenplay for* The Cotton Club. *Kennedy talked for most of a Saturday afternoon at his home outside of Averill Park, a small community east of Albany and the Hudson River in a region of rolling hills where the landscape is sprinkled with picturesque lakes, meadows, and woods. A second interview was conducted in Spring 1988.*

*The Kennedys live in a handsome nineteenth-century farmhouse, a large white clapboard house with green trim and shutters, shaded and decorated on three sides by mature blue spruce, Norway spruce, and sugar maple trees. At the back of the house is a wooden deck, and across an expanse of lawn a swimming pool that was a sparkling invitation in the hot July sun on the day of the first interview session.*

*Kennedy, tall and fit, looking younger than his then fifty-seven years, in spite of the fact that his Irish red hair showed signs of thinning on top, appeared at the front door wearing a red-and-white striped sport shirt with rolled-up sleeves, white cotton pants, and white dress shoes.*

*Born and bred in the city, a well-traveled, cosmopolitan man, he gave the clear impression of being very much at home in the country.*

*After a short excursion outside in the midday heat, Kennedy suggested that we go to his air-conditioned writing studio, a spacious corner room on the second floor.*

*Shelves of nonfiction works lined one side of the upstairs hallway, and his studio was filled from floor to ceiling with books against three of the walls: fiction, poetry, plays, and one large section of books on film and film criticism. A large wooden desk took up most of the space between two windows that looked out on the spruce and maple trees in the yard. Bookcases at each end of the desk were filled with reference books. The top of a cedar chest on the green shag rug was covered by more piles of books and papers, and nearby were boxes of letters Kennedy had received from his readers.*

*Collages of memorabilia decorated the back of the door to the hallway and the wall behind the desk: a poster of Francis Phelan from the cover of* Ironweed; *announcements of public readings Kennedy had given; a poster announcement of a reading by Saul Bellow at the Writers Institute; award plaques, and an honorary doctorate of letters; and photographs from Kennedy's days as a newsman.*

*A straw hat with a black band hung from one of the curtain rods. It belonged to William Kennedy, Sr., who wore it in the 1920s. Another link to family and the past was Kennedy's typewriter, set on a sturdy wooden leaf pulled out from the desk—a black L. C. Smith & Corona, 1934 vintage, that belonged to his mother, Mary Kennedy. Although he now uses a word processor for revisions, Kennedy still composes on this machine.*

*Kennedy sat at his desk in a wooden swivel chair that creaked slightly when he leaned back. Choosing his words with precision, he was often pensive with a serious, faraway look in his eyes as he talked of his life and his work.*

INTERVIEWER: Can you explain the circumstances under which you got the MacArthur Award?

WILLIAM KENNEDY: Well, in January I got a call from this man named Dr. Hope, and he asked me, was I William Kennedy, the writer, and I said I was. He said, Congratulations, you have just been awarded a MacArthur Fellowship, which will give you $264,000 tax-free over the next five years. I'd gotten a Chinese fortune cookie that week which said, this is your lucky week. I thought it had to do with the fact that I was getting reviewed in about five different major places in the same week. I thought that was good enough, but then I got the MacArthur. Quite a week!

INTERVIEWER: Is there any particular achievement to which they give recognition?

KENNEDY: They give it to you with no strings attached; they give it to all sorts of people—scientists, historians, translators, poets. Their first award to a writer that got widespread recognition was given to Robert Penn Warren. They give it to you on the basis of what you've done, but more important, I think, is their belief that you are going to do a lot more. It's an award given with faith that the person is going to be productive. You don't have to do anything for it; it just all of a sudden comes at you, like a health plan to cradle and protect you.

INTERVIEWER: Has the award changed your life?

KENNEDY: The change is that I have more options now to do things that have nothing to do with writing. Everybody wants me to become a fund-raiser or a public speaker or a teacher or go back to journalism or sit still and be interviewed. I've also become a correspondent. I've got something like a thousand letters, and the only thing I can do is try to answer some of them. Some I'll never get to, but I keep trying. All this is very time-consuming. The fact is that it's also very pleasant. I'm solvent, I can travel, I've been able to rewire the house, dig a new well, install a new furnace, put in a pool. Somebody accused me of going Hollywood in Averill Park, but that's not accurate. I wanted a pool for twenty years. If I have a pool I'll swim in it. If I don't have a pool I won't swim. And I don't exercise. I don't do anything . . . I never walk. I tend to dance at parties, which is a good way of having a heart attack if your feet still think you're a nineteen-year-old jitterbug. The change has been very pleasant. People ask will I change the way I write, and I don't believe I will. The work is based on what I see in the world, what's around me and what I take home from that. It's a superficial response if you change your writing because of a temporary change in your personal condition.

INTERVIEWER: Success came to you very late. *Ironweed* was turned down by thirteen publishing houses. How could a book which won the Pulitzer Prize be turned down by so many publishers?

KENNEDY: Yes. Thirteen rejections. Remember that character in "Li'l Abner," Joe Btfsplk, who went around with a cloud over his head? Well, I was the Joe Btfsplk of modern literarture for about two years. What happened was that I sold this book, then my editor left publishing; so that threw the ball game into extra innings. They gave me an editor in Georgia and I said, "I don't want an editor in Georgia; I want an editor in New York." They didn't like that. She was a very good editor, but she only came to New York every two months. Georgia is even more remote from the center of literary activity than Albany. She was living on a pecan farm, as I recall. So that got the publisher's nose out of joint. My agent was not very polite with them and finally we separated. In the meantime, my first editor came back to publishing and, finding that Joe Btfsplk cloud hanging over my head, was not terribly enthusiastic about taking me back. So I went over to Henry Robbins whom I had met at a cocktail party. Henry at that point was a very hot New York editor. He had just gone over to Dutton. Everybody was flocking to him. He was John Irving's editor. Joyce Carol Oates moved over there. Doris Grumbach moved in; so did John Gregory Dunne. It looked like Dutton was about to become the Scribner's of the new age. So anyway, at the cocktail party he said, "Can I see your book?" And I said, "Of course." I sent it to him and he wrote me back this wonderful letter saying that he loved the idea of adding me to their list. I picked up the paper a week later and he had just dropped dead in the subway on his way to work. So I then went over to another publisher where a former editor of mine had been; she was somewhat enthusiastic, thought we might be able to make it if there were some changes in the book. And then she was let go. I bounced about nine more times. Then fate intervened in the form of an assignment for *Esquire* to do an interview with Saul Bellow, who had been a teacher of mine for a semester, in San Juan. He had really encouraged me at a very early age to become a writer. So he took it upon himself—I didn't urge him, and I was very grateful to him for doing it—to write my former editor at Viking, saying that he didn't think it was proper for his former publisher to let a writer like Kennedy go begging. Two days later I got a call from Viking saying that they wanted to publish *Ironweed* and what did I think of the possibility of publishing *Legs* and *Billy Phelan* again at the same time.

INTERVIEWER: It would seem that Bellow was the answer.

KENNEDY: I think he's probably had several manuscripts sent to him since then. As have I.

INTERVIEWER: During this there must have been an immense amount of frustration. Did that experience give you ideas for changes that can or should be made in the publishing industry to encourage the writing of first-rate serious fiction?

KENNEDY: I don't know what to do to change the world that way, except to generate a running sense of shame in their attitudes toward their own behavior so that the next time they might pay more serious attention to the work at hand. So much of the publishing world is run on the basis of *marketplace* success, and so when a book is rejected as a financial loser, it immediately has a cloud over it, especially if the writer is already established with one publishing house and this house chooses not to take his next novel. That carries a stigma; you're like a leper. You go from house to house, and they say, well, why didn't so-and-so publish it? They published your last book. So you live under that cloud until you find some editor who understands the book and is willing to take a chance on it. I don't know how to change human nature about this. I'm very pessimistic about it. I just see one good writer after another in deep trouble.

INTERVIEWER: So the difficulty in getting books like *Ironweed* published is not necessarily due to the lack of good editors at the major publishing houses, but might be more closely tied to the prevailing corporate policy you're speaking of?

KENNEDY: I think there's a casualness about the way things are read. I think subject matter tends to play a large part. If you have a novel of intrigue or romance, with adultery or exotic locale, or a spy thriller, you probably won't have too much trouble getting published. If you have a major reputation, you're not going to have any problem getting published. But it's the writers who fall in the middle, who write serious books about subjects that are not the stuff of mass marketing, they have the problem—the so-called "mid-list" phenomenon. If the publishers don't think it's going to sell past a certain amount of copies, then they're not interested. And I would think that that was the case with *Ironweed*. People had decided it was a depressing book, set in the Depression, about a bum, a loser, a very downbeat subject. Who wants to read a book about bums? So they chose not to accept it. Yet it's not a downbeat book. It's a book about family, about redemption and perseverance, it's a book about love, faded violence, and any number of things. It's about the Irish, it's about the church.

So, again, I don't see how you're going to change the way editors think. They can't contravene the commercial element in their publishing house. They're as good as the books they bring in, and if those books don't make money, what good are the editors? Very sad.

INTERVIEWER: All these years of being turned down with books and short stories . . . I understand even the *Paris Review* turned down one story.

KENNEDY: That's true. You did give me a rejection slip, although I must say it wasn't as nice as the one I got from *The Atlantic*. That one said, "You write with a facility that has held our attention." But my story had their coffee drippings on it, even so.

INTERVIEWER: You started as a journalist in Albany. What was your favorite aspect of journalism? Why did it appeal to you?

KENNEDY: It was the uncertainty of general assignment that was terrific: the police stories, the disaster stories, the politics, the squirrelly interviews with some guy who had just walked across the country from Montana wearing a taillight and the dopester who had a perfect system to beat the horses and wanted the world to know about it, but he was broke because he was unlucky. That sort of thing was fun, but Albany, I thought, was moribund. I had exhausted the city in a certain way—at that age—and so along came the possibility to go down to the tropics and work in San Juan. That seemed very exotic. I applied and got the job. I went down in April 1956 and started to work on a newspaper called *The Puerto Rican World Journal*. It had existed during the war years as a publication for soldiers and sailors who were stationed in Puerto Rico and for the American civilian component. It was a stepchild of the major Spanish language daily, *El Mundo*. It only lasted nine months, but it was a valuable experience. I love Puerto Rico. I had a great time socially, as a columnist, and I wound up being assistant managing editor when the city editor went to lunch one day and never came back. When the newspaper died, I got married. I met Dana just when the paper was on its last legs. Then I went over for an interview with *The Miami Herald* and got a job writing about Cuban exiles, Castro in the hills, the C.I.A., revolutionaries, political thieves. It was great stuff.

INTERVIEWER: What, other than journalism, were you writing at the time?

KENNEDY: Having failed miserably as a short-story writer, I decided it was time to go out and fail as a novelist. I started in Miami, and I realized that I couldn't do it full-time—the job was very time consuming. I was writing good things for the paper, but I was bored, really. Some of the stories I was writing were not unlike what I had done at the *Times-Union*—a story on a cop giving a ticket to a little kid in a kiddie car, an escaped jaguar attacking a tomato plant in a woman's backyard. I stayed with the coverage for seven months and then decided that it was as deadly as everything else I was doing and I really had to get out. So I quit, went back to Puerto Rico, and wrote a rotten novel. It went around to an agent or two and nobody liked it. So I put it on the shelf and it hasn't seen the daylight since.

INTERVIEWER: What influence did Saul Bellow have on you?

KENNEDY: I met Saul in Puerto Rico when he was teaching at the university at Rio Piedras. I was managing editor of another brand new daily paper, the *San Juan Star*, but was writing yet another novel before and after work. I sent it to Bellow and he accepted me in his class. It was an important development and I took his criticism very seriously. He would explain that my writing was "fatty"—I was saying everything twice and I had too many adjectives. He said it was also occasionally "clotty"—it was imprecision he was talking about, an effort to use a word that wasn't quite as precise and so screwed up the clause or sentence. When he pointed that out to me, I would go back through the whole book and slash—it turned me into a real fiction editor of my own copy, and it later helped when *I* became a teacher. If I was ruthless with my own stuff, why shouldn't I be with everybody else's? Bellow also talked about being prodigal. He said that a writer shouldn't be parsimonious with his work, but "prodigal, like nature." He said just think of nature and how many billions of sperm are used when only one is needed for creating life. And that principle was, it seemed, at the heart of *Augie March*, a novel that exploded with language and ideas. I never became that kind of writer, but I think the effusion, the principle was important. I was never afraid of writing too much, never thought that just because you've written a sentence it means something, or that it's a good sentence just because you've written it. You know,

I wrote *Legs* eight times, and it was taller than my son when both he and the manuscript were six years old. I have a picture of them together. One day Bellow was reading this section of a story where I had gone back and rewritten the things he had suggested I change. He looked up at me, and he said, "Hey, this is publishable!" Nobody had ever said that about anything I had written before, so I went out and bought a bottle of champagne and went back and had a party with my wife and some friends. Having come that distance—twelve years of writing in the dark—then having somebody of value suddenly say that, well it put me onto a different level of existence as a writer. It verified the apprenticeship, moved me into journeyman status. And I kept writing.

INTERVIEWER: Because of your isolation and all the rejections, did you ever think: This is not my profession. I should really be doing something else.

KENNEDY: No, I never thought that. As I used to say on Thursday afternoons—when I was on my day off from the *Albany Times-Union* and waiting for the muse to descend and discovering that it was the muse's day off too—you have to beat the bastards. I didn't even know who the bastards were, but you have to beat somebody. You have to beat your own problematic imagination to discover what it is you're saying and how to say it and move forward into the unknown. I always knew that (a) I wanted to be a writer and (b) if you persist in doing something, that sooner or later you will achieve it. It's just a matter of persistence—and a certain amount of talent. You can't do anything without talent, but you can't do anything without persistence either. Bellow and I once talked about that. We were talking in general about writing and publishing and so on, and he said there's a certain amount of talent that's necessary. All sorts of people are out there with no talent trying very hard and nothing comes of it. You must have some kind of talent. But after that, it's character. I said, "What do you mean by character?" And he smiled at me, and never said anything. So I was left for the rest of my life to define what he meant that night. What I concluded was that character is equivalent to persistence. That if you just refuse to give up, the game's not over. You know, I had had enormous success in everything I'd done in life, up until the time I decided to be a writer. I was a good student; I was a good soldier. I got a hole-in-one one day on the golf course. I bowled 299, just like Billy Phelan. I was a very good newspaperman. Anything I wanted to do in journalism, it seemed to work; it just fell into place. So I didn't understand why I was so successful as a journalist and zilch as a novelist and short-story writer. It was just that time was working against me. You just have to learn. It's such complicated craft . . . such a complicated thing to understand what you're trying to bring out of your own imagination, your own life.

INTERVIEWER: Did you find yourself getting better and better at it?

KENNEDY: Well, I thought I was terrific when I wrote *The Ink Truck* and they published it—Jesus! But then I wrote *Legs* and everybody kept saying, "This is not good." People would turn it down; my own editor, who wanted to publish it, kept saying, "This is not working." I couldn't figure it out. It was six years of figuring and discovering. *Legs* was the novel where I really learned how to write a novel. And it takes you a long time to discover that, to probe whatever it is that you have in you. Where is your talent, where is your voice, where is your style? It was a complicated and sometimes painful struggle. To have an editor say to you, "We think you should turn this into a *biography* of Legs Diamond"—well, I immediately left that bind and went off on my own. And that was the night I sat down and decided to write *Legs* one more time, and that was the one that worked.

INTERVIEWER: What was the solution?

KENNEDY: I had been trying to do the book in a multiplicity of ways. I began thinking I would write it as a film-in-process, because the gangster had been such a charismatic presence in movies; I wanted to make a literary artifact in which the film would be a significant element. That became a silly gimmick. I tried to make it a surrealistic novel. I tried to pattern it totally on the Tibetan Book of the Dead; those chapters are pretty wild. The process of elimination left me with the Henry Jamesian wisdom that I really needed a point of view on this. I tried to write it from inside Diamond and it didn't work and I tried to write from outside Diamond with a chorus of voices and it didn't work. And then I discovered that if I used the lawyer who was in the book from the beginning as this intelligent presence who could look at Diamond and intersect with him at every level of his life, then I would be able to have a perspective on what was going on inside the man. So I did that and it made all the difference. It also made a difference that I spent three months just talking to myself, trying to figure out every character and defining the plot from scratch, narrowing it down. I had five years' worth of paper at that time but that three months' worth of work made all the difference. Then the book began to define itself. That's when you really understand craft.

INTERVIEWER: It is a technical problem.

KENNEDY: Absolutely. That's what I was up against. I had so much research, so much knowledge about this man, so many possible directions I could go in. I had done a massive amount of research because I wanted to discover what his life was really like. It turned out to be very complicated. He had been a celebrity quite apart from anything I had imagined of any gangster. I knew about the notoriety of Al Capone and I had heard of Legs Diamond, but it wasn't until I really began to go after him that I saw how much he had occupied the front pages of the newspapers of the country and the world. He was notorious, front-page stories about him every day, for weeks at a time. As a fugitive crossing the Atlantic on an ocean liner he was the cynosure of international news coverage. I knew he was a son of a bitch but even a life like his is worthy of attention in fiction. If you fix seriously on the transition from one life form to another, from defensible street life to the indefensible, where somebody begins to be a willfully cruel human being, that's worth doing. I wanted to understand the man but also the age, and I did not want to offer up another novel that would be historically inaccurate. So many books and films about Diamond and his kind were travesties. And so I got hooked on research, couldn't get out from under the library's microfilm machine until I finally realized I was doing myself a great disservice; because your imagination can't absorb all that new material and synthesize it easily. If you're trying to transform the material, which is what fiction must do or else it remains journalism, or biography, then you have to let your imagination have a little rest. So I quit. I could have done another six months of research on Diamond, but I gave up. That's when I sat down, slowly absorbed all that I'd collected, and invented Diamond—a brand new Legs Diamond—from scratch. Authentic but new.

INTERVIEWER: Would he recognize himself?

KENNEDY: Oh yes, he already has. After I finished the book and it was about to be published, my wife had a dream: Legs Diamond came up to our front door and knocked on the door. Then he got down on the lawn, laid back and rolled around and kicked his legs in the air. He said to Dana, "Bill got it just right."

INTERVIEWER: What a relief! Do you get letters from people who are historians of the twenties who say, "No, no, you didn't get that right"?

KENNEDY: Every once in a while, somebody writes me and says I didn't get the death of Legs Diamond right, but I never defined who killed him. That's still a mystery.

INTERVIEWER: How important is a sense of place in your fiction? How did Puerto Rico and Albany affect your fiction?

KENNEDY: The Puerto Rico short stories I wrote seemed to have no resonance, I suppose because I lacked a full historical sense of the place. They represented what Eudora Welty once called "the Isle of Capri novel," the transient story that could be set in Paris or Honolulu, all events taking place in a villa or a resort. The shallowness is evident; soap opera, really. I was leaving out the density of life in a given place and I came to know it. I kept reading Faulkner's *The Sound and The Fury* over and over, trying to understand how he'd done it. It was extraordinary to see how he knew so much about a group of people and at the same time reflected an entire cosmos, and with such remarkable language and invention. I wanted to understand any place I wrote about in the same way; and I believe that book more than any other led me to the sense of place in a novel. I started to write about Albany when I was still in San Juan and I realized how little I knew even of my own home town. When I came back to Albany to live I immersed myself in its history and I still can't get enough of the place. Some people have said that *Ironweed* could have been set anywhere because it has a universality about it; and that's nice to hear. But it couldn't have taken place in Capri, or Honolulu; not every town has a skid row and a mission, or trolley strikes with the heavy violence that made Francis Phelan what he was. Even being Irish Catholic—it's not the same even in Ireland as it is in Albany.

INTERVIEWER: How would you assess your development as a stylist?

KENNEDY: Somewhere back in the late sixties a friend of mine named Gene McGarr—we were sitting in The Lion's Head in Greenwich Village one afternoon—said to me, "You know, Irishmen are people who sit around trying to say things good." That is the purest expression of style I've ever come across. I remember being enormously impressed by Damon Runyon's style when I was a kid because it was so unique. It just leaped out at you and said, "Look at me! I'm a style!" and Hemingway had a style. These people were egregiously stylish. Then

I read Graham Greene and I couldn't find a style. I thought, why doesn't this man have a style? I liked his stories enormously, and his novels, but what was his style? Of course he has an extraordinary style in telling a story, great economy and intelligence. Obviously these were adolescent attitudes toward style, valuing ways of being singular. I admired journalists who had style, Red Smith and Mencken. You wouldn't mistake their writing, you'd know it right away. What I set out to do very early on, in college, was to mold a style; and then I realized it was an artificial effort. I was either imitating Red Smith or Hemingway, or Runyon, or whomever, and I gave up on it. I realized that was death. Every time I'd reread it, I'd say that's not you, that's somebody else. As I went on in journalism I was always trying to say something in a way that was neither clichéd nor banal, that was funny if possible, or dramatic if possible. I began to expand my language: sentences grew more complicated, the words became more arcane. I used the word "eclectic" once in a news story and it came out "electric." It was a willful strain at being artsy, so I gave up that too. And as soon as I gave up, I wrote the only thing that I could write, which was whatever came to my head in the most natural possible way. And I evolved into whatever it is I've become. If I have a style, I don't know how to evaluate it. I wouldn't know what to say about my style. I think *The Ink Truck* is an ambitious book in language. I think certain parts of *Legs* are also; but Marcus is still telling that story in a fairly offhanded way, using the vernacular in large measure. *Billy Phelan* goes from being inside Martin Daugherty's mind, which is a far more educated mind, to Billy Phelan's, and the narration is really only in service of representing those two minds. This was very different from what I came to in *Ironweed*, where I set out at the beginning to use the best language at my disposal. I thought my third person voice was me at first, but the more I wrote, the more I realized that the third person voice was this ineffable level of Francis Phelan's life, a level he would never get to consciously, but which was there somehow. And that became the style of the telling of the story; and the language became as good as I could make it whenever I felt it was time for those flights of rhetoric up from the sidewalk, out of the gutter. Francis moves in and out of those flights sometimes in the same sentence. A word will change the whole attitude toward what he's thinking, or talking about, or just intuiting silently. I think that as soon as you abandon your overt efforts at style, that's where you begin to find your own voice. Then it becomes a matter of editing out what doesn't belong—a subordinate clause that says, "That's Kafka," or "That's Melville," whoever it might be. If you don't get rid of that, every time you reread that sentence you think: petty larceny.

INTERVIEWER: The first chapter of *Ironweed* sets the tone for the rest of the book by showing us Francis Phelan through the eyes of the dead, and through his own encounters in memory with the ghosts from his past, with many shifts back and forth in time. The first chapter has a literary magic about it that persists throughout the book and makes the book work in a unique way—but I wonder if you encountered any editorial resistance to the narrative technique when you took *Ironweed* to publishers.

KENNEDY: Considerable. There was one editor who said it was not credible to write this kind of a story and put those kinds of thoughts into Francis Phelan's mind, because no bum thinks that way. That's so abjectly ignorant of human behavior that it really needs no comment except that that man should not be allowed anywhere near a manuscript. Congress should enact a law prohibiting that man from being an editor. I also sent the first few chapters to *The New Yorker* and an editor over there said it was a conventional story about an Irish drunk and they'd had enough of that sort of thing in the past, and they wished me well and thought it was quite well done, and so on. That seemed very wrong-headed. It's hardly a conventional story about an Irish drunk when he's talking to the dead, when he's on an odyssey of such dimensions as Francis is on. I'd never read a book like it, and it seems to me that that's a comment I hear again and again. But again, you have to put up with editors who don't know what they're reading. One editor said there were too many bums in the book and I should get rid of some. And a friend of mine said, "I understand, I love this chapter, but there's an awful lot of negative things in it, there's vomit and a lot of death and violence and there's a lot of sadness, you know, and it's such a downbeat chapter that editors won't want to buy it. Maybe you should alter it to get the editors past the first chapter." Well, there was no way I could take his advice; I had written the book, and it was either going to stand or fall on what it was. I also felt that there was no real merit in the advice, although it was an astute observation about the way some editors are incapable of judging serious literature seriously.

There were also people who just said, "I don't like it." Somebody said, "I could never sell it." Somebody else said, "It's a wonderful book, nobody's ever written anything better about this subject than you have, but I can't add another book to my list that won't make any money." These were more mundane, these were money considerations, but I think those other, more pretentious rejections had the same basis; they just didn't believe a book about bums was ever going to make it in the marketplace, but they didn't dare say so out loud. It's not a book about bums, you know, but that's the way it was perceived. I got a letter from Pat Moynihan after I won the Pulitzer and a story had come out on the AP wire, describing *Ironweed* as a book about a baseball player who turns out to be a murderer. Moynihan quoted that back to me in the letter, and he said, "Perhaps you will have a better understanding of what we poor politicians are up against."

INTERVIEWER: The most prominent characters in your novels are seekers after a truth or meaning or experience beyond the repetitive patterns of daily life. Do you find that your own world view changes as a result of creating these characters and moving them through a series of life experiences?

KENNEDY: I think that my world view changes as I write the book. It's a discovery. The only thing that's really interesting to me is when I surprise myself. It's boring to write things when you know exactly what's going to happen. That's why language was so important to me in journalism. It was the only way you could heighten the drama, or make it funny, or surprising. In *Legs* I was endlessly fascinated to learn how we look at gangsters. I discovered what I thought about mysticism and coincidence when I wrote *Billy*. I feel that *Ironweed* gave me a chance to think about a world most people find worthless. Actually, anybody who doesn't have an idea about what it is to be homeless, or on the road, or lost and without a family, really hasn't thought very much at all. Even though I'd written about this, the small details of that life weren't instantly available to my imagination until I began to think seriously about what it means to sleep in the weeds on a winter night, then wake up frozen to the sidewalk. Such an education becomes part of your ongoing frame of reference in the universe. And if you don't develop Alzheimer's disease or a wet brain, you might go on to write better books. I think that some writers, after an early peaking, go into decline. Fitzgerald seems to me a good example of that. He was writing an interesting book at the end of his life, *The Last Tycoon*, but I don't think it would have been up to his achievement in *Gatsby* or *Tender Is the Night*. But if you don't die, and you're able to sustain your seriousness, I don't think there's any rule that you can't supersede your own early work. I remember an essay by Thomas Mann about Theodor Fontane, the prolific German novelist who believed he was all done somewhere around the age of thirty-nine. But he lived to be a very old man, and published his masterpiece, *Effi Briest*, at age seventy-six. I believe in the capacity of the imagination to mature and I am fond of insisting that I'm not in decline, that the next book is going to be better than the last. It may or may not be, but I have no doubt I know more about how to write a novel, more about what it means to be alive, than I ever have. Whether another dimension of my being has faded, and will refuse to fire my brain into some galvanic achievement, I can't say. We may know more about this when the next book is published.

INTERVIEWER: Did your work in journalism hinder you in writing novels, or was it primarily helpful?

KENNEDY: It was both. It was very difficult to overcome the fact that I was a journalist for a long time. It had to do with the way I looked at material—my feeling that the world was there to be reported upon. Even when I was inventing in those early books—I'm not talking about the ones that were published, I mean the early ones I wrote that weren't published, and all the early stories—I tended to believe that experience alone would save me, that I'd encounter life and therefore be able to report more clearly on it. But the journalist must report on life objectively, and the novelist must reinvent life utterly, and the work has to come up from below instead of down from the top as a journalist receives it. The feeling of insufficient experience was strong for a long time. But experience alone will produce only commonplace novels. The real work is a blend of imagination and language. On the other hand, journalism serves you extraordinarily well because it forces you into situations you would not normally encounter. It thrusts you into spectacles, disasters, high crimes and high art. It forces you to behave in ways that you would not normally behave: being objective in the face of a lying politician, or a movie goddess, or some celebrity figure whose work you've valued all your life, such as Satchmo when I interviewed him. I partly educated myself in writing by interviewing writers. When

I came back to live up here from Puerto Rico in 1963, after seven years away, I left most of my literary friends behind in San Juan. I reentered the society here as a freelance and part-time journalist, trying to write novels, and the first thing I did was seek out people like John Cheever, Bernard Malamud, James Baldwin, and Arthur Miller for interviews. I could speak with these men about what was most important to me —literature. That kind of cachet that you have as a journalist is very valuable. Also, journalism forces you into an ethical stance through objectivity. You're forced into understanding that the world is not as you would like it to be. Yet you certainly cannot report on it your way, unless you become some sort of advocate for a cause. Even when you disagree with a cause you have to give it its due, and that presents you with a chance to understand complexities of human behavior that might otherwise take you a long time to come to. The other thing is that you use the language every day, and one of the pleasures of journalism to me was always being able to see the thing in print the next day or have somebody say, "Hey, that was a good story!" Daily journalism to me was writing as fast as you could, still trying to be some sort of interpreter and entertainer as well as objective reporter. And I was always, from very early on, imbued with the kind of journalism that flowered in the twenties and thirties and forties. People like Mencken, Don Marquis, Westbrook Pegler—I'm not speaking of Pegler's hate-ridden politics, just his ability to turn a sentence—or Red Smith, or so many of the reporters at the *Herald-Tribune* in the forties and fifties, a remarkable newspaper. Some people have this kind of monolithic feeling toward their art and rightfully so. I really consider myself a novelist preeminently but I came out of journalism and I would never in any way try to disown it the way Hemingway did. I think he was wrong-headed from the beginning about the destructive quality of journalism—it was a kind of snobbery; he had elevated himself above it. But what about Stephen Crane, James Agee, and García Márquez? What about Michael Herr and his Vietnam book *Dispatches*? What a piece of work that is.

INTERVIEWER: Do you have any advice for young writers, a way of starting, or a way of looking at one's work as it matures?

KENNEDY: I would think that he or she should discover language and discover the world, a sense of place, and not try to base his or her work only on personal experience. Personal experience as a young person is very limited. We have the great line from Faulkner that the problems of children are not worth writing about. This applies to adolescence and early sexhood as well. It's not that children in trouble are not great subjects, but what you need is a world and a way of approaching the world. If you have these two things, everything is interesting. It's not what you say, it's the way that you say it. It's a sense of the person's existence, and not the person's experience. It's the matrix translated into language. It's the sense of response, as opposed to problem. So much great literature exists on that level of response, the essential element of some great moderns. Leopold and Molly Bloom respond to their worlds with the most remarkable language of thought. Nabokov's language is everything. Take Cheever's language away and the work dribbles off into absurdity; yet with those golden sentences he's the most durable of writers.

INTERVIEWER: Is sex something that's easy to write about in a book? Why do writers have so much difficulty with it?

KENNEDY: I think writers should research sex in the same way they research historical characters. It's not difficult to write about. What is difficult to write about is the actual pornographical element of sex. That ceases to be interesting. What you need to do is find the surrounding elements, the emotional content of the sexual encounters. Yet another struggle of the genitals is hardly worth writing about. It's done on every street-corner, fifty-five times a magazine. So, you know that's not the point. On the contrary, it's when you discover a character like Kiki Roberts who is Legs Diamond's girlfriend and you look at her and discover this incredible beauty, obviously a great sex object for Diamond, who endangered his life many times for her. And she, reciprocating constantly. She was a fugitive from justice with him. When you look at that woman, you can begin to imagine what it was about her that led Diamond to behave that way. So that was quite a pleasant thing for me, to re-imagine Kiki Roberts.

INTERVIEWER: Do characters have a way of taking off on their own?

KENNEDY: I recall Nabokov looked on his characters as his galley slaves. But they do have a way of asserting themselves. Hemingway's line was that everything changes as it moves; and that that is what makes the movement that makes the story. Once you let a character speak or act you now know that he acts this way and not another. You dwell on why this is so and you move forward to the next page. This is my method. I'm not interested in formulating a plot to which characters are added like ribbons on a prize cow. The character is the key and when he does something which is new, something you didn't know about or expect, then the story percolates. If I knew, at the beginning, how the book was going to end, I would probably never finish. I knew that Legs Diamond was going to die at the end of the book, so I killed him on page one.

INTERVIEWER: You said before that you don't write novels to make money. Why do you write novels?

KENNEDY: I remember in 1957 I was reading in *Time* magazine about Jack Kerouac's success with *On the Road*. I felt I wasn't saying what I wanted to say in journalism, wasn't saying it in the short stories I'd been writing either. I had no compelling vision of anything, yet I knew the only way I would ever get it would be to give my imagination the time and space to spread out, to look at things in the round. I also felt that not only did I want to write one novel, I wanted to write a series of novels that would interrelate. I didn't know how, but this is a very old feeling with me. I came across a note the other day that I wrote to myself about "the big Albany novel." This was way back, I can't even remember when—long before I wrote *Legs*, even before *The Ink Truck*. It had to be in the middle sixties. It was a consequence of my early confrontation with the history of Albany when I did a series of articles on the city's neighborhoods in 1963 and 1964. I began to see how long and significant a history we had had, and as I moved along as a part-timer at the *Times-Union*, writing about blacks and civil rights and radicals, I began to see the broad dimension of the city, the interrelation of the ethnic groups. The politics were just incredible—Boss Machine politics, the most successful in the history of the country in terms of longevity. And I realized I could never tell it all in one book.

INTERVIEWER: Is this enormous sort of Yoknapatawpha County in your mind? Do the characters emerge as you think about them? You give the picture of being able to dip into this extraordinary civilization.

KENNEDY: Every time out it's different, but one of the staples is the sense that I have a column of time to work with; for example a political novel that could move from about 1918 to maybe 1930; and in there is a focal point on a character, probably the political boss. But that's not always enough, having a character. I once wrote a novel's worth of notes about three characters and I couldn't write the first sentence of the book. It was all dead in the water. There has to be a coalescence of influences that ignite and become viable as a story.

INTERVIEWER: What do you think the ignition thing is? It's rather frightening that you work on these things and do not know whether it's going to come together. How do you know?

KENNEDY: You don't. It's an act of faith.

INTERVIEWER: *Ironweed*, *Billy Phelan*, and *Legs* were reviewed and marketed as a trilogy of Albany novels.

KENNEDY: Trilogy was never my word and I don't want it to be the word. Cycle is my word. It started with *The Ink Truck*, and continues with *Quinn's Book*, the newest novel. I called it a cycle because I don't know when I'm going to stop. As long as I write books, it seems I have enough variety of intention, both in subject matter and in approach to the material, that I'm not going to be bored by my opportunities. People say, "Why don't you write about someplace else?" Well, I don't think that there's anyplace any more interesting to write about. I don't *have* to go anyplace else. The more I stay here, the more interesting the cycle becomes. If I'm able to convey a society in transition or a society in embryo, that's worth doing. In one way I'm really trying to write history. But history is only a tool to ground me in telling a story about what it means to be alive.

INTERVIEWER: What is the feeling when you're done with a book?

KENNEDY: I remember the day I finished *Ironweed*. I came down and I said, "I'm finished." My wife was there and one of my good friends; they had read most of the book along the way and they sat down and read the ending. Somehow they didn't respond the way I wanted them to respond. I was thinking of an abstract reader who would say what every writer wants you to say to him: "This is the best thing I ever read in my life." I knew something was wrong, though I didn't know what; I knew the elements of the ending should be very powerful. I thought about it and their lack of proper response. After dinner I went back upstairs and rewrote the ending, adding a page and a half. I brought that down and then they said, "This is the best thing I've ever read in my life."

DOUGLAS R. ALLEN
MONA SIMPSON
July 1984
Spring 1988

# 8. *Maya Angelou*

Maya Angelou is perhaps best known for the autobiographical series she launched in 1970 with *I Know Why the Caged Bird Sings*—an immediate success, receiving a National Book Award nomination. In it, Angelou depicts her growing up in the segregated town of Stamps, Arkansas, where she had been sent by her divorced parents. In *Gather Together in My Name* (1974), Angelou recounts the first four years of her life as a single mother. *Singin' and Swingin' and Gettin' Merry Like Christmas* (1976) chronicles her life into the 1950s. *The Heart of a Woman* (1981) and *All God's Children Need Traveling Shoes* (1986) describes her journey to Africa, as well as her involvement in the civil rights movement in the United States.

Angelou's first volume of poetry, *Just Give Me a Cold Drink of Water 'fore I Die* (1971), was nominated for the Pulitzer Prize. Other collections include *Oh Pray My Wings Are Gonna Fit Me Well* (1975) and *And Still I Rise* (1978). *I Shall Not Be Moved* was published in 1990.

Throughout her life, Angelou's involvement in the performing arts has been varied and outstanding. She has danced under the tuition of Martha Graham, Pearl Primus, and Ann Halprin; she was the first black woman to have an original screenplay produced (*Georgia, Georgia*, 1971) and was the first black American woman to direct films.

Angelou has held academic posts at several universities in the United States, including the University of California and Wichita State. She has been honored by Smith College (1975), Mills College (1975), and Lawrence University (1976). In 1981 Wake University in Winston-Salem, North Carolina, appointed her to a lifetime position as the first Reynolds Professor of American Studies. In 1991, Angelou was named Distinguished Visiting Professor at Exeter University, England.

1

Before a long journey begins, which includes crossing boundaries and time zones, the prudent traveler checks her maps checks, addresses and travel documents, passport, Visa, medical innoculations, makes certain that her clothes will fit the weather, and that she has apt currencies for the destination. If the journey include crossing regional & national boundaries and time zones, the traveller checks the validity of her

The less careful traveler is not so superb in her planning, and as a result frequently encounters delays, disruptions and disappointment and despair. Still Once the journey commences she unfailingly reaches some destination, although possibly not the one of her choice.

It is The desperate traveler who experiences the greatest surprises and the most exquisite thrills, her sole preparation for is the fierce determination to leave where she is, and her only certain destination is somewhere other than where she has been.

"I got the key to the Highway,

Booked down and I'm bound to go

*A manuscript page from a tribute to Oprah Winfrey by Maya Angelou.*

© Tim Richmond/Katz Pictures

# *Maya Angelou*

*This interview was conducted on the stage of the YMHA on Manhattan's upper East Side. A large audience, predominantly women, was on hand, filling indeed every seat, with standees in the back . . . a testament to Maya Angelou's drawing-power. Close to the stage was a small contingent of black women dressed in the white robes of the Black Muslim order. Her presence dominated the proceedings. Many of her remarks drew fervid applause, especially those which reflected her views on racial problems, the need to persevere, and "courage." She is an extraordinary performer and has a powerful stage presence. Many of the answers seemed as much directed to the audience as to the interviewer so that when Maya Angelou concluded the evening by reading aloud from her work —again to a rapt audience—it seemed a logical extension of a planned entertainment.*

INTERVIEWER: You once told me that you write lying on a made-up bed with a bottle of sherry, a dictionary, *Roget's Thesaurus*, yellow pads, an ashtray, and a Bible. What's the function of the Bible?

MAYA ANGELOU: The language of all the interpretations, the translations, of the Judaic Bible and the Christian Bible, is musical, just wonderful. I read the Bible to myself; I'll take any translation, any edition, and read it aloud, just to hear the language, hear the rhythm, and remind myself how beautiful English is. Though I do manage to mumble around in about seven or eight languages, English remains the most beautiful of languages. It will do anything.

INTERVIEWER: Do you read it to get inspired to pick up your own pen?

ANGELOU: For melody. For content also. I'm working at trying to be a Christian, and that's serious business. It's like trying to be a good Jew, a good Muslim, a good Buddhist, a good Shintoist, a good Zoroastrian, a good friend, a good lover, a good mother, a good buddy: it's serious business. It's not something where you think, "Oh, I've got it done. I did it all day, hotdiggety." The truth is, all day long you try to do it, try to be it, and then in the evening, if you're honest and have a little courage, you look at yourself and say, "Hmm. I only blew it eighty-six times. Not bad." I'm trying to be a Christian, and the Bible helps me to remind myself what I'm about.

INTERVIEWER: Do you transfer that melody to your own prose? Do you think your prose has that particular ring that one associates with the King James version?

ANGELOU: I want to hear how English sounds; how Edna St. Vincent Millay heard English. I want to hear it, so I read it aloud. It is not so that I can then imitate it. It is to remind me what a glorious language it is. Then, I try to be particular, and even original. It's a little like reading Gerard Manley Hopkins or Paul Laurence Dunbar, or James Weldon Johnson.

INTERVIEWER: And is the bottle of sherry for the end of the day, or to fuel the imagination?

ANGELOU: I might have it at 6:15 A.M. just as soon as I get in, but usually it's about eleven o'clock when I'll have a glass of sherry.

INTERVIEWER: When you are refreshed by the Bible and the sherry, how do you start a day's work?

ANGELOU: I have kept a hotel room in every town I've ever lived in. I rent a hotel room for a few months, leave my home at six and try to be at work by 6:30. To write, I lie across the bed, so that this elbow is absolutely encrusted at the end, just so rough with callouses. I never allow the hotel people to change the bed, because I never sleep there.

I stay until 12:30 or 1:30 in the afternoon, and then I go home and try to breathe; I look at the work around five; I have an orderly dinner: proper, quiet, lovely dinner; and then I go back to work the next morning. Sometimes in hotels I'll go into the room, and there'll be a note on the floor which says, "Dear Miss Angelou, let us change the sheets. We think they are moldy." But I only allow them to come in and empty wastebaskets. I insist that all things are taken off the walls. I don't want anything in there. I go into the room, and I feel as if all my beliefs are suspended. Nothing holds me to anything. No milkmaids, no flowers, nothing. I just want to *feel* and then when I start to work I'll remember. I'll read something, maybe the Psalms, maybe, again, something from Mr. Dunbar, James Weldon Johnson. And I'll remember how beautiful, how pliable the language is, how it will lend itself. If you pull it, it says, "Okay." I remember that, and I start to write. Nathaniel Hawthorne says, "Easy reading is damn hard writing." I try to pull the language in to such a sharpness that it jumps off the page. It must look easy, but it takes me forever to get it to look so easy. Of course, there are those critics—New York critics as a rule—who say, "Well, Maya Angelou has a new book out and, of course, it's good but then she's a natural writer." Those are the ones I want to grab by the throat and wrestle to the floor because it takes me forever to get it to sing. I *work* at the language. On an evening like this, looking out at the auditorium, if I had to write this evening from my point of view, I'd see the rust-red used worn velvet seats, and the lightness where people's backs have rubbed against the back of the seat so that it's a light orange; then, the beautiful colors of the people's faces, the white, pink-white, beige-white, light beige and brown and tan—I would have to look at all that, at all those faces and the way they sit on top of their necks. When I would end up writing after four hours or five hours in my room, it might sound like: "It was a rat that sat on a mat. That's that. Not a cat." But I would continue to play with it and pull at it and say, "I love you. Come to me. I love you." It might take me two or three weeks just to describe what I'm seeing now.

INTERVIEWER: How do you know when it's what you want?

ANGELOU: I know when it's the best I can do. It may not be the best there is. Another writer may do it much better. But I know when it's the best I can do. I know that one of the great arts that the writer develops is the art of saying, "No. No, I'm finished. Bye." And leaving it alone. I will not write it into the ground. I will not write the life out of it. I won't do that.

INTERVIEWER: How much revising is involved?

ANGELOU: I write in the morning, and then go home about midday and take a shower, because writing, as you know, is very hard work, so you have to do a double ablution. Then I go out and shop—I'm a serious cook—and pretend to be normal. I play sane: "Good morning! Fine, thank you. And you?" And I go home. I prepare dinner for myself and if I have houseguests, I do the candles and the pretty music and all that. Then, after all the dishes are moved away, I read what I wrote that morning. And more often than not, if I've done nine pages I may be able to save two and a half, or three. That's the cruelest time you know, to really admit that it doesn't work. And to blue pencil it. When I finish maybe fifty pages, and read them—fifty acceptable pages—it's not too bad. I've had the same editor since 1967. Many times he has said to me over the years, or asked me, "Why would you use a semicolon instead of a colon?" And many times over the years I have said to him things like: "I will never speak to you again. Forever. Goodbye. That is it. Thank you very much." And I leave. Then I read the piece and I think of his suggestions. I send him a telegram that says, "OK, so you're right. So what? Don't ever mention this to me again. If you do, I will never speak to you again." About two years ago I was visiting him and his wife in the Hamptons. I was at the end of a dining room table with a sit-down dinner of about fourteen people. Way at the end I said to someone, "I sent him telegrams over the years." From the other end of the table he said, "And I've kept every one!" Brute! But the editing, one's own editing, before the editor sees it, is the most important.

INTERVIEWER: The five autobiographical books follow each other in chronological order. When you started writing *I Know Why the Caged Bird Sings* did you know that you would move on from that? It almost works line by line into the second volume.

ANGELOU: I know, but I didn't really mean to. I thought I was going to write *Caged Bird* and that would be it and I would go back to playwriting and writing scripts for television. Autobiography is awfully seductive; it's wonderful. Once I got into it I realized I was following a tradition established by Frederick Douglass—the slave narrative—speaking in the first-person singular talking about the first-person plural, always saying "I" meaning "we." And what a responsibility! Trying to work with that form, the autobiographical mode, to change it, to make it bigger, richer, finer, and more inclusive in the twentieth century has been a great challenge for me. I've written five now, and I really hope—the works are required reading in many universities and colleges in the United States—that people *read* my work. The greatest compliment I receive is when people walk up to me on the street or in airports and say, "Miss Angelou, I *wrote* your books last year and I really—I mean I *read* . . ." That is it: that the person has come into the books so seriously, so completely, that he or she, black or white, male or female, feels, "That's my story. I told it. I'm making it up on the spot." That's the great compliment. I didn't expect, originally, that I was going to continue with the form. I thought I was going to write a little book and it would be fine, and I would go on back to poetry, write a little music.

INTERVIEWER: What about the genesis of the first book? Who were the people who helped you shape those sentences that leap off the page?

ANGELOU: Oh well, they started years and years before I ever wrote, when I was very young. I loved the black American minister. I loved the melody of the voice, and the imagery, so rich, and almost impossible. The minister in my church in Arkansas, when I was very young, would use phrases such as "God stepped out, the sun over his right shoulder, the moon nestling in the palm of his hand." I mean, I just loved it, and I loved the black poets, and I loved Shakespeare, and Edgar Allan Poe, and I liked Matthew Arnold a lot, still do. Being mute for a number of years, I read, and memorized, and all those people have had tremendous influence . . . in the first book, and even in the most recent book.

INTERVIEWER: Mute?

ANGELOU: I was raped when I was very young. I told my brother the name of the person who had done it. Within a few days the man was killed. In my child's mind—seven and a half years old—I thought my voice had killed him. So I stopped talking for five years. Of course I've written about this in *Caged Bird*.

INTERVIEWER: When did you decide you were going to be a writer? Was there a moment when you suddenly said, "This is what I wish to do for the rest of my life."

ANGELOU: Well, I had written a television series for PBS, and I was going out to California. I thought I was a poet and playwright. That was what I was going to do the rest of my life. Or become famous as a real estate broker. This sounds like name-dropping, and it really is —but James Baldwin took me over to dinner with Jules and Judy Feiffer one evening. All three of them are great talkers. They went on with their stories and I had to fight for the right to play it good. I had to insert myself to tell some stories too. Well, the next day, Judy Feiffer called Bob Loomis, an editor at Random House, and suggested that if he could get me to write an autobiography, he'd have something. So he phoned me and I said, "No, under no circumstances; I certainly will not do such a thing." So I went out to California to produce this series on African and black American culture. Loomis called me out there about three times. Each time I said no. Then he talked to James Baldwin. Jimmy gave him a ploy which always works with me—though I'm not proud to say that. The next time he called, he said, "Well, Miss Angelou. I won't bother you again. It's just as well that you don't attempt to write this book, because to write autobiography as literature is almost impossible." I said, "What are you talking about? I'll do it." I'm not proud about this button which can be pushed and I will immediately jump.

INTERVIEWER: Do you select a dominant theme for each book?

ANGELOU: I try to remember times in my life, incidents in which there was the dominating theme of cruelty, or kindness, or generosity, or envy, or happiness, glee . . . perhaps four incidents in the period I'm going to write about. Then I select, the one which lends itself best to my device and which I can write as drama without falling into melodrama.

INTERVIEWER: Did you write for a particular audience?

ANGELOU: I thought early on if I could write a book for black girls it would be good, because there were so few books for a black girl to read that said "This is how it is to grow up." Then, I thought "I'd better, you know, enlarge that group, the market group that I'm trying to reach." I decided to write for black boys, and then white girls, and then white boys.

But what I try to keep in mind mostly is my craft. That's what I really try for; I try to allow myself to be impelled by my art—if that doesn't sound too pompous and weird—accept the impulse, and then try my best to have a command of the craft. If I'm feeling depressed, and losing my control, then I think about the reader. But that is very rare—to think about the reader when the work is going on.

INTERVIEWER: So you don't keep a particular reader in mind when you sit down in that hotel room and begin to compose or write. It's yourself.

ANGELOU: It's myself . . . and my reader. I would be a liar, a hypocrite, or a fool—and I'm not any of those—to say that I don't write for the reader. I do. But for the reader who hears, who really will work at it, going behind what I seem to say. So I write for myself and that reader who will pay the dues. There's a phrase in West Africa, in Ghana; it's called "deep talk." For instance, there's a saying: "The trouble for the thief is not how to steal the chief's bugle, but where to blow it." Now, on the face of it, one understands that. But when you really think about it, it takes you deeper. In West Africa they call that "deep talk." I'd like to think I write "deep talk." When you read me, you should be able to say "Gosh, that's pretty. That's lovely. That's nice. Maybe there's something else? Better read it again." Years ago I read a man named Machado de Assis who wrote a book called *Dom Casmro: Epitaph of a Small Winner*. Machado de Assis is a South American writer—black mother, Portuguese father—writing in 1865, say. I thought the book was very nice. Then I went back and read the book and said, "Hmm. I didn't realize all that was in that book." Then I read it again, and again, and I came to the conclusion that what Machado de Assis had done for me was almost a trick: he had beckoned me onto the beach to watch a sunset. And I had watched the sunset with pleasure. When I turned around to come back in I found that the tide had come in over my head. That's when I decided to write. I would write so that the reader says, "That's so nice. Oh boy, that's pretty. Let me read that again." I think that's why *Caged Bird* is in its twenty-first printing in hardcover and its twenty-ninth in paper. All my books are still in print, in hardback as well as paper, because people go back and say, "Let me read that. Did she *really* say that?"

INTERVIEWER: The books are episodic, aren't they? Almost as if you had put together a string of short stories. I wondered if, as an autobiographer, you ever fiddled with the truth to make the story better.

ANGELOU: Well, sometimes. I love the phrase "fiddle with." It's so English. Sometimes I make a character from a composite of three or four people, because the essence in any one person is not sufficiently strong to be written about. Essentially though, the work is true though sometimes I fiddle with the facts. Many of the people I've written about are alive today, and I have them to face. I wrote about an ex-husband—he's an African—in *The Heart of a Woman*. Before I did, I called him in Dar-es-Salaam and said, "I'm going to write about some of our years together." He said, "Now before you ask, I want you to know that I shall sign my release, because I know you will not lie. However, I am sure I shall argue with you about your interpretation of the truth."

INTERVIEWER: Did he enjoy his portrait finally, or did you argue about it?

ANGELOU: Well, he didn't argue, but I was kind, too.

INTERVIEWER: I would guess this would make it very easy for you to move from autobiography into novel, where you can do anything you want with your characters.

ANGELOU: Yes, but for me, fiction is not the sweetest form. I really am trying to do something with autobiography now. It has caught me. I'm using the first-person singular, and trying to make that the first-person plural, so that anybody can read the work and say, "Hmm, that's the truth, yes, *uh-huh*," and live in the work. It's a large ambitious dream. But I love the form.

INTERVIEWER: Aren't the extraordinary events of your life very hard for the rest of us to identify with?

ANGELOU: Oh my God, I've lived a very simple life! You can say, "Oh yes, at thirteen this happened to me, and at fourteen . . ." But those are facts. But the facts can obscure the truth, what it really felt like. Every human being has paid the earth to grow up. Most people don't grow up. It's too damn difficult. What happens is most people get older. That's the truth of it. They honor their credit cards, they find parking spaces, they marry, they have the nerve to have children, but they don't grow up. Not really. They get older. But to grow up costs the earth, the *earth*. It means you take responsibility for the time you take up, for the space you occupy. It's serious business. And you find out what it costs us to love and to lose, to dare and to fail. And maybe even more, to succeed. What it costs, in truth. Not superficial costs—anybody can have that—I mean in truth. That's what I write. What it really is like. I'm just telling a very simple story.

INTERVIEWER: Aren't you tempted to lie? Novelists lie, don't they?

ANGELOU: I don't know about lying for novelists. I look at some of the great novelists, and I think the reason they are great is that they're telling the truth. The fact is they're using made-up names, made-up people, made-up places, and made-up times, but they're telling the truth about the human being—what we are capable of, what makes us lose, laugh, weep, fall down and gnash our teeth and wring our hands and kill each other and love each other.

INTERVIEWER: James Baldwin, along with a lot of writers in this series, said that "when you're writing you're trying to find out something you didn't know." When you write do you search for something that you didn't know about yourself or about us?

ANGELOU: Yes. When I'm writing, I am trying to find out who I am, who we are, what we're capable of, how we feel, how we lose and stand up, and go on from darkness into darkness. I'm trying for that. But I'm also trying for the language. I'm trying to see how it can really sound. I really love language. I love it for what it does for us, how it allows us to explain the pain and the glory, the nuances and the delicacies of our existence. And then it allows us to laugh, allows us to show wit. Real wit is shown in language. We need language.

INTERVIEWER: Baldwin also said that his family urged him not to become a writer. His father felt that there was a white monopoly in publishing. Did you ever have any of those feelings: that you were going up against something that was really immensely difficult for a black writer?

ANGELOU: Yes, but I didn't find it so just in writing. I've found it so in all the things I've attempted. In the shape of American society, the white male is on top, then the white female, and then the black male, and at the bottom is the black woman. So that's been always so. That is nothing new. It doesn't mean that it doesn't shock me, shake me up. . . .

INTERVIEWER: I can understand that in various social stratifications, but why in art?

ANGELOU: Well, unfortunately, racism is pervasive. It doesn't stop at the university gate, or at the ballet stage. I knew great black dancers, male and female, who were told early on that they were not shaped, physically, for ballet. Today, we see very few black ballet dancers. Unfortunately, in the theater and in film, racism and sexism stand at the door. I'm the first black female director in Hollywood; in order to direct, I went to Sweden and took a course in cinematography so I would understand what the camera would do. Though I had written a screenplay, and even composed the score, I wasn't allowed to direct it. They brought in a young Swedish director who hadn't even shaken a black person's hand before. The film was *Georgia, Georgia* with Diane Sands. People either loathed it or complimented me. Both were wrong, because it was not what I wanted, not what I would have done if I had been allowed to direct it. So I thought, well, what I guess I'd better do is be ten times as prepared. That is not new. I wish it was. In every case I know I have to be ten times more prepared than my white counterpart.

INTERVIEWER: Even as a writer where . . .

ANGELOU: Absolutely.

INTERVIEWER: Yet a manuscript is what arrives at the editor's desk, not a person, not a body.

ANGELOU: Yes. I must have such control of my tools, of words, that I can make this sentence leap off the page. I have to have my writing so polished that it doesn't look polished at all. I want a reader, especially an editor, to be a half-hour into my book before he realizes it's reading he's doing.

INTERVIEWER: But isn't that the goal of every person who sits down at a typewriter?

ANGELOU: Absolutely. Yes. It's possible to be overly sensitive, to carry a bit of paranoia along with you. But I don't think that's a bad thing. It keeps you sharp, keeps you on your toes.

INTERVIEWER: Is there a thread one can see through the five autobiographies? It seems to me that one prevailing theme is the love of your child.

ANGELOU: Yes, well, that's true. I think that that's a particular. I suppose, if I'm lucky, the particular is seen in the general. There is, I hope, a thesis in my work: we may encounter many defeats, but we must not be defeated. That sounds goody two-shoes, I know, but I believe that a diamond is the result of extreme pressure and time. Less time is crystal. Less than that is coal. Less than that is fossilized leaves. Less than that it's just plain dirt. In all my work, in the movies I write, the lyrics, the poetry, the prose, the essays, I am saying that we may encounter many defeats—maybe it's imperative that we encounter the defeats—but we are much stronger than we appear to be, and maybe much better than we allow ourselves to be. Human beings are more alike than unalike. There's no real mystique. Every human being, every Jew, Christian, back-slider, Muslim, Shintoist, Zen Buddhist, atheist, agnostic, every human being wants a nice place to live, a good place for the children to go to school, healthy children, somebody to love, the courage, the unmitigated gall to accept love in return, someplace to party on Saturday or Sunday night, and someplace to perpetuate that God. There's no mystique. None. And if I'm right in my work, that's what my work says.

INTERVIEWER: Have you been back to Stamps, Arkansas?

ANGELOU: About 1970, Bill Moyers, Willie Morris, and I were at some affair. Judith Moyers as well—I think she was the instigator. We may have had two or three scotches, or seven or eight. Willie Morris was then with *Harper's* magazine. The suggestion came up: "Why don't we all go back South." Willie Morris was from Yazoo, Mississippi. Bill Moyers is from Marshall, Texas, which is just a hop, skip, and a jump—about as far as you can throw a chitterling—from Stamps, my hometown. Sometime in the middle of the night there was this idea: "Why don't Bill Moyers and Maya Angelou go to Yazoo, Mississippi, to visit Willie Morris? Then why don't Willie Morris and Maya Angelou go to Marshall, Texas, to visit Bill Moyers?" I said, "Great." I was agreeing with both. Then they said Willie Morris and Bill Moyers would go to Stamps, Arkansas, to visit Maya Angelou, and I said, "No way, José. I'm not going back to that little town with two white men! I will not do it!" Well, after a while Bill Moyers called me—he was doing a series on "creativity"—and he said, "Maya, come on, let's go to Stamps." I said, "No way." He continued, "I want to talk about creativity." I said, "You know, I don't want to know where it resides." I really don't, and I still don't. One of the problems in the West is that people are too busy putting things under microscopes and so forth. Creativity is greater than the sum of its parts. All I want to know is that creativity is there. I want to know that I can put my hand behind my back like Tom Thumb and pull out a plum. Anyway, Moyers went on and on and so did Judith and before I knew it, I found myself in Stamps, Arkansas. Stamps, Arkansas! With Bill Moyers, in front of my grandmother's door. My God! We drove out of town: me with Bill and Judith. Back of us was the crew, a New York crew, you know, very "Right, dig where I'm comin' from, like, get it on," and so forth. We got about three miles outside of Stamps and I said, "Stop the car. Let the car behind us pull up. Get those people in with you and I'll take their car." I suddenly was taken back to being twelve years old in a southern, tiny town where my grandmother told me, "Sistah, never be on a country road with any white boys." I was two hundred years older than black pepper, but I said, "Stop the car." I did. I got out of the car. And I knew these guys—certainly Bill. Bill Moyers is a friend and brother-friend to me; we care for each other. But dragons, fears, the grotesques of childhood always must be confronted at childhood's door. Any other place is esoteric and has nothing to do with the great fear that is laid upon one as a child. So anyway, we did Bill Moyers's show. And it seems to be a very popular program, and it's the first of the "creativity" programs. . . .

INTERVIEWER: Did going back assuage those childhood fears?

ANGELOU: They are there like griffins hanging off the sides of old and tired European buildings.

INTERVIEWER: It hadn't changed?

ANGELOU: No, worse if anything.

INTERVIEWER: But it was forty years before you went back to the South, to North Carolina. Was that because of a fear of finding griffins everywhere, Stamps being a typical community of the South?

ANGELOU: Well, I've never felt the need to prove anything to an audience. I'm always concerned about who I am to me first, to myself and God. I really am. I didn't go south because I didn't want to pull up whatever clout I had, because that's boring, that's not real, not true; that doesn't tell me anything. If I had known I was afraid, I would have gone earlier. I just thought I'd find the South really unpleasant. I have moved south now. I *live* there.

INTERVIEWER: Perhaps writing the autobiographies, finding out about yourself, would have made it much easier to go back.

ANGELOU: I know many think that writing sort of "clears the air." It doesn't do that at all. If you are going to write autobiography, don't expect that it will clear anything up. It makes it more clear to you, but it doesn't alleviate anything. You simply know it better, you have names for people.

INTERVIEWER: There's a part in *Caged Bird* where you and your brother want to do a scene from *The Merchant of Venice*, and you don't dare do it because your grandmother would find out that Shakespeare was not only deceased but white.

ANGELOU: I don't think she'd have minded if she'd known he was deceased. I tried to pacify her—my mother knew Shakespeare, but my grandmother was raising us. When I told her I wanted to recite—it was actually Portia's speech—Mama said to me, "Now, sistah, what are you goin' to render?" The phrase was so fetching. The phrase was: "Now, little mistress Marguerite will render her rendition." Mama said, "Now, sistah, what are you goin' to render?" I said, "Mama, I'm going to render a piece written by William Shakespeare." My grandmother asked me, "Now, sistah, who is this very William Shakespeare?" I had to tell her that he was white, it was going to come out. Somebody would let it out. So I told Mama, "Mama, he's white, but he's dead." Then I said, "He's been dead for centuries," thinking she'd forgive him because of this little idiosyncracy. She said, "No Ma'am, little mistress you will not. No Ma'am, little mistress you will not." So I rendered James Weldon Johnson, Paul Laurence Dunbar, Countee Cullen, Langston Hughes.

INTERVIEWER: Were books allowed in the house?

ANGELOU: None of those books were in the house; they were in the school. I'd bring them home from school, and my brother gave me Edgar Allan Poe because he knew I loved him. I loved him so much I called him "EAP." But as I said, I had a problem when I was young: from the time I was seven and a half to the time I was twelve and a half I was a mute. I could speak, but I didn't speak for five years, and I was what was called a "volunteer mute." But I read and I memorized just masses—I don't know if one is born with photographic memory, but I think you can develop it. I just have that.

INTERVIEWER: What is the significance of the title, *All God's Children Need Traveling Shoes*?

ANGELOU: I never agreed, even as a young person, with the Thomas Wolfe title *You Can't Go Home Again*. Instinctively I didn't. But the truth is, you can never *leave* home. You take it with you; it's under your fingernails; it's in the hair follicles; it's in the way you smile; it's in the ride of your hips, in the passage of your breasts; it's all there, no matter where you go. You can take on the affectations and the postures of other places, and even learn to speak their ways. But the truth is, home is between your teeth. Everybody's always looking for it: Jews go to Israel; black-Americans and Africans in the Diaspora go to Africa; Europeans, Anglo-Saxons go to England and Ireland; people of Germanic background go to Germany. It's a very queer quest. We can kid ourselves; we can tell ourselves, "Oh yes, honey, I live in Tel Aviv, actually. . . ." The truth is a stubborn fact. So this book is about trying to go home.

INTERVIEWER: If you had to endow a writer with the most necessary pieces of equipment, other than, of course, yellow legal pads, what would these be?

ANGELOU: Ears. Ears. To hear the language. But there's no one piece of equipment that is most necessary. Courage, first.

INTERVIEWER: Did you ever feel that you could not get your work published? Would you have continued to write if Random House had returned your manuscript?

ANGELOU: I didn't think it was going to be very easy, but I knew I was going to do something. The real reason black people exist at all today is because there's a resistance to a larger society that says, "You can't do it. You can't survive. And if you survive, you certainly can't thrive. And if you thrive, you can't thrive with any passion or compassion or humor or style." There's a saying, a song which says, "Don't you let nobody turn you 'round, turn you 'round. Don't you let nobody turn you 'round." Well, I've always believed that. So knowing that, knowing that nobody could turn me 'round, if I didn't publish, well, I would design this theater we're sitting in. Yes. Why not? Some human being did it. I agree with Terence. Terence said, "*Homo sum: humani nihil a me alienum puto.*" I am a human being. Nothing human can be alien to me. When you look up Terence in the encyclopedia, you see beside his name, in italics: "Sold to a Roman senator, freed by that Senator." He became the most popular playwright in Rome. Six of his plays and that statement have come down to us from 154 B.C. This man, not born white, not born free, without any chance of ever receiving citizenship, said, "I am a human being. Nothing human can be alien to me." Well, I believe that. I ingested that, internalized that at about thirteen or twelve. I believed if I set my mind to it, maybe I wouldn't be published, but I would write a great piece of music, or do something about becoming a real friend. Yes, I would do something wonderful. It might be with my next-door neighbor, my gentleman friend, with my lover, but it would be wonderful as far as I could do it. So I never have been very concerned about the world telling me how successful I am. I don't need that.

INTERVIEWER: You mentioned courage . . .

ANGELOU: . . . the most important of all the virtues. Without that virtue you can't practice any other virtue with consistency.

INTERVIEWER: What do you think of white writers who have written of the black experience: Faulkner's *The Sound and the Fury*, or William Styron's *Confessions of Nat Turner*?

ANGELOU: Well, sometimes I am disappointed—more often than not. That's unfair, because I'm not suggesting the writer is lying about what he or she sees. It's my disappointment, really, in that he or she doesn't see more deeply, more carefully. I enjoy seeing Peter O'Toole or Michael Caine enact the role of an upper-class person in England. There the working class has had to study the upper-class, has been obliged to do so, to lift themselves out of their positions. Well, black Americans have had to study white Americans. For centuries under slavery, the smile or the grimace on a white man's face, or the flow of a hand on a white woman could inform a black person: "You're about to be sold, or flogged." So we have studied the white American, where the white American has not been obliged to study us. So often it is as if the writer is looking through a glass darkly. And I'm always a little—not a little—saddened by that poor vision.

INTERVIEWER: And you can pick it up in an instant if you . . .

ANGELOU: Yes, yes. There are some who delight and inform. It's so much better, you see, for me, when a writer like Edna St. Vincent Millay speaks so deeply about her concern for herself, and does not offer us any altruisms. Then when I look through her eyes at how she sees a black or an Asian my heart is lightened. But many of the other writers disappoint me.

INTERVIEWER: What is the best part of writing for you?

ANGELOU: Well, I could say the end. But when the language lends itself to me, when it comes and submits, when it surrenders and says "I am yours, darling"—that's the best part.

INTERVIEWER: You don't skip around when you write?

ANGELOU: No, I may skip around in revision, just to see what connections I can find.

INTERVIEWER: Is most of the effort made in putting the words down onto the paper, or is it in revision?

ANGELOU: Some work flows, and you know, you can catch three days. It's like . . . I think the word in sailing is "scudding"—you know, three days of just scudding. Other days it's just awful—plodding and backing up, trying to take out all the ands, ifs, tos, fors, buts, wherefores, therefores, howevers; you know, all those.

INTERVIEWER: And then, finally, you write "The End" and there it is; you have a little bit of sherry.

ANGELOU: A lot of sherry then.

GEORGE PLIMPTON
Summer 1990

# 9. Harold Bloom

No critic in the English language since Samuel Johnson has been more prolific than Harold Bloom. Born to Russian and Polish immigrants in New York City on July 11, 1930, Bloom attended the Bronx High School of Science, where he did poorly, and Cornell, where he finished at the top of his class. After spending a year at Pembroke College, Cambridge, as a research fellow, and receiving a Ph.D. in English from Yale in 1955, he joined the Yale faculty and has remained there ever since. He provided the introductions to some five hundred volumes in the Chelsea House Library of Literary Criticism, of which he is general editor, and he has written over twenty books. The best known: *The Visionary Company* (1961), which helped restore English Romantic poetry to the canon and to the syllabi of college courses in literature. Part of a tetralogy, *The Anxiety of Influence* (1973) attempts to redefine poetic tradition as a series of willful "misreadings" of their precursors on the part of "strong," ephebe poets. Taking its title from the Greek word for struggle, *Agon* (1982) further explores the subject of influence and originality and provides some illustrations. *Ruin the Sacred Truths* (1989) looks broadly at the continuities and discontinuities of the Western tradition, from the Bible to Beckett, insisting that the distinction between sacred and secular literature is a wholly societal one, with no literary consequences whatsoever: from a literary standpoint, the Bible can be no more sacred than Beckett. *Poetics of Influence* (1988), edited and with an introduction by John Hollander, provides a fine selection of Bloom's work.

Simultaneously having residences at Yale and at Harvard, where Bloom was Charles Eliot Norton Professor of Poetry in 1987, was a warm-up for his current act: twin appointments as Sterling Professor of the Humanities at Yale and Berg Professor of English at N.Y.U.

GATSBY
INTRO
1

# Introduction

It is reasonable to assert that Jay Gatsby is *the* major literary character of the United States in the Twentieth Century. No single figure created by Faulkner or Hemingway, or by our principal dramatists, is as central a presence in our national mythology as Gatsby. There are few living Americans, of whatever gender, race, ethnic origin, or social class, who do not have at least a little touch of Gatsby in them. Whatever the American Dream has become, its truest contemporary representative remains Jay Gatsby, at once a gangster and a Romantic idealist, and above all a victim of his own High Romantic, Keatsian dream of love. Like his creator, Scott Fitzgerald, Gatsby is the American hero of romance, a vulnerable quester whose fate has the aesthetic dignity of the romance mode at its strongest. Gatsby is neither pathetic nor tragic, because as a quester he meets his appropriate fate, which is to die still lacking in the knowledge that would destroy the spell of his enchantment. His death preserves his greatness, and justifies the title of his story, a title that is anything but ironic.

Gatsby, dream-eager yet desiring a perfect love, or perhaps dream-eager but

*A manuscript page from the introduction to* Major Literary Characters: Gatsby, *edited and with an introduction by Harold Bloom.*

# Harold Bloom

*Recently, Harold Bloom has been under attack not just in scholarly journals and colloquia, but also in newspapers, on the op-ed page, on television and radio. The barrage is due to the best-seller* The Book of J, *in which Bloom argues that the J-Writer, the putative first author of the Hebrew Bible, not only existed (a matter under debate among Bible historians for the last century) but, quite specifically, was a woman who belonged to the Solomonic elite and wrote during the reign of Rehoboam of Judah in competition with the Court Historian. The attacks have come from Bible scholars, rabbis, and journalists, as well as from the usual academic sources, and Bloom has never been more isolated in his views or more secure in them. He has become, by his own description, "a tired, sad, humane old creature," who greets his many friends and detractors with an endearing, melancholy exuberance.*

*He is happy to talk about most anything—politics, romance, sports—although he admits he is "too used to" some topics to get into them. One sets out to disagree with him, and the response is, "Oh, no, no, my dear. . . ." In a class on Shakespeare, a mod-dressed graduate student suggests that Iago may be sexually jealous of Othello; Bloom tilts his furry eyebrows, his stockinged feet crossed underneath him, his hand tucked in his shirt, and cries out, "That will not do, my dear. I must protest!" Not surprisingly, it is by now a commonplace of former students' articles and lectures to start off with a quarrel with Bloom, and, in his view, this is only as it should be. He likes to quote the Emersonian adage: "That which I can gain from another is never tuition but only provocation."*

*The interview was conducted at the homes he shares with his wife, Jeanne, in New Haven and New York—the one filled with four decades' accrual of furniture and books, the other nearly bare, although stacks of works-in-progress and students' papers are strewn about in both. If the conversation is not too heavy, Bloom likes to have music on, sometimes Baroque, sometimes jazz. (His New York apartment, which is in Greenwich Village, allows him to take in more live jazz.) The phone rings non-stop. Friends, former students, colleagues drop by. Talk is punctuated by strange exclamatories: "Zoombah," for one—Swahili for "libido"—is an all-purpose flavoring particle, with the accompanying, adjectival "zoombinatious" and the verb "to zoombinate." Bloom speaks as if the sentences came to him off a printed page, grammatically complex, at times tangled. But they are delivered with great animation, whether ponderous or joyful—if also with finality. Because he learned English by reading it, his accent is very much his own, with some New York inflections: "You try and learn English in an all Yiddish household in the East Bronx by sounding out the words of Blake's* Prophecies,*" he explains. Often, he will start a conversation with a direct, at times personal question, or a sigh: "Oh, how the Bloomian feet ache today!"*

INTERVIEWER: What are your memories of growing up?

HAROLD BLOOM: That was such a long time ago. I'm sixty years old. I can't remember much of my childhood that well. I was raised in an Orthodox East European Jewish household where Yiddish was the everyday language. My mother was very pious, my father less so. I still read Yiddish poetry. I have a great interest and pleasure in it.

INTERVIEWER: What are your recollections of the neighborhood in which you grew up?

BLOOM: Almost none. One of my principal memories is that I and my friends, just to survive, had constantly to fight street battles with neighborhood Irish toughs, some of whom were very much under the influence of a sort of Irish-American Nazi organization called the Silver Shirts. This was back in the 1930s. We were on the verge of an Irish neighborhood over there in the East Bronx. We lived in a Jewish neighborhood. On our border, somewhere around Southern Boulevard, an Irish neighborhood began, and they would raid us, and we would fight back. They were terrible street fights, involving broken bottles and baseball bats. They were very nasty times. I say this even though I've now grown up and find that many of my best friends are Irish.

INTERVIEWER: Do you think your background helped in any way to shape your career?

BLOOM: Obviously it predisposed me toward a great deal of systematic reading. It exposed me to the Bible as a sort of definitive text early on. And obviously too, I became obsessed with interpretation as such. Judaic tradition necessarily acquaints one with interpretation as a mode. Exegesis becomes wholly natural. But I did not have very orthodox religious beliefs. Even when I was quite a young child I was very skeptical indeed about orthodox notions of spirituality. Of course, I now regard normative Judaism as being, as I've often said, a very strong misreading of the Hebrew Bible undertaken in the second century in order to meet the needs of the Jewish people in a Palestine under Roman occupation. And that is not very relevant to matters eighteen centuries later. But otherwise, I think the crucial experiences for me as a reader, as a child, did not come reading the Hebrew Bible. It came in reading poetry written in English, which can still work on me with the force of a Bible conversion. It was the aesthetic experience of first reading Hart Crane and William Blake—those two poets in particular.

INTERVIEWER: How old were you at this point?

BLOOM: I was preadolescent, ten or eleven years old. I still remember the extraordinary delight, the extraordinary force that Crane and Blake brought to me (in particular Blake's rhetoric in the longer poems) though I had no notion what they were about. I picked up a copy of the *Collected Poems* of Hart Crane in the Bronx Library. I still remember when I lit upon the page with the extraordinary trope, "O Thou steeled Cognizance whose leap commits/ The agile precincts of the lark's return." I was just swept away by it, by the Marlovian rhetoric. I still have the flavor of that book in me. Indeed it's the first book I ever owned. I begged my oldest sister to give it to me, and I still have the old black and gold edition she gave me for my birthday back in 1942. It's up on the third floor. Why is it you can have that extraordinary experience (preadolescent in my case as in so many other cases) of falling violently in love with great poetry . . . where you are moved by its power before you comprehend it? In some, a version of the poetical character is incarnated and in some like myself the answering voice is from the beginning that of the critic. I suppose the only poet of the twentieth century that I could secretly set above Yeats and Stevens would be Hart Crane. Crane was dead at the age of thirty-two, so one doesn't really know what he would have been able to do. An immense loss. As large a loss as the death of Shelley at twenty-nine or Keats at twenty-five. Crane had to do it all in only seven or eight years.

INTERVIEWER: Did you read children's stories, fairy tales?

BLOOM: I don't think so. I read the Bible, which is, after all, a long fairy tale. I didn't read children's literature until I was an undergraduate.

INTERVIEWER: Did you write verse as a child?

BLOOM: In spite of my interest, that never occurred to me. It must have had something to do with the enormous reverence and rapture I felt about poetry, the incantatory strength that Crane and Blake had for me from the beginning. To be a poet did not occur to me. It was indeed a threshold guarded by demons. To try to write in verse would have been a kind of trespass. That's something that I still feel very strongly.

INTERVIEWER: How was your chosen career viewed by your family?

BLOOM: I don't think they had any idea what I would be. I think they were disappointed. They were Jewish immigrants from Eastern Europe with necessarily narrow views. They had hoped that I would be a doctor or a lawyer or a dentist. They did not know what a Professor of Poetry was. They would have understood, I suppose, had I chosen to be a rabbi or a Talmudic scholar. But finally, I don't think they cared one way or the other.

When I was a small boy already addicted to doing nothing but reading poems in English, I was asked by an uncle who kept a candy store in Brooklyn what I intended to do to earn a living when I grew up. I said I want to read poetry. He told me that there were professors of poetry at Harvard and Yale. That's the first time I'd ever heard of those places or that there was such a thing as a professor of poetry. In my five- or six-year-old way I replied, "I'm going to be a professor of poetry at Harvard or Yale." Of course, the joke is that three years ago I was simultaneously Charles Eliot Norton Professor of Poetry at Harvard and Sterling Professor of the Humanities at Yale! So in that sense I was prematurely overdetermined in profession. Sometimes I think that is the principal difference between my own work and the work of many other critics. I came to it very early, and I've been utterly unswerving.

INTERVIEWER: You are known as someone who has had a prodigious memory since childhood. Do you find that your power of recall was triggered by the words themselves, or were there other factors?

BLOOM: Oh no, it was immediate and it was always triggered by text, and indeed always had an aesthetic element. I learned early that a test for a poem for me was whether it seemed so inevitable that I could remember it perfectly from the start. I think the only change in me in that regard has come mainly under the influence of Nietzsche. It is the single way he has influenced me aesthetically. I've come to understand that the quality of memorability and inevitability which I assumed came from intense pleasure may actually have come from a kind of pain. That is to say that one learns from Nietzsche that there is something painful about meaning. Sometimes it is the pain of difficulty, sometimes the pain of being set a standard that one cannot attain.

INTERVIEWER: Did you ever feel that reading so much was an avoidance of experience?

BLOOM: No. It was for me a terrible rage or passion which was a drive. It was fiery. It was an absolute obsession. I do not think that speculation on my own part would ever convince me that it was an attempt to substitute a more ideal existence for the life that I had to live. It was love. I fell desperately in love with reading poems. I don't think that one should idealize such a passion. I certainly no longer do. I mean, I still love reading a poem when I can find a really good one to read. Just recently, I was sitting down, alas for the first time in several years, reading through Shakespeare's *Troilus and Cressida* at one sitting. I found it to be an astonishing experience, powerful and superb. That hasn't dimmed or diminished. But surely it is a value in itself, a reality in its own right; surely it cannot be reduced or subsumed under some other name. Freud, doubtless, would wish to reduce it to the sexual thought, or rather, the sexual past. But increasingly it seems to me that literature, and particularly Shakespeare, who is literature, is a much more comprehensive mode of cognition than psychoanalysis can be.

INTERVIEWER: Who are the teachers who were important to you? Did you study with the New Critics at Yale?

BLOOM: I did not study with any of the New Critics, with the single exception being William K. Wimsatt. Bill was a formalist and a very shrewd one, and from the moment I landed in the first course that I took with him, which was in theories of poetry, he sized me up. His comment on my first essay for him was, "This is Longinian criticism. You're an instance of exactly what I don't like or want." He was quite right. He was an Aristotelian; as far as I was concerned, Aristotle had ruined Western literary criticism almost from the beginning. What I thought of as literary criticism really *did* begin with the pseudo-Longinus. So we had very strong disagreements about that kind of stuff. But he was a remarkable teacher. We became very close friends later on. I miss him very much. He was a splendid, huge, fascinating man, almost seven feet tall, a fierce, dogmatic Roman Catholic, very intense. But very fair-minded. We shared a passion for Dr. Samuel Johnson. I reacted so violently against him that antithetically he was a great influence on me. I think that's what I meant by dedicating *The Anxiety of Influence* to Bill. I still treasure the note he wrote me after I gave him one of the early copies of the book. "I find the dedication extremely surprising," he said, and then added mournfully: "I suppose it entitles you to be Plotinus to Emerson's Plato in regard to American neo-Romanticism, a doctrine that I despise." Oh, yes, we had serious differences in our feelings about poetry.

INTERVIEWER: What were your earliest essays like?

BLOOM: I don't think I wrote any essays until I was an undergraduate at Cornell. But then a few years ago Bob Elias, one of my teachers there, sent me an essay I had written on Hart Crane (which I had completely forgotten about) when I was a Cornell freshman of sixteen or seventeen. I couldn't get myself to read it. I even destroyed it. I shouldn't have. I should have waited until I could bear to look at it. I'm very curious as to what kind of thing it was.

INTERVIEWER: Are there other literary figures who were important to you early on?

BLOOM: A real favorite among modern critics, and the one I think influenced me considerably, though no one ever wants to talk about him, was George Wilson Knight. He was an old friend. Utterly mad. He made Kenneth Burke and Harold Bloom look placid and mild. George died quite old. He was very interested in spiritualism, and in survival after death. He told me a couple of times that he believed it quite literally. There is a moment in *The Christian Renaissance* which I think is the finest moment in modern criticism, because it is the craziest. He is citing a spiritualist, F. W. H. Myers, and he quotes something that Myers wrote and published, and then he quotes something from a séance at which Myers "came back" and said something through a medium, this astonishing sentence, which I give to you verbatim: "These quotations from F. W. H. Myers, so similar in style, composed before and after his own earthly 'death,' contain together a wisdom which our era may find it hard to assimilate." I mean, perfectly straight about it! But the early books of Wilson Knight are very fine indeed—certainly one of the most considerable figures of twentieth-century criticism, though he's mostly forgotten now.

*At this point we wander into the kitchen, where Mrs. Bloom is watching the evening news.*

BLOOM: Now let's wait for the news about this comeback for the wretched Yankees. I've been denouncing them. They haven't won since 1979. That's ten years and they're not going to win this year. They're terrible . . . What's this?

> TV: THE YANKEES WITH THEIR MOST DRAMATIC WIN OF THE YEAR THIS AFTERNOON . . . AND THE TIGERS LOST AGAIN.

BLOOM: Oh my God! That means we're just four games out. How very up-cheering.
MRS. BLOOM: Jessica Hahn.
BLOOM: Jessica Hahn is back!

> TV: . . . HIRED ON AS AN ON-AIR PERSONALITY AT A TOP 40 RADIO STATION IN PHOENIX.

BLOOM: How marvelous!

TV: PLAYBOY MAGAZINE HAS COUNTED ON HAHN TO COME THROUGH. SHE APPEARED NUDE IN A RECENT ISSUE.

BLOOM: Splendid. . . . Let us start again, Antonio. What were we talking about?

*We return to the living room.*

INTERVIEWER: We were talking about your teachers and I was going to ask about the poets you've known over the years.

BLOOM: Auden I knew pretty well, mostly through John Hollander. Eliot I never met. Stevens I met just once. I was still a Cornell undergraduate. I came up to Yale to hear him read the shorter version of "Ordinary Evening in New Haven." It was the first time I was ever in New Haven or at Yale for that matter. I got to talk to him afterwards. It was a formidable experience meeting him. We talked about Shelley, and he quoted a stanza of the "Witch of Atlas" to me, which impressed me. "Men scarcely know how beautiful fire is," it starts. It's a chilly, rather beautiful poem. Robert Penn Warren and I were close friends. Miss Bishop was of that younger generation also. Archie Ammons and I are very close. There are quite a few others. Sometimes I used to correspond with James Merrill when he was writing *The Changing Light at Sandover*. He kept sending parts to me as it went along, and I kept writing him letters saying "can't we have more J.M. and less of this stuff in capital letters?" He said this was the way it had to be, this was the way it was actually coming to him. I realized I was going against my cardinal rule, which is don't argue with it, just appreciate it.

INTERVIEWER: Are there any authors you'd like to have known, but haven't?

BLOOM: No. I should like to have known fewer authors than I have known, which is to say nothing against all my good friends.

INTERVIEWER: Because it interferes with an honest assessment?

BLOOM: No. It's just that as one gets older, one is doomed, in this profession, to know personally more and more authors. Most of them are in fact quite nice ladies and gentlemen, but they have trouble—even one's very close friends—talking to the tired, sad, humane old creature that one is. They seem to be more conscious of one's profession as literary critic than one is necessarily conscious of their profession as novelist or poet.

INTERVIEWER: Are there characters you would like to have known?

BLOOM: No, no. The only person I would like to have known, whom I have never known, but it's just as well, is Sophia Loren. I have been in love with Sophia Loren for at least a third of a century. But undoubtedly it would be better never to meet her. I'm not sure I ever shall, though my late friend Bart Giamatti had breakfast with her. Judging by photographs and recent film appearances, she has held up quite well, though a little too slender now—no longer the same gorgeous Neapolitan beauty, now a much more sleek beauty.

INTERVIEWER: Could you give us your opinion of some novelists? We could start with Norman Mailer.

BLOOM: Oh, I have written on Norman a lot. I reviewed *Ancient Evenings* at some length in the *New York Review of Books* and I came forth with a sentence that did not please Norman which I'm still proud of. It was, "Subscribers to the Literary Guild will find in it more than enough humbuggery and bumbuggery to give them their money's worth." I had counted up the number of homosexual and heterosexual bumbuggeries; I was rather impressed by the total, including, unless I misremember, at one point the protagonist or perhaps it was the god-king successfully bumbuggering the lion. But then Norman is immensely inventive in this regard. He told me the last time I saw him that he is completing a manuscript of several thousand pages on the CIA. That should be an amazing nightmare of a book since Norman's natural grand paranoid vision is one of *everything* being a conspiracy. So I should think that might be very interesting indeed. What can one say? Mailer is an immense imaginative energy. One is not persuaded that in the sheer mode of the fantastic, he has found his proper mètier. Beyond a doubt his most impressive single book is *The Executioner's Song*, and that is, of course, very close indeed to a transcript of what we want to call reality. So it's rather ironic that Norman should be more effective in the mode of Theodore Dreiser, giving us a kind of contemporary *American Tragedy* or *Sister Carrie* in the *Executioner's Song* than in the modes he himself has wanted to excel in. I would think that he is likely to impress future literary historians as having been a knowing continuator of Dreiser, which is not an inconsiderable achievement.

INTERVIEWER: And William Gaddis?

BLOOM: Like everyone else, I've never gotten over *The Recognitions*, but I differ from those who have found the other two books worthy of him. I have had great difficulty working my way through them. I assume that there is more to be heard from him, but I am afraid that he is an instance of someone who in that vast initial anatomy of a book, to use Mister Frye's phrase for that kind of fictional writing, seems to have surpassed himself at the start . . . which is, of course, in the famous American tradition.

INTERVIEWER: And Saul Bellow?

BLOOM: He's an enormous pleasure but he does not make things difficult enough for himself or for us. Like many others, I would commend him for the almost Dickensian exuberance of his minor male characters who have carried every one of his books. The central protagonist, always being some version of himself, even in *Henderson*, is invariably an absurd failure, and the women, as we all know, are absurdities; they are third-rate pipe-dreams. The narrative line is of no particular interest. His secular opinions are worthy of Allan Bloom, who seems to derive from them. And I'm not an admirer of the "other Bloom," as is well known. In general, Bellow seems to me an immensely wasted talent though he certainly would not appreciate my saying so. I would oppose to him a most extraordinary talent: Philip Roth. It does seem to me that Philip Roth goes from strength to strength and is at the moment startlingly unappreciated. It seems strange to say Philip is unappreciated when he has so wide a readership and so great a notoriety, but *Deception* was not much remarked upon and it's an extraordinary tour-de-force.

INTERVIEWER: It was seen as an experiment or a sort of a leftover from—

BLOOM: From *The Counterlife*. Well, *The Counterlife*, of course, deserved the praise that it received. It's an astonishing book, though I would put it a touch below the *Zuckerman Bound* trilogy with its marvelous Prague Orgy postlude or coda. I still think *My Life as a Man* as well as, of course, *Portnoy's Complaint* are remarkable books. There's the great episode of Kafka's whore in *The Professor of Desire*. I've written a fair amount about Philip. After a rather unfortunate personal book called *The Facts*, which I had trouble getting through, he has written a book about his late father called *Patrimony*, which is both beautiful and immensely moving, a real achievement. The man is a prose artist of great accomplishment. He has immense narrative exuberance, and also—I would insist upon this—since it's an extremely difficult thing, as we all know, to write successful humorous fiction and, though the laughter Philip evokes is very painful indeed, he is an authentic comic novelist. I'm not sure at the moment that we have any other authentic comic novelist of the first order.

INTERVIEWER: You have written that poetry is in an especially strong stage now. Is the same true of fiction?

BLOOM: Although I've been reading extensively and writing about it over the last few years, it is very difficult for me to get a steady fix on the current kaleidoscope of American fiction. Our most distinguished living writer of narrative fiction—I don't think you would quite call him a novelist—is Thomas Pynchon, and yet that recent book *Vineland* was a total disaster. In fact, I cannot think of a comparable disaster in modern American fiction. To have written the great story of Byron the lightbulb in *Gravity's Rainbow*, to have written *The Crying of Lot 49* and then to give us this piece of sheer ineptitude, this hopelessly hollow book which I read through in amazement and disbelief and which has not got in it a redeeming sentence, hardly a redeeming phrase, is immensely disheartening.

INTERVIEWER: Do you have any response to the essay Tom Wolfe wrote urging the big, Victor Hugo-like novel?

BLOOM: He is, of course, praising his own *Bonfire of the Vanities*, which is a wholly legitimate thing for an essayist-turned-novelist to do. But with all honor to Tom Wolfe, a most amiable fellow and a former classmate of mine at Yale, and as someone who enjoyed reading *The Bonfire of the Vanities*, I found very little difference between it and his book of essays. He has merely taken his verve and gift for writing the journalistic essay and moved it a little further over the edge; but the characters are names on the page—he does not try to make them more than that. The social pressure is extraordinarily and vividly conveyed. But he's always been remarkable for that. He's still part of that broad movement which has lifted a particular kind of high-pitched journalism into a realm that may very nearly be aesthetic. On the other hand, I must say I would rather reread *The Bonfire of the Vanities* than reread another Rabbit volume by Mister Updike. But then Mister Updike and I, we are not a mutual admiration society.

INTERVIEWER: Have you had run-ins with friends or writers whose books you've reviewed?

BLOOM: I wouldn't say run-ins exactly. Mister Styron, who has, of course, his difficulties and I sympathize with them, once at Robert Penn Warren's dinner table, when I dared to disagree with him on a question of literary judgment, spoke up and said, "Your opinion doesn't matter, you are only a schoolteacher," which still strikes me as perhaps the most memorable single thing that has been said to me by any contemporary novelist.* I felt that Warren's poetry was greatly preferable to his recent novels, and was trying to persuade Red to stop writing novels. *A Place to Come to*, which Red to his dying day thought was a novel of the eminence of *World Enough and Time, At Heaven's Gate, All the King's Men*, and *Night Rider*, is a stillborn book and a terrible bore, though I say that with great sadness. Whereas Red Warren's poetry from the *Incarnations* in 1966 down to the end (he stopped writing poetry in the last few years because he was too ill) was consistently the work of a great poet.

INTERVIEWER: Are there younger writers you enjoy reading?

BLOOM: I like this fellow Ted Mooney. I think something is going on there. *Traffic and Laughter*, which I've just read through, certainly has éclat: it certainly has a lot of intensity. I don't know; there are so many that it is difficult to choose among them. It's easier on the whole these days to think of poets than novelists. It's very difficult for a novelist to break through. The form is not showing a great deal of fecundity, except perhaps in Don DeLillo, who is a superb inventor.

INTERVIEWER: What direction do you see the form taking?

BLOOM: I would suppose that in America we are leaning more and more towards terrible millennial visions. I would even expect a religious dimension, a satiric dimension, an even more apocalyptic dimension than we have been accustomed to. I would expect the mode of fantasy to develop new permutations.

INTERVIEWER: Do you think that fiction—or poetry for that matter—could ever die out?

BLOOM: I'm reminded of that great trope of Stevens's in "The Auroras

* Mr. Styron wishes to point out that his annoyance was not with H.B.'s critical views—with which he agrees—but that they were offered in Penn Warren's presence. [—Ed.]

of Autumn," when he speaks of a "Great shadow's last embellishment." There's always a further embellishment. It looks like a last embellishment and then it turns out not to be—yet once more, and yet once more. One is always saying farewell to it, it is always saying farewell to itself, and then it perpetuates itself. One is always astonished and delighted. When I introduced John Ashbery, at one of the poetry readings in the old days at Yale, I heard, for the first time, "Wet Casements." How it ravished my heart away the moment I heard it! Certainly when I recite that poem myself and remember the original experience of hearing him deliver it, it's hard to see how any poem could be more adequate. Clearly it is not a diminished or finished art form as long as a poem like "Wet Casements" is still possible.

INTERVIEWER: I wanted to ask you about a period of time in the mid-sixties, which you have described as a period of great upheaval and transition for you. You were immersed in the essays of Emerson.

BLOOM: Yes, I started reading him all day long, every day, and pretty much simultaneously reading Freud. People would look at me with amazement, and say, "Well, what about Thoreau? He at least counts for something." And I would look back at them in amazement and tell them what indeed was and is true, that Thoreau is deeply derivative of Emerson, and very minor compared to him. Emerson is God.

INTERVIEWER: You were in analysis during this period. How did that go?

BLOOM: As my distinguished analyst said to me at the end, there had never been a proper transference.

INTERVIEWER: You were unable to accept his authority?

BLOOM: I thought and still think that he is a very nice man, but as he wryly remarked, I was paying him to give him lectures several times a week on the proper way to read Freud. He thought this was quite self-defeating for both of us.

INTERVIEWER: Can a successful therapy ever be so closely allied to a reading of Freud?

BLOOM: I take it that a successful therapy is an oxymoron.

INTERVIEWER: It's always interminable?

BLOOM: I do not know anyone who has ever benefited from Freudian or any other mode of analysis, except by being, to use the popular trope for it, so badly shrunk, that they become quite dried out. That is to

say, all passion spent. Perhaps they become better people, but they also become stale and uninteresting people with very few exceptions. Like dried-out cheese, or wilted flowers.
INTERVIEWER: Were you worried about losing your creativity?
BLOOM: No, no. That was not the issue at all.
INTERVIEWER: You were having trouble writing at the time.
BLOOM: Oh yes. I was having all kinds of crises. I was, in every sense, "in the middle of a journey." On the other hand, this has been recurrent. Here I am sixty years old and as much as ever I'm in the middle of the journey. That is something that goes with the territory. One just keeps going.
INTERVIEWER: Do you see yourself as a difficult critic, in the sense that you qualify certain poets and prose fiction writers as "difficult"?
BLOOM: I would think, my dear, that most people these days might be kind enough to call me difficult. The younger members of my profession and the members of what I have called the School of Resentment describe me, I gather, as someone who partakes of a cult of personality or self-obsession rather than their wonderful, free, and generous social vision. One of them, I understand, refers to me customarily as "Napoleon Bonaparte." There is no way of dealing with these people. They have not been moved by literature. Many of them are my former students and I know them all too well. They are now gender and power freaks.

But, no. *The Anxiety of Influence* is a difficult book. So is *Kabbalah and Criticism*. They're books in which one is trying to discover something. But *Ruin the Sacred Truths* is a very different book from these earlier ones, a very simple book, to me quite transparent. Besides the aging process, and I hope the maturing process, the major reason is that I am writing more for that Johnsonian ideal (which, of course, does not exist anymore)—the Common Reader. I wouldn't dream of using a too technical word or term now if I could possibly help it, and I don't think there are any in *Ruin the Sacred Truths* except for "facticity." I use that term and then dismiss it. I don't think that any of my own special vocabulary, for which I have been condemned in the past (and which was meant to expose how arbitrary all critical and rhetorical terminology always is and has to be) is in that book. Nor do I think it's necessary to have read *Kabbalah and Criticism* or *A Map of Misreading* or any other to understand the book. It is general literary criticism.

INTERVIEWER: How do you account historically for the "School of Resentment?"

BLOOM: In the universities, the most surprising and reprehensible development came some twenty years ago, around 1968, and has had a very long-range effect, one that is still percolating. Suddenly all sorts of people, faculty members at the universities, graduate and undergraduate students, began to blame the universities not just for their own palpable ills and malfeasances, but for all the ills of history and society. They were blamed, and to some extent still are, by the budding School of Resentment and its precursors, as though they were not only representative of these ills, but weirdly enough, as though they had somehow helped *cause* these ills, and even more weirdly, quite surrealistically, as though they were somehow capable of ameliorating these ills. It's still going on—this attempt to ascribe both culpability and apocalyptic potential to the universities. It's really asking the universities to take the place that was once occupied by religion, philosophy, and science. These are our conceptual modes. They have all failed us. The entire history of Western culture, from Alexandrian days until now, shows that when a society's conceptual modes fail it, then willy-nilly it becomes a literary culture. This is probably neither good nor bad, but just the way things become. And we can't really ask literature, or the representatives of a literary culture, in or out of the university, to save society. Literature is not an instrument of social change or an instrument of social reform. It is more a mode of human sensations and impressions, which do not reduce very well to societal rules or forms.

INTERVIEWER: How does one react to the School of Resentment? By declaring oneself an aesthete?

BLOOM: Well, I do that now, of course, in furious reaction to their School and to so much other pernicious nonsense that goes on. I would certainly see myself as an aesthete in the sense advocated by Ruskin, indeed to a considerable degree by Emerson, and certainly by the divine Walter and the sublime Oscar. It is a very engaged kind of mode. Literary criticism in the United States increasingly is split between very low level literary journalism and what I increasingly regard as a disaster, which is literary criticism in the academies, particularly in the younger generations. Increasingly scores and scores of graduate students have read the absurd Lacan but have never read Edmund Spenser; or have read a great deal of Foucault or Derrida but scarcely read Shakespeare or Milton. That's obviously an absurd defeat for literary study. When I was a young man, back in the fifties, starting out on what was to be my career, I used to proclaim that my chosen profession seemed to consist of secular clergy or clerisy. I was thinking, of course, of the highly Anglo-Catholic New Criticism under the sponsorship or demigodness of T. S. Eliot. But I realized in latish middle age, that, no better or worse, I was surrounded by a pride of displaced social workers, a rabblement of lemmings, all rushing down to the sea carrying their subject down to destruction with them. The School of Resentment is an extraordinary sort of mélange of latest-model feminists, Lacanians, that whole semiotic cackle, latest-model pseudo-Marxists, so-called New Historicists, who are neither new nor historicist, and third generation deconstructors, who I believe have no relationship whatever to literary values. It's really a very paltry kind of a phenomenon. But it is pervasive, and it seems to be waxing rather than waning. It is a very rare thing indeed to encounter one critic, academic or otherwise, not just in the English speaking world, but also in France or Italy, who has an authentic commitment to aesthetic values, who reads for the pleasure of reading, and who values poetry or story as such, above all else. Reading has become a very curious kind of activity. It has become tendentious in the extreme. A sheer deliquescence has taken place because of this obsession with the methods or supposed method. Criticism starts—it *has* to start—with a real passion for reading. It can come in adolescence, even in your twenties, but you must fall in love with poems. You must fall in love with what we used to call "imaginative literature." And when you are in love that way, with or without provocation from good teachers, you will pass on to encounter what used to be called the sublime. And as soon as you do this, you pass into the agonistic mode, even if your own nature is anything but agonistic. In the end, the spirit that makes one a fan of a particular athlete or a particular team is different only in degree, not in kind, from the spirit that teaches one to prefer one poet to another, or one novelist to another. That is to say there is some element of competition at every point in one's experience as a reader. How could there not be? Perhaps you learn this more fully as you get older, but in the end you choose between books, or you choose between poems, the way you choose between people. You can't become friends with every acquaintance you make, and I would not think that it is any different with what you read.

INTERVIEWER: Do you foresee any change, or improvement, in the critical fashions?

BLOOM: I don't believe in myths of decline or myths of progress, even as regards to the literary scene. The world does not get to be a better or a worse place; it just gets more senescent. The world gets older, without getting either better or worse and so does literature. But I do think that the drab current phenomenon that passes for literary studies in the university will finally provide its own corrective. That is to say, sooner or later, students and teachers are going to get terribly bored with all the technocratic social work going on now. There will be a return to aesthetic values and desires, or these people will simply do something else with their time. But I find a great deal of hypocrisy in what they're doing now. It is tiresome to be encountering myths called "The Social Responsibility of the Critic" or "The Political Responsibility of the Critic." I would rather walk into a bookstore and find a book called "The Aesthetic Responsibilities of the Statesman," or "The Literary Responsibilities of the Engineer." Criticism is not a program for social betterment, not an engine for social change. I don't see how it possibly could be. If you look for the best instance of a socially radical critic, you find a very good one indeed in William Hazlitt. But you will not find that his social activism on the left in any way conditions his aesthetic judgments, or that he tries to make imaginative literature a machine for revolution. You would not find much difference in aesthetic response between Hazlitt and Dr. Samuel Johnson on Milton, though Dr. Johnson is very much on the right politically, and Hazlitt, of course, very much an enthusiast for the French Revolution and for English Radicalism. But I can't find much in the way of a Hazlittian or Johnsonian temperament in life and literature anywhere on the current scene. There are so many tiresomenesses going on. Everyone is so desperately afraid of being called a racist or a sexist that they connive—whether actively or passively—the almost total breakdown of standards which has taken place both in and out of the universities, where writings by blacks or Hispanics or in many cases simply women are concerned.

INTERVIEWER: This movement has helped focus attention on some great novels, though. You're an admirer, for example, of Ralph Ellison's *Invisible Man*.

BLOOM: Oh, but that is a very, very rare exception. What else is there like *Invisible Man*? Zora Neale Hurston's *Their Eyes Were Watching God* has a kind of superior intensity and firm control. It's a very fine book indeed. It surprised and delighted me when I first read it and it has sustained several rereadings since. But that and *Invisible Man* are the only full scale works of fiction I have read by American blacks in this century which have survival possibilities at all. Alice Walker is an extremely inadequate writer, and I think that is giving her the best of it. A book like *The Color Purple* is of no aesthetic interest or value whatsoever, yet it is exalted and taught in the academies. It clearly is a time in which social and cultural guilt has taken over.

INTERVIEWER: I know you find this to be true of feminist criticism.

BLOOM: I'm very fond of feminist critics, some of whom are my close friends, but it is widely known I'm not terribly fond of feminist criticism. The true test is to find work, whether in the past or present, by women writers which we had undervalued, and thus bring it to our attention and teach us to study it more closely or more usefully. By that test they have failed, because they have added not one to the canon. The women writers who mattered—Jane Austin, George Eliot, Emily Dickinson, Edith Wharton, Willa Cather, and others who have always mattered on aesthetic grounds—still matter. I do not appreciate Elizabeth Bishop or May Swenson any more or less than I would have appreciated them if we had no feminist literary criticism at all. And I stare at what is presented to me as feminist literary criticism and I shake my head. I regard it at best as being well-intentioned. I do not regard it as being literary criticism.

INTERVIEWER: Can it be valued as a form of social or political literary criticism?

BLOOM: I'm not concerned with political or social criticism. If people wish to practice it, that is entirely their business. It is not mine, heavens! If it does not help me to read a work of aesthetic value then I'm not going to be interested in it at all. I do not for a moment yield to the notion that any social, racial, ethnic, or "male" interest could determine my aesthetic choices. I have a lifetime of experience, learning, and insight which tells me this.

INTERVIEWER: What do you make of all this recent talk of the "canonical problem"?

BLOOM: It is no more than a reflection of current academic and social politics in the United States. The old test for what makes a work canonical is if it has engendered strong readings that come after it, whether as overt interpretations or implicitly interpretive forms. There's no way the gender and power boys and girls, or the New Historicists, or any of the current set are going to give us new canonical works, any more than all the agitation of feminist writing or nowadays what seems to be called African-American writing is going to give us canonical works. Alice Walker is not going to be a canonical poet no matter how many lemmings stand forth and proclaim her sublimity. It really does seem to me a kind of bogus issue. I am more and more certain that a great deal of what now passes for literary study of the so-called politically correct variety will wash aside. It is a ripple. I give it five years. I have seen many fashions come and go since I first took up literary study. After forty years one begins to be able to distinguish an ephemeral surface ripple from a deeper current or an authentic change.

INTERVIEWER: You teach Freud and Shakespeare.

BLOOM: Oh yes, increasingly. I keep telling my students that I'm not interested in a Freudian reading of Shakespeare but a kind of Shakespearean reading of Freud. In some sense Freud has to be a prose version of Shakespeare, the Freudian map of the mind being in fact Shakespearean. There's a lot of resentment on Freud's part because I think he recognizes this. What we think of as Freudian psychology is really a Shakespearean invention and, for the most part, Freud is merely codifying it. This shouldn't be too surprising. Freud himself says "the poets were there before me," and the poet in particular is necessarily Shakespeare. But you know, I think it runs deeper than that. Western psychology is much more a Shakespearean invention than a Biblical invention, let alone, obviously, a Homeric, or Sophoclean, or even Platonic, never mind a Cartesian or Jungian invention. It's not just that Shakespeare gives us most of our representations of cognition as such; I'm not so sure he doesn't largely invent what we think of as cognition. I remember saying something like this to a seminar consisting of professional teachers of Shakespeare and one of them got very indignant and said, "You are confusing Shakespeare with God." I don't see why one shouldn't, as it were. Most of what we know about how to represent cognition and personality in language was permanently altered by Shakespeare. The principal insight that I've had in teaching and writing about Shakespeare is that there isn't anyone before Shakespeare who actually gives you a representation of characters or human figures speaking out loud, whether to themselves or to others or both, and then brooding out loud, whether to themselves or to others or both, on what they themselves have said. And then, in the course of pondering, undergoing a serious or vital change, they become a different kind of character or personality and even a different kind of mind. We take that utterly for granted in representation. But it doesn't exist before Shakespeare. It doesn't happen in the Bible. It doesn't happen in Homer or in Dante. It doesn't even happen in Euripides. It's pretty clear that Shakespeare's true precursor—where he took the hint from—is Chaucer, which is why I think the Wife of Bath gets into Falstaff, and the Pardoner gets into figures like Edmund and Iago. As to where Chaucer gets that from, that's a very pretty question. It is a standing challenge I have put to my students. That's part of Chaucer's shocking originality as a writer. But Chaucer does it only in fits and starts, and in small degree. Shakespeare does it all the time. It's his common stock. The ability to do that, and to persuade one that this is a natural mode of representation, is purely Shakespearean and we are now so contained by it that we can't see its originality anymore. The originality of it is bewildering.

By the way, I was thinking recently about this whole question as it relates to the French tradition. I gave what I thought was a remarkable seminar on *Hamlet* to my undergraduate Shakespeare seminar at Yale. About an hour before class, I had what I thought was a very considerable insight, though I gather my students were baffled by it. I think that I was trying to say too much at once. It had suddenly occurred to me that the one canon of French neoclassical thought which was absolutely, indeed religiously followed, by French dramatists—and this means everyone, even Molière and Racine—was that there were to be no soliloquies and no asides. No matter what dexterity or agility had to be displayed, a confidante had to be dragged onto the stage so that the protagonist could have someone to whom to address cogitations, reflections. This accounts not only for why Shakespeare has never been properly absorbed by the French, as compared to his effect on every other European culture, language, literature, dramatic tradition, but also for the enormous differences between French and Anglo-American modes of literary thought. It also helps account for why the French modes, which are having so absurd an effect upon us at this time, are so clearly irrelevant to our literature and our way of talking about literature. I can give you a further illustration. I gave a faculty seminar a while ago, in which I talked for about two hours about my notions of Shakespeare and originality. At the end of it, a woman who was present, a faculty member at Yale, who had listened with a sort of amazement and a clear lack of comprehension, said, with considerable exasperation, "Well you know Professor Bloom, I don't really understand why you're talking about originality. It is as outmoded as, say, private enterprise in the economic sphere." An absurdity to have put myself in a situation where I had to address a member of the School of Resentment! I was too courteous, especially since my colleague Shoshana Felman jumped in to try to explain to the lady what I was up to. But I realized it was hopeless. Here was a lady who came not out of Racine and Molière but in fact out of Lacan, Derrida, and Foucault. Even if she *had* come out of Racine and Molière, she could never have hoped to understand. I remember what instantly flashed through my head was that I had been talking about the extraordinary originality of the way Shakespeare's protagonists ponder to themselves and, on the basis of that pondering, change. She could not understand this because it never actually happens in the French drama; the French critical mind has never been able to believe that it is appropriate for this to happen. Surely this is related to a mode of apprehension, a mode of criticism in which authorial presence was never very strong anyway, and so indeed it could die.

INTERVIEWER: Can you explain how you came to notice this about Shakespeare's protagonists?

BLOOM: Yes, I can even remember the particular moment. I was teaching *King Lear*, and I'd reached a moment in the play which has always fascinated me. I suddenly saw what was going on. Edmund is the most remarkable villain in all Shakespeare, a manipulator so strong that he makes Iago seem minor in comparison. Edmund is a sophisticated and sardonic consciousness who can run rings around anyone else on the stage in *King Lear*. He is so foul that it takes Goneril and Regan really to match up to him. . . . He's received his death wound from his brother; he's lying there on the battlefield. They bring in word that Goneril and Regan are dead: one slew the other and then committed suicide for his sake. Edmund broods out loud and says, quite extraordinarily (it's all in four words), "Yet Edmund was belov'd." One looks at those four words totally startled. As soon as he says it, he starts to ponder out loud: What are the implications that, though two monsters of the deep, the two loved me so much that one of them killed the other and then murdered herself. He reasons it out. He says, "The one the other poison'd for my sake/ And after slew herself." And then he suddenly says, "I pant for life," and then amazingly he says, "Some good I mean to do/ despite of mine own nature," and he suddenly gasps out, having given the order for Lear and Cordelia to be killed, "Send in time," to stop it. They don't get there in time. Cordelia's been murdered. And then Edmund dies. But that's an astonishing change. It comes about as he hears himself say, in real astonishment, "Yet Edmund was belov'd," and on that basis, he starts to ponder. Had he not said that, he would not have changed. There's nothing like that in literature before Shakespeare. It makes Freud unnecessary. The representation of inwardness is so absolute and large that we have no parallel to it before then.

INTERVIEWER: So that the Freudian commentary on Hamlet by Ernest Jones is unnecessary.

BLOOM: It's much better to work out what Hamlet's commentary on the Oedipal complex might be. There's that lovely remark of A. C. Bradley's that Shakespeare's major tragic heroes can only work in the play that they're in—that if Iago had to come onto the same stage with Hamlet, it would take Hamlet about five seconds to catch onto what Iago was doing and so viciously parody Iago that he would drive him to madness and suicide. The same way, if the ghost of Othello's dead father appeared to Othello and said that someone had murdered him, Othello would grab his sword and go and hack the other fellow down. In each case there would be no play. Just as the plays would make mincemeat of one another if you tried to work one into the other, so Shakespeare chops up any writer you apply him to. And a Shakespearean reading of Freud would leave certain things but not leave others. It would make one very impatient, I think, with Freud's representation of the Oedipal complex. And it's a disaster to try to apply the Freudian reading of that to Hamlet.

INTERVIEWER: Have you ever acted Shakespeare?

BLOOM: Only just once, at Cornell. I was pressed into service because I knew Father Falstaff by heart. But it was a disaster. I acted as though there were no one else on stage, something that delights my younger son when I repeat it. As a result, I never heard cues, I created a kind of gridlock on stage. I had a good time, but no one else did. Not long ago President Reagan, who should be remembered only for his jokes because his jokes I think are really very good, was asked how it was he could have managed eight years as President and still look so wonderful. Did you see this?

INTERVIEWER: No.

BLOOM: It was in the *Times*. He said, "Let me tell you the story about the old psychiatrist being admired by a young psychiatrist who asks, 'How come you still look so fresh, so free of anxiety, so little worn by care, when you've spent your entire life sitting as I do every day, getting worn out listening to the miseries of your patients?' To which the older psychiatrist replies, 'It's very simple, young man. I never listen.' " Such sublime, wonderful, and sincere self-revelation on the part of Reagan! In spite of all one's horror at what he has done or failed to do as President, it takes one's breath away with admiration. That's the way I played the part of Falstaff. I'm occasionally asked by old friends, who don't yet know me well enough, if I had ever considered becoming a psychoanalyst. I look at them in shock and say "Psychoanalyst! My great struggle as a teacher is to stop answering my own questions!" I still think, though no one in the world except me thinks so, and no one's ever going to give me an award as a great teacher, I'm a pretty good teacher, but only in terms of the great Emersonian maxim: "That which I can receive from another is never tuition but only provocation." I think that if the young woman or man listens to what I am saying, she or he will get very provoked indeed.

INTERVIEWER: Do you ever teach from notes? Or do you prefer to improvise?

BLOOM: I have never made a note in my life. How could I? I have internalized the text. I externalized it in different ways at different times. We cannot step even once in the same river. We cannot step even once in the same text.

INTERVIEWER: What do you think of creative writing workshops?

BLOOM: I suppose that they do more good than harm, and yet it baffles me. Writing seems to me so much an art of solitude. Criticism is a teachable art, but like every art it too finally depends upon an inherent or implicit gift. I remember remarking somewhere in something I wrote that I gave up going to the Modern Language Association some years ago because the idea of a convention of twenty-five or thirty thousand critics is every bit as hilarious as the idea of going to a convention of twenty-five thousand poets or novelists. There *aren't* twenty-five thousand critics. I frequently wonder if there are *five* critics alive at any one time. The extent to which the art of fiction or the art of poetry is teachable is a more complex problem. Historically, we know how poets become poets and fiction writers become fiction writers. They read. They read their predecessors, and they learn what is to be learned. The idea of Herman Melville in a writing class is always distressing to me.

INTERVIEWER: Do you think that the word processor has had or is having any effect on the study of literature?

BLOOM: There cannot be a human being who has fewer thoughts on the whole question of word processing than I do. I've never even seen a word processor. I am hopelessly archaic.

INTERVIEWER: Perhaps you see an effect on students' papers then?

BLOOM: But for me the typewriter hasn't even been invented yet, so how can I speak to this matter? I protest! A man who has never learned to type is not going to be able to add anything to this debate. As far as I'm concerned, computers have as much to do with literature as space travel, perhaps much less. I can only write with a ballpoint pen, with a "Rolling Writer," they're called, a black "Rolling Writer" on a lined yellow legal pad on a certain kind of clipboard. And then someone else types it.

INTERVIEWER: And someone else edits?

BLOOM: No one edits. I edit. I refuse to be edited.

INTERVIEWER: Do you revise much?

BLOOM: Sometimes, but not often.

INTERVIEWER: Is there a particular time of day when you like to write?

BLOOM: There isn't one for me. I write in desperation. I write because the pressures are so great, and I am simply so far past a deadline that I must turn out something.

INTERVIEWER: So you don't espouse a particular work ethic on a daily basis?

BLOOM: No, no. I lead a disordered and hurried life.

INTERVIEWER: Are there days when you do not work at all?

BLOOM: Yes, alas, alas, alas. But one always thinks about literature. I don't recognize a distinction between literature and life. I am, as I keep moaning, an experimental critic. I've spent my life proclaiming that what is called "critical objectivity" is a farce. It is deep subjectivity which has to be achieved, which is difficult, whereas objectivity is cheap.

INTERVIEWER: What is it that you think keeps you from writing when you're unable to write?

BLOOM: Despair, exhaustion. There are long periods when I cannot write at all. Long, long periods, sometimes lasting many years. Sometimes one just has to lie fallow. And also, you know, interests change. One goes into such different modes. What was incredibly difficult was the commentary on the J-Writer, which underwent real change for me as I became more and more convinced that she was a woman, which made some considerable difference. I mean, obviously it's just a question of imagining it one way or another. No one will ever demonstrate it, that he was a man or she was a woman. But I find that if I imagine it that J was a woman, it produces, to me, more imaginatively accurate results than the other way around.

INTERVIEWER: But do you think that the importance of the J-Writer's being a woman has been exaggerated?

BLOOM: Oh, immensely exaggerated. In an interview that was published in the *New York Times*, the extremely acute Richard Bernstein allowed me to remark at some length on my strong feeling, more intense than before, that on the internal, that is to say psychological and literary evidence, it is much more likely to have been a woman than a man. I also said—I believe this quite passionately—that if I had it to do over again, I wouldn't have mentioned the putative gender of the author. It has served as a monstrous red herring which has diverted attention away from what is really controversial and should be the outrage and scandal of the book, which is the fact that the god—the literary character named Yahweh or God—has absolutely nothing in common with the God of the revisionists in the completed Torah and therefore of the normative Jewish tradition and of Christianity and Islam and all their branches.

INTERVIEWER: Certainly that aspect of the book has caught the notice of the normative Jewish reviewers.

BLOOM: The normative Jewish reviewers have reacted very badly, in particular Mister Robert Alter. And the other Norman Podhorrors-type review was by his henchman, Neil Kozody, a subscriber to the Hotel Hilton Kramer criteria. (The marvelous controversialist Gore Vidal invariably refers to that dubiety as the Hotel Hilton Kramer.) Mister Kozody, in playing Tonto to the Lone Ranger, went considerably further than Mister Alter in denouncing me for what he thought was my vicious attack on normative Judaism. And indeed, I've now heard this from many quarters, including from an absurd rabbinical gentleman who reviewed it in *Newsday* and proclaimed, "What makes Professor Bloom think there was such a thing as irony 3,000 years ago?"—which may be the funniest single remark that anyone could make about this or any other book.

But I'm afraid it isn't over. It's just beginning. There was a program at Symphony Space, where Claire Bloom and Fritz Weaver read aloud from the Bible, and I spoke for ten minutes at the beginning and end. I got rather carried away. In the final ten minutes I allowed myself not only to answer my normative Jewish critics, but to start talking about what I feel are the plain spiritual inadequacies for a contemporary intellectual Jewry. It has been subsequently broadcast, and all hell may break loose. Many a rabbi and Jewish bureaucrat has been after my scalp.

INTERVIEWER: What did you say?

BLOOM: Well, I allowed myself to tell the truth, which is always a great mistake. I said that I could not be the only contemporary Jewish intellectual who was very unhappy indeed that the Holocaust had been made part of our religion. I did not like this vision of six million versions of what the Christians call Jesus, and I did not believe that if this was going to be offered to me as Judaism it would be acceptable. I also allowed myself to say that the god of the J-Writer seems to me a god in whom I scarcely could fail to believe, since that god was all of our breath and vitality. Whereas what the Redactor, being more a censor than an author of the Hebrew Bible, and the priestly authors and those that came after in Jewish, Christian, and Islamic tradition, gave us are simply not acceptable to a person with literary sensibility or any high spirituality at this time.

INTERVIEWER: How have you found being in the public eye? *The Book of J* is your first book on the best-seller list.

BLOOM: Though it's the first time, I'm informed, that a work of literary criticism or commentary has been on the best-seller list, it has not been a pleasant experience.

INTERVIEWER: How so?

BLOOM: I did not, on the whole, relish the television and radio appearances, which I undertook because of the plain inadequacies of the publisher. The people who work for that publisher did the best they could, but they were under-staffed, under-manned, never printed enough books, and have most inadequate advertising. I know that all authors complain about that, but this is manifest.

INTERVIEWER: You were on *Good Morning America* of all things.

BLOOM: I was on *Good Morning America*, I was on Larry King, and many others. I must say that I came away with two radically opposed insights. One is the remarkably high degree of civility and personal civilization of both my radio and TV interlocutors. In fact, they're far more civilized and gentlemanly or gentlewomanly than journalistic interviewers usually are, and certainly more so than the so-called scholarly and academic reviewers, who are merely assassins and thugs. But also, after a lifetime spent teaching, it was very difficult to accept emotionally that huge blank eye of the TV camera, or the strange bareness of the radio studio. There is a terrible unreality about it which I have not enjoyed at all.

INTERVIEWER: You have mentioned you might write on the aesthetics of outrage as a topic.

BLOOM: Yes, the aesthetics of *being* outraged. But I don't mean being outraged in that other sense, you know, that sort of post-sixties phenomenon. I mean in the sense in which Macbeth is increasingly outraged. What fascinates me is that we so intensely sympathize with a successful or strong representation of someone in the process of being outraged, and I want to know why. I suppose it's ultimately that we're outraged at mortality, and it is impossible not to sympathize with that.

INTERVIEWER: This is a topic that would somehow include W. C. Fields.

BLOOM: Oh yes, certainly, since I think his great power is that he perpetually demonstrates the enormous comedy of being outraged. I have never recovered from the first time I saw the W. C. Fields short, "The Fatal Glass of Beer." It represents for me still the high point of cinema, surpassing even Groucho's *Duck Soup*. Have you seen "The Fatal Glass of Beer"? I don't think I have the critical powers to describe it. Throughout much of it, W. C. Fields is strumming a zither and singing a song about the demise of his unfortunate son, who expires because of a fatal glass of beer which college boys persuade the abstaining youth to drink. He then insults a Salvation Army lassie, herself a reformed high-kicker in the chorus line, and she stuns him with a single high kick. But to describe it in this way is to say that *Macbeth* is about an ambitious man who murders the King.

INTERVIEWER: So in addition to being an outrageous critic, are you an outraged critic, in that sense?

BLOOM: No, no. I hope that I am not an outrageous critic, but I suppose I am. But that's only because most of the others are so dreadfully tame and senescent, or indeed are now politically correct or content to be social reformers who try to tell us there is some connection between literature and social change. Outraged? No, I am not outraged. I am not outraged as a person. I am beyond it now. I'm sixty years and seven months old. It's too late for me to be outraged. It would really shorten my life if I let myself be outraged. I don't have the emotional strength anymore. It would be an expense of spirit that I cannot afford. Besides, by now nothing surprises me. You know, the literary situation is one of a surpassing absurdity. Criticism in the universities, I'll have to admit, has entered a phase where I am totally out of sympathy with ninety-five percent of what goes on. It's Stalinism without Stalin. All the traits of the Stalinist in the 1930s and 1940s are being repeated in this whole resentment in the universities in the 1990s. The intolerance, the self-congratulation, smugness, sanctimoniousness, the retreat from imaginative values, the flight from the aesthetic. It's not worth being truly outraged about. Eventually these people will provide their own antidote, because they will perish of boredom. I will win in the end. I must be the only literary critic of any eminence who is writing today (I cannot think of another, I'm sad to say, however arrogant or difficult this sounds) who always asks about what he reads and likes, whether it is ancient, modern, or brand new, or has always been laying around, who always asks "How good is it? What is it better than? What is it less good than? What does it mean?" and "Is there some relation between what it means and how good or bad it is, and not only how is it good or bad, but why it is good or bad?" Mister Frye, who was very much my precursor, tried to banish all of that from criticism, just as I tried to reintroduce a kind of dark sense of temporality, or the sorrows of temporality, into literary criticism as a correction to Frye's Platonic idealism. I have also raised more explicitly than anyone else nowadays or indeed anyone since Johnson or Hazlitt, the question of, "Why does it matter?" There has to be some relation between the way in which we matter and the way in which we read. A way of speaking and writing about literature which addresses itself to these matters must seem impossibly naive or old-fashioned or not literary criticism at all to the partisans of the School of Resentment. But I believe that these have been the modes of Western literary criticism ever since Aristophanes invented the art of criticism by juxtaposing Euripides with Aeschylus (to the profound disadvantage of Euripides), or indeed ever since Longinus started to work off his own anxieties about Plato by dealing with Plato's anxieties about Homer. This is the stuff literary criticism has always done and, if it is finally to be of any use to us, this is what I think it must get back to. It really must answer the questions of good and bad and how and why. It must answer the question of what the relevance of literature is to our lives, and why it means one thing to us when we are one way and another thing to us when we are another. It astonishes me that I cannot find any other contemporary critic who still discusses the pathos of great literature, or is willing to talk about why a particular work does or does not evoke great anguish in us. This is of course dismissed as the merest subjectivity.

INTERVIEWER: Can essays like Hazlitt's or Ruskin's or Pater's still be written today?

BLOOM: Most people would say no. I can only say I do my best. That's as audacious a thing as I can say. I keep saying, though nobody will listen, or only a few will listen, that criticism is either a genre of literature or it is nothing. It has no hope for survival unless it is a genre of literature. It can be regarded, if you wish, as a minor genre, but I don't know why people say that. The idea that poetry or, rather, verse writing, is to take priority over criticism is on the face of it absolute nonsense. That would be to say that the verse-writer Felicia Hemans is a considerably larger figure than her contemporary William Hazlitt. Or that our era's Felicia Hemans, Sylvia Plath, is a considerably larger literary figure than, say, the late Wilson Knight. This is clearly not the case. Miss Plath is a bad verse writer. I read Knight with pleasure and profit, if at times wonder and shock. These are obvious points but obviously one will have to go on making them. Almost everything now written and published and praised in the United States as verse isn't even verse, let alone poetry. It's just typing, or word processing. As a matter of fact, it's usually just glib rhetoric or social resentment. Just as almost everything that we now call criticism is in fact just journalism.

INTERVIEWER: Or an involvement with what you refer to as the "easier pleasures." What are these easier pleasures?

BLOOM: Well, I take the notion from my friend and contemporary Angus Fletcher, who takes it from Shelley and Longinus. It's perfectly clear some very good writers offer only easier pleasures. Compare two writers exactly contemporary with one another—Harold Brodkey and John Updike. Updike, as I once wrote, is a minor novelist with a major style. A quite beautiful and very considerable stylist. I've read many novels by Updike, but the one I like best is *The Witches of Eastwick*. But for the most part it seems to me that he specializes in the easier pleasures. They are genuine pleasures, but they do not challenge the intellect. Brodkey, somewhat imperfectly perhaps, does so to a much more considerable degree. Thomas Pynchon provides very difficult pleasures, it seems to me, though not of late. I am not convinced, in fact, that it was he who wrote *Vineland*. Look at the strongest American novelist since Melville, Hawthorne, and James. That would certainly have to be Faulkner. Look at the difference between Faulkner at his very best in *As I Lay Dying* and at his very worst in *A Fable*. *A Fable* is nothing but easier pleasures, but they're not even pleasures. It is so easy it becomes, indeed, vulgar, disgusting, and does not afford pleasure. *As I Lay Dying* is a very difficult piece of work. To try to apprehend Darl Bundren takes a very considerable effort of the imagination. Faulkner really surpasses himself there. It seems to me an authentic instance of the literary sublime in our time. Or, if you look at modern American poetry, in some sense the entire development of Wallace Stevens is from affording us easier pleasures, as in "The Idea of Order at Key West," and before that "Sunday Morning," to the very difficult pleasures of "Notes toward a Supreme Fiction" and then the immensely difficult pleasures of a poem like "The Owl in the Sarcophagus." You have to labor with immense intensity in order to keep up. It is certainly related to the notion propounded by both Burckhardt and Nietzsche, which I've taken over from them, of the agonistic. There is a kind of standard of measurement starting with Plato on through Western thought where one asks a literary work, implicity, to answer the question, "More, equal to, or less than?" In the end, the answer to that question is the persuasive force enabling a reader to say, "I will sacrifice an easier pleasure for something that takes me beyond myself." Surely that must be the difference between Marlowe's *The Jew of Malta* and Shakespeare's *The Merchant of Venice*, an enigmatic and to me in many ways unequal play. I get a lot more pleasure out of Barabas than I do out of the equivocal Shylock, but I'm well aware that my pleasure in Barabas is an easier pleasure, and that my trouble in achieving any pleasure in reading or viewing Shylock is because other factors are getting in the way of apprehending the Shakespearean sublime. The whole question of the fifth act of *The Merchant of Venice* is for me one of the astonishing tests of what I would call the sublime in poetry. One has the trouble of having to accommodate oneself to it.

INTERVIEWER: You recently completed a stint as General Editor for the Chelsea House series, a sort of encyclopedia of literary criticism, consisting of some five hundred volumes.

BLOOM: I haven't completed it, but it has slowed down. It has been a very strange kind of a process. It swept me away in a kind of fantastic rush. I couldn't do it again like that and I wouldn't want to do it again, but it was very intense while it lasted. When it reached its height I was writing fifteen of those introductions a month, so that every two days I had to write another. I had to reread everything, and crystallize my views very quickly. But I like that kind of writing. I learned a great deal doing it, because you couldn't waste any time. You had to get to the kernel of it immediately, and in seven to twelve pages say what you really thought about it without wasting time on scholarly outreaches or byways.

INTERVIEWER: How do you manage to write so quickly? Is it insomnia?

BLOOM: Partly insomnia. I think I usually write therapeutically. That is what Hart Crane really taught one. I was talking to William Empson about this once. He never wrote any criticism of Crane, and he didn't know whether he liked his poetry or not, but he said that the desperation of Crane's poetry appealed to him. Using his funny kind of parlance, he said that Hart Crane's poetry showed that poetry is now a mug's game, that Crane always wrote every poem as though it were going to be his last. That catches something in Crane which is very true, that he writes each lyric in such a way that you literally feel he's going to die if he can't bring it off, that his survival not just as a poet but as a person depends upon somehow articulating that poem. I don't have the audacity to compare myself to Crane, yet I think I write criticism in the spirit in which he wrote poems. One writes to keep going, to keep oneself from going mad. One writes to be able to write the next piece of criticism or to live through the next day or two. Maybe it's an apotropaic gesture, maybe one writes to ward off death. I'm not sure. But I think in some sense that's what poets do. They write their poems to ward off dying.

INTERVIEWER: You were for some time writing a major work on Freud to be called *Transference and Authority*. What's become of that?

BLOOM: Well, it's a huge, yellowing manuscript. I don't know whether I would have finished it, but for the five years before the Chelsea House New Haven factory closed down I increasingly had to give my work to writing those introductions. I don't regret it, since it allowed me for the first time to become a really general literary critic. But I had to set the Freud aside. Perhaps in four or five years I'll get back to it. I would still like to write a book on Freud, but I don't think it will be the *Transference and Authority* book. I've got a huge manuscript which tries to comment on every important essay or monograph of Freud's, but I don't think I would want to publish it. I would not want to write on Freud as though he were a kind of scripture. I would have to rethink the whole thing. The title was a giveaway, I now realize. I could never work out my own transference relationship with regard to the text of Freud, and I could never decide how much authority it did or didn't have for me. I suppose I foundered upon that, so it's a kind of tattered white elephant. It's up in the attic—seven or eight hundred pages of typescript. But I think I have abandoned in manuscript more books and essays than I've ever printed. The attic is full of them. Eventually I may make a bonfire of the whole thing.

INTERVIEWER: You've also referred to a sequel to *Flight to Lucifer*, your one novel.

BLOOM: I wrote about half the sequel to it, called *The Lost Travellers' Dream*, about a changeling child, a kind of gnostic concept, though it was much less doctrinal than *A Flight to Lucifer*. I thought it was a much better piece of writing, and a couple of people whom I showed it to thought it had real promise. But I brooded on it one night, about 1981 or 1982, and I shut my notebook, took the manuscript, and put it up in the attic; it's still up there, and if I ever live long enough and there are no changes in my life I might take it down. *Flight to Lucifer* is certainly the only book which I wish I hadn't published. It was all right to have composed it, but I wish I hadn't published it. I sat down one night, six months after it came out, and read through it. I thought it was—particularly in the last third or so—quite well-written, but I also felt it was an atrociously bad book. It failed as narrative, as negative characterization. Its overt attempt to be a sort of secret sequel to that sublime and crazy book *A Voyage to Arcturus* failed completely. It had no redeeming virtues. It was a kind of tractate in the understanding of gnosticism. It clearly had many obsessive critical ideas in it. *The Flight to Lucifer* now reads to me as though Walter Pater were trying to write *Star Wars*. That's giving it the best of it.

INTERVIEWER: Do you find you have "slowed down" at all since your incredibly prolific period in the seventies?

BLOOM: I don't know that I'm a burned-out husk but one becomes so dialetically aware of the history of literature that one requires some multiple consciousness of oneself in regard to the total work of others. One gets more and more addicted to considering the relationship between literature and life in teaching and writing. In fact, there are certain things which had been possible at an early age which are not possible anymore. I find that anything of any length I'm now trying to write is what once would have been called religious. I'm writing this book called *The American Religion: A Prophecy*, whose title, of course, echoes Blake's *America: A Prophecy*. It is meant to be a somewhat outrageous but I hope a true and useful book. It begins with our last election and leads into the whole question of the American spirit and American literature and above all the American religion—which existed before Emerson but to which Emerson gave the decisive terms. The religion of the United States is not Christianity; perhaps it never was Christianity, but is a curious form of American gnosis. It is a mighty queer religion, exhilarating in some ways but marked by destructiveness. It seems to me increasingly that George Bush won hands down and had to win because of the two candidates he more nearly incarnated the ideals and visions of the American religion. Our foreign policy basically amounts to making the world safe for gnosticism.

INTERVIEWER: You've written that the Christian Bible is, on the whole, a disappointment.

BLOOM: The aesthetic achievement is so much less than that of the Old—or Original—Testament. The New Testament is a very curious work from a literary point of view. So much of it is written by writers who are thinking in Aramaic and writing in demotic Greek. And that curious blend of Aramatic syntax with a Greek vocabulary is a very dubious medium. It's particularly egregious in the Revelation of St. John the Divine, the Apocalypse, which is a very bad and hysterical and nasty piece of writing. Even the most powerful parts of the New Testament from a literary point of view—certain epistles of Paul and the Gospel of John—are not works which can sustain a close aesthetic comparison with the stronger parts of the Hebrew Bible. It is striking how the Apocalypse of John has had an influence out of all proportion to its aesthetic, or for that matter, I would think, its spiritual value. It is not only an hysterical piece of work, but a work lacking love or compassion. In fact, it is the archetypal text of resentment, and it is the proper foundation for every School of Resentment ever since.

INTERVIEWER: Is belief anything more than a trope for you now?

BLOOM: Belief is not available to me. It is a stuffed bird, up on the shelf. So is philosophy, let me point out, and so, for that matter, is psychoanalysis—an institutional church founded upon Freud's writings, praxis, and example. These are not live birds that one can hold in one's hand. We live in a literary culture, as I keep saying. This is not necessarily good—it might even be bad—but it is where we are. Our cognitive modes have failed us.

INTERVIEWER: Can belief be as individual and idiosyncratic as fiction?

BLOOM: The religious genius is a dead mode. Belief should be as passionate and individual a fiction as any strong, idiosyncratic literary work, but it isn't. It almost never is. Religion has been too contaminated by society, by human hatreds. The history of religion as an institutional or social mode is a continuous horror. At this very moment we see this with the wretched Mister Rushdie, who, by the way, alas, is not much of a writer. I tried to read *Midnight's Children* and found myself quite bored; I have tried to read *The Satanic Verses*, which seems to me very wordy, very neo-Joycean, very much an inadequate artifice. It is not much better than an upper-middle brow attempt at serious fiction. Poor wretched fellow, who can blame him? There's no way for him to apologize because the world is not prepared to protect him from the consequences of having offended a religion. All religions have always been pernicious as social, political and economic entities. And they always will be.

INTERVIEWER: Are you still watching the TV evangelists?

BLOOM: Oh yes, I love the TV evangelists, especially Jimmy Swaggart. I loved above all his grand confession starting, "I have sinned . . ." which he delivered to all of America with his family in the front row of the auditorium. One of the most marvelous moments in modern American culture! I enjoyed it immensely. It was his finest performance. And then the revelation by the lady, when she published her article, that he never touched her! And he was paying her these rather inconsiderable sums for her to zoombinate herself while he watched. Oh dear. It's so sad. It's so terribly sad.

INTERVIEWER: I've heard that you occasionally listen to rock music.

BLOOM: Oh sure. My favorite viewing, and this is the first time I have ever admitted it to anyone, but what I love to do, when I don't watch evangelicals, when I can't read or write and can't go out walking, and don't want to just tear my hair and destroy myself, I put on, here in New Haven, cable channel 13 and I watch rock television endlessly. As a sheer revelation of the American religion it's overwhelming. Yes, I like to watch the dancing girls too. The sex part of it is fine. Occasionally it's musically interesting, but you know, 99 out of 100 groups are just bilge. And there hasn't been any good American rock since, alas, The Band disbanded. I watch MTV endlessly, my dear, because what is going on there, not just in the lyrics but in its whole ambience, is the real vision of what the country needs and desires. It's the image of reality that it sees, and it's quite weird and wonderful. It confirms exactly these two points: first, that no matter how many are on the screen at once, not one of them feels free except in total self-exaltation. And second, it comes through again and again in the lyrics and the way one dances, the way one moves, that what is best and purest in one is just no part of the Creation: that myth of an essential purity before and beyond experience never goes away. It's quite fascinating. And notice how pervasive it is! I spent a month in Rome lecturing and

I was so exhausted at the end of each day that my son David and I cheerfully watched the Italian MTV. I stared and I just couldn't believe it. Italian MTV is a sheer parody of its American counterpart, with some amazing consequences: the American religion has made its way even into Rome! It is nothing but a religious phenomenon. Very weird to see it take place.

INTERVIEWER: Has the decision to be a critic . . . or it's not really a decision, I suppose.

BLOOM: It's not a decision, it's an infliction.

INTERVIEWER: Has the vocation of criticism been a happy one?

BLOOM: I don't think of it in those terms.

INTERVIEWER: Satisfying?

BLOOM: I don't think of it in those terms.

INTERVIEWER: Inevitable only?

BLOOM: People who don't like me would say so. Denis Donoghue, in his review of *Rain the Sacred Truths*, described me as the Satan of literary criticism. That I take as an involuntary compliment. Perhaps indeed it was a voluntary compliment. In any case, I'm delighted to accept that. I'm delighted to believe that I am by merit raised to that bad eminence.

INTERVIEWER: Are there personal costs to being the Satan of literary criticism?

BLOOM: I can't imagine what they would be. All of us are, as Mister Stevens said, "condemned to be that inescapable animal, ourselves." Or as an even greater figure, Sir John Falstaff, said, " 'Tis no sin for a man to labor in his vocation." I would much rather be regarded, of course, as the Flagstaff of literary criticism than as the Satan of literary criticism. Much as I love my Uncle Satan, I love my Uncle Falstaff even more. He's much wittier than Satan. He's wiser than Satan. But then, Shakespeare's an even better poet than Milton.

INTERVIEWER: Is there anything you feel especially required to complete right now, as a teacher or as a critic? Something just beyond view?

BLOOM: Well, I intend to teach Shakespeare for the rest of my life. I would like to write a general, comprehensive study on Shakespeare, not necessarily commenting on every play or every scene, but trying to arrive at a total view of Shakespeare. One always wants to write about Shakespeare. But by then I may be too old I think.

INTERVIEWER: Are you being fruitfully misread, as you would say, by anyone?

BLOOM: I hope that somewhere in the world there is a young critic or two who will strongly misread me to their advantage. Lord knows, one is not Samuel Johnson or William Hazlitt or John Ruskin, or even Walter Pater or Oscar Wilde as critic. But, yes, I hope so.

You know, I've learned something over the years, picking up copies of my books in secondhand bookstores and in libraries, off people's shelves. I've written so much and have now looked at so many of these books that I've learned a great deal. You also learn this from reviews and from things that are cited in other people's books and so on, or from what people say to you: What you pride yourself on, the things that you think are your insight and contribution . . . no one ever even *notices* them. It's as though they're just for you. What you say in passing or what you expound because you know it too well, because it really bores you, but you feel you have to get through this in order to make your grand point, *that's* what people pick up on. *That's* what they underline. *That's* what they quote. *That's* what they attack, or cite favorably. *That's* what they can use. What you really think you're doing may or may not be what you're doing, but it certainly isn't communicated to others. I've talked about this to other critics, to other writers; they haven't had quite my extensive sense of this, but it strikes an answering chord in them. One's grand ideas are indeed one's grand ideas, but there are none that seem to be useful or even recognizable to anyone else. It's a very strange phenomenon. It must have something to do with our capacity for not knowing ourselves.

ANTONIO WEISS
Fall 1990

# 10. Tom Wolfe

Tom Wolfe's work is often representative of the style he dubbed himself as the "New Journalism," combining detailed factual reportage with an involved personal viewpoint. In his introduction to the book *The New Journalism,* Wolfe embraced the idea that the future of the novel lies in this type of highly detailed writing. An example is his own *Bonfire of the Vanities,* his only novel to date, and which first appeared in serial form in *Rolling Stone* magazine. The book was published in 1987 to considerable critical acclaim and was the nation's top best-seller, both in hardcover and paperback, for many weeks.

A native of Virginia, Wolfe attended Washington and Lee University and received his doctorate of American studies from Yale. The paper he worked for initially was the *Springfield Union* in Massachusetts; he later reported for the *Washington Post* and the *New York Herald Tribune* as well. Many of his first magazine articles appeared in *New York* magazine, and he wrote numerous pieces for *Rolling Stone, Esquire,* and *Harper's.* In 1965 *The Kandy-Kolored Tangerine-Flake Streamline Baby* was published; three years later *The Pump House Gang* and *The Electric Kool-Aid Acid Test* appeared simultaneously. In 1975, *The Painted Word,* Wolfe's controversial look at the world of modern art, came out and, a year later, *Mauve Gloves & Madmen, Clutter & Vine,* his look at popular American culture. His book about the early astronauts, *The Right Stuff,* which was made into a movie, won the American Book Award for general non-fiction. In *From Bauhaus to Our House* he critiqued contemporary architecture and in 1982 compiled a selection of his writings from the sixties and seventies, entitled *The Purple Decades.*

Wolfe lives in New York City with his wife, son, and ten-year-old daughter.

XII:
10 WOLFE

fool enough to stand around in the asphalt mush of Downtown at noon watching a parade was obviously defective to begin with. The parade plowed on, however, through wave after wave of catatonia and rippling lassitude.

After about an hour of this the fellows and their families noticed, with considerable misgiving, that the parade was heading back into that hole in the ground underneath the Coliseum. The air conditioning hit them like a wall. Everybody's bone marrow congealed. It made you feel like your teeth were loose. It turned out that this was where the little cocktail party was going to take place: in the Houston Coliseum. They led them up to the floor of the coliseum, which was like a great indoor bowl. There were thousands of people milling around, and some sort of incredible smell and a storm of voices and the occasional insane cackle. There were five thousand extremely loud people on the floor eager to tear into roast cow and wash it

*Although marked "XII," this is actually a manuscript page from chapter XIII of* The Right Stuff, *by Tom Wolfe.*

© Thomas Victor

# Tom Wolfe

*One of Tom Wolfe's favorite restaurants in New York City is the Isle of Capri on the East Side, specializing, as one might expect, in Italian cuisine; indeed, the menu does not condescend to non-Italian speaking customers: an extensive list of choices is not identified in English. The table set aside for Wolfe is in a corner of a patio-like glassed-in enclosure facing Third Avenue. Clusters of potted plants hang from its rafters. The author arrived wearing the white ensemble he is noted for—a white modified homburg, a chalk-white overcoat—but to the surprise of regular customers looking up from their tables, he removed the coat to disclose a light-brown suit set off by a pale lilac tie. Questioned about the light-brown suit, he replied: "Shows that I'm versatile." He went on to point out that his overcoat only had one button—rare in overcoats, quite impractical, obviously, in a stiff wind. "One must occasionally suffer for style." At the table he ordered bottled water and calamari. Squid. His accent is more cosmopolitan than southern though he grew up in the South (Richmond, Virginia) and went to school there (Washington and Lee). His face is pale, fine-featured. During the interview a young woman nervously approached the table for an autograph. She announced that she hoped to become a writer and that he had been her idol from the first. Wolfe thanked her and asked where she was from. North Carolina. While he worked the pen across the paper (Wolfe's autograph is a decorative scrawl which if stretched out straight would measure a foot.) the two chatted about her home state, which he knows well—his mother and sister live there. The young woman went on to say that she found New York City wonderful and looked forward to moving. Wolfe nodded, and afterwards remarked how pleasing it was to hear from someone not swayed by the bad publicity, least of all by reading his novel,* The Bonfire of the Vanities.

*Part of the interview which follows was conducted before the public under the auspices of the West Side* YMCA *in Manhattan.*

INTERVIEWER: When did you first realize that you had a knack for writing?

TOM WOLFE: Very early. When I was six or seven years old. My father was the editor of an agricultural magazine called *The Southern Planter.* He didn't think of himself as a writer. He was a scientist, an agronomist, but I thought of him as a writer because I'd seen him working at his desk. I just assumed that I was going to do that, that I was going to be a writer. There's an enormous advantage in having (mistakenly or not) the impression that you have a vocation very early because from that time forward you begin to focus all of your energies towards this goal. The only other thing I ever considered from six on was to become an artist, something my mother had encouraged me to do.

INTERVIEWER: Regarding writing, was there any particular book which influenced you?

WOLFE: I was greatly struck by Emil Ludwig's biography of Napoleon, which is written in the historical present. It begins as the mother sits suckling her babe in a tent.

INTERVIEWER: And that impressed you?

WOLFE: It impressed me so enormously that I began to write the biography of Napoleon myself, though heavily cribbed from Emil Ludwig. I was eight at the time.

INTERVIEWER: Did it start the same way, with a babe being suckled in . . .

WOLFE: It did, though no one would tell me what "suckled" meant. I only knew that that was what Napoleon did at the start. I always liked Napoleon from when I was six on because he was small and had ruled the world and at the time I was small. I liked Mozart for the same reason.

INTERVIEWER: What about Thomas Wolfe? Did he float into your consciousness at all?

WOLFE: Yes, he did. I can remember that on the shelves at home there were these books by Thomas Wolfe. *Look Homeward Angel* and *Of Time and the River. Of Time and the River* had just come out when I was aware of his name. My parents had a hard time convincing me that he was no kin whatsoever. My attitude was, "Well, what's he doing on the shelf then?" But as soon as I was old enough I became a tremendous fan of Thomas Wolfe and remain so to this day. I ignore his fluctuations on the literary stock market.

INTERVIEWER: You started off writing for newspapers. . . .

WOLFE: The first newspaper I worked on was the *Springfield Union* in Springfield, Massachusetts. I wrote over a hundred letters to newspapers asking for work and got three responses, two no's.

INTERVIEWER: Style is pretty much dictated in newspaper work, isn't it? Can you say something about the development of your style, which is certainly one of the more unique in American letters?

WOLFE: The newspaper is, in fact, very bad for one's prose style. That's why I gravitated towards feature stories where you get a littlc more leeway in the writing style. When I started writing magazine pieces for *Esquire* I had to unlearn newspaper restraints and shortcuts. Working on newspapers, you're writing to a certain length, often very brief pieces; you tend to look for easy forms of humor: "Women can't drive," things like that. That's about the level of a lot of newspaper humor. It becomes a form of laziness. But I wouldn't give anything for the years I spent on newspapers because it forces you, it immerses you, in so many different sides of life. I did try to cut up as much as I could; I think I was a lively newspaper writer, but that's a long way from being a good writer.

INTERVIEWER: Did editors tend to say, "Come now, you can't do this sort of thing?"

WOLFE: Yes, if the subject was serious. The greatest promotion I ever had on a newspaper was when the *Washington Post* suddenly promoted me from cityside general assignment reporter to Latin-American correspondent and sent me off to Cuba. Fidel Castro had just come to power. It was a very exciting assignment, but also very serious. Every time I tried to write about the veins popping out on the forehead of a Cuban revolutionary leader it was just stricken from the copy because all they wanted was, "Defense Minister Raul Castro said yesterday that . . ."

INTERVIEWER: When did the breakthrough come?

WOLFE: Well, this happened really in two stages. While I was in graduate school at Yale I came upon a group of early Soviet writers called the Brothers Serapion. These were people like Boris Pilnyak who wrote a book called *The Naked Year*, and especially Eugene Zamiatin, probably best known for his novel *We*, upon which George Orwell's *1984* is based. He is a brilliant writer who was exiled from the Soviet Union in 1927, I believe. These were Russian writers writing about the Soviet revolution; they were heavily influenced by French Symbolism, so you had all the preciousness and aestheticism of the Symbolists converging upon a very raw subject, namely the Revolution. I began imitating the Brothers Serapion in the short pieces I was writing for myself. I even tried to sneak these things into my newspaper work. I never got very far with it.

INTERVIEWER: What sort of thing?

WOLFE: For example, one of the things they did was experiment with punctuation. In *We*, Zamiatin constantly breaks off a thought in mid-sentence with a dash. He's trying to imitate the habits of actual thought, assuming, quite correctly, that we don't think in whole sentences. We think emotionally. He also used a lot of exclamation points, a habit I picked up and which I still have. Someone counted them in *The Bonfire of the Vanities*—some enormous number of exclamation points, up in the thousands. I think it's quite justified, though I've been ridiculed for it. Dwight Macdonald once wrote that reading me, with all these exclamation points, was like reading Queen Victoria's diaries. He was so eminent at the time, I felt crushed. But then out of curiosity I looked up Queen Victoria's diaries. They're childhood diaries. They're full of exclamation points. They are so much more readable than the official prose she inflicted on prime ministers and the English people in the years thereafter. Her diaries aren't bad at all. I also made a lot of use of the historical present (getting back to Emil Ludwig) in my early magazine work, along with eccentric images and metaphors. These were things that I began to use as soon as I had a truly free hand. That was when I began to do magazine work in 1963 for *Esquire*—which was that rarest of things: an experimental mass-circulation magazine.

INTERVIEWER: Presumably there was an editor at *Esquire* who supported what you were up to. . . .

WOLFE: Well, Byron Dobell was the first editor I had at *Esquire*. I've written about this in the introduction to *The Kandy-Kolored Tangerine-Flake Streamline Baby*. The piece about car customizers in Los Angeles was the first magazine piece I ever wrote. I was totally blocked. I now know what writer's block is. It's the fear you cannot do what you've announced to someone else you can do, or else the fear that it isn't worth doing. That's a rarer form. In this case I suddenly realized I'd never written a magazine article before and I just felt I couldn't do it. Well, Dobell somehow shamed me into writing down the notes that I had taken in my reporting on the car customizers so that some competent writer could convert them into a magazine piece. I sat down one night and started writing a memorandum to him as fast as I could, just to get the ordeal over with. It became very much like a letter that you would write to a friend in which you're not thinking about style, you're just pouring it all out, and I churned it out all night long, forty typewritten, triple-spaced pages. I turned it in in the morning to Byron at *Esquire*, and then I went home to sleep. About four that afternoon I got a call from him telling me, "Well, we're knocking the 'Dear Byron' off the top of your memo, and we're running the piece." That was a tremendous release for me. I think there are not many editors who would have done that, but *Esquire* at that time was a very experimental magazine. Byron Dobell was and remains a brilliant editor, and it worked out.

INTERVIEWER: Is it hazardous to have a style as distinctive as that?

WOLFE: It became so. At the outset I didn't think of myself as having something called a "Tom Wolfe Style." Many of my first pieces were for the *Herald Tribune*'s new Sunday magazine which was called *New York* and is now an independent magazine. Sunday supplements at that time were like brain candy, easily thrown away. I never had the feeling that there were any standards to writing for a Sunday supplement. So you could experiment in any fashion you wished, which I began to do. Still, I didn't think of it as a "Tom Wolfe Style." Finally, after *The Kandy-Kolored Tangerine-Flake Streamline Baby* came out as a book, and I began to get a lot of publicity, people began to write about me and about this style. Suddenly I would start writing an article and I'd say, "Wait a minute. Is this really a 'Tom Wolfe Style'?" Now that is fatal, I assure you. I wrote a number of pieces in the year 1966 that were so bad that, although I'm a great collector of my own pieces, I have never collected them.

INTERVIEWER: Readers have always followed your fascination with clothes, material goods, and so forth. Where does that come from?

WOLFE: I couldn't tell you in any analytical fashion, but I assume I realized instinctively that if I were going to write vignettes of contemporary life, which is what I was doing constantly for *New York*, I wanted all the sounds, the looks, the feel of whatever place I was writing about to be in this vignette. Brand names, tastes in clothes and furniture, manners, the way people treat children, servants, or their superiors, are important clues to an individual's expectations. This is something else that I am criticized for, mocked for, ridiculed for. I take some solace in the fact that the leading critic of Balzac's day, Sainte-Beuve, used to say the same thing about Balzac's fixation on furniture. You can learn the names of more arcane pieces of furniture reading Balzac than you can reading a Sotheby's catalogue. Sainte-Beuve said, "If this little man is so obsessed with furniture why doesn't he open up a shop and spare us these so-called novels of his?" So I take solace in this. After all, we are in a brand name culture.

INTERVIEWER: Do you read catalogues, for example, to keep up on shoes and so forth?

WOLFE: I must confess to having read furniture-auction catalogues so that if I walked into somebody's living room I'd be able to tell you what these articles of furniture were. When I wrote *Radical Chic*, as a matter of fact, about a party for the Black Panthers at Leonard Bernstein's apartment, I noticed that the platters upon which the Panthers were being served Roquefort cheese balls were gadrooned. They had this little sort of ribbing around the edges of the trays. You may think that's a small point, but I think that small points like that can really make a piece, particularly at the beginning. There's something about a gadrooned platter being served to the Black Panthers that really gives a piece a bite, particularly at the beginning. It doesn't matter if your audience doesn't know what a gadrooned platter is. Often people are flattered to have an unusual word thrust upon them. They say, "Well, that author thinks I know what he's talking about!"

INTERVIEWER: At that party did you remember such things or do you have to whisk a notebook out and write a note down in the bathroom or wherever?

WOLFE: At that party I did take notes very openly. I was not the only person in the room doing so, incidentally. Charlotte Curtis of *The New York Times* was taking notes a mile a minute, and she did write about the party too. If it's a situation in which it's impossible or very awkward to take notes, I will try to write down everything I can remember before going to sleep. I find that memory decay is very rapid. Even going to sleep and waking up the next day, there's an awful lot that simply doesn't come back. At least it doesn't come back accurately. So I do it as soon as I can.

INTERVIEWER: Are memorable stories like that assigned to you by editors? How do you pick your subjects?

WOLFE: A great many stories that I did, particularly early in the game, were assigned to me, often things that I had no interest in covering at first. For example, after I did the piece on customized cars, *Esquire* assigned me a piece on the then Cassius Clay, which I did want to do very much, and then a piece on Las Vegas. I felt that Las Vegas was the most tired story imaginable, but I wanted to be in *Esquire* again. And I wanted the money. So I went off to Las Vegas, and the place was a wonderland in a way that I had never expected. It turned out to be a very successful story as well; other stories were assigned. There's probably never been a better originator of story ideas in journalism than Clay Felker. Harold Hayes and Byron Dobell at *Esquire* were both very good. I did a story on a stockcar driver in North Carolina, Junior Johnson, who had been a whiskey runner for his father. That was an idea that came from an *Esquire* editor. On the other hand, *Radical Chic*, which was about the party at Leonard Bernstein's, was my own.

INTERVIEWER: Between journalism and fiction, which is the more difficult and which the more satisfying?

WOLFE: The problems are enormous with each, and I wouldn't say that one is any easier than another. I found it extremely difficult to shift from nonfiction to fiction and for reasons that surprised me. One was that I didn't face up to the most obvious thing of all . . . which is that in nonfiction you are handed the plot. You are handed the characters. It just didn't dawn on me how much I was now depriving myself of. The other thing that surprised me when I first started writing *The Bonfire of the Vanities* was that I was not nearly as free technically and in terms of style as I had been in nonfiction. I would have assumed it would be the opposite, since you have carte blanche in fiction, this tremendous freedom. What happened was that all the rules of composition I had been taught about fiction in college and graduate school came flooding back: Henry James's doctrine of point of view, Virginia Woolf's theory of the inner psychological glow. All things were suddenly laws. I was on an unfamiliar terrain and so I'd better obey. My first time around writing *The Bonfire of the Vanities* for *Rolling Stone* I was not nearly as free as I should have been. It took me a long time to realize that I could enjoy the kind of freedom that I'd had in nonfiction where I was operating without any rules to speak of. I finally began to appreciate the enormous flexibility of fiction, but it really took some doing.

INTERVIEWER: I believe you'd always wanted to do a huge nonfiction book about New York, and somehow you changed your mind. Why did you decide to do the book as fiction?

WOLFE: There were two things. One was personal. Practically everyone my age who wanted to write somehow got the impression in college that there was only one thing to write, which was a novel and that if you went into journalism, this was only a cup of coffee on the road to the final triumph. At some point you would move into a shack—it was always a shack for some reason—and write a novel. This would be your real métier. But by the time I got to the *Herald Tribune* a lot of things were happening in nonfiction. Gay Talese was doing amazing work; so were Jimmy Breslin and people like Tom Morgan at *Esquire* and many others. This was exciting to me and I started writing nonfiction, borrowing heavily, as others did, from the techniques of fiction writers. All along, even though I felt this was where things were happening, there was always a silent and perhaps not-so-silent rebuke from others that said, "This is an elaborate screen you're constructing to avoid the great challenge, which is the novel." So I decided I didn't want to reach the end of my career and look back and say, "Well, gee, I wonder what would have happened if I had tried the novel." I didn't want others saying, "Well, he ducked it. He never faced up to it."

Also, I had developed a theory about the future of the novel which I had elaborated to some extent in the introduction to the book *The New Journalism* in which I said that I felt the novel had taken a lot of wrong turns since 1950 in the United States and that its future would be highly detailed realism, a kind of hypernaturalism, to borrow a term from Zola. So I knew from the beginning that the type of novel I wanted to write would be that kind.

INTERVIEWER: *The Bonfire of the Vanities* was first published in *Rolling Stone* as a serial. McCoy, the main character, was originally a writer. Why did you want to write it as a serial novel? Was that another challenge?

WOLFE: For eight months I had sat at my typewriter every day, intending to start this novel and nothing had happened. I felt that the only way I was ever going to get going on it was to put myself under deadline pressure. I knew that if I *had* to, I could produce something under deadline pressure. I found the only marvelous maniac in all of journalism willing to let me do such a thing. That was Jann Wenner at *Rolling Stone*. This book would have never been written if Jann Wenner had not said, "Okay, let's do it. Let's see what happens."

INTERVIEWER: Was it the first fiction you had ever tried?

WOLFE: I had done a short story for *Esquire* called "Oh, the Big-Time, Game-Time, Show-Time Roll" in 1974. It was based on a couple of actual incidents about a black baseball star making a commercial here in New York. It was okay. I didn't see it in the O. Henry collection or anything.

INTERVIEWER: So, you started doing the serial for Jann Wenner . . .

WOLFE: Yes. I wrote three chapters at the outset thinking that I would have a two-chapter cushion. In case I got in trouble in a subsequent issue I had something to fall back on. Well, Jann wanted me to get off to a glorious start, so he published all three in the first issue! From that time on I was scrambling desperately.

INTERVIEWER: Well, did you have any grand design? Did you know where you were going?

WOLFE: Well, yes and no. I'm a great believer in outlines. The outline for *The Right Stuff*, for example, my nonfiction book about the astronauts, was three hundred pages, cross-indexed. So I did a very thorough outline for *The Bonfire of the Vanities*. Jann Wenner had read it and liked it. Then at the last moment I began to think of what I considered important changes. For example, in the outline everything took place in Manhattan. I began hearing these amazing stories about the Bronx, so I shifted my scene of operations from the Manhattan Criminal Court Building at 100 Centre Street up to the Bronx County Courthouse at 161st Street and the Grand Concourse. I changed the nature of the crime that the story was to pivot upon—actually a Class E felony, not much of a crime—to an automobile accident in the Bronx. Then, at the very last moment, I had gone down to Wall Street and I'd gotten entrée to one of the great investment-banking houses and what I'd seen was so exciting that I said to myself, "Well, maybe I'll change Sherman McCoy from a writer"—which he was in this long outline that I had—"to some kind of Wall Street figure." If anyone cares to look back at the first three chapters of the *Rolling Stone* version of *The Bonfire of the Vanities*, he'll find that Sherman McCoy has no occupation. I was going to give myself the flexibility in the fourth chapter to make him a Wall Street figure. Then I got cold feet because I didn't really have the time to work this whole thing out. He remained a writer, a rather boring figure for the most part. He's not right in that version. I hate stories in which a person has an occupation and you never see him working at it, like all those marvelous Cary Grant movies where he's a surgeon, and you never see him in the operating room.

INTERVIEWER: Was the serialization carried out to the end?

WOLFE: Yes, it was. I'm proud of this. It continued for twenty-seven issues. The magazine comes out every two weeks . . . a year and a week over. At the outset I began to wonder if my work would be more like Zola's, Dostoyevski's, or Dickens's . . . all serial novel writers. By the fourth chapter the only thing I wondered about was, would the hole be filled? I was out on Long Island in Southampton where there's a church in the middle of town that chimes the hours all through the night. I can remember it so well. I would go to sleep exhausted about ten o'clock at night. I'd wake up about 11:30 or midnight; I'd always hear the midnight bells, all twelve of those chimes. I had terrible insomnia for about six weeks. I finally realized that, in fact, I could fill the hole, that I would be spared the ignominy of not making the issue.

INTERVIEWER: What a terrifying experience. Did you ever feel like going to Jann Wenner and saying, "This is too much. To hell with it"?

WOLFE: Well, I didn't really put it quite that way, but to myself many times I said, "Why did I do this? I don't need to do it. I could have written a sequel to *The Right Stuff*." After all, *The Right Stuff* was only the story of the astronauts doing the Mercury program. I could have written a book called *Gemini*. It *was* terrifying. I don't think I had the courage to tell Jann that we had to call it off!

INTERVIEWER: How many words did that mean you had to produce in, let's say, a day?

WOLFE: That wasn't so much the problem. I had to produce about six thousand words every two weeks. That isn't a terrible amount if you're sure of what you're doing, but it's difficult if you don't, especially if you're trying to construct something with real coherence to it. At the beginning it was terrible. Just changing the locale from Manhattan to the Bronx was something that meant an unraveling of all sorts of things in the plot. This is something that happens in fiction. It doesn't happen in nonfiction. You can change the structure of a nonfiction book and, no matter how awkward, it's like an enormous Erector set. It may lurch into ungainly forms, but it's going to hold together because you're dealing with actual facts. On the other hand, when you start playing with your structure in fiction, it's like pulling a thread in a sweater. Everything begins to go in ways you never dreamed of. So I had a continual problem with that; I found myself reworking and rethinking chapters on the spot. I became very much interested in how people had done this successfully. I read a lot of Zola and Dickens and Dostoyevski with this in mind. I came to the conclusion that the master of the form was Zola. Typically Zola would write four or five chapters ahead of time, four or five out of twelve to fourteen chapters. Pick almost any novel by Zola and you'll see that it runs twelve to fourteen chapters because he had a contract to write a novel in the year for a monthly magazine. Now, if you've done that, written forty percent of a novel, by this time you have worked out the most difficult problems. You know your characters by now. You know the real course of your plot. You know how you're going to create suspense. By the end of twelve chapters he would have spent his cushion, and he'd now be writing against deadline pressure to finish the book. But that's not so bad. The last half of any book, particularly a book of fiction, is not nearly so difficult as the first half. At the very end, you often see Zola speeding up recklessly. Read the last chapter of that marvelous book *Nana*. Here's a guy who either is terribly tired or had a day and a half to finish . . . to finish a book! But if I had to do it over again, I would make sure I had written thirty-three to forty percent of the book ahead of time.

INTERVIEWER: But would you ever want to subject yourself again to serialization?

WOLFE: I don't think I would.

INTERVIEWER: What's the point of it really?

WOLFE: In this day and age there isn't much point to it. People do not read that way. If people want stories serially they'll go to television.

INTERVIEWER: How close are the characters of the novel to real people?

WOLFE: Only two characters are actually based on real people—Tommy Killian was based on Counsellor Eddie Hayes, and the character of Judge Kovitsky is based on Burton Roberts, who is now the chief administrative and chief criminal judge of the Bronx. Otherwise I steered clear of the roman à clef game. I think that's a game of very limited usefulness. In some cases I have composites. For example, Reverend Bacon, the activist minister from Harlem, was based on the sort of figure I had begun seeing as early as 1969, shortly after the poverty program had gotten started.

INTERVIEWER: For research and background, did you go to the holding pens in the Bronx?

WOLFE: I did. I managed to get entrée to the pens, just to see what's going on. I found that, though there were a great many colorful things happening before my eyes, I had no way of getting inside the mind of someone who was in that predicament. Even if you masquerade as a prisoner, you know you're going to be let out. Then I realized that I had to interview people who had been through it. By this time I had met a number of lawyers. They put me in touch with a few middle-class professional defendants—white defendants who had been through something like McCoy. I eventually met four men, one of whom was tremendously helpful. He told me that the most humiliating part of this experience for him came when he was marched through a metal detector which he kept setting off. They kept taking more of his clothes away from him. He still kept setting off the metal detector. Finally, the policeman in charge of the metal detector had a hunch. He told him to lean over and just put his head in the metal detector. This set the thing off. Then he said, "Open your mouth," and he said, "Oh, look at that! You've got a mouth like a coin-changer!" It was the fillings in his teeth. He began calling the other policemen over. He'd say, "Look at this guy. Hey, do it again." He wasn't abusive in language. He didn't lay a hand on him. Suddenly the fact that these police—whom the man had always regarded as his protectors and protectors particularly of people like himself—were now, not in any perverse or bad way, treating him like an object, an object of sport. It was crushing. It crushed what last defenses he had in this situation. Now this is something I could not have gotten except through interviewing. I don't think the unaided imagination of the writer—and I don't care who the writer is—can come up with what is obtainable through research and reporting. I'm firmly convinced of that, particularly in an age like this and particularly if you choose to write about a large city.

INTERVIEWER: I can't resist asking whether, when you were in the holding pens talking to criminals and so forth, you wore the white suit.

WOLFE: Now we're getting down to cases! I'd like to be able to say that I went attired all in white. I didn't. I always wore a suit though and usually a double-breasted suit. That was pushing my luck enough right there! I found early in the game that for me there's no use trying to blend in. I might as well be the village information-gatherer, the man from Mars who simply wants to know. Fortunately the world is full of people with information-compulsion who want to tell you their stories. They want to tell you things that you don't know. They're some of the greatest allies that any writer has.

INTERVIEWER: *The Bonfire of the Vanities* ends with an epilogue—a shattering epilogue, one page long or so, where you find out that a year later McCoy's back in exactly the same predicament. Was that always in the design?

WOLFE: No, it wasn't. That was one part of the outline that I hadn't worked out. I didn't know whether to make it a happy or an unhappy ending. I could have made it a happy ending, but I felt that this would not have been true to the criminal-justice system in New York! Having gotten their hooks into a highly publicized figure like McCoy—and I think this is one of the sad sides of the interaction of the press and the criminal-justice system in large cities—they were not going to humiliate themselves by letting this man off completely if there were any way to hold him. McCoy had committed a Class E felony—leaving the scene of an accident where there has been personal bodily injury. That can be considered an important crime or a very minor crime depending on the mood of the hour. In the case of someone in a highly publicized case, given his background, it would have been treated severely. He would have probably drawn a year in jail and would have ended up having to serve most of it. I had a choice of either giving it a happy ending or spending several more chapters to follow him through the maw and the innards of the criminal-justice system—the hearings, the various court appearances and appeals and all the rest of it. I felt that would be anticlimactic. So I came up with this device of the epilogue—a newspaper article written by the *New York Times*. My model—and this may seem farfetched—was the epilogue to Fitzgerald's *Tender Is the Night* in which the Divers are seen from afar by someone who says, "The last time I saw them they were sitting in a terrace of a hotel having a drink. I should have stopped to say something to them and I never did." It's very poignant. I decided to have this type of monologue-from-afar in the form of a newspaper piece in the *New York Times*. I'm not sure it worked, but that was my solution.

INTERVIEWER: Did it bother you at all that the book was criticized for having so few, if any, sympathetic characters?

WOLFE: Well, I don't like to be criticized, but it didn't bother me a great deal because I felt that this was a book about vanity in New York in an age of money fever. In fact, those who triumph in an age like that are seldom what we usually consider heroic and admirable characters. I also looked back at novels about cities that I admire tremendously, John O'Hara's *Butterfield 8*, Zola's *Nana*, Balzac's *Cousin Bette*, and it's hard to find any major character in them who is sympathetic in the usual meaning of that term. Somewhere I ran into a theory which I'd never heard of before, that without love from the author a character is not noble. I was being called incapable of love for the characters. Actually, I was in awe of the characters. I couldn't very well love them.

INTERVIEWER: Thinking back, would you make any changes now?

WOLFE: I might change the ending. The epilogue. Looking back on it I felt it had a somewhat gimmicky quality about it. I still couldn't give it a happy ending. That wouldn't be right.

INTERVIEWER: How long was the title *The Bonfire of the Vanities* in your mind?

WOLFE: A long time. I once took an American Express bus tour of Florence. We reached the Piazza della Signoria where there is a wonderful statue of Mercury by Cellini. The driver who was also the guide told the story of the "bonfires of the vanities," which had taken place there. At the end of the fifteenth century the Florentines had just been through a hog-wallowing, hog-stomping, baroque period, and when suddenly this ascetic monk, Savonarola, came forward and said, "Get rid of your evil ways, strip down, get rid of your vanities." A bonfire was built. Most of the things were thrown into the fire voluntarily. Some things weren't but most of them were—nonreligious paintings, books by Boccaccio, plus wigs and false eyelashes and all kinds of silver, gold. At first, the citizenry loved it. It's sort of like the granola period we're going into right now. They loved the asceticism of it. Then after two of these bonfires, they'd really gotten very bored with the whole process and besides the Pope was getting a little jealous of Savonarola who was really running the city, and so he was the victim of the third bonfire. Anyway, this idea of a bonfire of the vanities stuck in my mind, intrigued me, and I said to myself how some day I'd write a book called that.

INTERVIEWER: There was nothing in your book that really reflects this title.

WOLFE: No. I started to write an epigraph that would explain this reference, sort of the way John O'Hara in *Appointment in Samarra* has this epigraph by way of an historical note. But every time I wrote it, I came off as Savonarola. So I finally said, to hell with it. The connection is more the fiery itch of vanity. It was a far-fetched analogy. But that was in my mind.

INTERVIEWER: Does criticism bother you? I seem to remember that your book *The Painted Word* about the art world caused a great stir.

WOLFE: Yes. It was the most vitriolic response I've ever had anywhere, much more so than *Radical Chic* or *Bonfire of the Vanities*. The things that I was called in print were remarkable. In fact, there were so many, I started categorizing them. One was "psychiatric insults"—the usual thing: This man is obviously sick. Then there were the "political insults"—usually I was called a fascist but occasionally a communist, a commissar. And then there were the curious round of insults I called the "X-rated insults," all taking the same form which was, "This man who wrote the book is like a six-year-old at a pornographic movie; he can follow the motions of the bodies but he cannot comprehend the nuances." I always thought it was a very strange sort of insult because it cast contemporary art as pornography and I was the child. In various forms this metaphor was repeated by several different reviewers. Robert Hughes used it. He had the full image, the six-year-old, the grunts and groans, the pornographic movie and the rest of it. In the *Times* John Russell referred to me as a eunuch at the orgy. I think he was afraid that too many of his readers would be overstimulated by the thought of a six-year-old at a pornographic movie. So I became a eunuch at an orgy. Because of the similarity of the sexual metaphors, I was curious about this and was told later on that there had been a dinner in Bedford, New York, shortly after *The Painted Word* came out . . . a number of art world figures, including Robert Motherwell, in somebody's fancy home. The subject of *The Painted Word* came up and Motherwell supposedly said, "You know, this man Wolfe reminds me of a six-year-old at a pornographic movie. He can follow the motion of the bodies but he can't comprehend the nuances." If it's true, it shows what a small world the art world is. Actually that was one of the points I was trying to *make* in *The Painted Word*—that three thousand people, no more than that certainly, with roughly three hundred who live outside of the New York metropolitan area, determine all fashion in art. As far as I can tell, it was Motherwell's conceit; he is an influential, major figure, and it spread from this dinner table in Bedford overnight, as it were.

INTERVIEWER: What was it that outraged them more than anything else in *The Painted Word*?

WOLFE: Now maybe I'm flattering myself, but I think what made a bigger impact than the usual diatribe was that what I wrote was a history; there's not a single critical judgment in the piece. It's a history of taste, and I think that approach—it's pitted on the level of a history of fashion—was infuriating. The art world can deal very easily with anybody who says they don't like Pollock or they don't like Rauschenberg, so what if you don't. But to say these people blindly follow Clement Greenberg's or Harold Rosenberg's theories, which is pretty much what *The Painted Word* is saying, and that a whole era was not visual at all but literary, now that got them.

INTERVIEWER: Do you have any artwork hanging at home?

WOLFE: Yes. Not a lot but I have some. Most of it is by my friend Richard Merkin. I don't know how to characterize his work. His work has titles such as "Van Lingle Mungo Enters Havana." So he's right on my wavelength. He has a very strong palette. Outside his work and a few others, my real passion is caricature. Mostly from the turn of the century and from a couple of magazines, for example *Simplicissimus*, which had artists like Bruno Paul, Rudolf Wilke, and Olaf Gulbransson. These were satirical magazines with brilliant illustrators.

INTERVIEWER: It wouldn't be a *Paris Review* interview unless we asked you about your work habits.

WOLFE: To tell you the truth, I always find that a fascinating part of the *Paris Review* interviews. That's the kind of thing writers always want to know: What are other writers doing? I use a typewriter. My wife gave me a word processor two Christmases ago which still stares at me accusingly from a desk in my office. One day I am going to be compelled to learn how to use it. But for the time being, I use a typewriter. I set myself a quota—ten pages a day, triple-spaced, which means about eighteen hundred words. If I can finish that in three hours, then I'm through for the day. I just close up the lunch box and go home—that's the way I think of it anyway. If it takes me twelve hours, that's too bad, I've got to do it. To me, the idea "I'm going to work for six hours" is of no use. I can waste time as handily at the desk as I can window-shopping, which is one of my favorite diversions. So I try to be very methodical and force myself to stick to that schedule.

INTERVIEWER: Is there any mnemonic device to get you going?

WOLFE: I always have a clock in front of me. Sometimes, if things are going badly, I will force myself to write a page in a half an hour. I find that can be done. I find that what I write when I force myself is generally just as good as what I write when I'm feeling inspired. It's mainly a matter of forcing yourself to write. There's a marvelous essay that Sinclair Lewis wrote on how to write. He said most writers don't understand that the process begins by actually sitting down.

INTERVIEWER: Hemingway stood up when he wrote. Used the top of his bureau.

WOLFE: Well, actually, so did my namesake, Thomas Wolfe. He wrote using the top of the refrigerator he was so tall. . . .

INTERVIEWER: What about your confidence as you write?

WOLFE: You go to bed every night thinking that you've written the most brilliant passage ever done which somehow the next day you realize is sheer drivel. Sometimes it's six months later that it dawns on you that it doesn't work. It's a constant hazard. I can sympathize with Ken Kesey who once said that he stopped writing because he was tired of being a seismograph—an instrument which measures rumblings from a great distance. He said he wanted to be a lightning rod—where it all happens at once, quick, and decisive. Perhaps this applies to painters, though I don't know. I suspect there are some awful dawns for them too.

INTERVIEWER: Is there any characteristic the fiction writer has that means perhaps more power, more of an effect than can be achieved by the journalist or the essayist? Why fiction, is what I'm really trying to ask.

WOLFE: In answering this, I'm inevitably promoting my own theory of fiction: that you can dramatize reality in fiction so easily and with such economy, bring so many strands of a society onto one plotline. You can have a real impact with fiction provided that you deal with reality, provided you want to show how society works, how it fits together. This has been true at many points in our literary history, most notably in the thirties, with books like *The Grapes of Wrath.* It's hard to remember today the impact of a book like *The Grapes of Wrath.* We're in an age that cries out, I think, for that type of fiction. Instead, most of that impact has come from nonfiction; it's a great time for nonfiction writers because the main terrain—realism—was largely abandoned by an entire generation of talented writers. It's a worldwide phenomenon. When I was in Germany last year I became interested in the Berlin Wall—obviously one of the historical epicenters of the twentieth century, this fantastic, medieval wall built in the mid-twentieth century dividing a city, a whole country in two, literally dividing brothers and sisters from brothers and sisters on the other side. So I asked about the great novels about the Wall written in Germany. I came up with a list of zero! Talented writers weren't going to look at the Wall. Amazing! What are the great Italian novels from the whole era of the kidnapping of Moro, the rest of the terrorist experience? Or what were the great French novels about the North African adventures?

INTERVIEWER: Or Vietnam novels in our country?

WOLFE: Finally now they begin to appear, usually written by people who had not gone to college with the slightest notion of becoming writers, such as our recently resigned Secretary of the Navy, James Webb, who wrote what I consider the finest of the Vietnam novels, *Fields of Fire.* A career military officer, who happened to go to Vietnam and just wanted to write about it.

INTERVIEWER: What denotes a "good" novel?

WOLFE: To me, it's a novel that pulls you inside the central nervous system of the characters . . . and makes you feel in your bones their motivations as affected by the society of which they are a part. It is folly to believe that you can bring the psychology of an individual successfully to life without putting him very firmly in a social setting. After *The Bonfire of the Vanities* came out I was accused of the negative stereotyping of just about every ethnic and racial type known to New York City. I would always challenge anyone who wrote that to give me one example. I have been waiting ever since. I think what I actually did was to violate a rule of etiquette—that it's all right to bring up the subject of racial and ethnic differences, but you must treat it in a certain way. Somewhere in the tale you must find an enlightened figure, preferably from the streets, who shows everyone the error of his or her ways; a higher synthesis is created and everyone leaves the stage perhaps sadder but a good deal wiser and a good deal kinder and more compassionate. Well, this just simply isn't the way New York works. The best you can say is that New York is held together by competing antagonisms which tend to cancel one another out. I tried to face up to that as unflinchingly as I could.

INTERVIEWER: What's been the effect of film on your writing?

WOLFE: I've never been consciously affected by film—that is, I've never said to myself, I should set this scene the way it would be done in a movie. I *do* very consciously, however, think about how to set up a scene—whether fiction or nonfiction—and often it may coincide with cinematographic technique. For example, I'm often drawn to start a story with a long shot—as they would say in the cinema. It's an instinctive way of setting up a scene. A wonderful example is the way Truman Capote begins *In Cold Blood*—a very long shot of a Kansas wheat field, gradually focusing in on a solitary farmhouse on the horizon. Another way is to start with a very tight close-up—which I've done especially in my nonfiction. *Radical Chic*, for example, starts with a description of the aforementioned gadrooned silver platter with cheeseballs on it, and then pulls back—to use another cinematic metaphor—and you see that a person down whose gullet the cheeseball is disappearing is one of the leaders of the Black Panthers.

INTERVIEWER: How would you categorize your political outlook? After

*Radical Chic* and to a certain extent after *The Bonfire of the Vanities* you were called reactionary, conservative.

WOLFE: I think of myself as a seer! Those two words, "reactionary" and "conservative," are part of the etiquette of intellectual life in New York City—simply a way of saying "you're bad" or "I disagree with you." Some time ago I attended the twenty-fifth anniversary of the *National Review* at a big party at the Plaza. About 2,500 people there. A reporter came up and asked if I would say that this was a gathering of the neoconservative clan. First I asked him if he spelt clan with a "K." When he assured me he was going to use a "C," I answered him. I said that what we were looking at in the room were 2,500 people, most of whom had never laid eyes on each other, who for one reason or another had not gone along with the official gag for the last quarter-century. I think that's about what it amounts to.

GEORGE PLIMPTON
November 17, 1989

# 11. *Mario Vargas Llosa*

Mario Vargas Llosa was born in 1936 in Arequipa, a small town in southern Peru. His parents divorced in his infancy and he moved to Cochabamba, Bolivia, to live with his mother's grandparents. In 1945 he returned to Peru, where he attended the Leonico Prado Military Academy and studied law and literature at the University of San Marcos in Lima. At nineteen he married his aunt by marriage, Julia Urquid Illanes, who was twelve years his senior; it was a union he would later use as fodder for his novel *Aunt Julia and the Scriptwriter* (1982). Upon finishing his studies in Lima, Vargas Llosa went into a sixteen-year, self-imposed exile from Peru, during which he lived in France, England, and Spain and traveled in the Amazon. He worked as a journalist and lecturer, having received his doctorate in Madrid, and it was during this period that he began writing novels. Exile, he feels, afforded him the necessary distance to free himself in order to transform reality with an understanding of what was essential to an experience and with the nostalgia which "fertilizes" the memory. *The Time of the Hero,* Vargas Llosa's first novel, was published in Spain in 1963 and is based on his experiences in the military academy. His other novels include *The Green House* (1963), *Conversation in the Cathedral* (1969), and *The War of the End of the World* (1981), his personal favorite. In 1990 Penguin released *The Storyteller* and Syracuse University *A Writer's Reality. In Praise of the Stepmother* was published that same year.

Vargas Llosa is also a part-time politician, playwright, and essayist and has produced a weekly interview program on Peruvian television. He has been the recipient of numerous international literary awards and was the president of PEN from 1976 to 1979. He has three children and lives with his second wife, Patricia, in Lima, in an apartment overlooking the Pacific.

122

Pero, aunque nunca admitiría en voz alta semejante cosa, cuando a solas, como ahora, Doña Lucrecia se preguntaba si el niño no estaba efectivamente descubriendo la vida, el despuntar del deseo, la poesía del cuerpo, aliéndose de ella como maestra. La actitud de Alfonsito la intrigaba. ?Era con= ciente de que, al echarle los brazos como lo hacía, al besarla en el cuello de esa manera remolona y buscarle los labios, infringía los límites de lo tolerado? Imposible saberlo. Tenía una mirada tan franca, tan directa, que a Do= ña Lucrecia le párecía imposible que aquella cabecita rubicun= da pudiera albergar pensamientos sucios, escabrosos.

"Pens mientos sucios, susurró, la boca contra la almohada, escabrosos ¡Jajajá!" Se sentía de buen humor y un calorcito delicioso corría por sus venas, como si la sangre se hubiera transubstanciado en vino tibio. No, seguramente el niño no sospechaba que aquello era jugar con fuego, seguramente que esas efusiones las dictaba un oscuro instinto, un tropismo inconsciente. Pero, aun así, no dejaban de ser juegos peli= grosos verdad, Lucrecia? Porque cuando lo veía, pequeñín, arrodillado en el suelo, contemplándola arrobado como si fue= ra una aparición, o cuando sus bracitos y su cuerpo frágil se soldaban a ella y sus labios delgados, casi invisibles, se

A *manuscript page from* Mario Vargas Llosa's *most recent novel,* In Praise of the Stepmother.

© Jerry Bauer

# Mario Vargas Llosa

*In this interview Mario Vargas Llosa speaks of the inviolable mornings he spends in his office writing, seven days a week. In the fall of 1988, however, he decided to interrupt this otherwise strictly kept schedule to run as the Libertad party candidate for the presidency of Peru. Vargas Llosa has long been outspoken on the subject of Peruvian politics and has made Peruvian political issues the subject of several of his novels. Yet until the most recent elections he had always resisted suggestions that he run for political office. During the campaign he mentioned his difficulty with the empty emotionalism and rhetoric that are the language of electoral politics. Following the multiparty election, he lost a runoff to Alberto Fujimori on June 10, 1990.*

INTERVIEWER: You are a well-known writer and your readers are familiar with what you've written. Will you tell us what you read?

MARIO VARGAS LLOSA: In the last few years, something curious has happened. I've noticed that I'm reading less and less by my contemporaries and more and more by writers of the past. I read much more from the nineteenth century than from the twentieth. These days, I lean perhaps less toward literary works than toward essays and history. I haven't given much thought to why I read what I read. . . . Sometimes it's professional reasons. My literary projects are related to the nineteenth century: an essay about Victor Hugo's *Les Misérables*, or a novel inspired by the life of Flora Tristan, a Franco-Peruvian social reformer and "feminist" *avant-la-lettre*. But then I also think it's because at fifteen or eighteen, you feel as if you have all the time in the world ahead of you. When you turn fifty, you become aware that your days are numbered and that you have to be selective. That's probably why I don't read my contemporaries as much.

INTERVIEWER: But among your contemporaries that you do read, whom do you particularly admire?

VARGAS LLOSA: When I was young, I was a passionate reader of Sartre. I've read the American novelists, in particular the lost generation—Faulkner, Hemingway, Fitzgerald, Dos Passos—especially Faulkner. Of the authors I read when I was young, he is one of the few who still means a lot to me. I have never been disappointed when I reread him, the way I have been occasionally with, say, Hemingway. I wouldn't reread Sartre today. Compared to everything I've read since, his fiction seems dated and has lost much of its value. As for his essays, I find most of them to be less important, with one exception perhaps: "Saint Genet: Comedian or Martyr," which I still like. They are full of contradictions, ambiguities, inaccuracies, and ramblings, something that never happened with Faulkner. Faulkner was the first novelist I read with pen and paper in hand, because his technique stunned me. He was the first novelist whose work I consciously tried to reconstruct by attempting to trace, for example, the organization of time, the intersection of time and place, the breaks in the narrative, and that ability he has of telling a story from different points of view in order to create a certain ambiguity, to give it added depth. As a Latin American, I think it was very useful for me to read his books when I did because they are a precious source of descriptive techniques that are applicable to a world which, in a sense, is not so unlike the one Faulkner described. Later, of course, I read the nineteenth-century novelists with a consuming passion: Flaubert, Balzac, Dostoyevsky, Tolstoy, Stendhal, Hawthorne, Dickens, Melville. I'm still an avid reader of nineteenth-century writers.

As for Latin American literature, strangely enough, it wasn't until I lived in Europe that I really discovered it and began to read it with great enthusiasm. I had to teach it at the university in London, which was a very enriching experience because it forced me to think about Latin American literature as a whole. From then on I read Borges, whom I was somewhat familiar with, Carpentíer, Cortázar, Guimaraes Rosa, Lezama Lima—that whole generation except for García Márquez. I discovered him later and even wrote a book about him: *García Márquez: Historia de un Decidio.* I also began reading nineteenth-century Latin American literature because I had to teach it. I realized then that we have extremely interesting writers—the novelists perhaps less so than the essayists or poets. Sarmiento, for example, who never wrote a novel, is in my opinion one of the greatest storytellers Latin America has produced; his *Facundo* is a masterwork. But if I were forced to choose one name, I would have to say Borges, because the world he creates seems to me to be absolutely original. Aside from his enormous originality, he is also endowed with a tremendous imagination and culture that are expressly his own. And then of course there is the language of Borges, which in a sense broke with our tradition and opened a new one. Spanish is a language that tends toward exuberance, proliferation, profusion. Our great writers have all been prolix, from Cervantes to Ortega y Gasset, Valle-Inclán, or Alfonso Reyes. Borges is the opposite—all concision, economy, and precision. He is the only writer in the Spanish language who has almost as many ideas as he has words. He's one of the great writers of our time.

INTERVIEWER: What was your relationship to Borges?

VARGAS LLOSA: I saw him for the first time in Paris where I lived in the early sixties. He was there giving seminars on the literature of the fantastic and *gauchesca* literature. Later I interviewed him for the Office de Radio Television Française where I was working at the time. I still remember it with emotion. After that, we saw each other several times in different parts of the world, even in Lima, where I gave a dinner for him. At the end he asked me to take him to the toilet. When he was peeing he suddenly said, "The Catholics, do you think they are serious? Probably not."

The last time I saw him was at his house in Buenos Aires; I interviewed him for a television show I had in Peru and I got the impression he resented some of the questions I asked him. Strangely, he got mad because, after the interview—during which, of course, I was extremely attentive, not only because of the admiration I felt for him but also because of the great affection I had for the charming and fragile man that he was—I said I was surprised by the modesty of his house, which had peeling walls and leaks in the roof. This apparently deeply offended him. I saw him once more after that and he was extremely distant. Octavio Paz told me that he really resented that particular remark about his house. The only thing that might have hurt him is what I have just related, because otherwise I have never done anything but praise him. I don't think he read my books. According to him, he never read a single living writer after he turned forty, just read and reread the same books. . . . But he's a writer I very much admire. He's not the only one, of course. Pablo Neruda is an extraordinary poet. And Octavio Paz—not only a great poet, but a great essayist, a man who is articulate about politics, art, and literature. His curiosity is universal. I still read him with great pleasure. Also, his political ideas are quite similar to mine.

INTERVIEWER: You mention Neruda among the writers you admire. You were his friend. What was he like?

VARGAS LLOSA: Neruda adored life. He was wild about everything—painting, art in general, books, rare editions, food, drink. Eating and drinking were almost a mystical experience for him. A wonderfully likable man, full of vitality—if you forget his poems in praise of Stalin, of course. He lived in a near-feudal world, where everything led to his rejoicing, his sweet-toothed exuberance for life. I had the good fortune to spend a weekend on Isla Negra. It was wonderful! A kind of social machinery worked around him: hordes of people who cooked and worked—and always quantities of guests. It was a very funny society, extraordinarily alive, without the slightest trace of intellectualism. Neruda was exactly the opposite of Borges, the man who appeared never to drink, smoke, or eat, who one would have said had never made love, for whom all these things seemed completely secondary, and if he had done them it was out of politeness and nothing more. That's because ideas, reading, reflection, and creation were his life, the purely cerebral life. Neruda comes out of the Jorge Amado and Rafael Alberti tradition that says literature is generated by a sensual experience of life.

I remember the day we celebrated Neruda's birthday in London. He wanted to have the party on a boat on the Thames. Fortunately, one of his admirers, the English poet Alastair Reid, happened to live on a boat on the Thames, so we were able to organize a party for him. The moment came and he announced that he was going to make a cocktail. It was the most expensive drink in the world with I don't know how many bottles of Dom Pérignon, fruit juices, and God knows what else. The result, of course, was wonderful, but one glass of it was enough to make you drunk. So there we were, drunk every one of us, without exception. Even so, I still remember what he told me then; something that has proven to be a great truth over the years. An article at the time—I can't remember what it was about—had upset and irritated me because it insulted me and told lies about me. I showed it to Neruda. In the middle of the party, he prophesied: "You are becoming famous. I want you to know what awaits you: the more famous you are, the more you will be attacked like this. For every praise, there will be two or three insults. I myself have a chest full of all the insults, villainies, and infamies a man is capable of withstanding. I wasn't spared a single one: thief, pervert, traitor, thug, cuckold . . . everything! If you become famous, you will have to go through that."

Neruda told the truth; his prognosis came absolutely true. I not only have a chest, but several suitcases full of articles that contain every insult known to man.

INTERVIEWER: What about García Márquez?

VARGAS LLOSA: We were friends; we were neighbors for two years in Barcelona, we lived on the same street. Later, we drifted apart for personal as well as political reasons. But the original cause for the separation was a personal problem that had no relation whatsoever to his ideological beliefs—which I don't approve of either. In my opinion, his writing and his politics are not of the same quality. Let's just say that I greatly admire his work as a writer. As I've already said, I wrote a six-hundred-page book on his work. But I don't have much respect for him personally, nor for his political beliefs which don't seem serious to me. I think they're opportunistic and publicity-oriented.

INTERVIEWER: Is the personal problem you mentioned related to an incident at a movie theater in Mexico where you allegedly fought?

VARGAS LLOSA: There was an incident in Mexico. But this is a subject that I don't care to discuss; it has given rise to so much speculation that I don't want to supply more material for commentators. If I write my memoirs, maybe I'll tell the true story.

INTERVIEWER: Do you choose the subjects of your books or do they choose you?

VARGAS LLOSA: As far as I'm concerned, I believe the subject chooses the writer. I've always had the feeling that certain stories imposed themselves on me; I couldn't ignore them, because in some obscure way, they related to some kind of fundamental experience—I can't really say how. For example, the time I spent at the Leonico Prado Military School in Lima when I was still a young boy gave me a real need, an obsessive desire to write. It was an extremely traumatic experience which in many ways marked the end of my childhood—the rediscovery of my country as a violent society, filled with bitterness, made up of social, cultural, and racial factions in complete opposition and caught up in sometimes ferocious battle. I suppose the experience had an influence on me; one thing I'm sure of is that it gave rise to the great need in me to create, to invent.

Up until now, it's been pretty much the same for all my books. I never get the feeling that I've decided rationally, cold-bloodedly to write a story. On the contrary, certain events or people, sometimes dreams or readings, impose themselves suddenly and demand attention. That's why I talk so much about the importance of the purely irrational elements of literary creation. This irrationality must also, I believe, come through to the reader. I would like my novels to be read the way I read the novels I love. The novels that have fascinated me most are the ones that have reached me less through the channels of the intellect or reason than bewitched me. These are stories capable of completely annihilating all my critical faculties so that I'm left there, in suspense. That's the kind of novel I like to read and the kind of novel I'd like to write. I think it's very important that the intellectual element, whose presence is inevitable in a novel, dissolves into the action, into the stories that must seduce the reader not by their ideas but by their color, by the emotions they inspire, by their element of surprise, and by all the suspense and mystery they're capable of generating. In my opinion, a novel's technique exists essentially to produce that effect: to diminish and if possible abolish the distance between the story and the reader. In that sense, I am a writer of the nineteenth century. The novel for me is still the novel of adventures, which is read in the particular way I have described.

INTERVIEWER: What's become of the humor in your novels? Your most recent novels seem far from the humor of *Aunt Julia and the Scriptwriter*. Is it hard to practice humor today?

VARGAS LLOSA: It's never occurred to me to ask myself whether today I will write a funny book or a serious one. The subjects of the books I've written in the last few years just didn't lend themselves to humor. I don't think *War of the End of the World* and *The Real Life of Alejandro Mayta* or the plays I've written are based on themes that can be treated humorously. And what about *In Praise of the Stepmother*? There's plenty of humor there, isn't there?

I used to be "allergic" to humor because I thought, very naively, that serious literature never smiled; that humor could be very dangerous if I wanted to broach serious social, political, or cultural problems in my novels. I thought it would make my stories seem superficial and give my reader the impression that they were nothing more than light entertainment. That's why I had renounced humor, probably under the influence of Sartre who was always very hostile to humor, at least in his writing. But one day, I discovered that in order to effect a certain experience of life in literature, humor could be a very precious tool. That happened with *Pantaleon and the Special Service*. From then on, I was very conscious of humor as a great treasure, a basic element of life and therefore of literature. And I don't exclude the possibility that it will play a prominent role again in my novels. As a matter of fact it has. This is also true of my plays, particularly *Kathie and the Hippopotamus*.

INTERVIEWER: Can you tell us about your work habits? How do you work? How does a novel originate?

VARGAS LLOSA: First of all, it's a daydream, a kind of rumination about a person, a situation, something that occurs only in the mind. Then I start to take notes, summaries of narrative sequences: somebody enters the scene here, leaves there, does this or that. When I start working on the novel itself, I draw up a general outline of the plot—which I never hold to, changing it completely as I go along, but which allows me to get started. Then I start putting it together, without the slightest preoccupation with style, writing and rewriting the same scenes, making up completely contradictory situations. . . .

The raw material helps me, reassures me. But it's the part of writing I have the hardest time with. When I'm at that stage, I proceed very warily, always unsure of the result. The first version is written in a real state of anxiety. Then once I've finished that draft—which can sometimes take a long time: for *The War of the End of the World,* the first stage lasted almost two years—everything changes. I know then that the story is there, buried in what I call my "magma." It's absolute chaos but the novel is in there, lost in a mass of dead elements, superfluous scenes that will disappear or scenes that are repeated several times from different perspectives, with different characters. It's very chaotic and makes sense only to me. But the story is born under there. You have to separate it from the rest, clean it up, and that's the most pleasant part of the work. From then on I am able to work much longer hours without the anxiety and tension that accompanies the writing of that first draft. I think what I love is not the writing itself, but the rewriting, the editing, the correcting. . . . I think it's the most creative part of writing. I never know when I'm going to finish a story. A piece I thought would only take a few months has sometimes taken me several years to finish. A novel seems finished to me when I start feeling that if I don't end it soon, it will get the better of me. When I've reached saturation, when I've had enough, when I just can't take it anymore, then the story is finished.

INTERVIEWER: Do you write by hand, on the typewriter, or do you alternate?

VARGAS LLOSA: First, I write by hand. I always work in the morning, and in the early hours of the day, I always write by hand. Those are the most creative hours. I never work more than two hours like this—my hand gets cramped. Then I start typing what I've written, making changes as I go along; this is perhaps the first stage of rewriting. But I always leave a few lines untyped so that the next day, I can start by typing the end of what I'd written the day before. Starting up the typewriter creates a certain dynamic—it's like a warm-up exercise.

INTERVIEWER: Hemingway used that same technique of always leaving a sentence half-written so he could pick up the thread the next day. . . .

VARGAS LLOSA: Yes, he thought he should never write out all he had in mind so that he could start up more easily the next day. The hardest part, it always seems to me, is starting. In the morning, making contact again, the anxiety of it . . . But if you have something mechanical to do, the work has already begun. The machine starts to work. Anyway, I have a very rigorous work schedule. Every morning until two in the afternoon, I stay in my office. These hours are sacred to me. That doesn't mean I'm always writing; sometimes I'm revising or taking notes. But I remain systematically at work. There are, of course, the good days for creation and the bad ones. But I work every day because even if I don't have any new ideas, I can spend the time making corrections, revising, taking notes, et cetera. . . . Sometimes I decide to rewrite a finished piece, if only to change the punctuation.

Monday through Saturday, I work on the novel in progress, and I devote Sunday mornings to journalistic work—articles and essays. I try to keep this kind of work within the allotted time of Sunday so that it doesn't infringe on the creative work of the rest of the week. Sometimes I listen to classical music when I take notes, as long as there's no singing. It's something I started doing when I lived in a very noisy house. In the mornings, I work alone, nobody comes up to my office. I don't even take phone calls. If I did, my life would be a living hell. You cannot imagine how many phone calls and visitors I get. Everyone knows this house. My address unfortunately fell into the public domain.

INTERVIEWER: You never let go of this spartan routine?

VARGAS LLOSA: I can't seem to, I don't know how to work otherwise. If I started to wait for moments of inspiration, I would never finish a book. Inspiration for me comes from a regular effort. This routine allows me to work, with great exultation or without, depending on the days.

INTERVIEWER: Victor Hugo, among other writers, believed in the magical force of inspiration. Gabriel García Márquez said that after years of struggling with *One Hundred Years of Solitude,* the novel wrote itself in his head during a trip to Acapulco in a car. You have just stated that inspiration is for you a product of discipline, but have you never known the famous "illumination"?

VARGAS LLOSA: It's never happened to me. It's a much slower process. In the beginning there's something very nebulous, a state of alert, a wariness, a curiosity. Something I perceive in the fog and vagueness which arouses my interest, curiosity, and excitement and then translates itself into work, note cards, the summary of the plot. Then when I have the outline and start to put things in order, something very diffuse, very nebulous still persists. The "illumination" only occurs during the work. It's the hard work that, at any given time, can unleash that . . . heightened perception, that excitement capable of bringing about revelation, solution, and light. When I reach the heart of a story I've been working on for some time, then, yes, something does happen. The story ceases to be cold, unrelated to me. On the contrary, it becomes so alive, so important that everything I experience exists only in relation to what I'm writing. Everything I hear, see, read seems in one way or another to help my work. I become a kind of cannibal of reality. But to reach this state, I have to go through the catharsis of work. I live a kind of permanent double life. I do a thousand different things but I always have my mind on my work. Obviously, sometimes it becomes obsessive, neurotic. During those times, seeing a movie relaxes me. At the end of a day of intense work, when I find myself in a state of great inner turmoil, a movie does me a great deal of good.

INTERVIEWER: Pedro Nava, the memorialist, went as far as to draw some of his characters—their face, their hair, their clothes. Do you ever do that?

VARGAS LLOSA: No, but in certain cases, I do make up biographical sheets. It depends on the way I sense the character. Although the characters do sometimes appear to me visually, I also identify them by the way they express themselves or in relation to the facts surrounding them. But it does happen that a character is defined by physical characteristics that I have to get down on paper. But despite all the notes you can take for a novel, I think that in the end what counts is what the memory selects. What remains is the most important. That's why I have never taken a camera with me on my research expeditions.

INTERVIEWER: So, for a certain time, your characters are not related to each other? Each has his or her own personal history?

VARGAS LLOSA: In the beginning, everything is so cold, so artificial and dead! Little by little, it all begins to come alive, as each character takes on associations and relationships. That's what is wonderful and fascinating: when you begin to discover that lines of force already exist naturally in the story. But before getting to that point, it's nothing but work, work, and more work. In everyday life, there are certain people, certain events, that seem to fill a void or fulfill a need. Suddenly you become aware of exactly what you need to know for the piece you're working on. The representation is never true to the real person, it becomes altered, falsified. But that kind of encounter only occurs when the story has reached an advanced stage, when everything seems to nourish it further. Sometimes, it's a kind of recognition: "Oh, that's the face I was looking for, that intonation, that way of speaking. . . ." On the other hand, you can lose control of your characters which happens to me constantly because mine are never born out of purely rational considerations. They're expressions of more instinctual forces at work. That's why some of them immediately take on more importance or seem to develop by themselves, as it were. Others are relegated to the background, even if they weren't meant to, to begin with. That's the most interesting part of the work, when you realize that certain characters are asking to be given more prominence, when you begin to see that the story is governed by its own laws which you cannot violate. It becomes apparent that the author cannot mold characters as he pleases, that they have a certain autonomy. It's the most exciting moment when you discover life in what you've created, a life you have to respect.

INTERVIEWER: Much of your work was written outside of Peru, in what one might call a voluntary exile. You stated once that the fact Victor Hugo wrote out of his own country contributed to the greatness of a novel like *Les Misérables*. To find oneself far from "the vertigo of reality" is somehow an advantage for the reconstruction of that same reality. Do you find reality to be a source of vertigo?

VARGAS LLOSA: Yes, in the sense that I've never been able to write about what's close to me. Proximity is inhibiting in the sense that it doesn't allow me to work freely. It's very important to be able to work with enough freedom to allow you to transform reality, to change people, to make them act differently, or to introduce a personal element into the narrative, some perfectly arbitrary thing. It's absolutely essential. That's what creation is. If you have the reality before you, it seems to me it becomes a constraint. I always need a certain distance, timewise, or better still, in time and place. In that sense, exile has been very beneficial. Because of it, I discovered discipline. I discovered that writing was work, and for the most part, an obligation. Distance has also been useful because I believe in the great importance of nostalgia for the writer. Generally speaking, the absence of the subject fertilizes the memory. For example, Peru in *The Green House* is not just a depiction of reality, but the subject of nostalgia for a man who is deprived of it and feels a painful desire for it. At the same time, I think distance creates a useful perspective. It distills reality, that complicated thing which makes us dizzy. It's very hard to select or distinguish between what's important and what is secondary. Distance makes that distinction possible. It establishes the necessary hierarchies between the essential and the transient.

INTERVIEWER: In an essay you published a few years ago, you wrote that literature is a passion, and that passion is exclusive and requires all sacrifices to be made and makes none of its own. "The primary duty is not to live but to write," which reminds me of something Fernando Pessoa, the Portuguese poet, wrote: "To navigate is necessary, to live is unnecessary."

VARGAS LLOSA: You could say that to write is necessary and to live is unnecessary. . . . I should probably tell you something about me, so that people will understand me better. Literature has been very important to me ever since I was a child. But even though I read and wrote a lot during my school years, I never imagined that I would one day devote myself exclusively to literature, because at the time it seemed too much of a luxury for a Latin American, especially a Peruvian. I pursued other things: I planned to go into law, to be a professor or a journalist. I had accepted that what was essential to me would be relegated to the background. But when I arrived in Europe with a scholarship after finishing university, I realized that if I continued to think that way, I would never become a writer, that the only way would be to decide officially that literature would be not only my main preoccupation, but my occupation. That's when I decided to devote myself entirely to literature. And since I couldn't support myself on it, I decided I would look for jobs that would leave me time to write and never become priorities. In other words, I would choose jobs in terms of my work as a writer. I think that decision marked a turning point in my life because from then on I had the power to write. There was a psychological change. That's why literature seems more like a passion to me than a profession. Obviously, it is a profession because I make my living off it. But even if I couldn't support myself on it, I would still continue to write. Literature is more than a *modus vivendi*. I believe the choice a writer makes to give himself entirely to his work, to put everything at the service of literature instead of subsuming it to other considerations is absolutely crucial. Some people think of it as a kind of complementary or decorative activity in a life devoted to other things or even as a way of acquiring prestige and power. In those cases, there's a block, it's literature avenging itself, not allowing you to write with any freedom, audacity, or originality. That's why I think it's so important to make an absolutely total commitment to literature. What's strange is that in my case, when I made that decision, I thought it meant I chose a hard life, because I never imagined that literature could make me enough to live on, not to mention to live well. It seems like a kind of miracle. I still can't get over it. I didn't have to deprive myself of anything essential in order to write. I remember feeling much more frustrated and unhappy with myself when I couldn't write, when I was living in Peru before I left for Europe. I married when I was very young and I had to take any job I could get. I had as many as seven at a time! It was of course practically impossible for me to write. I wrote on Sundays, on holidays, but most of my time was spent on dreary work that had nothing to do with literature and I felt terribly frustrated by it. Today, when I wake up in the morning, I'm often amazed at the thought that I can spend my life doing what gives me the greatest pleasure, and furthermore, live off it, and well.

INTERVIEWER: Has literature made you rich?

VARGAS LLOSA: No, I'm not a rich man. If you compare a writer's income to a company president's, or to a man who has made a name for himself in one of the professions, or in Peru, to a toreador's or a top athlete's, you'll find that literature has remained an ill-paid profession.

INTERVIEWER: You once recalled that Hemingway felt empty, sad, and happy at the same time after he finished a book. What do you feel in those circumstances?

VARGAS LLOSA: Exactly the same thing. When I finish a book, I feel an emptiness, a malaise, because the novel has become a part of me. From one day to the next, I see myself deprived of it—like an alcoholic who quits drinking. It's something that isn't simply accessory; life itself is suddenly torn from me. The only cure is to throw myself immediately into some other work, which isn't hard to do since I have a thousand projects to attend to. But I always have to get back to work immediately, without the slightest transition, so that I don't allow the void to dig itself deeper between the previous book and the next one.

INTERVIEWER: We've mentioned some of the writers whose work you admire. Now let's talk about your own work. You've said several times that *The War of the End of the World* is your best book. Do you still think that?

VARGAS LLOSA: It's the novel I put the most work into, the one I gave the most of myself for. It took me four years to write it. I had to do enormous research for it, read enormous amounts, and overcome great difficulties because it was the first time I was writing about a different country from my own, in an era that wasn't mine, and working with characters who spoke in a language which wasn't the book's. But never has a story excited me as much as that one did. Everything about the work fascinated me, from the things I read to my trip across the Northeast. That's why I feel a singular tenderness for that book. The subject also allowed me to write the kind of novel I've always wanted to write, an adventure novel, where the adventure is essential—not a purely imaginary adventure but one profoundly linked to historical and social problematics. That's probably why I consider *The War of the End of the World* my most important book. Of course, these kinds of judgments are always so subjective. An author isn't capable of seeing his work objectively enough to establish these kinds of hierarchies. The novel became a terrifying challenge that I wanted to overcome. In the beginning, I was very apprehensive. The colossal amount of research material made me feel dizzy. My first draft was enormous, certainly twice the size of the novel. I asked myself how I was going to coordinate the whole mass of scenes, the thousands of little stories. For two years, I was filled with anxiety. But then, I made the trip through the Northeast, throughout the Sertao, and that was the turning point. I had already done an outline. I had wanted to imagine the story first, on the basis of the research material, and then do the trip. The trip confirmed a number of things and offered new insights on others. A lot of people also helped me. Originally, the subject was not meant for a book but for a film directed by Ruy Guerra. At the time, Paramount in Paris was run by someone I knew who called me one day and asked me if I wanted to write the screenplay for a movie they were producing for Guerra. I had seen one of his movies, *Tender Warriors*, that I had liked very much; so I went to Paris and met him. He explained to me what he wanted to do. He told me what he had in mind was a story having to do in one way or another with the war at Canudos.* We

* In 1897, a large group of disaffected villagers led by the messianic preacher Antonio Maciel occupied the town of Canudos in the Brazilian Sertoa of Bahia. Under the control of Maciel, who was also known as "the Councelor," they declared the village an independent state. The uprising was finally put down by an expedition commanded by the Brazilian minister of war, after several other police and military efforts to suppress it had failed.

couldn't make a movie about Canudos, the subject was too broad, but about something that was in some way related to it. I didn't know anything about the war at Canudos, I'd never even heard of it. I started to research it, to read about it, and one of the first things I read in Portuguese was *Os Sertões* by Euclides da Cunha. It was one of the great revelations in my life as a reader, similar to reading *The Three Musketeers* as a child, or *War and Peace, Madame Bovary*, and *Moby Dick* as an adult. Truly a great book, a fundamental experience. I was absolutely stunned by it; it is one of the greatest works Latin America has produced. It's a great book for many reasons but most of all because it's a manual for "Latin Americanism"—you discover for the first time what Latin America isn't. It isn't the sum of its imports. It's not Europe, Africa, pre-Hispanic America, or indigenous societies—but at the same time, it's a mixture of all these elements which coexist in a harsh and sometimes violent way. All this has produced a world that few works have captured with as much intelligence and literary marvel as *Os Sertões*. In other words, the man I truly owe for the existence of *The War of the End of the World* is Euclides da Cunha.

I think I read practically everything ever published about the war at Canudos up until that time. First, I wrote a screenplay for the movie which was never produced because of various problems it ran into, inherent to the film industry. The project reached a very advanced stage, production had already started, but one day Paramount decided the movie wouldn't be made and it wasn't. It was a disappointment for Ruy Guerra, but I was able to continue working on a subject that had kept me fascinated for so long for a measly result—a screenplay isn't much after all. So I started to read again, to do research, and I reached a peak of enthusiasm that few books have inspired in me. I used to work ten to twelve hours a day on it. Still, I was afraid of Brazil's response to it. I worried it would be considered meddling in a private affair . . . especially since a classic Brazilian writer had already covered the subject. There were some unfavorable reviews of the book, but on the whole, it was received with a generosity and an enthusiasm—by the public as well—that touched me. I felt rewarded for my efforts.

INTERVIEWER: What do you think of the succession of misunderstandings that characterize Canudos: the republican partisans seeing in the rebels the upheaval of the monarchy and British imperialism, while the rebels themselves believed they were fighting the devil. Could one call this a metaphor of sorts for ideology?

VARGAS LLOSA: Perhaps that's where the value of Canudos lies for a Latin American because the reciprocal blindness produced by a fanatical vision of reality is also the one that prevents us from seeing the contradictions between reality and theoretical visions. The tragedy of Latin America is that, at various points in history, our countries have found themselves divided and in the midst of civil wars, massive repressions, massacres like the one at Canudos because of that same reciprocal blindness. Perhaps one of the reasons I was fascinated by Canudos is that the phenomenon could be observed in miniature, in the laboratory, as it were. But obviously, it's a general phenomenon: fanaticism and intolerance weigh heavily on our history. Whether it's messianic rebellions, socialist or utopian rebellions, or struggles between the conservatives and the liberals. And if it isn't the English at work, it's the Yankee imperialists, or the Freemasons, or the devil. Our history has been marked by our inability to accept differences of opinion.

INTERVIEWER: You wrote once that none of your other works had lent themselves as well to the chimeric ideal of the novel as this book. What did you mean by that?

VARGAS LLOSA: I think the novel as a genre tends toward excess. It tends towards proliferation, the plot develops like a cancer. If the writer follows a novel's every lead, it becomes a jungle. The ambition to tell the whole story is inherent in the genre. Although I've always felt there comes a moment when you have to kill the story so it won't go on indefinitely, I also believe that storytelling is an attempt to reach that ideal of the "total" novel. The novel I went the farthest with in that respect is *The War of the End of the World*, without a doubt.

INTERVIEWER: In *Mayta* and *The War of the End of the World*, you said you wanted to lie in full knowledge of the truth. Can you explain?

VARGAS LLOSA: In order to fabricate, I always have to start from a concrete reality. I don't know whether that's true for all novelists, but I always need the trampoline of reality. That's why I do research and visit the places where the action takes place, not that I aim simply to reproduce reality. I know that's impossible. Even if I wanted to, the result wouldn't be any good, it would be something entirely different.

INTERVIEWER: At the end of *Mayta*, the narrator tells us that the main character, now owner of a bar, has trouble remembering the events that are so important to the narrator. Did that really happen? Did the man really exist?

VARGAS LLOSA: Yes, he exists, though he isn't exactly what the book made of him. I changed and added a lot. But for the most part, the character corresponds to someone who was once a militant Trotskyite and was imprisoned several times. I got the idea for the last chapter when I spoke to him and was surprised to find that what I considered a crucial time in his life had become secondary to him—an adventure among others in a checkered life. It really struck me when I realized during our conversation that I knew more about the affair than he did. He had already forgotten certain facts and there were things he never even knew about. I think the last chapter is crucial because it changes the whole sense of the book.

INTERVIEWER: Tell us about Pedro Camacho in *Aunt Julia and the Scriptwriter* who writes serials for the radio and starts mixing up his own plots.

VARGAS LLOSA: Pedro Camacho never existed. When I started to work for the radio in the early fifties, I knew a man who wrote radio serials for Radio Central in Lima. He was a real character who functioned as a kind of script machine: he wrote countless episodes with incredible ease, hardly taking the time to reread what he'd written. I was absolutely fascinated by him, maybe because he was the first professional writer I'd ever known. But what really amazed me was the vast world that seemed to escape from him like an exhalation; and I became absolutely captivated by him when he began to do what Pedro Camacho does in the book. One day, the stories he wrote started overlapping and getting mixed up and the radio station received letters from the audience alerting them to certain irregularities like characters traveling from one story to the next. That's what gave me the idea for *Aunt Julia and the Scriptwriter*. But obviously, the character in the novel goes through many transformations; he has little to do with his model, who never went crazy. I think he left the station, took a vacation. . . . The ending was much less dramatic than the novel's.

INTERVIEWER: Isn't there also a kind of meta-language in the novel in the sense that Varguitas, who is modeled after you, lives a life as farcical as the lives of Camacho's serial characters?

VARGAS LLOSA: That's about right. When I wrote *Aunt Julia*, I thought I was only going to tell Pedro Camacho's story. I was already well into the novel when I realized it was turning into a kind of mind game and wouldn't be very believable. And, as I've said before, I have a kind of realism mania. So, as a counterpoint to the absurdity of the Pedro Camacho story, I decided to create another more realistic plot that would anchor the novel in reality. And since I was living a kind of soap opera myself at the time—my first marriage—I included that more personal story and combined it with the other, hoping to establish an opposition between a world of fantasy and one that is almost documentary. In the process of trying to achieve this, I realized that it was impossible to do when you write a piece of fiction, a hint of unreality always seeps into it, against the author's will. The personal story became as delirious as the other. Language itself is capable of transforming reality. So Varguitas's story has autobiographical elements in it that were profoundly altered, as it were, by contagion.

INTERVIEWER: In several articles from recent years, you have made certain assertions that seem very pessimistic. In 1982, for example, you wrote: "Literature is more important than politics. Writers should become involved in politics only in the sense of opposing its dangerous schemes and putting them in their place." Isn't that a pessimistic vision of what politics can do to bring about progress?

VARGAS LLOSA: No. I meant that literature has more to do with what is lasting than politics do, that a writer cannot put literature and politics on an equal footing without failing as a writer and perhaps also as a politician. We must remember that political action is rather ephemeral whereas literature is in for the duration. You don't write a book for the present day; in order for a work to exert influence over the future, time must play its role, which is never or rarely the case for political actions. However, even as I say this, I never stop passing judgments on the political climate or implicating myself by what I write and what I do. I believe that a writer cannot avoid political involvement, especially in countries like mine where the problems are difficult and the economic and social situation often has dramatic aspects. It's very important that writers act in one way or another, by offering criticism, ideas, by using their imagination in order to contribute to the solution of the problems. I think it's crucial that writers show—because like all artists, they sense this more strongly than anyone—the importance of freedom for the society as well as for the individual. Justice, which we all wish to rule, should never become disassociated from freedom; and we must never accept the notion that freedom should at certain times be sacrificed in the name of social justice or national security, as totalitarians from the extreme left and reactionaries from the extreme right would have us do. Writers know this because every day they sense the degree to which freedom is necessary for creation, for life itself. Writers should defend their freedom as a necessity like a fair salary or the right to work.

INTERVIEWER: But I was quoting your statement for its pessimistic view of what politics can do. Should or can writers limit themselves to voicing their opposition?

VARGAS LLOSA: I think it's important that writers participate, make judgments, and intervene, but also that they not let politics invade and destroy the literary sphere, the writer's creative domain. When that happens, it kills the writer, making him nothing more than a propagandist. It is therefore crucial that he put limits on his political activities without renouncing or stripping himself of his duty to voice his opinion.

INTERVIEWER: How is it that a writer who has always shown a great distrust of politics became a candidate for the presidency of Peru in the 1990 elections?

VARGAS LLOSA: A country can sometimes find itself in a state of emergency, in a war for example, in which case there is no alternative. The situation in Peru today is catastrophic. The economy is foundering. Inflation has reached record highs. Over the first ten months of 1989, the population lost half its buying power. Political violence has become extreme. Paradoxically, in the midst of this enormous crisis, there appears to be the possibility of making great changes toward democracy and economic freedom. We can rethink the collectivist, socialist model for the state which has been used in Peru since 1968. We shouldn't miss this chance to restore what we've been fighting for these last years: liberal reform and the creation of a real market economy. Not to mention the renewal of the political culture in Peru responsible for the crisis that is sweeping the country. All these reasons made me overcome any reservations I had and led to my involvement in the political struggle—a very naive illusion, after all.

INTERVIEWER: As a writer, what do you think is your greatest quality and your biggest fault?

VARGAS LLOSA: I think my greatest quality is my perseverance: I'm capable of working extremely hard and getting more out of myself than I thought was possible. My greatest fault, I think, is my lack of confidence, which torments me enormously. It takes me three or four years to write a novel—and I spend a good part of that time doubting myself. It doesn't get any better with time; on the contrary, I think I'm getting more self-critical and less confident. Maybe that's why I'm not vain: my conscience is too strong. But I know that I'll write until the day I die. Writing is in my nature. I live my life according to my work. If I didn't write, I would blow my brains out, without a shadow of a doubt. I want to write many more books and better ones. I want to have more interesting and wonderful adventures than I've already had. I refuse to admit the possibility that my best years are behind me, and would not admit it even if faced with the evidence.

INTERVIEWER: Why do you write?

VARGAS LLOSA: I write because I'm unhappy. I write because it's a way of fighting unhappiness.

RICARDO A. SETTI
translated, 1989, by Susannah Hunnewell

# 12. Tom Stoppard

Tom Stoppard's first major play, *Rosencrantz and Guildenstern Are Dead*, was staged at the Edinburgh Festival in 1966 by a group of Oxford students. A local reviewer dismissed it as "an off-putting piece of non-theater," but the drama critic of *The Observer* wrote, "This is erudite comedy, punning, farfetched, leaping from depth to dizziness. It is the most brilliant debut by a young playwright." On his return to London, Stoppard found a telegram from Kenneth Tynan, then the National Theatre's dramaturge, asking to see his play. Eight months later it was produced at the National to the highest critical and popular acclaim and in 1990 was made into a film, which Stoppard directed.

Tom Stoppard was born Tomas Straussler in Zlin, Czechoslovakia, in 1937. In 1938 the Strausslers went to Singapore. When the Japanese invasion of the island became imminent, the women and children were put on boats to Australia and India. Tom and his elder brother and mother were sent to India. His father, Eugene Straussler, remained behind and was killed. Tom spent the rest of the war in different parts of India, ending up at school in Darjceling. After the war, his mother married a British officer, Kenneth Stoppard, whose name the two boys took after the family arrived in England in 1946. On leaving school at seventeen Tom began working as a journalist at a local newspaper in Bristol, where his family lived.

In addition to stage plays—including *Jumpers*, *Travesties* (which received a Tony in 1976), *Night and Day*, *The Real Thing* (which received a Tony in 1984), and *Hapgood*—he has written a number of radio and television plays, filmscripts (including *Empire of the Sun*), and adaptations, and is now one of the world's best-known and most respected contemporary playwrights.

12.11/4–

... Secret bloody service! – if you're it I'm learning Russian.
And you switch as if you're half way through the course, no wonder you're confused. You're out on a limb for a boy she put there. While she was making the world safe for him to talk properly in and lose like a gentleman: what a pal, I said for a friend like you.
she never played with dolls.

Ridley: Yeah. You'd better be sure, Ernie ~~and ...~~. It's only skat

Hapgood: ~~You'd better be sure.~~
~~... Ernie, it's only ... you haven't got~~

Ridley: Yeah.
– and I'm haven't got a prayer. ~~Ernest.~~

Hapgood: ~~You'd better be sure ...~~ If you think she's lying
~~... you haven't got a prayer.~~
walk away. If you think bringing back her son will make you her type, walk away. You won't get in the money, women like her don't pay out – take my advice and open the box–

Ridley: Who the hell are you?

Hapgood: I'm your dream-girl, Ernie. Hapgood without the brains or the taste.

She plays without a board.

You haven't got a prayer–

You'd better be sure, Ernie, it's only skat and she plays without a board.

A *manuscript page from Tom Stoppard's play* Hapgood.

# Tom Stoppard

*At the time of this interview, Stoppard was near the end of rehearsals for his new play,* Hapgood, *which opened in London in March 1988. For the duration of the rehearsals Stoppard had rented a furnished apartment in central London in order to avoid commuting, and although he had said, "I would never volunteer to talk about my work and myself more than ninety seconds," he was extremely generous with his time and attention. Stoppard is tall and exotically handsome, and he speaks with a very slight lisp.*

INTERVIEWER: How are the rehearsals going?

TOM STOPPARD: So far they are conforming to pattern, alas! I mean I am suffering from the usual delusion that the play was ready before we went into production. It happens every time. I give my publisher the finished text of the play so that it can be published not too long after the opening in London, but by the time the galleys arrive they're hopelessly out of date because of all the changes I've made during rehearsals. This time I gave them *Hapgood* and told them that it was folly to pretend it would be unaltered, but I added, "I think it won't be as bad as the others." It turned out to be worse. Yesterday I realized that a chunk of information in the third scene ought to be in the second scene, and it's like pulling out entrails: as in any surgery there's blood. As I was doing it I watched a documentary about Crick and Watson's discovery of the structure of DNA—the double helix. There was only one way all the information they had could fit but they couldn't figure out what it was. I felt the same. So the answer to your question is that the rehearsals are going well and enjoyably, but that I'm very busy with my pencil.

INTERVIEWER: What provokes the changes? Does the transfer from your imagination to the stage alter your perception? Or do the director and the actors make suggestions?

STOPPARD: They make a few suggestions which I am often happy to act upon. In the theater there is often a tension, almost a contradiction, between the way real people would think and behave, and a kind of imposed dramaticness. I like dialogue which is slightly more brittle than life. I have always admired and wished to write one of those 1940s filmscripts where every line is written with a sharpness and economy which is frankly artificial. Peter Wood, the director with whom I've worked for sixteen years, sometimes feels obliged to find a humanity, perhaps a romantic ambiguity, in scenes which are not written like that but which, I hope, contain the possibility. I like surface gloss, but it's all too easy to get that right for the first night only to find that *that* was the best performance of the play; from then on the gloss starts cracking apart. The ideal is to make the groundwork so deep and solid that the actors are continually discovering new possibilities under the surface, so that the best performance turns out to be the last one. In my plays there are usually a few lines which Peter loathes, for their slickness or coldness, and we have a lot of fairly enjoyable squabbles which entail some messing about with the text as we rehearse. In the case of *Hapgood* there is a further problem which has to do with the narrative mechanics, because it's a plotty play, and I can't do plots and have no interest in plots.

INTERVIEWER: Yet you have produced some complex and plausible plots. So why the aversion?

STOPPARD: The subject matter of the play exists before the story and it is always something abstract. I get interested by a notion of some kind and see that it has dramatic possibilities. Gradually I see how a pure idea can be married with a dramatic event. But it is still not a play until you invent a plausible narrative. Sometimes this is not too hard—*The Real Thing* was fairly straightforward. For *Hapgood* the thing that I wanted to write about seemed to suit the form of an espionage thriller. It's not the sort of thing I read or write.

INTERVIEWER: What was the original idea that made you think of an espionage thriller?

STOPPARD: It had to do with mathematics. I am not a mathematician but I was aware that for centuries mathematics was considered the queen of the sciences because it claimed certainty. It was grounded on some fundamental certainties—axioms—which led to others. But then, in a sense, it all started going wrong, with concepts like non-euclidean geometry—I mean, looking at it from Euclid's point of view. The mathematics of physics turned out to be grounded on *un*certainties, on probability and chance. And if you're me, you think—there's a play in that. Finding an idea for a play is like picking up a shell on a beach. I started reading about mathematics without finding what I was looking for. In the end I realized that what I was after was something which any first-year physics student is familiar with, namely quantum mechanics. So I started reading about that.

INTERVIEWER: It is said that you research your plays thoroughly.

STOPPARD: I don't think of it as research. I read for interest and enjoyment, and when I cease to enjoy it I stop. I didn't research quantum mechanics but I was fascinated by the mystery which lies in the foundation of the observable world, of which the most familiar example is the wave/particle duality of light. I thought it was a good metaphor for human personality. The language of espionage lends itself to this duality—think of the double agent.

INTERVIEWER: You seem to think the success of the play has so much to do with its production. Do you, therefore, get involved with the lighting, costumes, etc.? Please give examples, anecdotes.

STOPPARD: It is obvious that a given text (think of any classic) can give rise to a satisfying event or an unsatisfying one. These are the only relative values which end up mattering in the theater. A great production of a black comedy is better than a mediocre production of a comedy of errors. When the writing is over, the event is the thing. I attend the first rehearsal of a new play and every rehearsal after that, as well as discussions with designers, lighting designers, costume designers . . . I like to be there, even though I'm doing more listening than talking. When *Hapgood* was being designed, I kept insisting that the shower in the first scene wouldn't work unless it was in the middle of the upper stage, so that Hapgood could approach us facing down the middle. Peter and Carl insisted that the scene wouldn't work unless the main entrance doors were facing the audience. They were quite right, but so was I. We opened out of town with the shower in the wings, and it didn't work at all, so we ended up having to find a way to have both the doors and the shower in view of the audience. The look of the thing is one thing. The sound of it is more important. David Lean was quoted as saying somewhere that the hardest part of making films is knowing how fast or slow to make the actors speak. I suddenly saw how *horribly* difficult that made it to make a film. Because you can't change your mind. When you write a play, it makes a certain kind of noise in your head, and for me rehearsals are largely a process of trying to reproduce that noise. It is not always wise to reproduce it in every instance, but that's another question. The first time I met Laurence Olivier, we were casting *Rosencrantz and Guildenstern.* He asked me about the Player. I said the Player should be a sneaky, snake-like sort of person. Olivier looked dubious. The part was given, thank God, or Olivier, to Graham Crowden who is about six-foot four and roars like a lion. Olivier came to rehearsal one day. He watched for about fifteen minutes, and then, leaving, made one suggestion. I forget what it was. At the door he turned again, twinkled at us all, and said, "Just the odd pearl," and left.

INTERVIEWER: Is it a very anxious moment for you, working up to the first night?

STOPPARD: Yes. You are trying to imagine the effect on people who know nothing about what is going on and whom you are taking through the story. In a normal spy thriller you contrive to delude the reader until all is revealed in the dénouement. This is the exact opposite of a scientific paper in which the dénouement—the discovery—is announced at the beginning. *Hapgood* to some extent follows this latter procedure. It is not a whodunit because we are told who has done it near the beginning of the first act, so the story becomes *how* he did it.

INTERVIEWER: Did you draw on some famous spies, like Philby or Blunt, for your characters?

STOPPARD: Not at all. I wasn't really interested in authenticity. John Le Carré's *A Perfect Spy* uses the word "joe" for an agent who is being run by somebody, and I picked it up. I have no idea whether it is authentic or invented by Le Carré.

INTERVIEWER: What happens on the first night? Do you sit among the audience or in a concealed place at the back? And what do you do afterwards?

STOPPARD: The first *audience* is more interesting than the first night. We now have previews, which makes a difference. Actually, my play *The Real Inspector Hound* was the first to have previews in London, in 1968. Previews are essential. The idea of going straight from a dress-rehearsal to a first night is frightening. It happened with *Rosencrantz and Guildenstern* and we got away with it, but for *Jumpers* we had several previews by the end of which I had taken fifteen minutes out of the play. I hate first nights. I attend out of courtesy for the actors and afterwards we all have a drink and go home.

INTERVIEWER: How does the London theater world differ from New York?

STOPPARD: Theater in New York is nearer to the street. In London you have to go deep into the building, usually, to reach the place where theater happens. On Broadway, only the fire doors separate you from the sidewalk and you're lucky if the sound of a police car doesn't rip the envelope twice a night. This difference means something, I'm not quite sure what. Well, as Peter Brook will tell you, the theater has its roots in something holy, and perhaps we in London are still a little holier than thou. The potential rewards of theater in New York are really too great for its own good. One bull's-eye and you're rich and famous. The rich get more famous and the famous get richer. You're the talk of the town. The taxi drivers have read about you and they remember you for a fortnight. You get to be photographed for *Vogue* with new clothes and Vuitton luggage, if that's your bag. If it's a new play, everyone owes the writer, they celebrate him—the theater owners, the producers, the actors. Even the stage doorman is somehow touched by the wand. The sense of so much depending on success is very hard to ignore, perhaps impossible. It leads to disproportionate anxiety and disproportionate relief or disappointment. The British are more phlegmatic about these things. You know about British phlegm. The audiences, respectively, are included in this. In New York, expressions of appreciation have succumbed to galloping inflation—in London only the Americans stand up to applaud the actors, and only American audiences emit those high-pitched barks which signify the highest form of approval. But if you mean the difference between what happens on stage in London and New York, there isn't much, and there's no difference between the best. Cross-fertilization has evened out what I believe used to be quite a sharp difference between styles of American and British acting, although it is probably still a little harder to find American actors with an easy command of rhetoric, and British actors who can produce that controlled untidiness which, when we encountered it a generation ago, seemed to make acting life-like for the first time.

INTERVIEWER: I have heard that in New York people sit up and wait for *The New York Times* review, which makes or breaks a show. It is not like that in London, but do you worry all night until the reviews come out the next day?

STOPPARD: Certainly I'm anxious. One is implicated in other people's fortunes—producers, directors, actors—and one wants the play to succeed for their sake as much as for one's own. If there is a favorable consensus among the reviewers, you accept it as a reasonable judgment. If you get mixed reviews, you are heartened by those who enjoyed it and depressed by the rejections. What one is anxious about is the judgment on the event rather than the play. None of us would have worked so hard if we didn't believe in the play, and so we don't need a critic to tell us whether we liked it, but whether we succeeded in putting it across. For the text is only one aspect of an evening at the theater; often the most memorable moments have little to do with the words uttered. It is the totality—to use the jargon—which is being judged. A favorable judgment means that on that occasion the play has worked, which does not mean that it always will.

INTERVIEWER: Do critics matter as much?

STOPPARD: In the long term, not at all. In the short term they give an extra push, or conversely give you more to push against; but favorable reviews won't save a play for long if the audiences don't like it, and vice versa. The play has to *work*.

INTERVIEWER: I would like to know what you mean by "work."

STOPPARD: It has to be truthful. The audience must believe. But the play is also a physical mechanism. Getting that mechanism to work takes an awful lot of time and preoccupation. The way music comes in and out, lights vary, etc. When you've got all that right you can get back to the text. Otherwise, the fact that it seems right on paper won't help you.

INTERVIEWER: Do you change things according to what the reviews say?

STOPPARD: No. But I change things according to what happens to the play, and what I think of it. Sometimes one is involved in a revival and one wants to change things because one has changed oneself, and what used to seem intriguing or amusing might now strike one as banal. Any revival in which I am involved is liable to change.

INTERVIEWER: It has been said that Kenneth Tynan was the last critic who had a definite point of view and was bold enough to express it, thereby influencing the direction of the theater. So perhaps critics do make a difference?

STOPPARD: Ken had enthusiasms. Some lasted longer than others and while he had them he pushed them. But you have to read critics critically and make the necessary adjustment according to what you know about them. When I was a critic—on my local paper in Bristol and later for a magazine in London—I floundered between pronouncing what I hoped were magisterial judgments and merely declaring my own taste. If I might quote myself from a previous interview—"I was not a good critic because I never had the moral character to pan a friend." I'll rephrase that—"I had the moral character never to pan a friend."

INTERVIEWER: But Tynan introduced into England what one associates with French intellectual life—a kind of intellectual terrorism, when suddenly one author or school is "in" and another "out," and woe betide he who disagrees! He destroyed people like Terrence Rattigan and Christopher Fry and all those he called "bourgeois" playwrights, and you had to love Osborne and Brecht or else! But I recently saw Rattigan's *Separate Tables* and thought it very good indeed, infinitely better than some of the plays Ken had praised and made fashionable.

STOPPARD: Which shows that he didn't destroy them. However, I know what you mean, and one or two of my close friends thoroughly disapproved of Ken. But I hope they know what I mean when I stick up for him. The first time I met Ken was when I was summoned to his tiny office when the National Theatre offices consisted of a wooden hut on waste ground, and I was so awed by being in a small room with him that I began to stutter. Ken stuttered, as you know. So we sat stuttering at each other, mainly about his shirt which was pale lemon and came from Turnbull and Asser in Jermyn Street. This was in the late summer of 1966 when we wore roll-neck shirts.

INTERVIEWER: You have been praised for your eloquence, your use of language—your aphorisms, puns, epigrams—as if you invented them, wrote them down and put them into your characters' mouths. Do you?

STOPPARD: No. They tend to show up when I need them. But perhaps it is significant that very often a particular line is more or less arbitrarily attached to a particular character. I can take a line from one character and give it to another. As I just told you, there was something in the third scene of *Hapgood* which I had to put in the second scene. But the dialogue was not between the same two people—only one of them was the same. So the lines of a female character became those of a male, and it made no difference. In *Night and Day* I had to invent an African dictator, but there was no way I could do it unless he was the only African dictator who had been to the London School of Economics. You don't have to be African or a dictator to make those observations about the British press. I rely heavily on an actor's performance to help individualize a character.

INTERVIEWER: Do you act out all the characters as you write?

STOPPARD: Sometimes. I walk around the room speaking the dialogue.

INTERVIEWER: Once you've got the idea and devised the narrative, do you take notes while you're reading up on the subject?

STOPPARD: Not really. Sometimes, over the course of several months, I might cover a page with odds and ends, many of which might find their way into the play. But I don't write down in notebooks, nor jot down what I overhear—nothing like that.

INTERVIEWER: In the course of writing the play, do you get surprises, because for example, you don't know what a character is going to do next, or how the story will end?

STOPPARD: Absolutely.

INTERVIEWER: What about the order of the play, the number of acts and scenes?

STOPPARD: I don't work out the whole plot before I begin, just the general outline. The play alters as you write it. For example, in *Jumpers* the end of the first act in my scheme turned out to be the end of the second act, followed by only an epilogue. *Hapgood* was in three acts and is now in two. The reason for the change is partly intrinsic and partly circumstantial. Managements prefer two-act plays because they think that audiences like only one interval, and Peter thought it would be better for the play. It shows how pragmatic the theater is, perhaps the most pragmatic art form, apart from advertising. For example, the male secretary, Maggs, used to be Madge, a woman. But when we came to choose the understudies we realized that if the secretary were male he could understudy so-and-so. It turned out to be better for the play also, because then Hapgood is the only woman surrounded by all these men. But at first it was a question of casting.

INTERVIEWER: Having got your outline, do you proceed from the beginning to the end chronologically?

STOPPARD: Yes I do. I write plays from beginning to end, without making stabs at intermediate scenes, so the first thing I write is the first line of the play. By that time I have formed some idea of the set but I don't write that down. I don't write down anything which I can keep in my head—stage directions and so on. When I have got to the end of the play—which I write with a fountain pen; you can't scribble with a typewriter—there is almost nothing on the page except what people say. Then I dictate the play, ad-libbing all the stage directions, into a tape machine from which my secretary transcribes the first script.

INTERVIEWER: What are the pitfalls on the way? Things that might get you stuck?

STOPPARD: It is not like playing the violin—not difficult in that way. The difficulties vary at different stages. The first is that you haven't got anything you wish to write a play about. Then you get an idea, but it might be several ideas that could belong to two or three plays. Finally, if you are lucky, they may fit into the same play. The next difficulty, as I said before, is to translate these abstract ideas into concrete situations. That is a very long and elaborate period. Another difficulty is knowing when to start; it's chicken-and-egg—you don't know what you're going to write until you start, and you can't start until you know. Finally, in some strange, quantum mechanical way, the two trains arrive on the same line without colliding, and you can begin. The following stage is not exactly pleasant but exciting and absorbing—you live with the fear that "it" may go away. There is a three-month period when I don't want to say good morning to anyone lest I miss the thought that would make all the difference.

INTERVIEWER: Once the play begins to take shape, what do you feel?
STOPPARD: Tremendous joy. Because whenever I finish a play I have no feeling that I would ever have another one to write.
INTERVIEWER: Do you disappear from home to write?
STOPPARD: I disappear into myself. Sometimes I go away for a short period, say a week, to think and concentrate, then I come back home to carry on.
INTERVIEWER: Where do you work and when?
STOPPARD: I have a very nice long room, which used to be the stable. It has a desk and lots of paper, etc. But most of my plays are written on the kitchen table at night, when everybody has gone to bed and I feel completely at peace. During the day, somehow I don't get much done; although I have a secretary who answers the phone, I always want to know who it is, and I generally get distracted.
INTERVIEWER: Do you have an ideal spectator in mind when you write?
STOPPARD: Perhaps I do. Peter Wood has quite a different spectator in mind, one who is a cross between Rupert Bear and Winnie the Pooh. He assumes bafflement in order to force me to explain on a level of banality. If I had an ideal spectator it would be someone more sharp-witted and attentive than the average theatergoer whom Peter thinks of. A lot of changes in rehearsals have to do with reconciling his spectator with mine.
INTERVIEWER: You have said that all the characters talk like you. Does that mean that you have trouble creating female characters? You once said, "There is an aura of mystery about women which I find difficult to penetrate." Yet the eponymous character of your new play, *Hapgood*, is a woman.
STOPPARD: I wonder when I said that! It is not what I feel now. When I said I wasn't interested by plot or character I meant that they are not the point for me. Before writing *Night and Day* I thought, I'm sick of people saying there are no good parts for women in my plays, so I'll do one. It turned out not to be just about a woman, and I thought, well, one day I'll do a Joan of Arc. But I never think, "I'm writing for a woman so it had better be different."
INTERVIEWER: How important are curtain lines?
STOPPARD: Very important, because they define the play's shape, like the spans of a bridge. It's like architecture—there is a structure and a

conscious architect at work. Otherwise you could decide to have an interval at 8:30, and whatever was being said at that moment would be your curtain line. It wouldn't do.

INTERVIEWER: You said that you have worked with Peter Wood for sixteen years, but are you always closely involved with your plays' productions?

STOPPARD: In this country, yes. In America I was involved with the production of *The Real Thing*, which was directed by Mike Nichols. But who knows what's going on elsewhere? You are pleased the plays are being done and hope for the best.

INTERVIEWER: You have been accused of superficiality; some people say that your plays are all linguistic pyrotechnics, dazzling wordplay, intelligent punning, but that they don't have much substance. How do you react to that charge?

STOPPARD: I suppose there is a certain justice in it, insofar as if I were to write an essay instead of a play about any of these subjects it wouldn't be a profound essay.

INTERVIEWER: Nowadays fame has become a thing in itself. In French the word is "gloire," which is nicer because it denotes achievement; it has connotations of glory. But fame doesn't: you can be famous just for being famous. Now that you are, do you still feel excited by it, or do you think it isn't that important?

STOPPARD: Oh, I like it. The advantages are psychological, social, and material. The first because I don't have to worry about who I am—I am the man who has written these plays. The social advantages appeal to half of me because there are two of me: the recluse and the fan. And the fan in me is still thrilled to meet people I admire. As for the material side, I like having some money. The best way to gauge wealth is to consider the amount of money which you can spend *thoughtlessly*—a casual purchase which simply doesn't register. The really rich can do it in Cartier's; I'm quite happy if I can do it in a good bookshop or a good restaurant.

INTERVIEWER: What about the company of your peers. Harold Pinter?

STOPPARD: The first time I met Harold Pinter was when I was a journalist in Bristol and he came down to see a student production of *The Birthday Party*. I realized he was sitting in the seat in front of me. I was tremendously intimidated and spent a good long time working out how to engage him in conversation. Finally, I tapped him on the shoulder and said, "Are you Harold Pinter or do you just look like him?" He said, "What?" So that was the end of that.

INTERVIEWER: Going back to your work, *Jumpers* was about moral philosophy, and in it you attacked logical positivism and its denial that metaphysical questions are valid. . . .

STOPPARD: Ah, but remember that I was attacking a dodo—logical positivism was over by the time I wrote the play. I was amused to see Freddy [Sir Alfred] Ayer being interviewed on television. The interviewer asked him what were the defects of logical positivism, and Freddy answered, "I suppose its main defect was that it wasn't true." The play addressed itself to a set of attitudes which people didn't think of as philosophical but which in fact were. At the same time, it tried to be a moral play, because while George has the right ideas, he is also a culpable person; while he is defending his ideas and attacking the opposition, he is also neglecting everyone around him and shutting out his wife who is in need, not to mention shooting his hare and stepping on his tortoise.

INTERVIEWER: In the play you say that the Ten Commandments, unlike tennis rules, can't be changed, implying that there are fundamental moral principles which are eternally valid because of their transcendental provenance—their foundation in religion. Do you believe that?

STOPPARD: Yes, I do.

INTERVIEWER: Are you religious?

STOPPARD: Well, I keep looking over my shoulder. When I am asked whether I believe in God, my answer is that I don't know what the question means. I approve of belief in God and I try to behave as if there is one, but that hardly amounts to faith. I don't know what religious certainty would consist of, though many apparently have it. I am uneasy with religious ceremonials, because I think intellectually, and the case for God is not an intellectual one. However, militant humanism grates on me much more than evangelism.

INTERVIEWER: I would like to ask you about your early influences. What about the angry young men and the kitchen-sink school of the fifties, or Beckett, whom you are quoted as saying had the greatest impact on you?

STOPPARD: There were good plays and not-so-good plays. I was moved by and interested by John Osborne's *Look Back in Anger*, Beckett's

*Waiting for Godot*, *The Birthday Party* by Pinter, *Next Time I'll Sing To You* . . . I mean when I was starting to write plays. I'd be wary of calling them influences. I don't write the way I write because I liked them. I liked them because of the way I write, or despite it.

INTERVIEWER: So if we forget about "influence," who are the writers you admire and go back to?

STOPPARD: I had a passion for Hemingway and Evelyn Waugh, and I think I will always return to them, apart from anyone else.

INTERVIEWER: Does it annoy you that people compare you to George Bernard Shaw?

STOPPARD: I don't think they do very much. I find the comparison embarrassing, by which I mean flattering. Shaw raises conversation to the power of the drama, and he does it for three acts. I sometimes do it for three pages, though the tone is very different; but my theatrical impulses are flashier. The result can be exhilarating when things go right, and pathetic when things go wrong. Anyway, one's admirations don't have much to do with the way one likes to write. I've been going around for years saying that Alan Bennett is one of the best playwrights we've had this century, and he does exactly what I don't do and can't do; he makes drama out of character study. The fact that his jokes are very good helps but he's really a social anthropologist who prefers to report in the form of plays. Incidentally, I think Bennett's comparative lack of recognition among the academically minded has most to do with a snobbishness about television—where much of his best work appears. David Mamet is another great enthusiasm of mine, and another writer who has almost nothing in common with me.

INTERVIEWER: What actually led you to write plays? Could you describe the genesis of your plays other than *Hapgood* and *Jumpers*?

STOPPARD: I started writing plays because everybody else was doing it at the time. As for the genesis of plays, it is never the story. The story comes just about last. I'm not sure I can generalize. The genesis of *Travesties* was simply the information that James Joyce, Tristan Tzara, and Lenin were all in Zurich at the same time. Anybody can see that there was some kind of play in that. But what play? I started to read Richard Ellman's biography of Joyce, and came across Henry Carr, and so on and so on. In the case of *Night and Day*, it was merely that I had been a reporter, that I knew quite a lot about journalism, and that I should have been writing another play about *something* and that therefore it was probably a good idea to write a play about journalists. After that, it was just a case of shuffling around my bits of knowledge and my prejudices until they began to suggest some kind of story. I was also shuffling a separate pack of cards which had to do with sexual attraction. Quite soon I started trying to integrate the two packs. And so on.

INTERVIEWER: There's another aspect of your work which I would like to talk about, that is adaptations of other playwrights' plays. Are the two activities very different?

STOPPARD: Yes, they are. I don't do adaptations because I have a thing about them, but to keep busy. I write a play every three or four years and they don't take that long—perhaps a year each.

INTERVIEWER: Does someone do the literal translation for you from the original language first?

STOPPARD: Yes, since I don't read any other languages. I have done two plays by Arthur Schnitzler, *Dalliance* and *Undiscovered Country*, one by Molnar, *Rough Crossing*, and a play by Johann Nestroy which became *On The Razzle*.

INTERVIEWER: Do you tinker with the original text?

STOPPARD: There is no general rule. *Undiscovered Country* was pretty faithful. I thought of Schnitzler as a modern classic, not to be monkeyed about with. But you're not doing an author a favor if the adaptation is not vibrant. So in the end I started "helping," not because Schnitzler was defective but because he was writing in 1905 in Vienna. When you are writing a play you use cultural references by the thousands, and they all interconnect like a nervous system. In the case of *Dalliance*, Peter Wood started with the idea that the third act should be transferred to the wings of the opera. He did it beautifully and it worked very well. The number of critics who suddenly turned out to be Schnitzler purists was quite surprising. As for *On The Razzle*, that had a wonderful plot—which wasn't Nestroy's own anyway—and I invented most of the dialogue. The Molnar play was set in an Italian castle and I put it on an ocean liner called *The Italian Castle*. And I also made up nearly all the dialogue. So you can see there's a difference between "translation" and "adaptation."

INTERVIEWER: So far your adaptations have been of plays. Have you ever thought of adapting a novel, or a book of testimony, into a play or a series of plays? For example, Primo Levi's *If This Is a Man*, or

Nadezhda Mandelstam's *Hope Against Hope?* I mention these because I know you admire them as much as I do.

STOPPARD: I think Nadezhda Mandelstam's books are two of the greatest books written in this century. But what would be the point of turning them into plays?

INTERVIEWER: To make them accessible to a larger audience, the way Olivia Manning's *The Balkan Trilogy* was resurrected and became a bestseller after it was shown on television as a six-part series.

STOPPARD: It would be admirable if it made people turn to the Mandelstam books. I quite agree that television would be the way to do it.

INTERVIEWER: Let's talk about another of your activities—writing filmscripts. You have never written an original one. Why not?

STOPPARD: Because I don't have any original ideas to spare.

INTERVIEWER: What if someone gave you the idea?

STOPPARD: That is possible, but it would be pure accident if you gave me the right one. The reason is that all you know about me is what I have written so far; it has nothing to do with what I want to do next because I don't know, either.

INTERVIEWER: What is the difference between writing a play and writing a filmscript?

STOPPARD: The main difference is that in films the writer serves the director, and in the theater the director serves the writer—broadly speaking.

INTERVIEWER: Now for the first time you are going to direct your own film version of *Rosencrantz and Guildenstern*. Are you looking forward to it?

STOPPARD: The reason why I agreed to do it myself was that the producers gave me a list of twenty possible directors and I couldn't see why any of them should or should not do it, since I had no idea what each would wish to do. So I suggested myself, because it was the line of least resistance, and also because I am the only director willing to commit the necessary violence to the play—I've thrown masses of it out, and I've added things.

INTERVIEWER: You are friendly with Czech playwrights, like Václav Havel and others. Do you feel any special affinity with them as a result of your own Czech origin?

STOPPARD: This whole Czech thing about me has gotten wildly out of hand. I wasn't two years old when I left the country and I was back one week in 1977. I went to an English school and was brought up in English. So I don't feel Czech. I like what Havel writes. When I first came across his work, I thought *The Memorandum* was a play I'd have liked to have written, and you don't think that of many plays. And when I met him I loved him as a person. I met other writers there I liked and admired, and I felt their situation keenly. But I could have gotten onto the wrong plane and landed in Poland or Paraguay and felt the same about writers' situations there.

INTERVIEWER: I wanted to ask you about radio plays, because you started out writing some, and before *Rosencrantz* had a number of them produced on the radio. It is always astonishing that despite television, radio is still so popular, especially for plays. What are your feelings about radio—its technique, possibilities, and differences from other dramatic forms?

STOPPARD: Radio plays are neither easier nor harder. I'm supposed to be writing one now, and the hard part is simply finding a play to write. The pleasant part will be writing it. There is nothing much to be said about radio technique except what is obvious—scene setting through dialogue and sound effects. I'd like to write a radio play which consisted entirely of sound effects but I suppose it would be rather a short one.

INTERVIEWER: After you have seen *Hapgood* through, what are you going to do?

STOPPARD: I would like to write a very simple play, perhaps with two or three people in one setting. A literature play rather than an event play. Getting *Hapgood* ready was exhausting and frustrating—it has as many scene changes, light cues, sound cues, etc., as a musical. I'd like to write a play where all the time and the energy can be devoted to language, thought process, and emotion.

INTERVIEWER: It is often said that a writer's output is the product of a psychosis, of self-examination. Is there any indication of this in your case?

STOPPARD: You tell me!

INTERVIEWER: What is the most difficult aspect of playwriting?

STOPPARD: Structure.

INTERVIEWER: And the easiest?

STOPPARD: Dialogue.

INTERVIEWER: What about the curtain lines? Do they come first and then you work your way towards them, or do they arrive in the natural progression of writing the dialogue?

STOPPARD: Curtain lines tend to be produced under the pressure of the preceding two or three acts, and usually they seem so dead right, to me anyway, that it really is as if they were in the DNA, unique and inevitable.

INTERVIEWER: What are some of your favorite curtain lines—and not necessarily those in your own plays?

STOPPARD: "The son of a bitch stole my watch" [from *The Front Page*]—I quote from memory—and "You that way; we this way" [from *Love's Labour's Lost*].

INTERVIEWER: Not to put you to the test, but can you provide a curtain line for this interview?

STOPPARD: "That's all, folks."

SHUSHA GUPPY
May–October 1986

# Notes on the Contributors

ZOLTÁN ABÁDI-NAGY *(Interview with Walker Percy)* is an associate professor of English at Kossuth University, Debrecen, Hungary. His books include *Swift: The Satirist as Projector* and a study of American fiction of the 1960s, *Crisis and Comedy.* He has been a research fellow at Duke University, and has translated the works of Banks, Barth, Barthelme, Brautigan, Coover, De Vries, Federman, and Percy.

DOUGLAS R. ALLEN *(Interview with William Kennedy)* is the coauthor of *Shaker Furniture Makers* (University Press of New England). He resides with his wife and sons in Chatham, New York. A speech- and scriptwriter by trade, Allen is currently working on a novel and a screenplay, having completed another screenplay, with Randy Fisher, for a vampire movie.

EDWINA BURNESS *(Interview with P. L. Travers)* was born in Edinburgh and now lives in the countryside near London. She has an M.A. from Cambridge and a Ph.D. from London University, both in English and American literature. She reviews for the *Times Educational Supplement*, contributes to the *Spectator* and *Harpers and Queen*, and teaches part-time at London University.

THOMAS FRICK *(Interview with Doris Lessing)* writes frequently for *Art in America* and other publications. He lives in Los Angeles.

JERRY GRISWOLD *(Interview with P. L. Travers)* is the author of *Audacious Kids: America's Favorite Children's Books* and *The Children's Books of Randall Jarrell.* He teaches at San Diego State University.

SHUSHA GUPPY *(Interview with Tom Stoppard)* is the London editor of the *Paris Review* and contributes regularly to *The Daily Telegraph* and *British Vogue,* among other periodicals. Her memoir, *The Blindfold Horse,* was published by Beacon Press. A collection of her interviews with British women of letters, *Looking Back,* was published by Paris Review Editions in 1991.

JAMES R. HEPWORTH *(Interview with Wallace Stegner)* is an assistant professor at Lewis–Clark State College and is the director of Confluence Press in Lewiston, Idaho. He is the co-editor of *Resist Much, Obey Little: Some Notes on Edward Abbey* (1985).

SUSANNAH HUNNEWELL *(Interview with Mario Vargas Llosa),* a former intern at the *Paris Review,* is on the staff of *The New York Times Magazine.*

ALFRED MACADAM *(Interview with Octavio Paz)* teaches Latin American literature at Barnard College–Columbia University. His most recent book is *Textual Confrontations* (University of Chicago Press), a comparative study of Latin American and Anglo-American writing. He is also editor of *Review,* a publication of the Americas Society.

GEORGE PLIMPTON *(Interviews with Maya Angelou and Tom Wolfe)* is the editor of the *Paris Review.* His most recent book is *The Best of Plimpton,* published by The Atlantic Monthly Press.

RICARDO A. SETTI *(Interview with Mario Vargas Llosa)* has written for numerous magazines and newspapers in Brazil and is the regional editor in São Paolo for *Journal do Brasil.* This interview is a condensed version of a longer interview with Vargas Llosa, published in book form in Spanish, French, and Portuguese.

LAWRENCE SHAINBERG *(Exorcising Beckett)* is the author of two novels, *One on One* and *Memories of Amnesia*, and the non-fiction book *Brain Surgeon: An Intimate View of His World*.

MONA SIMPSON *(Interview with William Kennedy)* is the author of *Anywhere But Here*, a novel published by Knopf. Her work has been anthologized in *The Best American Short Stories, The Pushcart Prize*, and *Twenty Under Thirty*. Her most recent novel, *The Lost Father*, was published by Knopf and Faber in January 1992. She is a Bard College Fellow and an advisory editor of the *Paris Review*.

ANTONIO WEISS *(Interview with Harold Bloom)*, a recent graduate of Yale University, is a financial analyst at Donaldson, Lufkin & Jenrette, an investment banking firm in Manhattan. He is also an advisory editor of the *Paris Review*.